Brutal Youth

Brutal Youth

Anthony Breznican

THOMAS DUNNE BOOKS

ST. MARTIN'S PRESS ✳ NEW YORK

To Jillo

for my wildflower,

these cruel shadows

THOMAS DUNNE BOOKS.
An imprint of St. Martin's Press.

BRUTAL YOUTH. Copyright © 2014 by Anthony Breznican. All rights reserved. Printed in the United States of America. For information, address St. Martin's Press, 175 Fifth Avenue, New York, N.Y. 10010.

www.thomasdunnebooks.com
www.stmartins.com

The Library of Congress Cataloging-in-Publication Data is available upon request.

ISBN 978-1-250-01935-6 (hardcover)
ISBN 978-1-250-01936-3 (e-book)

St. Martin's Press books may be purchased for educational, business, or promotional use. For information on bulk purchases, please contact Macmillan Corporate and Premium Sales Department at 1-800-221-7945, extension 5442, or write specialmarkets@macmillan.com.

First Edition: June 2014

10 9 8 7 6 5 4 3 2 1

1991

PROLOGUE:
THE BOY ON THE ROOF

The kid had taken a lot of punishment over the years, so he had much to give back.

A steel hatch on the roof of St. Michael the Archangel High School shuddered, then burst open, and the boy crawled out and collapsed against the gritty tarpaper surface, kicking the lid shut again with one sock-covered foot. He wore only his uniform gray slacks and a wide-open button-down shirt, streaked with blood that wasn't his. A black canvas book bag hung over one shoulder, swinging back and forth as he scrambled to his knees. He pressed his weight against the closed metal door to stifle the hollering and pandemonium rising from beneath it.

Next to the steel hatch was a bucket, steaming with hot tar. The janitor had been using it to seal sections of loose shingle that had been leaking water into the school during every springtime rainstorm. A grubby tar mop leaned against the bucket. The boy shifted his heavy bag and scooped up the mop, wedging it between the handles of the hatch, locking it shut. Then he fled back across the flat roof toward the ghostly concrete statues lining the edge.

The row of saints had stood watch over St. Michael's for as long as anyone alive could remember. Thomas, the doubter; Joseph, the foster father; Anthony, finder of lost things; Jude, devotee to the hopelesss; Francis of

Assisi, the lover of nature, who had a small concrete bird in his out-stretched hand, and a real drip of birdshit on his concrete head. At the center archway of the ledge high above the school's main entrance stood an even larger statue of a warrior angel, St. Michael himself, wings spread and sword raised against the satanic serpent being squashed beneath his foot.

The boy on the roof was named Colin Vickler. Not that it mattered. This was the end. This was good-bye. There was nowhere else to hide. He climbed up onto the short ledge, first steadying himself on St. Michael's wing, and then hugging its torso as he tried not to stare into the bone-shattering drop below. Behind him, the steel hatch shook again—a rumble of thunder on a sunny, spring afternoon. He heard screams rise from the open classroom windows on the face of the school below. Even out here, on the edge, he was surrounded.

He slumped against St. Michael, pressing his open mouth against the concrete figure's arm to make himself stop crying, tasting the stone that had weathered away to dust. The statue lurched, as if withdrawing from him, and he fell back as pieces of the crumbling base tumbled over the ledge.

Peering over the side, he saw a small group of classmates in gym clothes lingering on the school steps. The bits of stone lay scattered around their feet, and they stared up at him, shielding their eyes against the sun.

One of them pointed and said, "Hey, I think that's Clink." Another shouted: "Jump, Clink!" and the rest of them laughed. A girl's voice rose up in a singsong: "Cliiii-iiiink!"

Vickler stood up straight, staring back at them.

He rammed his shoulder against St. Michael. He beat the saint's back. He grabbed the figure's sword-wielding arm and rocked him back and forth, cracking the mortar. The statue lurched, and the rusted shaft of pipe protruding through the base cracked loose, splitting the serpent free from the avenging angel's foot.

St. Michael tipped off the ledge and spiraled to the sidewalk, diving toward its own shrinking shadow. It detonated against the concrete steps in a crackling explosion of dust and rocks as the gym students leaped for their lives, shrieking and scrambling over each other.

For the first time that day—for the first time in a long while—Colin Vickler smiled.

As those fresh screams rose up, he stared over the streets ahead, to the shopping center across the road, the receding clusters of homes, the green springtime slopes of the valley rising in the distance, the wide curve of the Allegheny River, an industrial artery slouching along the steel mills and gravelworks as it bent toward Pittsburgh. In the busy street beside the school, traffic crawled past the gas stations, fast-food joints, doctor's offices, and other storefronts that lined Tobinsville's main strip. Up here, it all looked like some toy village in a model train layout. Tiny. Unreal. It seemed harmless to him now. And he felt so much bigger than it.

The hatch shook again, but the mop handle held. Vickler watched it. Waited. Then nothing.

He stumbled toward the next saint, dragging his heavy behind him.

The bag. That's what got him here. Thick, full glass jars clattered inside the canvas. The strap cut into his hand, but he wouldn't let it leave his side again, not that it mattered now. The other kids had discovered what he kept inside, though they wouldn't understand. They couldn't. Not even he did, really. A kid had the right to some secrets, if only the ones he could carry. But these had just been taken from him.

He heard voices in the parking lot. More of the gym students were gathered below. His classmates. *Former* classmates now, he guessed.

One kick. One kick was all it took, and that surprised Vickler. One kick sent St. Francis toppling end-over-end to the ground. But the statue didn't deliver the satisfying explosion the angel had. Instead of the sidewalk, it landed with its touchdown-raised arms now stuck in a soft flower bed, its head buried: patron saint of ostriches. The kids standing around the garden looked at it with confusion.

Vickler dragged his bag to St. Thomas. He rattled the saint's head. Jars clinked madly in Vickler's bag. *Clink.* That's what they called him. Clink.

Three kicks later, and St. Thomas became an arrow to the earth. He hit the brick wall along the grand front steps and fractured in two at the waist. This time the kids ran.

St. Barnabas. Decades of hard weather had already crumbled the base of this statue. Vickler heaved him over.

St. Anthony—three shakes, two kicks—pray for us.

Vickler had black dust on his hands now. The filth smeared his face as he wiped away tears.

A man's voice bellowed below the roof hatch. Vickler whirled. The contents of his knapsack clattered: *clinkclink*. The steel sheet rocked once, then twice, as someone rammed it from the other side. The mop handle bent like rubber, flexing, beginning to crack. The next hit splintered it. The tar-bristled mop end flopped away from the jagged stick.

Vickler's hands crawled into his book bag and came out with a sealed glass jar. Trapped inside the clear fluid was a small swollen creature: a baby shark, curled in death, its little black eyes staring at him. He inched closer to the hatch, his shadow touching its edge.

The heavy steel door lifted. Below rose panicky shouts. A woman's voice barked, "Open it already!"

A little head, as white as a clover flower, rose up from the hole. Vickler arched his arm and hurled the jar into the face of Mr. Saducci, the school's mumble-mouthed elderly janitor.

Saducci squealed. One hand rose to shield his face too late. The other squeezed at the edge of the hatch for balance. The jar caromed off his brow and burst against the steel door, spraying the tumbling janitor's face in formaldehyde.

The old man's right hand grasped blindly as his eyes sizzled, and the steel lid slammed down, trapping his fingers. The janitor's wail echoed, seeming to plunge away in the distance as rounds of fresh screams erupted below.

Vickler dropped to the roof and scrambled forward on his hands and knees, pulling his bag after him. He picked up the sharpened end of the splintered mop handle and held it like a spear.

But the hatch didn't move. The janitor's trapped fingers didn't either.

Vickler's guts roared. His greasy black hair dangled around his eyes. He shifted his pack. *Clink. Clink.* His eyes darted. "Go ahead!" he yelled, his voice breaking. "Open it up. Pull in your hand. I won't hurt you!"

A thread of blood began to run along the hatch's crease.

Vickler waited. He lifted the mop handle and timidly poked at the fingertips.

They rolled off the ledge and bounced against the roof.

About twenty minutes before the saints began to fall, another boy, named Peter Davidek, was walking the crowded halls of St. Mike's and trying not to feel microscopic. His last name was pronounced *Davv-ah-deck*, which rhymed with "have a check"—and he had been repeating that all day. Still, most of the teachers got it wrong, even after he meekly corrected them. At first he thought it was on purpose, that they were messing with him. Then he realized they just didn't care enough to make the miniscule effort to remember. He wasn't sure which was worse.

Freshly fourteen years old and a foot shorter than most of the kids around him, the lost eighth-grader searched for the right place to be. It was St. Michael's annual open house for potential incoming students, and the stone halls of the Catholic high school were filled with miniature middle-schoolers like him, trying to make their way between the oafish St. Mike's guys, who seemed to be all shoulders wrapped in polyester blazers, and the equally intimidating sweet-smelling schoolgirls in their tantalizing navy blue sweaters and plaid skirts.

Davidek's heart pounded as he scanned the room numbers. He was supposed to be in Mrs. Apps's chemistry class, room 11-A, but had become separated from his group. There were no familiar faces here. All of Davidek's friends planned to attend Valley High next year, New Kensington's public high school. Only 316 kids in total attended St. Mike's, almost nothing compared to the thousands at Valley, where it was easier to lie low, and the students didn't have to wear stupid uniforms or go to church all the time or have weird priests and nuns watching every move.

Attending Valley was one of the few things Davidek and his parents agreed on. His father had attended St. Mike's for a year, though he hadn't graduated. The old man wanted to know why his son was even bothering to visit that school full of spoiled brats and know-nothings. For Davidek, it had seemed like a good excuse to escape regular class.

Three upperclassmen blundered by in the hallway, punching each other and swinging their book bags like maces. Davidek caught one behind the knee and hit the ground. His wrinkled paper schedule fluttered out of his hand. A girl stepped on his ankle, but she glanced over her shoulder at the guy behind her and apologized to him instead. "No problem," the guy said, stepping on Davidek's ankle, too. Only he did it on purpose.

Legs pistoned at the floor all around Davidek. A hand hooked under his arm to help him up, and that person handed him his schedule before stepping back into the crowd. "I owe you one," Davidek said, but the kid kept moving, giving Davidek a nod. The boy was a visitor, too, since he was wearing regular street clothes and not a St. Mike's uniform. Davidek didn't recognize him from his group, and he would have remembered—this boy had a band of scars on the left side of his face, with rosy tendrils linking the edge of his left eye to his neck.

Lockers slammed like gunfire. Every student seemed to be hauling both book bags and duffel bags as class changed. Some of them toted dirty sneakers. Gym class had just ended for seniors and was about to begin for juniors.

A chunky kid with greasy black hair staggered by Davidek and whacked him on the side with his black canvas bag. Glass jars clattered together inside. A smaller sack, a Pittsburgh Steelers gym bag, dangled at the greasy kid's side.

"Cliiiiiink!!" someone in the crowd shouted. A couple of girls giggled. Soon the hallway was a cacophony of voices muttering, whispering, and shouting the same word: *ClinkClinkClink*. All of a sudden, no one was moving. They were blockading him.

The greasy kid whirled around. "I got to get to my *locker*," he barked.

"Umm, can you help me?" Davidek pleaded to the faces around him, but they were all too amused blocking in the increasingly frustrated Clink. It was Davidek's first lesson at the school: When people didn't like you, they got in your way. When they didn't care about you, they let you get in your own way.

Clink clutched his clattering black bag like a battering ram, shoving through and disappearing as the change-of-class bell shrieked. Everyone still standing in the hall, including Davidek, was now officially late.

The students around him scattered, but Davidek had no one to follow. He had lost track of the scarred boy, but followed in that direction. He found a room 11 on the second floor, but it was an elderly nun teaching French—not Mrs. Apps's chemistry class.

In an empty stairwell, Davidek found a white-haired janitor hauling a hot tar bucket up to the roof on a retractable steel ladder. Davidek held out his paper schedule and asked, "Could you help me find where I'm supposed to be?"

The janitor glared at him, like he'd been tortured mightily by the children at this school, and was not now about to supply aid and comfort to the enemy. When he spoke, the Pittsburgh accent was so thick, it was almost another language: "Howen da'heckamye sposta know where yinz kids shubbee?" Davidek blinked. *How in the heck am I supposed to know where yinz kids should be.* Yinz. In the South, it was *y'all*, in New York it was *you's*. Around Pittsburgh, *yinz* was the plural of *you*, the telltale sign of someone born and raised in Pennsylvania's bottom left corner. The word was invisible most of the time, since everybody used it now and again.

"I'm looking for room 11-A," Davidek said. "But I can't—"

The janitor waved his free hand impatiently, counting out on fingers that would soon be separated from his hand. "A, B, C," he said. "Three letters, three floors. Unnerstann?"

Davidek thanked him and descended the steps. The janitor muttered as he carried his acrid-smelling tar bucket up the ladder.

At the bottom of the stairwell, the eighth-grader pushed open the doors to the first-floor hallway. "Lost?" a woman's voice said.

He turned to see a tall, plump woman in a long, royal blue dress, which swept the floor at her heels. She was pacing outside the closed door of the principal's office, apparently waiting for entry. He smiled at her, and she smiled back—thinly. He couldn't guess her age—anywhere from thirty to fifty. She was pretty in a sad way, a faded way. Once-delicate features had gone soft and round, slightly wrinkled, as if they had swollen and then deflated. "Are you a teacher?" Davidek asked. "I could use some help finding—"

"I'm the *guidance counselor*," she said, as if *teacher* were a slur. "Why are you wandering the halls?"

"Uh, I'm Peter Davidek, I'm—"

"Daffy-*what?*" she said.

"Daff-a-*deck*," he corrected, with a break in his voice. "I'm an eighth-grade visitor for the open house."

"I didn't ask your *name*. Why aren't you with your group?" Her voice was sharp, annoyed by default. Her eyes narrowed, which with her chubby cheeks, made her look like a grown-up baby.

"I'm supposed to be in 11-A, chemis—"

"Right there," she said, jabbing a finger down the hall. The nail was also painted royal blue. "You're *supposed* to be there."

Davidek was about to thank her and slink away when two boys emerged from the men's bathroom, both wearing shorts, T-shirts, and tennis shoes. A stout man—completely bald, lacking even eyebrows—emerged from the stairwell, also wearing shorts and a T-shirt (though his was tucked in.) He had a whistle around his neck, and blew it as he tossed the first boy a football and shoved open the bathroom door: "Ten more minutes, guys, out on the field!" The boys with the football ran off, and the bald gym teacher looked Davidek up and down, then turned to the blue woman. "So what's going on *here*, Ms. Bromine?" he asked, stroking his naked chin. *Bromine*. It was a name like chemicals in the mouth.

"I'm trying to get to the bottom of that myself, Mr. Mankowski," the guidance counselor sighed.

"Ahhhh . . . ," the bald man said, acting like this was serious business. "Should I get Sister Maria?" Sister Maria was the principal, and had welcomed all the visiting students in the assembly hall that morning. She had seemed nice. Davidek actually hoped they *would* get her.

Ms. Bromine nodded toward the principal's closed office door. "I'm waiting for Sister Maria myself—not that it ever matters for much. As you know," she said, her lips tightening. With a marble-sized mole near the right corner of her mouth, the expression was like a sideways exclamation point. She turned back to Davidek: "We don't appreciate visitors abusing the rules at St. Michael's, young man. Tell me your name again?"

"Peter *Daff*-ah-deck," the boy repeated, for the third time. "And I wasn't—"

A swell of laughter and a loud, horrified "Oh, God!" echoed from the men's bathroom, drawing a concerned look from Mr. Mankowski.

"All right," said Ms. Bromine. "You can go—*this time*. But if you find yourself hopelessly confused again in this simple three-story structure—"

"*Stop!*" a boy yelled from inside the restroom.

Laughter erupted again and there was more shouting. Feet scuffled; voices rose. A boy cried out in agony. Mr. Mankowski ran forward and shoved open the bathroom door just as something massive collided against the other side, smashing the door into his face. A clear fluid popped from his nose as he collapsed.

The bathroom door whooshed open and Davidek saw the greasy boy named Clink shamble out, his eyes bulging beneath tangles of hair. His black duffel bag, clattering with off-key chimes, swung around his belly like a disembowled organ. His uniform gray slacks were unbuttoned, and there was a splash of blood on his open white shirt.

A boy with a gaping mouth of crooked horse teeth darted from the bathroom, holding a small glass jar over his head. "Have this back, you fucking freak!" Horse-Teeth hollered, heaving the jar against the wall just over Clink's shoulder, spraying the brick with putrid yellow fluid.

A new figure emerged from the boys' room, a kid gushing blood and yelping panicked screams as he pawed delicately at the blunt end of a click-button pen jutting from his right cheek. The tip of the pen, dripping ribbons of scarlet saliva, poked out between his lips like a strange lizard tongue, clicking against his teeth as he moaned for help.

The contents of Colin Vickler's black bag had been a curiosity at St. Mike's for months. People began noticing the unusual glass clanking sound around the start of the school year, but whenever teachers had taken him aside and forcibly searched him, they never found anything. The rumors got more and more elaborate: It was a portable methamphetamine lab. Or, maybe was he smuggling bomb chemicals. Sickening theories arose: He carried his own urine in jars, filling them at school and keeping them on a shelf in his bedroom. But for what dark purpose could any of this be happening: perversion, paranoia, witchcraft?

Colin "Clink" Vickler didn't have a single friend at St. Mike's, though he had been a student there for three years. As a freshman, he was a lightning rod for the ninety-two-year-old school's hazing tradition, a yearlong, alleg-edly good-natured teasing of new students, which the school tacitly ap-proved of as a "fun" bonding exercise for the newcomers. Vickler had carried a disproportionate amount of the torment, with even his fellow freshmen bullying him, usually to impress or distract their own oppressors.

When he was as a sophomore, the teasing hadn't stopped. In one of the worst instances, a group of seniors ambushed him in the bathroom one day, held his arms, and snagged the rim of his underwear, ripping them off from underneath his pants and tearing into his groin. While he rolled in agony, someone went outside and ran the tattered threads up the school flagpole. For weeks, Vickler's classmates saluted him and hummed "The Battle Hymn of the Republic."

It wasn't the beautiful and so-called popular kids who did it to him, though they may have been laughing on the periphery. Everyone was, ba-sically. The boys who had attacked him in the bathroom were the most worthless, aimless, and friendless in the school. The cheerleaders, basket-ball players, theater kids, and science geeks (among countless other cliques at St. Mike's) all picked on kids within their own circles, venting their frustrations on weaker versions of themselves. Sometimes the cliques turned on each other, but that was rare. When one group did need an-other to beat up on, they all tended to turn on the same niche—the losers. Clink just happened to be the one the losers picked on.

He became a junior, but even with upperclassman status, the teasing never stopped. The worst were the girls laughing at him, girls he thought were cute. And he was no help for himself—dropping his eyes, muttering, not clever enough to return the insults, not strong enough to fight back. It never stopped. It never would.

Vickler's only protection was to hide.

St. Mike's was a strange old building, full of narrow corridors and stair-wells curling deep underground in a quiet labyrinth. To escape his jeering classmates when class wasn't in session, Vickler would sneak into the sub-basement and take sanctuary in the science storage room, where he would read comic books or video game magazines. There among the Bunsen burners and assorted carafes of chemicals, he found shelf after shelf of glass containers, each containing a preserved biological specimen: insects, birds, snakes, worms, lizards, fetal pigs, fish, frogs, mice. They stared forlornly at the greasy-haired boy hiding in their midst. Vickler studied them in the darkness. Even the prickly-legged giant centipedes had a mournful appearance, floating lifeless and tangled together in their preservative stew.

These beings could not escape, had no future, and existed only as peculiarities.

Vickler began smuggling away the jars, one by one, taking them to a place in the woods near his home to release the poor deceased creatures for burial. His parents became suspicious about him going to the woods each night, so he had to slow down. He knew he couldn't explain. He also couldn't stop. There were hundreds of jars in the storage basement, and he committed himself to removing them all.

The earth around his shallow burials became blighted. Weeds shriveled to brown husks as they absorbed the toxic preserving chemicals. To avoid detection, Vickler began to spread the bodies around more broadly through the woods, which only slowed his progress. Then the science faculty noticed that half their biology specimens had disappeared. Suspicion fell on the janitor for carelessly disposing them, and new ones were ordered from the Nebraska Scientific company. Colin Vickler's smuggling campaign started all over again.

Throughout this time, not a soul knew what "Clink" really carried in his bag. Not until the day of the open house.

Gym class at St. Mike's happened only on sunny days. This was because the school no longer had a gymnasium, and phys-ed classes had nowhere to take place when the weather was unkind. The old gymnasium had been converted into the parish's church when the original chapel burned down four years earlier. There had been no money to rebuild the church, so the gym was made into a substitute house of worship—at first temporarily, though it had since become dismayingly permanent. The old locker rooms had become dressing rooms for the priest and altar boys, so for gym class, the students changed out of their uniforms in the school bathrooms. Their calesthentics and games of dodgeball took place in the grassy field where the burned chapel once stood. (In the winter, or if it rained, they earned gym-class credit at a nearby bowling alley.)

On the day of the open house, while Davidek stood outside in the hall-way in the glare of Ms. Bromine, a junior in that boys' bathroom named Richard Mullen picked a fight with the only kid who was a bigger loser than he was. The bathroom was crowded, and Mullen was standing on one leg, leaning over at an odd angle, pulling at the tip of one socked foot as his open pants slipped down around his ankles. He stumbled backwards and landed hard on his ass, which drew loud laughs from the other boys— including creepy Clink Vickler.

Mullen had only one friend in the school, his dull, horse-toothed com-panion, Frank Simms—the only boy besides Clink whose existence was more pathetic than Mullen's. Since he was already so low in the pecking order, Mullen couldn't abide being laughed at by the shy, fat, fellow outcast.

In the hallway, Mr. Mankowski's whistle blew and his voice called out: "Ten more minutes, guys, out on the field!"

Everyone was still laughing as Mullen stood up, and he said to Clink, because he couldn't say it to anyone else: "Is that how your dad laughs when he's buttfucking you?" Mullen punctuated this with a swift kick to Clink's duffel bag, causing two glass jars, pregnant with fluid, to tumble out and roll slowly across the tile floor.

A handsome and popular boy named Michael Crawford lifted one of the jars toward the light, and a preserved fruit bat inside slid around to face him and his friends—its mouth open, wings undulating in the shaking water.

Horse-toothed Simms picked up the other jar. "Holy shit, this guy's pick-ling dead critters!" he cried, and Mullen shoved aside the layer of papers, books, pens, and pencils in Clink's bag to reveal a dozen more jars. He extracted one—an embryonic pig—and held it out. "Whatever this is, you're going to hell for it, sicko. . . ."

Vickler's mind went numb. An eternity passed. He had been trying to do something good, something merciful, but now he saw his collection with the same horror as the boys around him. There was nothing he could do, no explanation that would make sense. He heard the words *psycho, freak, disgusting,* and began to cry, squatting over his scattered papers, gathering them blindly.

Mullen stuck the specimen jar against Vickler's face. "Wait'll the girls find out what you did to P-p-p-porky Pig!"

That's when Vickler's groping hand found the ballpoint pen.

Before he even realized what was happening, Vickler was slicing it through the air, puncturing Mullen's cheek like a marshmallow.

Mullen screeched, and Clink seized him by the throat, shoving him backwards with blind fury and slamming him against the boys' room door as Mr. Mankowski pushed it open on the other side, crushing the teacher's sinus cavity and toppling him to the ground.

Clink tossed the bleeding, braying Mullen aside and grabbed his bag, yanking the strap over his shoulder as he fled out the door.

The first-floor hallway of St. Mike's yawned before Vickler like a giant stone throat. He was dimly aware of figures around him, two blurs—one giant and blue, the other small and insignificant—standing a few feet away, and a man—Mr. Mankowski—rolling in agony on the floor beside the lockers.

Horse-toothed Simms rushed out of the bathroom, hefting a jar with a floating tapeworm inside, and hurled it at Vickler, who shoved past Davidek and sprinted into the stairwell, up one floor, then another, until there was no one around him except the stunned-looking janitor standing beside a ladder leading to a square of blue sky.

He began to climb, terrified, thinking maybe he could hide, and realizing too late he was trapping himself.

With unwitting help from Ms. Bromine, Vickler soon learned he had trapped everyone else, too.

When the janitor became separated from his fingers, he plunged down like a pile of old clothes and smashed against the stairwell floor, squealing as he clutched the red nubs of his knuckles. He might have shattered his spine if Mr. Mankowski, staggering beneath the ladder with his bruised face, hadn't softened the fall.

Ms. Bromine tried to remain calm. She took a step back as the janitor's crimson-spritzing fingertips spray-painted the floor. The gym teacher was hysterical, whimpering beneath the crumpled janitor, his collarbone fractured. Davidek stood with the crowd of other gawking students and faculty as the two wounded men gibbered madly at the foot of the ladder. "This is going to be bad for enrollment," Davidek heard one of the teachers say.

Ms. Bromine, suddenly aware of the audience, tried to clear people away, but the crowd was too large for anyone to go anywhere. People in the back were yelling, "Sister Maria is trying to come through! Clear a path!" and Davidek looked over the railing to see the old woman on the stairs below, poking through the mob.

Bromine drew back against the wall. She couldn't be seen presiding over this chaos.

The red handle of a fire alarm was beside her. "We need to get everyone *out of here*," she said as her fingers reached for the switch.

On the roof, Colin Vickler, also known as Clink Vickler, also known in grade school as Creepy Colin, seventeen years old, still without a driver's license, pale-skinned, a prospect-less virgin, and utterly friendless, felt power for the first time in his life as he listened to the electric howl of the alarm and watched waves of his schoolmates gush out of St. Michael's arched entryway.

They were afraid. Of him.

Some turned their faces up, squinting against the sunlight, their expressions bent into question marks as they tried to see him. A few who'd witnessed what had happened were crying, not looking back—others were spreading the news, passing along a contamination of lies: Clink had been murdering animals, dismembering them, and hiding the remains in glass containers. One of the boys from the changing room said he'd looked into the bag and saw a human hand in one of the jars. A few visiting eighth-graders overheard a teacher say the boy on the roof had cut the school janitor's throat.

The actual truth was bad enough. Vickler knew he wasn't coming down again. There was no crawling back through the hatch. There was no apologizing. There was no explaining. He was over. Colin Vickler was gone. Now, he was just Clink. Weird. Psychotic. Dangerous.

But he kind of liked that last part.

The boy lifted his bag onto the ledge and ran his grubby fingers over the tops of the remaining jars, counting ten. He hefted one in his hand, looked down into the parking lot, and surveyed his targets.

From the outside, St. Michael the Archangel High School looked like a building that might devour other buildings. The style of traditional collegiate Gothic architecture seemed to have been fused with primitive battle fortifications to create an imposing, redbrick edifice that bulged up from the earth like some thorny, stone-shelled titan. Davidek looked back at the building as he fled with the other students. "Rubberneck later, man. Now you better run!" someone said, pulling him forward. It was the boy with the scar on his cheek, the one who had helped him in the hallway earlier.

The boy on the roof heaved a jar toward the crowd, smashing a spider-web into the windshield of a red Buick in the parking lot. Davidek and the scarred kid bolted together through the scattering mob as the second and third jar of scientific specimens exploded against the ground behind them.

Ms. Bromine stood in the center of the evacuation, conducting the mayhem to the street. A shuffling, heavyset kid, gushing sweat in his St. Mike's uniform, nudged in front of Davidek, huffing as he lurched forward, like a bull trying to run on its hind legs. A thin red tie drifted over his shoulder as a flash of light streaked out of the sky and exploded against the back of the chubby kid's skull. The glass jar had made a hissing sound as it cut the air, and the fat boy made the same noise as he faceplanted against the pavement.

Davidek tried to stop, tried to reach down and snag the fallen kid's shoulders, but the other students pushed him forward, with no time for anyone's rescue but their own. Davidek and the scarred boy reached the edge of school property, where cars cut back and forth along the street, honking furiously at the herd of students fleeing across the blacktop.

That's when Ms. Bromine began to yell, "Stop! *Stop!*"

For a moment, everyone did.

"*No one . . . can leave . . . school grounds,*" she said, the crowd swirling around her as she turned. Her blond puff of hair was wilting with sweat. "No leaving without a . . . a . . . permission slip."

The students of St. Mike's gawped at her. They began to argue in discordant unison. Then another jar streaked from the rooftop and sent them scattering for cover behind parked cars.

The school principal, Sister Maria Hest, was among the confused and cowering. She crawled through the hiding crowd, demanding information. "What's happening? . . . Why is the school being evacuated? . . . Who is throwing things from the roof?" Everyone tried to tell her at once, so she understood none of it.

Ms. Bromine did not speak up right away. She was formulating justifications. She wondered who, if anyone, had stayed behind with Mr. Mankowski and Mr. Saducci.

A UPS truck squealed smoke from its tires and jerked to a stop inches from some scampering freshmen who'd decided to ignore the rules and run off the property. As the driver drowned out his own obscenities with the blast of his horn, Bromine and Sister Maria saw more refugee trails of students flowing across the street, out of range from the boy on the roof.

The guidance counselor snapped her fingers at two of the other teachers. "Grab those kids. Keep them on school property! We can be sued if they get hurt in this traffic!"

A blond girl in gym clothes broke away from the group and stood her ground in the middle of the street, right in front of Bromine. Her kinky hair was tied up in two madwoman pigtails. "Are you a total fucking idiot?" the girl snapped. "What if we get hurt *on* school property?"

Bromine became aware of many eyes turning toward her. Her throat tightened. "Don't curse at me," she said.

The blonde raised two middle fingers at the guidance counselor. "How about some sign language, then?" she said, turning her back to leave. Bromine darted into the street, seizing the girl by one frazzled pigtail and dragging her back to the sidewalk.

A smattering of rocks fell against the cars at the far end of the parking lot. The boy on the roof was throwing chunks of broken brick at them now. Bromine ducked behind the trunk of a beat-up green Plymouth, still gripping the blond girl's hair. At the other corner of the lot, a cluster of boisterious seniors stood on the hood of a silver Honda, chortling piggishly as they pretended to shoot the projectiles out of the sky with invisible shotguns.

In the center of the parking lot, lying motionless in a widening pool of blood, was the unconscious boy who had charged in front of Davidek before getting beaned on the skull. With everyone else hiding, this still figure was now the easiest target for the boy on the roof.

Thuck. Thuck. Chunks of brick began to thwack against the facedown kid.

Davidek and his new friend with the scarred cheek were both crouched beside a Jeep, just a few spaces away. They could see glass mixed with blood on the back of the unconscious boy's head.

"Someone should help," Davidek said.

The scarred kid nodded. "You know, if that kid hadn't shoved us aside, maybe me or you would be lying there with our head split open. . . . You think he'd run out to save *us*?"

Davidek shrugged. "He's bleeding bad."

The scarred kid looked around doubtfully. "I'm not sure doing the right thing is the way to survive at this place." But Davidek was already edging out, getting ready to spring toward the wounded kid. "I could have grabbed that crazy kid in the hall, tried to slow him down," he said. "But I didn't. I just got out of the way. I was scared."

"Guilty conscience?" the scarred kid said with a laugh. "You're perfect for Catholic school." He put a hand out. "Hey, tough guy, before we charge into battle . . . my name's Noah Stein. My family calls me No for short. No Stein. That's weird, right?" Davidek said he guessed it was and shook the kid's hand distractedly.

A monstrous, skinny shape, tall and bent like a streetlamp, cast its long shadow over them. It was one of the teachers, a young guy with a stretched, gargoyle's face. "If you boys are planning a distraction, I could sure use one," he said, moving forward toward the school without stopping for a response. "Go, Mr. Zimmer!" the girl with the yellow pigtails screamed as Ms. Bromine's gripped loosened and she pulled free. Bromine staggered forward, watching her colleague steal the credit for saving the day.

. . .

Mr. Zimmer had been a student at St. Mike's more years ago than he cared to remember. He'd been a good kid, a quiet kid, one who never got in trouble—except once. Since he had long legs and stretchy arms, some guys had dared him to climb one of the brass waterspouts on the corner of the school building. The trick was to hold on to some of the brick outcroppings, but no one else could reach them. Nobody except Andy Zimmer and his praying mantis limbs.

Getting up through the rooftop hatch was impossible—the janitor had proved that—but that old waterspout was another fast way up, provided Vickler didn't notice until he was already over the ledge.

The sound of sirens rose in the distance. Police. Firefighters. Zimmer didn't want to think about what the cops would do if the boy on the roof started shoving statues over on them, too.

On the other side of the Jeep where Davidek and Stein were taking cover, a chubby black boy poked his head up. "Hey, I'm Hector. Hector Greenwill," he said, extending his hand, although neither boy was going to move from their hiding spot to shake it. "I'm another eighth-grade visitor, like you guys." He was dressed in tan pants and stuffed into an orange-and-black striped sweater. "When you do your thing, I'll help cause another distraction, try to draw his fire," he said.

Stein shrugged. "Perfect, dude. You *are* dressed as a bull's-eye."

Greenwill got into a squat, ready to run. "Just don't make someone else have to rescue *you*, all right?" he said, and lumbered off in the opposite direction from Mr. Zimmer, toward the grassy green field beside the school, where the burned-down church once stood.

"Okay, hero," Stein said, putting a hand on Davidek's back. "Let's go pretend we're the good guys."

A pair of sapphire-clawed hands seized them both by their collars. "You're too close!" Ms. Bromine growled, pulling them back. "Get down! Now!"

Davidek squirmed, pointing to the lifeless heap in the center of the lot. "We're going to help that kid!" Bromine peered in the unconscious boy's direction. "Carl!" she barked. "Carl LeRose! Stand up now and get over here!"

The boy was lifelessly disobedient. Davidek kept trying to pull away, but Stein was looking for something to distract her. In the same instant, the fat boy in the black-and-tangerine sweater made his move—running and yelling and waving his arms in the wide grassy field, drawing the attention of the boy on the roof, along with everyone else in the parking lot. On the opposite side of the building, Mr. Zimmer put one hand over the other and began to methodically climb the waterspout.

This was their moment. Stein watched Davidek struggle helplessly as the guidance counselor held him in place. He reached out and grabbed the blue lady's face between his hands, thrusting his face against hers in a smacking kiss.

Bromine opened her hands.

Davidek bolted free, his lungs gasping air as he dashed toward the unconscious boy, grabbing him by one arm and pulling him across the asphalt. It looked like the facedown kid had an urgent classroom question. Half of a brick cratered into the hood of a Volkswagen Beetle beside them. They'd been spotted again.

Davidek heaved the unconscious boy onto his own back and stumbled toward the sheltering cars, where Stein now rolled on the ground as a raving Ms. Bromine slapped him silly.

The wounded boy's head lolled, like his neck was a kitchen rag. One shoe fell off his foot. His eyes were open, drifting back toward the school. He raised a weak arm and pointed. "Fuckin' . . . *Spider-Man* . . . ," he groaned.

Mr. Zimmer, his shirttail dangling free, had reached the top of the school, his ropy arms grabbing for purchase along the stone ledge. The boy on the roof hadn't seen him yet. He was instead watching with panic as dual fire engines pulled up to the curb and police cars squealed into the parking lot. Hector Greenwill and his bull's-eye sweater were now close enough to hit.

Clink had one jar left, and intended to make it count by hurling it directly into the fat kid's face. There was no fluid in it, so it was light, and he aimed it ever so carefully. He shook the jar slightly, but nothing rattled inside. Clink held out the glass container, turning it at an angle. The world got very quiet for the boy on the roof.

There was nothing inside this one. The jar was empty—except for the image of the boy he was targeting, who with his black-and-orange striped sweater looked like a very exotic trapped bumblebee.

Clink unscrewed the jar's metal lid. He spilled the nothing over the side, where he imagined it was captured by the silent wind and carried away. He put the empty jar back in his bag and adjusted the strap around his shoulder.

On the other side of the school, Mr. Zimmer had clawed over the ledge and was surging forward, arms outstretched, his feet making gritty pulse-pounds against the surface of the roof.

Vickler's eyes were closed. He never even saw the teacher coming.

Down below, Davidek was cradling the wounded kid as paramedics swarmed around them. A few cars over, Bromine was dragging Stein by the front of his shirt. Then a hush swept over the crowd in the parking lot.

Everyone looked up to see Clink slip backwards off the ledge.

PART I

The Bad Hand

ONE

Six months later, Davidek stood again in St. Michael's parking lot, looking up through gray rainfall at the rooftop of the school. The destroyed saints had been replaced, glistening amid the surviving statues like new teeth in a decrepit smile. Water poured down the rust-colored stone walls of the school, turning the classroom windows into shimmering cascades of light.

It was the first day of the new school year, and Davidek stood silent and still, his gray slacks, white shirt, and blue blazer growing heavy in the falling rainwater. He couldn't believe he was here any more than his parents could believe *him* when he had come home from visiting St. Mike's with stories of stabbed faces, severed fingers, and projectile animal specimens.

"Don't make up stories," his father had said, showing him the local newspaper story about a janitor who was injured at St. Mike's in a roofing accident. "No mention of your daring rescue or a kid falling off the building."

"He fell, but he didn't *land,*" Davidek said, making his father groan and his mother sigh.

Clink's attempt at a gruesome end was stymied by his infamous black bag. When he tipped off the roof, it was that strap Mr. Zimmer snagged as he lunged toward the falling boy. Zimmer's long, ropy muscles strained to hold the teenager aloft as the shrieking boy slashed at his arms, pleading to fall. In desperation, Zimmer had made a fist of his free hand and thrust it down into the boy's face—one, two, three, very fast punches. Clink's face reeled backwards as he went limp, and the teacher grabbed a second hold on his shirt, heaving him back up to safety.

When the police took control of the scene, Ms. Bromine was still fuming over the kiss Stein had used to distract her so Davidek could break free. She wanted both the boys arrested. "They, uh . . . *kissed* you," the cop said flatly, more annoyed than amused. "Anybody else see this?"

Bromine demanded to see his superior officer.

The lieutenant who came over to her later told the ranting guidance counselor, "We got a kid with a stabbed face, a kid with a fractured skull, a guy with no fingers, a guy with a broken arm. And you've got—?"

"I've been sexually assaulted!" Bromine huffed. The lieutenant took a deep breath and closed his eyes. He said he'd bring it up with the principal, but Sister Maria had already heard the complaints and didn't believe them either. "I think Ms. Bromine is suffering a bit of anxiety," she said. The lieutenant nodded. "She can get in line," he sighed, and pretended to write in his notebook because Ms. Bromine was watching them.

Mr. Mankowski was taken away in a stretcher that held his neck between giant red pads. The janitor was wheeled away, moaning, reaching back toward another EMT, who carried a white towel with the old man's fingers inside.

After the unconscious boy Davidek had rescued was taken away in an ambulance, the lieutenant came over to talk to the visiting eighth-grader. He wore a silver name tag beneath his badge—BELLOWS. He wanted Davidek's name and address, but the boy told him he'd already given all that information to another officer.

"It's not for the report," Lieutenant Bellows said. "It's for somebody else."

"Who?"

The lieutenant shrugged. "Maybe someone wants to send you a thank-you card."

Davidek began reading the paper every day, knowing there had to be an update, some follow-up, some explanation about what had happened.

But there was nothing, not even a week later. "I think I saw something about it on CNN," Bill Davidek said at dinner. "'Playground fight at local school,' right?" The old man scratched his beard with a self-satisfied smile.

"Come on, Dad! That guy jumped *off the roof*! He almost killed himself!" Davidek said, his cheeks stuffed with food. "He chopped off a dude's fingers! . . ."

Davidek's mother clanged her fork and knife flat on the table. "For God's sake, we're eating fish sticks," she said.

The table went silent. After a while, June Davidek spoke to her husband without looking up. "You know, they say these private schools look better on a college application than ever before. Really helps a student stand out. I just saw something about that in *Reader's Digest*. . . ."

Her husband frowned. "We pay taxes. And those taxes pay for the public schools. You don't pay for groceries at one store, leave them there, and then go buy them again at another store, do you? So why would we pay for St. Mike's? Because they wear little suits and ties? Because they think they're smarter than everybody else?"

Davidek's mother was silent. Then she ventured: "If we *weren't* paying though . . . ," and Davidek's father stiffened.

"I said we're done talking about that," he said.

Their son asked, "Talking about what?"

Bill Davidek pointed a fork at Peter's plate. "Eat your fish dicks," he said, which made his son laugh, and made his wife clang down her silverware again.

Bill had once been a student at St. Mike's, but it was a sore subject—he dropped out after two years, though nowadays that was the only part he seemed proud of. He finished up at public school only because it was a requirement to get hired at the Kees-Northson Steel Mill over in Brackenridge, which was just down the hill from St. Mike's. It irritated him to see it every day as he left work, and irritated him more that his wife never stopped fetishizing the place.

She had always wanted to attend, though her parents refused. (It was one of the only things Bill liked about her family.) When the time came, June had insisted they enroll their older son, Charlie, in the school. Charlie was seven years older than Peter, who remembered those fights well from his hiding place under the dining room table. He even remembered the line his mother would use: "This is how we make our boy into something better than his father." Bill complained he was paying tuition only so June could brag to her card club. He was partly right. "It's expensive, but my Charles is worth it," she used to tell her friends. She always called him Charles around other people.

Davidek and Charlie weren't close, partly due to the age difference. Davidek's most vivid memories of his big brother were about getting pushed around by him. Charlie was always bigger, so all he needed to do was lie on top of his baby brother, smothering him, to win any fight. Then Davidek discovered a foolproof self-defense: The Purple Nurple, aka the Titty-Twister—a tried and true fight move every younger sibling learns after being repeatedly crushed by an overpowering foe. Charlie would rear back, clutching his aching areola, cursing his little brother's name. "Fucking, Peter . . . Fuck!"

Charlie's name was off-limits in the Davidek house now, except during arguments—which their dinner conversation was now turning into. "I just think private school would give Peter an advantage," June said. "It's an investment in the future."

Her husband jerked his thumb at the empty fourth seat beside the table, where Charlie used to sit. "That one turned out to be a real good investment in the future, too, didn't he?"

After St. Mike's, Charlie Davidek had spent the next four years getting drunk and fucking up. He flunked out of two colleges. Then he moved back home and spent a couple years working part-time for a landscaping company, and warring full-time with his parents. When they finally made him start paying rent and reimbursing them for whatever he ate out of the refrigerator, Charlie joined the Marines, fleeing Pittsburgh for Camp Pendelton outside San Diego. Enlistment made Charlie someone the Davideks could be proud of again.

They had Charlie's military portrait enlarged so it could hang in the center of their staircase. Beside it he hung a snapshot of Bill fishing with a six-year-old Charlie, and Charlie's scowling senior picture from St. Mike's. June kept a small version of the military portrait in her wallet, by her credit cards, which allowed her to accidentally-on-purpose show him off to random bank tellers and grocery store clerks.

Then, a year into his service, Charlie had gone AWOL. The family found out when some men from the local recruiting office visited the house to ask whether they'd had any contact with their missing son. Months later, a letter arrived from Arkansas—no return address—where Charlie said he was working in a garage. He said he was okay, and told them not to worry. He didn't explain why he'd gone AWOL, but nobody really wondered. Charlie (and another guy from his unit) had taken off in late summer of 1990, just a few weeks after Iraqi tanks rolled into Kuwait, and Americans started tying yellow ribbons around trees. When Davidek's father turned his son's letter over to the Marines, they offered to mail back a copy. "Don't bother," he said. "I never want to hear from that coward again."

All the pictures of Charlie were gone now, even the ones from when he was little. When Charlie's name did come up, it was usually as a way for Bill Davidek to trash the school he always hated. "Four years at St. Mike's. Thousands of dollars down the toilet," he said. "We might as well have burned it to warm the house."

Their younger son, Peter, was happy to go to Valley with the rest of his friends—Chad Junod; Billy Fularz; the Peters twins, Matt and Mark. It bothered him that his mother kept talking about the Catholic school like it was even a possibility. It bothered his father, too. "I don't want to talk to you about this anymore," he said.

June shrugged. She twirled a fish stick on her plate. Bill Davidek nodded at his son, who smiled when his dad said: "*Nobody's* going to St. Mike's."

The Big Texan changed that.

It was late July. Davidek noticed the silver Porsche parked in front of their house as he rode his bike around from the backyard. Nobody in their neighborhood drove a car like that, and if they did, they wouldn't park it in the street. The Davideks lived on a main strip through a part of town known as Parnassus, right along the Allegheny River. There was a sand and gravel company at the water's edge that sent massive dump trucks rumbling down their street all day, spilling flecks of grit and stones against the windshields and paint jobs of those too stupid not to use their driveways.

Through the living room window, Davidek could see a large man in an immaculate gray suit, with an open-collar ivory shirt and a tan bald head rimmed by a corona of gray hair. His teeth were huge and white and perfect.

Davidek immediately thought of him as The Big Texan. No one ever told the boy his real name, and he reminded Davidek of one of those cheerful tycoons featured in a glossy business magazines, one hand propped against an oil derrick and the other waving hundred-dollar bills in the wind.

When Davidek went inside, The Big Texan was laughing and assuring Davidek's parents that they were smart people for making a decision like this, very smart indeed. Davidek's father stood by the fireplace, his arms crossed, looking unconvinced. Davidek's mother sat on the couch, her hands folded primly in her lap, grinning like someone who'd just won an argument. For some reason, she was wearing the red cocktail dress that she saved for parties or formal occasions. Davidek's father was in dirty jeans and a UNITED STEELWORKERS LOCAL 1196 T-shirt, which had creases like it had just been taken out of the bottom of a drawer for this occasion.

The conversation stopped when they saw Peter.

"This must be the boy! I mean, the young *man*!" boomed The Big Texan, extending an arm and swallowing Davidek's hand in a grip that was surprisingly gentle, like a bodybuilder shaking hands with a baby. "Did your parents tell you about me?" the stranger asked.

Davidek's father fixed him with a hard expression and nodded his head slightly, so the boy said, "Uh . . . yeah, I think so."

The stranger looked very pleased. "Your mom and dad have been talking with me for a few weeks, but they drive a hard bargain," he said. "They're very protective of their little son. . . . But I think they've finally come around."

Davidek's father stared at the floor. His mother kept shaking her foot, like she wanted to dance. The stranger leaned down close, like he was sharing a secret. "Peter, I want you to know that school changed my life. And it changed your father's life, even if he doesn't like to admit it." He put a hand on Davidek's shoulder. "It's going to change your life, too."

Davidek studied his parents for some sign of what was happening. The

Big Texan leaned back and said, "We'll work out all the dollars and cents later. Cross the *i*'s and dot the *t*'s, and all that." He nudged Davidek, who laughed with him uncertainly.

Davidek's father extended his hand, albeit reluctantly, but the stranger surprised him with a bear hug instead, pinning his arms at his sides. "Been too long, Billy boy," The Big Texan said. "Too long, by half."

Moments later, the Porsche was roaring away into the sunset. Hi-yo, silver sportscar, away.

"Who the hell was that?" the boy demanded.

Davidek's father walked out of the room, while Davidek's mother explained, "That man was from the parish over at St. Michael's. He thinks you'd be a good student there."

Her voice dropped to a whisper. "He's been calling for *weeks*," she said. "He's friends with your father."

"We're not *friends*," Bill Davidek said, storming back into the room.

The boy narrowed his eyes, not understanding. "But . . . I'm already signed up at Valley." He looked back and forth between his mother and father. Neither one looked back at him.

That's how, on the first day of his first year of high school, Peter Davidek found himself in the rain outside St. Michael the Archangel.

He and his mother were fighting as she drove him into the parking lot. Not only was Davidek unhappy to be there, but his mother had also failed to buy him a standard uniform-regulation red tie. Instead, June had given him a hand-me-down clip-on from when Charlie was in grade school. "It's basically the same," she said.

It was *not* the same. It was too short, and too fat, and the little silver clip stuck out at the top, poking into Davidek's throat. It also hung crooked on his collar, no matter how much he fussed with it. "Please don't make me wear this," he said.

"Everybody at St. Mike's wears a tie," she answered, checking her lipstick in the rearview mirror. Behind them, a yellow school bus pulled into the lot, and a cluster of similarly uniformed kids shuffled out, scurrying to the school as they opened umbrellas or held book bags over their heads. "See!" June said. "Those boys have red ties."

"Mom, this isn't like those."

His mother pushed a button, unlocking the minivan doors. "Well, if you want a grown-up tie, start acting like a grown-up and we'll see."

"Mom . . . pl—," he said.

"Do I have to repeat that for you? Do I?" This was what she always said to end an argument. If he kept fighting, she'd just keep saying it. She'd keep *repeating* it—not her original point, but that phrase: *Do I need to repeat it for you? Do I need to repeat it for you?*

Davidek stepped out into the rainstorm. He reached up to his collar, clipped on the tie, and faced the school as his mother drove off, and prepared for the worst. The worst, however, was already prepared for him.

TWO

Lorelei Paskal awoke before her alarm on that same first day of the new school year. Her eyes opened wide in the dim light, and she listened to the rain hammering an irregular rhythm in the silence. She had seven minutes before the buzzer went off—a good omen. Lorelei sprang out of bed.

The past two years had been deeply unhappy ones for the fifteen-year-old. They were supposed to be uncomplicated times, seventh and eighth grade—silly, even. Carefree. Hers had been filled with broken friendships, loneliess, loss, ridicule. . . . Lorelei knew it all sounded melodramatic and petty, which was why she never talked about it. Not that she had any friends to confide in anymore, and adults never wanted to hear about the heartaches of children. They tended to doubt there was any such thing.

Across the shadowy room was a bulletin board, loaded with pictures of her old classmates from Burrell Middle School. They were smiling at her, many with funny little phrases written over their heads in word balloons painted with Wite-Out. Most of those girls had quit speaking to her long ago, but Lorelei never took their pictures down.

Lorelei walked barefoot over to the bulletin board without turning on the light. Gray bands of dawn peeked through the blinds of her water-streaked bedroom window, casting bars on the pictures. On the floor beside her dresser was a metal wastebasket with a dent on one side and a painting of a unicorn on the other. Lorelei picked it up and set it beneath the photos, then plucked off a three-year-old school portrait of Allison Ketalwan, who had been her best friend since kindergarten. Lorelei turned the photo in her hands and read the inscription on the back, written with ink that was supposed to smell like peaches: *Stay cool, but not 2 cool! Luvs and Hugs Friends4EVER! AK.* Lorelei smiled. Then she dropped the photo in the trash.

Life at home had never been wonderful for Lorelei, but despite that, she had always considered herself a happy girl. Allison had been a part of that, like a sister she trusted with every secret joy or hardship, making each better. Then it seemed like everything collapsed at once. The wrong boy fell for Lorelei, Allison turned on her, and soon after, her mother had a terrible accident, making an already unhappy home a lot more frightening.

Lorelei and her mother never got along much before that. Her mom acted like both her daughter and her perpetually unemployed husband were two pets she had gotten before realizing she was allergic. It helped Lorelei to have friends outside the house who cared about her, who made her feel like she mattered. And she always tried to do the same for them. When Allison had fallen for Nicholas Barani, the nicest and cutest boy in the class, Lorelei—like any good friend—worked hard to help get them together. A photo of Nicholas in his soccer uniform was tacked to the bulletin board in her room. Lorelei ripped it loose and dropped it in the trash, too.

"Dating" in the social circles of thirteen-year-olds was a complicated network of protocols, negotiated by friends of the boy and girl, whose respective entourages would haggle and argue and jab their fingers into their palms over the particulars of how much the one liked the other, whether they would agree to "go with" each other (which meant hanging out at lunch and before and after class), and—if the relationship continued to develop—if, where, and when they might actually kiss. One day, one of Nicholas's friends approached Lorelei with grave news: Nicholas had agreed to "go with" Allison only because she was friends with Lorelei. He truly did consider Lorelei the cutest of all the girls. He wanted her to like him back.

This flattered Lorelei and her heart soared at the prospect, but her parents didn't permit dating, and she told the emissary so. On her bulletin board, there was a picture of Nicholas and his guy friends, none of them as cute as him, laughing while stacked in a pyramid on the playground. Lorelei dropped the photo in her trash.

Allison became furious when she learned of Nicholas's betrayal, but rather than confront him and give up her hopeless crush, she declared Lorelei a backstabber, a liar, a whore, a bitch, and in one afternoon annihilated seven years of friendship, sleepovers, and barely concealed jealousies. Allison, humiliated, began a relentless campaign of ridicule: Lorelei's clothes, her hair, her makeup, the music she listened to, the cars her parents drove. To Lorelei's horror, her other friends joined in. They were terrified Allison would make fun of them, too. Kelli, Danielle, Samantha . . . Lorelei had a picture of the whole group at the zoo with their faces painted like tigers. She dropped it in the trash.

The nonstop teasing worked. Lorelei was isolated, and Nicholas soon abandoned his infatuation. She became toxic, but began fighting back, dubbing Allison "Chocolate Chips" for the sprinkling of moles on her face. The name actually caught on, and their opportunistic mutual friends were no longer sure whose side to choose for their own safety. For a while, it seemed like Lorelei was gaining the upper hand. She started to matter once more.

Then came her mother's accident.

Miranda Paskal worked as night manager at a hardware store, overseeing delivery and placement of plywood, drywall, and plumbing supplies in the back warehouse. She wasn't even supposed to work the night it happened, but it was February and the weekend shipments had been delayed by a snowstorm. Then they all came in at once. The warehouse roared with incoming trucks and racing forklifts.

They were overloading the lifts to get it all stacked a little faster. There was still a pending inquiry about whether Miranda Paskal had ordered them to break regulation, or whether it was something the workers did themselves out of haste. That's why her mother's settlement turned out to be so small.

One of the loads shifted when a lift operator backed up while the rack was extended, toppling the vehicle and two tons of PVC fence on top of

Miranda Paskal and a twenty-year-old stockroom worker, crushing and killing him instantly, while pinning Miranda back against the sideways forklift, its wheels still spinning against her outstretched arm.

Six surgeries later, the nurses and doctors tried to tell her how lucky she was to even be alive. Lorelei never forgot the look of rage on her mother's face when reminded of that during her long hospitalization. Lorelei made the mistake of saying it herself in the midst of one of mother's more sour moods during the recovery. Her mother had smacked her across the mouth—with her prosthetic. "I never want to hear that from you again," she said.

Lorelei's mother no longer worked, having left on permanent disability, and Lorelei's father—who had been chronically unemployed well before that—became her mother's perpetual nursemaid. The teachers at school were very sympathetic. The kids pretended to be, for a while.

Then Allison began calling Lorelei "Peter Pan." Lorelei didn't even understand this. Then the other girls started cackling: "What's it like having Captain Hook for a mom?" It made no difference when Lorelei, displaying infinite patience for a child, tried to explain: "It's more of a clamp than a hook."

"Don't touch Lorelei . . . or you'll get *the clamp*!" Allison warned the other girls gravely. "That's a sex disease. It makes hands fall off."

On her most recent birthday, Lorelei sat alone on the back deck of her house, watching a suitcase-sized ice cream cake slowly liquefy in the springtime sun. A handful of the less-hostile girls had said they would come, but didn't.

She hated what had happened to her life, to all the friends she used to have. It hadn't even been her fault. But now there was an escape. High school would be different.

Lorelei wanted to matter again.

St. Michael's population was fed by dozens of schools throughout the surrounding towns, though most of the kids in Lorelei's class were going to Shadyside Academy, an Ivy League prep school closer to Pittsburgh. The rest of her St. Margaret Mary classmates were heading to public school. No one Lorelei knew was going to St. Mike's.

That's when she began begging her parents to enroll her.

On that rainy first day of school, Lorelei looked at the remaining pictures on her bulletin board, then raked her fingers across them, clearing them all into her trash bin. Within the hour, she was showered, powdered, and dressed in her new uniform—all in near silence.

Her parents wouldn't wake for their daughter's first day of school. Mom tended to be unwell in the mornings, and Lorelei's father stayed up late and slept most of the day. It had been that way ever since the accident. That was okay. Lorelei was good at being on her own now.

In the hush of the house, she stood admiring herself in the full-length mirror on her closet door, smoothing the pleats of her skirt and measuring the evenness of the tuck on her white blouse. She welcomed the uniform, having too often found herself unarmed in the fashion wars at her old school. At St. Mike's, everyone would be the same.

She pulled her chestnut hair into a ponytail and smiled at her reflection, which did not smile back as sincerely as she hoped. Maturity and poise— she had spent the summer practicing.

In the space between her old life and this new one, Lorelei studied the elements of popularity. She analyzed teen coming-of-age movies and romantic comedies like an anthropologist, taking note of "the cute stumble," whereby a lovely and charming actress would trip, dropping a stack of plates or collapsing in a heap within sight of the leading man, who would smile and cradle her back to her feet. It was a chance to display vulnerability and a willingness to laugh at oneself. It always seemed to work.

Lorelei practiced tripping in front of her mirror, but was never fully satisfied with her technique. What if she cracked her forehead open on a bookshelf while trying to act cute? It sometimes felt like movies just made things up about romance.

She had scoured the top women's magazines for guidance, but they were either all about sex or all about recipes. So she crafted her own list of guidelines to make herself beloved:

1. Be pretty, but not gorgeous. (Other girls don't like being jealous.)
2. Get good grades, but don't act like a genius. (Others don't like to feel stupid.)

3. Don't be the class clown. (If you have to make jokes, try to make them about other people instead.)
4. Sit in the front of class. (Troublemakers take the back rows.)
5. Be generous, but don't be a pushover. (Show what a good person you are by befriending a crippled person.)

Besides that last one counting as a good deed, a crippled person would also be a greater target for teasing, drawing any ridcule away from Lorelei—though she didn't want to write that down. It seemed mean. She memorized it instead.

In the mirror, on the morning of her first day, Lorelei tried to pinpoint her own flaws, anything at all someone meeting her for the first time might make fun of. She fixated on the shape of her eyebrows, each of which had a hard little arch in the centers. If a mean girl noticed that, it could undermine months of preparation.

She found a set of silver tweezers in the mess of makeup, brushes, and lotions atop her dresser, and braced herself beside the mirror. There wasn't much time; the bus was supposed to arrive soon. She worked fast. Fresh tears appeared with each pluck.

Her distorted vision and hurried work prevented her from noticing right away that one brow was noticeably narrower than the other. *Damn it.*

She plucked again at the thicker one, but once again miscalculated—attacking the bottom half of the eyebrow instead of the top. They were the same thickness now, but one was higher than the other—making her look permanently skeptical.

She walked downstairs and then back up, paced the corners of her room, then settled in front of the mirror again. An eyebrow pencil wasn't solving the problem, so she washed her face and tried something risky.

Lorelei yanked her ponytail loose. Her hair was all one length, but a small pair of cuticle scissors were all she needed to trim a line of bangs across her forehead. Then, while attempting to curl them, she once again realized the perils of hasty grooming. She had cut too short, exposing the eyebrows anyway—and the line of bangs was painfully crooked.

For the next ten minutes, she made pass after pass with the scissors, shaving off dust-sized fragments. Her hands trembled.

Soon she was sprinting through the misty rain down her empty street, the rows of factory houses silent and dark. She rounded the corner past the warmly glowing windows of Mazziotti's Bakery, where she had intended to treat herself to a doughnut and hot chocolate for breakfast, if only she'd had enough time. Lorelei raced toward the corner of Constitution Boulevard, waving her arms and calling out as her bright yellow bus started to pull away. The brakes squealed, and the doors gasped open, inhaling the out-of-breath girl. Lorelei thanked the lumberjack-looking man behind the wheel and sulked into a seat—the first row, of course, right behind the driver. (Only troublemakers gravitated toward the back rows.) In the big rearview mirror, her wet bangs fell in something that looked like a chart illustrating economic decline. And they did nothing to hide her weirdly askew eyebrows.

The rusty little town of Arnold slid by outside her rainy window. Lorelei tried to look happy as the dim morning light cast shadows of trickling water down her face.

THREE

F irst class of the day: Religion.

Lorelei entered the classroom and found a seat in the center of the front row, placed a notebook and pen on the desktop, and crossed her ankles under her chair.

Her new classmates shuffled in behind her, and the boy who took the seat next to hers had a web of thin pink scars running from the corner of his eye, right down to his jawline. But he was still kind of cute. It made him look strong somehow, to be damaged.

Lorelei immediately remembered Rule No. 5 (befriend a cripple), and thought this might be a perfect opportunity. "Can I ask you . . . ," she said, tracing a finger near her own eye. The boy instinctively touched his scar. "Are you blind in that eye?" she asked.

The boy leaned in conspiratorially, smiling. "If I was, I'd have sat on the other side, so I could still see you."

Lorelei groaned. "I get it. So you're the guy who flirts with every girl in class?"

The boy with the scar shook his head. "No," he said. "Just the prettiest ones."

The chatter in the room was cut off by the slam of a door. Ms. Bromine stood with her hand clenched on the knob, in case she needed to slam it again. "Good morning," she said sweetly. She walked to the podium beside the teacher's desk. After more silence, she said: "Aren't you going to wish *me* a good morning?" which was followed by a disjointed response of "Good morn-ing, Miss-us Bromummum . . ."

"Bro-*myne*," the teacher corrected them, dashing her name on the chalk-board. "I am the school guidance counselor, and I also teach this class on Catholic catechism. This is not church, but it's *about* church, so I expect you to behave ac—" That's when she noticed the scarred boy. Their eyes locked. The lips he had once planted a mocking kiss on pursed. "Do you have a problem, young man?"

Stein looked behind him. Bromine said, "I'm talking to *you*. What is it you have there on the side of your face? Some kind of . . . rash?" As every eye in the classroom penetrated him, the teacher adjusted her little Ben Franklin glasses and said, "Oh. I'm sorry, I didn't realize that was just . . . well, how God made you." She put a hand to her mouth to cover a small smile, and coughed to clear her throat.

"You should see the other guy," Stein said. "And it wasn't *God*." The kids in the class chuckled, but Ms. Bromine no longer had a smile to hide. "Let's not talk out of turn," she said, unable to think of a better comeback.

A hulking, blue-eyed boy in the back row snorted one out for her. "Is that from when your mom tried to abort you?" Bromine pretended not to hear this. Stein turned to glare at the big kid, and mouthed: *Shut up, shit head.* The boy, who appeared too large for his desk, sat up straighter and hardened his gaze: *Make me, asshole.*

"In any case, where was I?" Bromine said. "Oh, yes. This class is where you learn right from wrong. This is *not* a place for you to sit around and dis-cuss what you *believe* is right, or what you don't *feel* is wrong. 'Believing' and 'feeling' aren't welcome in a mathematics course, and they're not welcome here either."

Bromine had them go to a table in the back and pick up a textbook, *Exploring Modern Faith*—or, as some of them had been vandalized by past students, *Exploding Modern Farts*. As the kids returned to their desks, the classroom door opened. Bromine looked over at the new arrival. *Good Lord Jesus. The other one, too?*

Davidek, his hair and blazer still dripping with rain, wandered in nervously, raising a freshly printed class schedule like a talisman to ward away evil. "The secretary gave me a sophomore list by mistake . . . ," he said.

"It's always somebody else's fault with you, isn't it?" Bromine said. She folded her arms. "Take a seat," she said. "And congratulations."

"For what?" Davidek asked, hunching toward the empty desk on the other side of Lorelei.

"For collecting the first detention of the year," Bromine said. "And in the first class of your first year, in the first minute you enter. You should be in the record books."

Davidek sank into his seat. Stein leaned forward to tip him a friendly salute that Davidek didn't feel energized enough to return.

"You'll need to get a textbook," Bromine said. When Davidek stood up, she snapped: "Play catch-up on your own time. You've already distracted me enough. Let's go around the room, and each of you say your name. And don't go changing seats after today. I can't remember who's who if you keep shifting around."

Bromine barely heard any of the kids saying their names. She was focused on the two hooligans, evidence of how things had changed for the worse around here since the days when she had worn the St. Mike's uniform.

When the scarred kid introduced himself as "Noah Stein," Bromine raised her pencil-thin eyebrows. "Noah, eh?" she said. "So, where's your ark?"

She basked as the class chuckled at her zinger (which had been her whole reason for the introductions), but Stein shot back: "Where's the second animal who matches you?" It was a reflex from a lifetime of dumb "Hey, Noah, where's your ark?" jokes.

Bromine's eyes went wide. "You," she said, "have earned yourself the second detention."

Stein shrugged. Bromine started scribbling the punishment slips at her desk. She didn't bother with the rest of the students' names.

When the bell rang, Lorelei turned to Davidek and reminded him to pick up his textbook from the back desk. He thanked her, and she noticed his gaze linger slightly above her face.

She raised a palm to her forehead, like she was taking her own temperature. "What?" she demanded, though she knew exactly what. The misshapen eyebrows, the crooked hair.

"*Nothing.* Just your hairdo is a little different. . . . But different is cool," Davidek added.

Lorelei, hand still on her forehead, told him acidly: "You know what else is cool? Your clip-on tie."

In Biology class, the students sat at long, high tables with gas pipes jutting out of the center for Bunsen burners. The scorched-egg smell of sulfur hung in the room—the ghost of experiments past. The Biology teacher, Mrs. Horgen, handed out textbooks and a set of copied notes, telling the students to pick a partner for the semester's lab work.

Davidek scanned the tables for a seat and saw Stein talking with Lorelei, and since he had so recently offended her, he settled at a different table beside another person he recognized: the chubby black kid, last seen dodging projectiles in his tangerine sweater. Davidek told him, "I remember you from that day in the parking lot. I wouldn't have guessed you'd come back after getting stuff thrown at you the first time."

The black kid looked amazed and flattered. "That was me, yeah. Hector Greenwill—but everybody calls me Green. . . . You and that Noah guy were the ones trying to help that hurt kid, right?"

Davidek nodded. Green said, "That was a weird day, all right. . . . My parents said this would be a good school for me, though. I'm really into music and stuff—I play guitar—and I want to learn about choirs and arrangements and all. The sucky part is the school's music teacher quit over the summer. Anyway, they say at a smaller school like this, you get more attention."

"When you're not dodging bricks," Davidek said, but Green waved it off.

"Honestly, that kid on the roof made me want to come here even more. It felt good helping that teacher, like I was a part of something, you know?"

Davidek shrugged. "What do you think happened to that kid anyway? The newspaper made it seem like nothing happened."

"He's probably down in a psych ward somewhere, banging his head in one of the padded rooms," Green said. "But I'll tell you this—that guy could *throw*. If the loony farm has an all-crazy softball team, he'd be an all-star."

Davidek said, "It's hard to pitch in a straitjacket."

Green contemplated this. "If a guy with four multiple personalities gets to home base, does that count as a grand slam?"

They started to laugh, and then they couldn't stop. It went on for so long, Mrs. Horgen told them they couldn't be lab partners, and separated them.

Computer Science class was taught by Mr. Zimmer, the human praying mantis who had scaled the side of the school and saved the boy on the roof. He was telling them they'd learn how to format term papers, and create spreadsheets and other programs.

The faces of the students blinked at him from behind their computer monitors.

"Okay," Zimmer said. "So you have an empty screen in front of you. Put your hands on the keyboard and start writing—it doesn't matter what. Swearwords, the Gettysburg Address . . . I just want to get a sense of your typing skills. But, seriously . . . don't type any swearwords. I was just kidding about that."

Zimmer prowled through the room, and when he got to Green, he asked softly: "Do you mind talking to me in the hall for a second?"

Green nodded mutely, and they walked out of the classroom and down the corridor near the main entrance, where there were two wooden trophy cases full of aging honors, and between them a large crucifix hanging on the wall. A long-departed priest, who had been pastor back when Sister Maria was only a student at St. Mike's, had commissioned the art class to paint wide white eyes on Jesus—an unsubtle reminder to students that they were always being watched. The Christ figure with the stark, crazy eyes loomed over Mr. Zimmer's shoulder, chest out, arms spread, like it was trying to taunt Green into a fight.

"I wanted to tell you, I'm glad you decided to come to school here," Zimmer said. "I never got a chance to thank you for running interference for me that day. You'd make an excellent running back—if we had a football team."

"I was glad to help," Green said.

Zimmer nodded. "I wanted to talk with you privately because . . . well, you're clearly a good kid and I'm a little worried. Maybe unnecessarily, but there are some things you should know. . . . Have you heard much about initiation and hazing at St. Mike's?"

Green said, "Sorta. Like in the movies where the frat brothers are all getting spanked and saying 'Thank you, sir, may I have another'?"

"Well, St. Mike's isn't quite *Animal House*." Zimmer laughed. "But it can get a little mean. Not all of us like it, but it's a part of the school's tradition. So, it's difficult to stop."

"It's just fun and games, right?" Green shrugged. "A little teasing?"

Zimmer proceeded cautiously. "St. Mike's is a good place, but . . . the seniors have a lot of pressures facing them. College applications to start, scholarships to fight for . . . It makes them a little—*severe*. Tempers are high, emotions can be, too. What troubles me is, well, you're *different* from the other freshmen—and that's a good thing. But when this hazing thing gets under way, I don't want anyone to take advantage of that difference. Do you understand what I'm trying to say?"

Green did, and he made it easy on the struggling teacher. "You think they'll come after me since I'm the only black kid."

Zimmer ran a hand on the back of his neck. "We've had other people of color at St. Mike's—not many, I'm afraid, but a few. None right now, though. Just you. Kids can say stupid things sometimes. If it ever happens, just know you can come to me for help, okay?"

Green studied his shoes, then looked up at the teacher with great hopefulness. "Can you stop them from making fat jokes, too?"

For a while after Zimmer left the computer classroom, there was only the raindrop sound of keyboards being tapped, and the actual rain, still blasting against the arched windows.

Davidek felt something tap his shoulder, and turned to see Noah Stein leaning across the side of his computer.

Stein squinted one eye, like someone appraising faulty merchandise. "Do you believe in the supernatural? Psychic prophecy? Karma, and that kind of stuff?"

All Davidek could say was: "What are you talking about—ghosts?"

"Nah." The scarred boy leaned closer, his voice hushed and urgent. "I'm talking about *big* weirdness. Strange coincidences. Haven't you noticed odd things happening?"

Davidek considered this. "Did a great big, fat bald man from the church come by and tell your parents to send you here, too?"

Now it was Stein's turned to be bewildered. "I never met any big, fat bald guy, but I did have a long conversation with *her* today." Stein gestured to a girl in the back row who had a short bob of unnaturally black hair and dark red lipstick that stuck to her teeth when she smiled at them. She wiggled her fingers in a wave, rattling the silver bands around her wrist.

Stein waved back and said to Davidek: "Her name's Zari, and she's into all that gypsy-type hocus-pocus. In homeroom this morning, she did a tarot reading for me, turning over all these creepy cards. She says, 'Sorry,' and tells me that there are lonely times ahead. That's her exact words: 'Lonely times ahead.' Then she turned over some more cards and said, 'Your old companions will not finish this journey with you.' I asked what that meant, and she said that I couldn't count on my girlfriend or my old buddies any- more. Well, I told her I don't have a girlfriend and I don't know anybody at this school. *That's* when I thought of *you!*"

"Why'd you think of *me?*" Davidek demanded, outraged to be drawn into someone else's metaphysical grief.

"Look what's happened to us so far," Stein said. "Our first class is with that teacher we pissed off—and she starts picking fights right away. You think that's going to get better the rest of the year?"

"We were bound to run into her again," Davidek said. Then, smiling, added: "At least I'm not the one who kissed her."

Stein flashed his eyebrows. "I learned that one from Bugs Bunny."

Davidek shrugged and sank back in his seat. "Tarot cards? . . . Forget about them. Don't those always deal you a bad hand? They always predict lonely times ahead for everybody."

Stein crossed his arms. "So, tell me, my doubting friend . . . what would you think if the walls of our new high school appeared to be bleeding?"

Stein gestured like a carnival presenter to the back corner of the room, where the plaster ceiling was bulging downward in a nebula of brown and red stains, and crimson tears trickled down the wall in a slow race to the bottom.

FOUR

The four stairwells of St. Mike's were like chambers of a brick and mortar heart, one at each corner, pumping a lifeblood of students through the building's armored body. On the ground level, stone passages led to the basement levels, like smaller capillaries, spiraling below to the subterranean auditorium; the solemn, silent library; and the deep-fried-chicken-smelling cafeteria. Davidek stood beside Stein in a traffic jam of students in one of the polished marble staircases, which curved heavenward along walls glowing with stained glass images of the saints.

Everyone was trying to move upstairs and deposit their books in lockers before rushing back downstairs for lunch. Scores of uniformed shoulders shoved and pushed. People leaned over the railings, trying to look up at the source of the blockade. On the ground floor, peering up through the center void in the stairwell, a group of senior boys sipped sodas casually, smiling and nudging each other over some secret joke.

Red water was trickling down the brick wall above.

"Hey, so, uh, what is this?" Davidek asked as he squeezed by the janitor, who was trying to clean up the mess on the landing between the second and third floors. "I'm pannin' for gold, smart stuff," the janitor said, shaking his mop in the air with his good hand. Davidek and Stein looked down at the nubs of the fingers on his other hand, which were still dark and swollen, and not quite healed, even after all these months. The janitor made no move to hide them. "Yinz wanna closer look?"

Davidek shook his head. "No, I mean . . . we were just wondering what are these leaks? We saw one in the computer room and—"

This news seemed to break Saducci's heart. "It's leakin' on the first floor awready?" he sputtered. "Jee-sus Christmas Christ." He slapped the mop against a dry part of the wall, making a splatter like someone had been shot in the skull. "Gawdamm roof. Little cracks is all it takes. . . . Chews up the brick, and spits it back outtagain. And whose gotta warsh it up? Yers truly!"

Davidek and Stein moved up the stairs, leaving the old man behind, not feeling any better that their new school was digesting itself from the inside out.

At lunch, Lorelei was very pleased. She had already become friendly with the pathological flirt Noah Stein, who had found a way to sit by her in every class that morning. Now it was time to charm her fellow girls.

The freshmen were the last to be served in the lunch line, and once Lorelei collected her plate of meat loaf and potatoes, she settled at a table full of skirts, approaching them the way a missionary approaches a group of savages. Lorelei came not to join, but to lead.

The girl beside her was Zari, the tarot-card reader, whom she'd seen cozying up to Stein in homeroom earlier, dealing her devil cards to him. "I love your dark lipstick," Lorelei said. "Where did you get it?" Zari's sleepily sarcastic expression perked up as she noticed Lorelei's peculiar bangs and eyebrows.

Lorelei reddened, but she'd been contemplating a defensive maneuver all morning. "I know, I know," she said, flipping her fingers casually through the uneven cut. "Looks strange, right? . . . But my stylist says it's the latest thing. Symmetry is so *yesterday*."

Zari said, "You're lying," and Lorelei, speaking faster than she was thinking, snapped: "The trend just hasn't hit Pittsburgh yet."

Zari rolled her eyes. "*Something* needs to hit Pittsburgh," she said. Lorelei didn't realize it was a joke at first. Then she laughed a little too loud. Zari just stared at her.

If she had given Lorelei a chance, she might have found they had a lot in common. Zari had also come from a school where she didn't have many friends, though at St. Michael's she didn't see many people she *wanted* as friends. But Zari had liked the scarred boy—Noah. She liked the mark on his face, which meant he understood pain, and made him different. Plus, that morning as she did his tarot reading, he made funny jokes about some of the uglier classmates. It meant he didn't think she was one of them.

Her reading for him had been bullshit. When she told him his closest friends wouldn't continue with him in this school, it was just a trick to find out whether he already had a girlfriend. She told him there would be "hard times" at St. Mike's and he would be lonely. Then she'd given him her phone number.

The very next class, she had seen Stein become preoccupied with this Lorelei, a much more conventional-looking bobblehead. Zari knew she could never compete with Lorelei's avant-garde eyebrows and esoteric grooming fashions.

She looked across the aisle to where Stein had settled for lunch at one of the boys-only tables. He was laughing with Davidek, who was irrelevant to Zari, and babbling about something—probably not her.

Lorelei followed her gaze. "He's cute, right?" she said.

Zari's teeth severed the tip of a french fry. "I heard him making fun of your hair earlier," she said, holding back a smile as Lorelei's fell.

Lorelei looked back over her shoulder at the boy's table. The look of worry wasn't caused by her irregular eyebrows this time.

Lord, the newcomers looked little.

Sister Maria Hest had been principal at St. Michael's for fifteen years and was a teacher for two decades before that. During her adolescence, what seemed like centuries ago, the now-sixty-year-old nun had been a student herself. How strong and wise she had seemed to herself then. Surely one of her withered old teachers had passed her at some moment and marveled at her smallness, too.

As the first day of class came to an end, Sister Maria stood in the hallway near the main doors, watching as the students departed, and noticed two boys: Davidek and Stein, the pair Ms. Bromine had complained about, escorting a lovely young classmate between them. Davidek was chattering at Lorelei, who was ignoring him in favor of locking eyes with Stein.

Sister Maria noticed the girl hesitate at the giant doors, then trip forward with a small cry. It had almost seemed deliberate. But why? . . . Sister Maria looked behind her, but the only other witness was that white-eyed crucifix over the trophy cabinet.

She might have understood better if she had seen the small smile of relief on Lorelei's face when both Stein and Davidek reached out to catch her.

FIVE

We should be afraid. . . .

W	e should be afraid. . . .
Sister Maria turned around in the empty hallway, as if she had heard those words spoken aloud, but no one was there, of course. The students and teachers were long gone. It had been an exhausting first day, and Sister Maria stood there alone, her eyes closed, listening to the distant drips of the school's many leaks. The stairwell. The third-floor girls' bathroom. The second-floor history classroom. And finally, the computer room, which would cost them dearly if the water ever touched those expensive machines.

Then she had heard those words. *We should be afraid . . . over how easy it is to go wrong, trying to make others do right.* These were words first spoken to her when she was a teenager in these same halls. It had been the saying of Sister Victor, who'd been the principal when Maria Hest was a teenager at St. Michael's and had inspired her, in fact, not only to join the sisterhood but follow the same vocation as an educator as well. The words had always haunted Sister Maria, though she never fully understood what her friend and mentor had meant. *Afraid?*

That was a word she heard a lot in the halls these days.

There were others, too: *Hazing. Initiation. Teasing. Torture. A little harmless fun.*

Sister Maria had heard the upperclassmen talking, almost gloating, about the only thing that seemed to excite them about returning for their final year at St. Mike's—the ritual of welcoming the freshmen by making sport of them.

It had already started. At lunch, she had seen a pair of large boys racing through the hall from opposite sides, like demolition balls, bashing together into crowds of freshmen boys, whose arms and legs jabbed in every direction, like crushed insects. She had found the seniors, scolded them, and they had smiled and said, "C'mon, Sister. . . . It's *our* turn!"

Our turn.

It was supposed to be just fun and games. That's what the faculty and parents and alumni association believed, which was why the tradition persisted. Hazing was regarded as a healthy bonding exercise for the freshmen, and no graduate who endured it thought anyone who came after should be spared. True enough, it was hardly a violation of the Geneva Conventions for the freshmen to serve a few days as butlers and waitresses to the senior class. A few pranks . . . maybe a snowball fight or two . . . the Hazing Picnic, with freshmen drafted into a series of sketches and songs designed to blur the boundary of being "laughed at" and "laughed with."

When Sister Maria became principal, she'd seen things getting more extreme. Maybe there was just more anxiety—to get into college, get into the *right* college, and find some way through the spartan landscape of scholarships, grants, and loans to pay for those futures. It was easier to be afraid now, easier to be angry. Meanwhile, St. Mike's had changed. Hungry for tuition dollars, it had begun to collect no small number of students who were kicked out of public school for violence, drugs, sex, and assorted other acts of delinquency, while the number of especially devout Catholic parents seemed to increase as well, filling the halls with their holier-than-thou (and painfully isolated) offspring. Hazing was always a pressure valve, but that pressure had become unbearable. As Sister Maria saw it, the tradition had turned into a form of sanctioned bullying.

Now came this new hunger: *Our turn* . . . As if these upperclassmen had suffered worse than any who came before. *Our turn* . . .

She thought of the boy on the roof last year, and what had made him snap. St. Mike's was a place that tried to do right, but as Sister Victor's voice reminded her . . . it was easy to go wrong that way, too. It was getting harder to make excuses to the people of the church.

Sister Maria stood at the school's first-floor side entrance, where there had once been a corridor leading to the great chapel of St. Michael the Archangel. Now the glass-and-steel door overlooked only a grassy field.

For almost ninety years, the red-stone chapel had stood on that ground, towering and majestic, with a steeple that cast a sundial shadow across the surrounding neighborhood. It had been built by the town's early immigrant families—the steelmen, the glassworkers, the housewives, the rail operators, the stonemasons, housepainters, barbers. . . . They had labored in poverty a century ago to build St. Mike's—a sanctuary for their families, a place for their children's weddings, their grandchildren's baptisms, and their own funerals.

It was meant to stand forever, but like so much from when Sister Maria was a girl, the chapel was gone now.

A fire had destroyed it before dawn one Christmas, several hours after a packed Midnight Mass. It had started on the fifty-foot pine trees decorating the altar, and faulty light strands were the official cause. The trees were dry, brittle, just waiting for a spark to become twin columns of flame, which quickly devoured the interior of the church.

Later that morning, as the smoke still rose, parishioners celebrated holiday Mass in a makeshift chapel in the school's basketball gymnasium. In his sermon from the free throw line, Father Mercedes, the parish's longtime pastor and a son of the school himself, vowed that St. Michael the Archangel's would stand again within the year. That had been four years ago.

In that time, the scoreboard and bleachers were removed. The retractable stage, previously used for school plays, became an altar, and a thin carpet was nailed over the pine flooring of the basketball court. Worn pews had been salvaged from a church in McKeesport, which was among several shuttered by the diocese as part of a series of parish closings and consolidations due to the shriveling population of the region's faithful. St. Michael's was not rebuilt, but it was the beneficiary of many secondhand baptismal fonts, pipe organs, choir loft risers, and assorted gilded candelabras.

Father Mercedes regularly explained to the restless congregation that he could not persuade the bishop to reconstruct their burned church when so many others were being forced to close their doors.

The gymnasium church remained, and it was there Sister Maria ended her after-hours walk.

She found she was no longer alone.

A slouching figure, clad entirely in black, knelt in the church pews.

His back was to her, his face turned up at a ceramic statue of the resurrected Christ, salvaged from one of the shuttered churches, suspended from the ceiling with its arms extended in the shape of the cross and a peculiar neutral expression on its face—less the throes of agony than the boredom of a minimum-wage employee at the end of a long day: *Don't ask me, I'm going off shift.*

The dark figure in the pews looked back at Sister Maria, an unlit cigarette hanging from his lips. His eyes were shadow pits, his thin gray hair neatly combed across his scalp, though a little damp with sweat. His face had a similar expression to the impatient Christ.

"Good afternoon, Father Mercedes," she said.

He smiled, and the cigarette bent upward toward his nose. "Sister," he said. "Let me guess—bad news?"

She walked toward him down the central aisle of the church. "The ceilings are leaking again—four of them," she said. "You've seen the problems, I take it?"

The priest's unlit cigarette danced as he spoke. "Oh, that and a lot more."

He held a gold-plated Zippo in his hands, sparking the flame, touching it to the tip of his cigarette, and exhaling a corona of blue haze into the air. She despised this about him, smoking in a church. He did it all the time when no one was around—no one he cared about, anyway.

Father Harold Mercedes was only seven years older than her, but always seemed much more ragged and tired. Many parishioners found his roguishness charming. To the students, his bad habits made him a maverick, a fellow rebel—the priest who bought rounds of beer at the P&M Bar, placed bets on the Steelers, took annual vacations to Vegas and Atlantic City, and occasionally let slip a curse word. His Friday-night poker buddies would tease the priest, "Ah, better go to confession, Father!" And he would close his eyes and say: "I forgive myself."

Behind his back, the older parishioners called him Diamond Hal. The kids called him Father Pimp.

"We'll need money to repair the damage, Father," Sister Maria said. She reminded him about the eroding brick and the past failures of temporary fixes. He smoked his cigarette and let her talk, not really listening. When she finished, he rose from the pew and shrugged. "Why bother fixing a school that may not exist in another year?"

The nun crossed her arms. "I don't think that's very funny, Father."

The priest blew smoke through his nose. "That's because it's not a joke, Sister. When I ask for things, when I ask for extra *money*—a special pass of the collection plate—our parish council tends to ask two questions. First is: 'Why are we supporting a school that only causes humiliation for the parish?' And the second question is: 'When will we finally rebuild our burned church?' My answer to the second one is, 'We can't afford it yet.' And so the parish council's response is to repeat the first question—'Why, why, why' . . . ," he said, exhaling smoke again. ". . . 'Why are we supporting a school nobody wants?'"

In the twelve years he'd served as pastor, Father Mercedes had proved himself adept at wielding the parish council like a bludgeon. He didn't need the panel's approval for much, but it was always easy enough for him to manipulate them into whatever cause he supported.

The nun's shoulder's sagged. "Shall I control the weather in the meantime?" she asked.

"I'd prefer you control your students," Father Mercedes snapped back. "What happened to the emergency funds I secured for you this summer?"

Sister Maria sighed. "You know the answer to that." That money had been scattered by the Boy on the Roof. Settlements, medical bills, pain and suffering payments for the staff injured that day. Money for secret scholarships for the hurt students—secret to prevent every enrollee from claiming psychological scarring. Luckily, the child who was most seriously wounded— the boy Davidek and Stein had rescued—came from a family with a near slavish devotion to the school, and they had helped coordinate the legal arrangements to keep everything hush-hush. It was a wealthy and influential family (made more wealthy by the payments they arranged, of course), but they had helped suppress the full story in the local newspaper, shielding the school's reputation . . . somewhat. That had cost a significant payout, too.

Only one student involved in the incident hadn't returned, and he was the one Sister Maria knew she had failed the most—The Boy on the Roof, himself. Mr. Zimmer had been the one who saved St. Michael's in that regard, and not just by grabbing the boy in the midst of his plunge. He had arranged something for the boy and his family that no one else could. He had settled the ugliness once and for all. The boy had disappeared. The boy's family was satisfied. St. Michael the Archangel soldiered on.

But they had paid for it. Paid mightily. Now Sister Maria was asking for more money.

"So how many more deranged students should we budget for this year?" Father Mercedes asked. He stubbed out his cigarette on the bottom of a pew, then looked in vain for a place to dispose of the butt.

"I thought perhaps, given the circumstances, the diocese might consider offering us a small—," Sister Maria began, but Father Mercedes cut her off.

"The diocese isn't going to give us any *more* money; it *collects* money. And we are becoming more valuable as real estate. Would you like to see St. Michael's become another *community theater*, or a Taco Bell?" The dead ember in his hand wavered near her face.

"The school is St. Michael's identity," the nun said quietly.

"The *empty field* out there is our identity now," he said. "St. Michael's is the church without a church. The parish that *could not* rebuild itself." His eyes scanned the gymnasium chapel with unmasked disgust. "If you want to keep this school, you'd better *force* these students to become something worth saving," he said. "Frankly, a lot of parishioners believe you're the worst principal we've ever had at St. Mike's. Do you like the idea of being the *last* one, too?"

The nun closed her eyes. The priest was waiting for an answer. "No," she said finally.

"Good." He nodded. "Then we're going to see some changes around here, yes?" He reached out his hand, and the nun shook it reluctantly. "Take care of that for me," he said.

As the priest left her, the silence of the empty school returned, that great after-hours stillness she had once found calming. For the first time, Sister Maria felt lost there—and, finally, afraid.

She sat down in the pew, opening the hand that had just shook the priest's.

In her palm was the blackened stub of his cigarette.

PART II

Our Turn

SIX

I was dead," said a kid at the freshman lunch table. "These senior guys slammed my tie in a locker and then put on the lock!" Davidek didn't know the name of the boy telling the war story. School was just a couple of weeks in, and he still didn't know everybody.

Green did: "Well, what'd you do, Mikey?"

"I was screaming for help, and the old French-teacher nun came out and made them unlock me," the kid told the serious faces around him. "If she hadn't come out, I would've been stuck there for good."

Stein was chewing a cookie. "Or until you figured out you could just loosen the loop around your neck and slip it off."

The boy telling the story hung his head. "I didn't think of that," he said quietly.

The freshman boys had finished their lunches, but no one was leaving the table. It was cool down here in the cafeteria, and safe—while outside, in the scorching September sun, the seniors had started a recess ritual of capturing freshman guys and swinging them by their ankles around the parking lot. They liked to make the human pinwheels slam into each other.

Anxiety had overtaken the newcomers. Everyone knew about the hazing, but no one was sure what to do about it, or how bad it would get. "Mr.

Zimmer said if we just go along with it, they'll get bored," Green said. "And it won't last long."

"Nuh-uh, it lasts all year," said another kid, J. R. Picklin, a self-professed graffiti artist who bragged that he spelled his name *JayArr* when he tagged objects around town. "And at the end of the year, there's this big gathering where they put you on a stage and *really* fuck you up."

"What do they make you do?" said a small voice. It was a girl, the only one at an empty table next to the one jammed with boys. The girl was tiny and abnormally thin, with a narrow wedge-shaped face that almost put her eyes on opposite sides of her head, like a fish. Her whitish blond hair fell in short, straight lines and she breathed through drooped lips. A small gold cross dangled from her neck, like the bell you'd attach to a cat.

JayArr shrugged at her. "It's some end-of-the-year picnic thing. I heard from my older brother that they march you out in front of the crowd, and everybody's chanting and yelling shit at you, and throwing stuff. And you're, like, the entertainment."

Stein asked, "So what? You sing a song or tootle on a kazoo, or something?"

"That's not scary. Just sounds lame," Davidek said.

"Yeah, but then they pull down your pants or make you wear girl's underwear or put ants down your shirt while you're doing it," JayArr emphasized. "My brother says there's no mercy."

"They can't do any of that," Davidek said. "The teachers wouldn't *let* them do that."

The fish-faced girl spoke softly again. "They did it to Jesus on the crucifixion. . . ." But the weird religious invocation just made everybody squirm.

"All seniors got their asses decapitated when they were freshmen, and it boils in them for years. Now they're gonna give it *back*," JayArr said. "My brother and his friends got stomped all year long. Then came the big finale—this picnic, which is so bad, they need to have it at a park away from school grounds, just so St. Mike's can't get sued, or something. The teachers pretend they don't even *know* about it."

"So what exactly did your brother say happened?" Davidek asked, wondering what his own brother, the marine deserter, could have told him about all this—if he were around.

"My brother and some other guys got covered in chocolate sauce and whip cream and had cherries dumped on their head. The sicko seniors turned them into a damned banana split! I'm not joking. All the people in the audience were pelting them with fruit and nuts and shit."

JayArr crossed his arms, leaning back in his chair. "And when *my* brother got to be a senior, you better believe he and his friends did the exact same thing to their freshmen. It's called *revenge,* dudes."

"Except the guys your brother squirted chocolate sauce on weren't the guys who did anything to him," Stein pointed out. "Sounds to me like he got his *just desserts.*" He leaned back, smiling proudly, awaiting accolades from the table for his cleverness—but nobody got it.

"I think you're getting hung up on the banna split thing," JayArr said.

Stein rolled his eyes. "No, I mean, what your brother did to those freshmen is not revenge. It just means your brother is a dickhead, same as the guys who did it to him for no good reason. Karma just happened to catch up with him ahead of time."

JayArr squinted. "What the hell's *karma?*"

Stein considered explaining, then shrugged. "You'll know it when you see it, pal."

At the head of the table, the large blue-eyed boy who always sat in the back row of class exhaled a loud, bored sigh. He was usually silent, his head hung—maybe listening to the others, maybe not. Davidek heard teachers say his name a couple times. Jim, or Jeff, or something.

The hulking boy's icy eyes glittered. "You know . . . I knew pussies had lips, but I never knew they could talk so much," he said.

The table went silent. Not only was the blue-eyed boy a head taller than most of his classmates, but he was also broad-shouldered and muscled in a way that made his thin-armed, scrawny-legged fellow freshmen look like stick drawings. The buttons of his shirt seemed taut, as if he had outgrown it that morning, and his rolled-up sleeves constrained python arms. He reminded Davidek of his old action figure toys: G.I. Joes were one size, and *Star Wars* toys were just a little smaller. You couldn't fit a big G.I. Joe in the little seat of a *Star Wars* X-wing fighter, and that was how the blue-eyed boy looked to him now: a bigger toy stuck into the universe of a smaller playset.

"You sissies whine and cry," the blue-eyed boy said. "But you're only scared because you can't protect your own self like—"

"Like what?" said a voice from behind him. It was an older boy, a grinning senior orbited by other upperclassmen who'd come in from the parking lot in search of their absentee prey. Davidek recognized him by the dime-sized pucker scar in the center of his cheek: it was Richard Mullen, the kid he'd seen stabbed through the face with a pen.

"So you know the secret of survival, huh, big boy?" said Mullen, jabbing the big kid in the back with his index finger. His horse-toothed friend, Frank Simms, who had once run out of the boy's restroom hurling a jar of preserved tapeworms, darted forward to make an impression. "Answer him," Simms demanded, swatting the huge freshman's head. "What's your name?"

The blue-eyed boy regarded them coolly, the muscles in his large shoulders shifting under his shirt. "Name's Smitty," he said.

"What happened, Smitty, to put such a big boy like you in a class of little boys?" Mullen asked. "You, like, a retard or something? One of those fat-fuck dinosaurs with a peanut brain?" The upperclassmen fell into each other, laughing so hard. Clusters of curious sophomores and juniors began wandering over, intrigued by the sight of conflict.

Smitty looked up, outnumbered, uncertain. The other freshmen—those he had just dubbed "talking pussies"—were chuckling a little, too.

Smitty pointed toward the neighboring table. "While we're making introductions, what's your name, skinny?" he asked.

The scrawny, fish-faced girl sitting alone had frozen. She pointed at her chest with a questioning expression.

"Yeah, I meant you," Smitty said, refocusing the attention of the threatening upperclassmen.

"I'm . . . Sarah," the skinny girl replied in a milky, half-swallowed voice.

"Sarah," Smitty repeated. "You got a last name?"

"You got a *first* name?" Mullen snapped at him, feeling his moment in the spotlight slipping away.

"John," Smitty answered curtly. "John Smith."

"John Smith? That's original," snorted Mullen's friend Simms, but nobody thought that was funny.

"Now, Sarah, you are one *skinny* little thing!" Smitty said. "I mean,

deadly skinny. Goddamn, it's like somebody just took a *slice* out of you—
lengthwise." Smitty made his hand into a blade, squinted one eye, and fil-
leted her in his field of vision. "It's like you're a goddamn fraction," he
said. "Seven-eighths of a person. Am I right?"

He looked around for support, and the seniors who had just been menacing him were nodding, laughing, and agreeing wholeheartedly. The girl,
meanwhile, seemed to be looking for a way to draw her arms, legs, and
head inside her body. "Please," she murmured, almost too low to be heard.
"Please, don't . . ."

Smitty's face softened in faux concern. "Hey, listen . . . you're not *sick*,
or anything, are you? Like . . . you've got that hatchet of a face because
you're *diseased*?"

The girl's fingers twined around her gold cross necklace. She shook her
head back and forth—no—which made Smitty lean backwards suddenly.
"Whoa! Whoa! Watch where you swing that thing!" The upperclassmen
roared laughter, and Smitty's face broke into a victorious smile, like a sheet
of ice breaking off a mountainside.

Mullen leaned in and put a finger in the girl's face. "That's your new
name—Seven-Eighths! Got it?" He looked around at his friends. "Seven-
Eighths, right?" Everybody was dying, repeating the name to each other.

"Hey, I got a nickname for you, too, " piped up a voice from the freshman
table. It was Stein, and all eyes fixed on him. He tapped the spot on his cheek
where Mullen's puckered scar was. "How about Asshole Face?"

Mullen shoved aside some chairs to get close to him. "What the fuck
did you call me?"

Stein tapped that spot on his cheek again. "Asshole Face. How's that?
Cute, right?" Simms shoved in front of his friend, overbite hanging open in
outrage, and yanked Stein out of his chair. "You best apologize, shithead."
Stein's face reeled back, staggered by the bad breath.

"What's going on over here, boys?" asked Mr. Zimmer, appearing out of
nowhere to walk over to the table. Simms let go of Stein's shirt, and the
older boys began to sidle away. They were repeating the nickname to each
other—not "Seven-Eighths," but "Asshole Face."

Mullen leaned in close to Stein. "You got some nerve with your face
full of scars, worse than mine, even."

Stein nodded, his fingers tracing the pink tendrils running along his jaw. "Yeah," he whispered, his mouth near Mullen's ear. "But mine doesn't look like a . . . *butt* . . . hole." Mullen shoved him—straight into Mr. Zimmer, who stepped in to separate them, herding the group of seniors back outside. Stein sat back in his seat, waiting for them all to clear; then he stood up and walked off with his tray. Seven-Eighths had vanished without anyone noticing.

Green glared at Smitty with contempt. "That what you meant by protecting yourself? Picking on some helpless girl instead?" The remaining freshmen grumbled agreement.

Smitty flashed a bemused expression at their after-the-fact outrage. "You were all quite the heroes when you were scared of being the next one to get picked on. I did what I had to do."

"You had to be a *dick?*" Green asked.

Smitty stood up, walked over, and leaned his arms on Davidek—not Green. "I like this kid," he said, ruffling Davidek's hair. "Keeps his mouth shut, lies low, and stays out of trouble." He walked on, looking up at the ceiling. "Now, the other guy—Stein? My hat's off to him, but I don't get the whole kamikaze thing." He shrugged. "Maybe he thinks old Seven-Eighths will let him put his fingers in that other narrow place of hers!" Smitty laughed at his own joke in the otherwise quiet cafeteria. "But you . . . ," he said, smiling and gesturing toward Green, like a lounge singer crooning to a fan in the front row: "*You're Mr. Fucking Nice Guy*—once all the trouble is gone. Makes you look like the hero, while I come off as the villain, right? Well, you and me are the same, Nice Guy," he said. "Except I'm not pretending to be tough to win friends—friends who will be very disappointed in how brave you are later, I'm sure."

Green tried to protest, but the school bell drowned him out.

Smitty, still the lounge singer, winked and pointed at Green as the others rose from their seats. "Just remember, boys, you always know where you stand with an honest asshole," he said, laying one hand flat over his heart. "It's the fake do-gooders you gotta watch out for." He turned his palm out and blew Green a kiss—then shoved the hand into Green's face as the boy was standing up, sprawling him backwards over his chair and onto his ass.

Davidek rushed over to help, but Smitty backed him off. "You try and help, you'll end up on top of him. I promise," Smitty said, almost politely. Davidek hestitated, looked down at Green, and waited in silence as the heavy boy squirmed and got up by himself. Smitty tipped an invisible hat at them and whistled as he walked away.

SEVEN

No rain fell for several weeks, and the leaks in St. Mike's walls dried to dusty stains. The only thunderous rumblings above the school came from the stub-fingered janitor as he dragged his metal tub of tar and tried to patch weak spots on the rooftop. All of September burned hot and dry, toasting the Allegheny Valley until the river went still, and the rolling hillsides of trees wilted like baked lettuce.

At the weekly faculty meetings, teachers suggested suspending part of the dress code so students could go without their blazers and sweaters (names for clothing that took on new meaning at such temperatures). Sister Maria was inclined to approve it, but Ms. Bromine argued that students who dressed better would behave better, and presented an article from a psychological magazine to back up the claim. Sister Maria, thinking of Father Mercedes's warning about discipline, decided to keep the uniform code intact.

Many students went without the blazers and sweaters anyway. Sister Maria instructed teachers to show no leniency, and since they were just as miserable in the heat, few were merciful. That led to a rash of daily detentions. There were more requests to leave the broiling classrooms and visit the water fountains and bathrooms, and fraternizing in the hallways and restrooms led to more conflict. Tempers rose along with the heat, punches flew more quickly, insults were sharper. Behavior worsened at an alarming rate.

The school had no air-conditioning, but it did have an industrial fan in the bay windows at the end of the third-floor hallway, which hauled a current of stale, hot air through the building, replacing it—mostly—with hot, stale air from outside. The squat steel drum jutted from the building like a jet engine, and the dirty propellers had become a tool of amusement for a particularly thuggish element of juniors known as the Fanboys, who clustered around it before class began each day. They had discovered the fan would flash sparks and utter an angry electrical wail if a fistful of pocket change was thrown through the protective grate into its churning, blurred maw. The gashed coins would flash out into the morning air, dimes and pennies and quarters pattering softly into the grass of the vacant church lot. Inside the hall, the screams of metal quickly drew teachers into the hallway, but it was too late to catch anyone in the act.

Led by a junior named James Mortinelli, the Fanboys spent every morning shaking down freshmen for coins, but they happily fed whatever—pens, tie-clips, math homework—through the blades if spare change wasn't available. They had found an ally in the large, intimidating freshman, Smitty. Rather than fight with the Fanboys, he had ingratiated himself by pointing out his classmates who had jangling pockets, or girls who kept small change purses in their book bags.

Impressed by the way Stein had stood up to him, Davidek told Smitty he thought he was being an asshole. The next day, two of the Fanboys were pressing Davidek's face against the fan grate, while Mortinelli searched his pockets. Morti was stubby, with little shoes and little hands. At seventeen, his hairline was already receding, which further enlarged a forehead that was already big enough to show a movie on. His eyes were like raisins sunk close together in a mound of bread dough. "Christ, what are you, on fucking welfare?" he said. "This is the third time I've turned out empty pockets on you."

Davidek said he had five dollars in his front blazer pocket. The whirling blades in front of his face chopped his syllables into vibrating staccato.

Morti spun him around, snatching the bill out of the pocket and holding it in front of the freshman's face. "This ain't a damn stick-up," he said. "We want coins, dumbass."

"*Change!*" another boy bellowed in Davidek's ear, filling the air with the smell of cheese curls. Mortinelli kept the fiver anyway. "Let's hit the cafeteria. They'll change this out for us," and the gang retreated down the stairs to the school's sublevels. Before leaving, Mortinelli's little eyes narrowed on Davidek, and his little hand tugged at the freshman's tie. "Really? A clip-on?" the runty junior asked, flashing his baby doll teeth in disgust. "What are you, in third grade?"

The junior snatched off the tie and threw it at the fan, where it sucked tight to the metal grate like it was magnetized, fluttering against the pull of the fan. As Davidek peeled it off, a girl's voice said: "Start keeping some pennies in your pockets. Then you can keep your five dollars."

Davidek looked up, refastening the clasp to his collar, and saw an older girl with scarlet hair cascading down one side of her face. She was standing about five lockers away, with an open bag at her feet, pinning her brilliant hair back. She stuck two barrettes between her lips, and the tips tilted skyward as she smiled at him. "If you start out letting people push you around, you'll always be at the mercy of losers like that," she said, her words muffled by her tight lips. She stuck the barrettes in her autumn-colored hair and fluffed her fingers through it.

"Well, maybe next time I'll shove Morti into the fan. See how tough the rest of them are when he squirts out the other side like Hawaiian Punch," Davidek said, his voice higher than usual for someone trying to talk tough.

The red-haired girl stepped before him, evaluating his serious expression. She put a hand on his cheek. "You're adorable," she said. Then a bell rang and the bustle in the hallway doubled as students rushed to homeroom, and the girl retreated into the crowd, carrying her bag. The spot where her hand had touched him was like a sweet poison melting into his skin.

Adorable.

It was better than any other name he'd been called at St. Mike's.

A week later, the seniors corralled a group of freshman girls for a lunch-time beauty contest. At first, it seemed like pretty lightweight treatment, considering the freshman boys were getting physically pulverized daily. But in addition to the coveted prettiest-girl honor of being chosen Miss St. Mike's, the other titles were the less-than-flattering Miss Skank, Miss Bug-Eyes, Miss 2-by-4 (for flattest chest), Miss Piggy, and Miss Looks-Like-a-Dude. The one everybody called Seven-Eighths was named Miss Fetus Head because of her abnormally thin hair.

Lorelei lingered behind most of the other freshman girls who were surrounded for this playground spectacle, keeping her head low. Careful daily micro-grooming had returned her bangs and eyebrows to a normal state, but she was still self-conscious, and when the taunting upperclassmen ordered her to the front, she stood with her ankles crossed, hands behind her back, staring at the ground.

They sent her back as a finalist for the one non-cruel award, and she smiled as a handful of other pretty girls lined up beside her, and smiled even more as, one by one, they all lost. The older boys hooted and whistled at Lorelei, while the upperclassman girls mostly rolled their eyes. Michael Crawford, the lazy-eyed but otherwise clean-cut-looking senior who served as the pageant's impromptu moderator, approached her holding an invisible microphone and talking in a rapid-1920s reporter voice.

"Tell us, young lass—how's it feel to be the prettiest girl in your class?" Behind him, some of his friends were singing, "Here she is . . . Miss Saint Miiii-Yie-Yikes!"

Lorelei was looking at the girls she had defeated, who looked disgusted with her, even though it wasn't her fault. "I'm sorry, I don't really care who's pretty and who's not," she said, loud enough for everyone around her to hear.

Michael Crawford smiled, his voice returning to its natural timbre. "The prettiest ones never do."

The end-of-lunch bell rang, and the crowd cleared after the stupid beauty pageant. As Lorelei joined the throng heading back inside the school, a hand reached in front of her, holding a fistful of plucked marigolds from a Virgin Mary shrine in one of the school's gardens. A boy's voice said: ". . . for the most beautiful girl." Lorelei spun around smiling, hoping it would be Michael Crawford. But it was Stein.

"I picked these for you," he said. "They kind of smell funny, though."

Lorelei took them, brushing a lock of fallen hair out of her face. She forced a smile. "That's very sweet." She looked at the flowers as long as she could, then back up at him. Stein was definitely cute, even with that weird scar on his cheek. She'd heard about him standing up for Seven-Eighths. She liked that, though it had led to the rumor Stein had a crush on Seven-Eighths. Secretly Lorelei wished he had stood up for *her* like that, though nothing bad had happened to her yet.

"I thought maybe we could go out sometime—if you want," Stein said.

Lorelei brushed nonexistent hair out of her face again as they walked inside. "How exactly does a date work for two kids who don't drive and have no money?"

"How do you know I'm not a millionaire?" Stein asked.

"Because you steal flowers from the Virgin Mary," she said.

Stein laughed. "My sister said she could drive us. I'd just have to do some of her chores."

"Okay . . . ," Lorelei said. "And where would we go?"

"We could just go down to Riverview Park in Tarentum, walk around, and climb on the war memorial cannons that are pointed over the river," Stein answered. "Maybe we could get one working and declare war on New Kensington."

Lorelei shook her head.

"Why?" Stein asked.

She said, "A lot of reasons." Stein said, "Give me one," but most of them she couldn't explain. Whenever Lorelei spent too much time with Stein in class, she noticed a coolness from some of the other girls, particularly the dark-haired soothsayer, Zari. Everyone thought Stein was cute—that was the problem—and Lorelei didn't want to derail her budding friendships over some stupid jealously, like last time.

"My mother doesn't allow me to date. Not until I'm eighteen," Lorelei said. That was one excuse she could give Stein.

"Maybe your mom will change her mind if she meets me," Stein said, flashing his eyebrows. "I'm pretty charming, you know."

Lorelei said no. Stein asked why again, but there were limits to what Lorelei was willing to explain. She hadn't told anyone at St. Mike's about her mother's accident at the warehouse, and the missing hand, her mother's sometimes explosive moods and . . . well, what could be called an increasingly serious dependence on self-medication.

Ms. Bromine was standing inside the doors, watching the students flow back inside. When she saw Lorelei, she snapped: "Did you pick those from the school grounds!"

Stein snatched the marigolds out of Lorelei's hands. "I gave them to her," he said.

Ms. Bromine's mouth tightened. She told him he could help replant those beds during his next detention.

EIGHT

The unofficial title of Miss St. Mike's didn't make Lorelei any new friends, but it made her some new enemies.

"Hey, Miss America . . . You smoke?"

She heard this after school while passing the Grough sisters—Mary, a senior, and Theresa, a sophomore—who shared the same Neanderthal brows and linebacker shoulders. They always hung out in the shadows of a cluster of yew bushes near the school's side exit with another senior, Anne-Marie Thomas, who was masculine enough to be known by the other students as an "honorary Grough." Lorelei had heard a little about them. The Grough sisters' mother forbade them from shaving their legs. ("It's what whores do. Be happy as God made you.") So they wore thick stockings on even the most sweltering days, and sweatpants during gym instead of shorts, to hide their bristly calves and thighs. But they had to *change clothes* for gym, which always brought fresh taunts of "Sasquatch! Sasquatch!"

The surly attitudes of the sisters reflected lifetimes of torment. Anne-Marie Thomas was just miserable by association.

Mary Grough beckoned Lorelei over to the bushes, where she held out a crumpled pack of cigarettes, and Lorelei, who knew it wasn't cool to smoke, but thought it might be cool to *pretend* to smoke, said, "Yes, sometimes I do. But not right now, thank you."

Mary turned the pack upside down, to show it was empty. "I wasn't asking for your company, beauty queen. I need to bum some."

Lorelei grinned, embarrassed. "I don't really smoke," she said. "I was just . . . kidding."

Anne-Marie advanced on her, flicking the smoldering butt of her cigarette at the freshman and singeing a hole in her white shirt. "You playing games with us, Miss Congeniality?" she said, grabbing Lorelei by her collar and shoving her backwards.

Lorelei's head spun around, but no one could see her in the clearing between the tall shrubs. "No, I—I just . . ." Anne-Marie unzipped Lorelei's book bag. The younger Grough, Theresa, stepped forward to dig through it.

"Nothing here," Theresa reported to her older sister.

Mary Grough dropped her own cigarette and ground it beneath a thick shoe. "You prissy cheerleader types are all the same," she said. "You tease, but you don't put out, right? Maybe that works with your boyfriends, but it just pisses me off."

Lorelei said, "I didn't mean to—," but Anne-Marie shook her by her collar again.

"We don't give a shit what you 'mean to,'" the older girl said.

Mary Grough told her, "All we know, girlie, is you owe us a pack—each. Make it a whole carton. Ten packs. You got it?"

Lorelei pursed her lips. "And what if I don't?"

Mary Grough opened and closed her middle and index fingers, like scissors. "You little bitch . . . I'm going to sneak up behind you and snip that ponytail off at the root." Anne-Marie gave Lorelei a final shove, and all three Groughs were laughing. The sophomore, Theresa, giggled. "We've done it before, bitch. And we'll do it to you, gladly."

Lorelei rejoined the flow of students heading toward the buses in the parking lot, her heart splashing in her chest. One hand found the end of her ponytail and held it close to her neck as she walked. Fast.

"*Screw* those hairy-assed smokestacks," Stein said the next day. *Screw them. Fuck them. Shit on them.* That was Stein's standard advice for most threats from the older kids. "I say give them one pack and inject each cigarette with a squirt of toilet bowl cleaner."

Murder by household chemical, however, was not a solution Lorelei would consider.

They were sitting in Mr. Zimmer's computer class, learning term paper format in Microsoft Word. Davidek was sitting at the computer behind Lorelei and interrupted: "Maybe you could find one of those cigarette-dispensing machines. They don't check ID, right?"

Stein insisted, "I wouldn't give them *anything*," but for Lorelei that wasn't an option. To her list of rules, she had made a mental addition: *No. 6. Don't fight over anything.*

"I haven't had any trouble before. And I don't want any now," she said, which made Stein turn away from her and back to his computer.

"If you're going to do what you want anyway, why'd you ask for help?" he told her.

"That's not why you're angry," she said.

Davidek was confused. "Then why *are* you angry, Stein?"

Nobody answered him.

Lorelei leaned over to Stein's computer and nudged his shoulder. "Don't be mad," she said. "Help me figure out what to do about the Groughs."

Stein didn't look away from his screen. "Why don't you ask your *mom*," he said softly. "Since she's so worried about who you hang out with."

Lorelei slumped in her seat, fingers resting on the keyboard but not moving. Davidek remained puzzled behind her. "Would your mom really help?" he asked.

Lorelei had learned about the dangers of cigarettes from the time of her first health class in grade school, and she had always worried about her mom, seeing the specters of cancer, emphysema, and heart disease floating in the white smoke that seeped out of her mother's nose and mouth. Now her mom's stash in the upper kitchen cabinet was her salvation.

Even before her accident, Miranda Paskal despised being preached to about her bad habits, but afterwards, when she shifted from one to two and a half packs a day and began subsisting more on rums-and-Cokes than any other fluid, her guilt was the one thing certain to provoke her temper. The haggard woman's once-thin face, sagging with extra weight from her now sedentary lifestyle, would tense whenever she sensed even unspoken judgment. Her eyes, usually bleary and lifeless, would flame to life. Once, after what had been an intensely unpleasant seventh-grade lesson on cancerous thyroids and blackened lungs, Lorelei made the mistake of saying simply: "I'm worried about how much you smoke, Mom."

Her mother had glowered at her. Her father, watching from the kitchen, had said, "Lorelei, don't criticize your mother."

Miranda Paskal had moved carefully to place her lit cigarette in the stainless steel clasp attached to her prosthetic forearm. She knew her daughter hated to see it without the fitted latex hand. Sometimes she left it bare on purpose.

Without Lorelei saying another word, her mother's outrage snowballed into irrational fury. "Everything in this house, every thread of clothing you're wearing, all the food you and your father eat—it's all paid for by this. My accident. *My hand!*" Her mother had lunged forward, moving with one quick swipe that made the sound of hard plastic connecting with flesh. Lorelei reeled backwards, holding her cheek. She never cried. It made her mother feel guilty when she cried, but that only made her angrier.

"A lifetime of paths poorly chosen . . ." That's something Miranda Paskal sometimes said aloud. She had lamented being a failure, long before she became one. She always said her parents should have been stricter with her, were right to be as harsh as they were, but did not go far enough. She had married poorly, settled too soon with a man who got her pregnant. She planned not to make the same mistake with her daughter. That was the source of her many random and unprovoked rules: no dating, and no driving until Lorelei was eighteen, either. No telephone calls after 8 P.M. (though no one ever called her daughter anyway).

After her handicapping, Miranda Paskal had real misery to fuel her self-pity, which made her explosive. When her husband and daughter failed to tiptoe around her moods, a simple dropped dinner plate or a coy answer to a question could elicit a smack across the face, for either of them. Lorelei tried to interfere when her mother's arguments with her father degenerated into thrown glassware or poundings on his back. He rarely did the same for his daughter.

The worse part was that her mother often hit with the arm she lost, using the hard prosthetic as a weapon. It's easier to hurt someone when you don't have to feel it back.

Lorelei never asked her to stop smoking again. Never mentioned the drinking, the overeating, the isolation of sitting in a dark house day after day, year after year.

On the afternoon after she was threatened by the Groughs, Lorelei stood on a kitchen chair and opened the small cabinet over the refrigerator. There were two cartons in there, one unopened, the other half-empty. Lorelei took what she thought wouldn't be noticed—two packs. The recycling bin by the trash was full of stale-smelling empty beer cans. When her mother drank that heavily, she sometimes forgot her quantity of consumption. Many times, Lorelei had seen her mom nursing a hangover and searching the couch cushions, demanding to know where her smokes went—ignoring the overflowing stinking ashtrays in the living room and back patio.

For the first time, Lorelei was happy to see that recycling bin so full.

That had been Friday. On the next Monday, Lorelei opened her backpack and took out two sealed packages—Morley Lights.

The Grough sisters stared at her. They were standing at their usual spot near the side entrance after school, shaded by the cover of the smoking bushes. Finally, Mary Grough spoke. "Morley?" she said. "And *lights?* What is this shit? I said I wanted Alpacas!"

"No, you didn't!" Lorelei cried back, holding the packages out like she was about to get an electric shock. "You said you wanted cigarettes. So here they are."

"Don't tell me what I said!" Mary snapped, nodding at her younger sister, Theresa, who stepped forward to snatch the packs out of Lorelei's hands. "And I told you I wanted a whole carton," Mary added. Anne-Marie Thomas snagged Lorelei's hair between her stubby fingers, yanked it once, and gave her a shove toward the sidewalk. Mary said: "You got till Friday. Either I'll be holding a whole carton in my hand, or your pretty little scalp."

After Lorelei hurried away, the Groughs stared at each other blankly. Theresa held the unopened cigarette packs between them—undeniable proof of what had just happened.

They menaced a lot of the younger girls. No one had ever taken them seriously before.

"Can we help somehow?" Davidek asked. He was hanging out with Lorelei and Stein on the second floor every morning now, glad to be out of sight of the Fanboys up on the third, where his homeroom group's lockers were. He had gradually ingratiated himself with Lorelei, who no longer rolled her eyes every time he spoke.

"Do either of your parents smoke?" she asked hopefully. Davidek shook his head. She looked at Stein, who was struggling with his locker clutter.

"You spend a lot more time worrying about people who treat you like crap, Lorelei," Stein said, his head in the metal box. "Not so much on the people who are actually your friends."

Lorelei crossed her arms. "My friends would help me instead of lecture me."

"How does giving those girls what they want make them stop?" Stein asked, still not looking at her. Lorelei groaned, scooping up her bag and stalking away down the hall.

Davidek watched her go. Stein didn't, but wanted to.

NINE

The next morning, Davidek failed to gather his stuff and move to the second floor fast enough. As a result, his face was now pressed against the fan grate again. His tie fluttered before him in the stainless steel drum, its tip nipped by the roaring whirl of the blades.

"Almost there!" Morti cried. "Push a little harder!" Two of the larger Fanboys shoved all their weight against Davidek's back. He felt the metal grate flex and shut his eyes, imagining the bars giving way and his face plunging into the gnawing metal.

That's when the tie caught. It drew tight on his collar, but only for an instant as the clasp popped open and the clip-on knot slipped easily through the bent grate, clattering around in a crimson blur before being ejected on the other side of the whirring blades.

The Fanboys fell back, cackling, hooting, and high-fiving each other. Morti had confiscated a freshman girl's change purse and opened the contents over Davidek's head, and the pennies, nickels, and dimes flashed against the blades in metallic agony as the older boys ran away.

Davidek slumped on the floor beside the fan, breathing heavily, wiping the dust lines from his face, spitting off the little bit that got between his lips.

"Are you the one throwing coins in there?" He looked up at Ms. Bromine, her hands on her purple-skirted hips. Mr. Mankowski was behind her, in the same pose.

"No, no," Davidek said, but she had already drawn out a pad of detention slips from the binder she was carrying. "You're out of uniform," she said, pointing a pen where his tie used to be. "That's a second detention."

When she was done writing them, Davidek walked down the stairs, down to the first floor, and slipped out the side entrance as the homeroom bell began to ring. He found his tie—a little ripped, but still intact—blowing across the long grass, whipped by the wind of the overcast morning. It was starting to rain.

Davidek reattached the clip-on to his collar and went back inside, where he was greeted again by Ms. Bromine. She had two more detention slips already waiting.

"For being late for class," she said. "And leaving the school without permission."

When Davidek got home that afternoon, the house was empty. His mother had gone shopping again, but that was good. In response to his begging, she had promised to buy him a proper tie. He heard the front door opening and ran to find her hauling six overstuffed Guess? shopping bags alongside her.

"Did you get it?" he asked.

His mother blew hair out of her eyes. "Get what?"

Davidek dropped his hands, his mouth, and his welcoming tone. "Mom— *the tie!*"

She groaned. "Peter, you're like a broken record sometimes. . . ."

"Mom!" he said, outraged, incredulous, infuriated. "Mom, you *promised!*"

"I *forgot!* I'm sorry!" she screamed. "Do I have to repeat it for you? Do I?"

Davidek sat watching TV that night, trying not to say a word to anyone, rehearsing his words, waiting to go off like a time bomb. Davidek looked at his mother's new Guess? shoes, propped up on the leg rest of her easy chair. The fresh white turtleneck she wore was Guess?, too. Over by the front door was a brand-new Guess? purse. Davidek stared at everything around him like he wanted it all to catch on fire.

"What's your problem tonight?" his father asked.

Davidek said, "Guess."

"I'm so tired of this attitude," his mother said, marching into the kitchen rather than defend herself.

"I'm still going to school with a clip-on tie!" Davidek bellowed after her. "I've asked you *every day*. And other kids make fun of me—*every day*. You've gone shopping, like, six times since school started!"

His mother rushed back into the living room, frowning at him. She had no defense, and knew it. "You sound just like *your brother* when you talk like that," she hissed, the ultimate put-down in their house.

Davidek's father suggested: "Don't I have ties upstairs you can wear?"

"Dad, freshmen have to wear red ties. It's the rules. Sophomores have blue and red stripes, and upperclassmen have blue."

His father said, "I have red ties. Did you look?"

Davidek sank deeper into the couch. "Yeah, they have Santa Claus on them."

His father turned up the TV volume. He was clueless about why any of this was relevant to him. "So, buy the stupid tie yourself and quit bellyaching."

"Can I have some money?" Davidek demanded.

His father said, "Not with that attitude. Find it yourself."

Davidek was telling this story at school the next morning, when Green said: "So it's lost treasure you need?" He smiled. "Wait here a second, I'll be right back."

When he returned, Green led Davidek outside. They were careful, secret-agent style, to avoid being spotted leaving the school without permission. Green didn't have any detentions, and Davidek couldn't handle any more.

Soon the boys' fingers were picking along the ground below the third-floor ventilation fan, overturning a penny, a nickel, two dimes. Black and gray clouds swirled above as Davidek crawled through the wet emerald grass of the empty church field, pausing to parse through the fistful of coins he had gathered. "Six dollars and thirty-five cents!" he called out to Green, who was bent over by the yew bushes where the Groughs tended to hang out, his arm searching the bare dirt beneath the shrubs.

"I only have nickels and dimes so far. Maybe four dollars' worth," Green said.

"This ought to be enough to get me some kind of regular tie," Davidek said. "This was a great idea, Green. I mean it. Thanks."

Green continued to probe under the shrubs. "It might be better than you know," he said. Davidek asked what he meant, and Green answered cryptically: "I tried to set something in motion when I left before. Let's see if it works." The two freshmen resumed their hunt, and had accumulated another two dollars between them when a sound of hollering and mad laughter drew their eyes up the side of the schoolhouse to the mouth of the industrial fan three stories up. Seconds later, a rumbling pitched into a piercing whine, and a cannon blast of coins exploded from the exhaust grate.

The widening column of metal disks spinning and flipping through space created a small galaxy of twinkling light across the dark morning clouds. Davidek and Green covered their heads as the coins showered around them.

Green was laughing to himself. He looked at Davidek. "I call heads!" he said.

Both boys swooped down to gather up the fallen fortune. "What *was* that?" Davidek asked. "There's, like, twenty bucks in coins here, at least!"

Green couldn't hide his pride. "The truth is . . . I got the idea to come out here from our friend—Mr. Smitty. Turns out he isn't just trying to curry favor with those Fanboys when he rats out all the kids who have spare change in their pockets. I saw him coming out here afterwards to gather up the money."

The boys were using their forearms to sweep together big piles of coins on the sidewalk. "Smitty had most of the money he gathered just sitting in two Ziploc bags in his locker," Green said. "So, before we came out here, I just went over and told Morti and his buddies to go have a look-see."

"You are an evil genius, Hector Greenwill," Davidek said. "But this is a lot of cash. Why wouldn't the Fanboys just keep those big bags of coins for themselves?"

Green sat up, thinking about it. "I guess because they're morons."

Davidek said that sounded about right. "You think Smitty will find out it was us?"

"I'm not sure *what* to make out of that guy," Green said. "But remember that big speech of his? The one about how people do bad stuff to get what they want, but people only do good stuff out of selfishness, too? Well, maybe he was wrong. Maybe sometimes, people just do . . . *stuff.* Because they don't know what else to do. Or out of pure craziness. Or who-knows-why."

The two freshmen hustled up the stairs, the change-filled pockets of their pants and blazers jangling like Christmas sleighs. "He was right about one thing," Davidek said, putting an arm over his friend's shoulder as they went inside. "Don't get on the bad side of a do-gooder like you."

In English class, Mr. McClerk was droning on about some Edgar Allan Poe story about a guy who keeps killing a black cat, but Davidek wasn't paying any attention. He was planning not to spend one more day with the stupid clip-on around his neck.

He had a study hall in the last period of the day and figured he could sneak away to hit the Kaufmann's department store down the street and still make it back in time for the bus. But he'd need another student to tell Mrs. Tunns, the study hall monitor, that he wasn't feeling well and had gone to the secretary's office to lie down. It would have to be somebody trustworthy, so Mrs. Tunns wouldn't feel obliged to check—that ruled out Stein, and maybe even Green.

"Lorelei . . . ," Davidek whispered to the table in front of his. Her head was hung over her open book, hair drooping down around her face. "Lorelei . . . hey . . ." She wasn't responding, so he strained forward and swatted her shoulder, then dropped back into his seat.

She surprised him, and everyone else in the room, with a startled cry of pain. Mr. McClerk turned around at the chalkboard to ask if she was okay. Lorelei winced, but said she was fine. The other kids sitting around Davidek glared at him: *What the hell did you do?* He wondered the same.

"Lorelei . . . ," he whispered, leaning forward across the table again. "Lorelei, I'm sorry. What was . . . ?" She pulled her hair forward to block him from view, and Davidek noticed a deep bruise of brown and purple creeping up her neck from the shoulder beneath her blue sweater. "Lorelei . . . what . . ."

She turned her face, looking at him through her hair. She wanted him to stop asking. "My mom caught me," she said. "Taking her cigarettes."

At lunch, Davidek thought Lorelei was avoiding him because he'd seen the bruises, but Lorelei just couldn't be bothered to sit down. She spent the lunch break going from table to table in dangerous territory, begging for help in the upperclassman sections. It was humiliating. It was terrifying. But she was desperate, and saw no other way.

Four very disinterested seniors listened to her plea: ". . . just a couple packs, and if you get me more, I can pay you back—eventually."

One of the guys shook his head, like a doctor diagnosing a terminal patient. "If you weren't a freshman . . . but I don't buy cigarettes for little kids."

Lorelei moved on to the next table, some middleclassmen, juniors and sophomores, a few of them girls. She hoped *they* would be sympathetic. "Hi," she said, forcing a perky expression into her sagging eyes. "I, uh, wondered if you could . . ." She explained about the Grough sisters. "You sophomores know what it's like, right? You put up with this last year. . . ."

One guy leered at her, spreading his knees. "So, how are you willing to pay me?" He jiggled his hips at her, and all his friends laughed. Even the girls.

Lorelei hurried away from them, running only a few steps before smacking into Davidek.

"Hey, everybody, it's Clip-On to the rescue!" said the Hip Jiggler, and everybody laughed again. The guy was on a roll.

"You're making this harder for me," Lorelei said. "What do you want?"

"I actually . . . need your help. To tell Mrs. Tunns I'm sick so I can skip out at study hall . . ." But Lorelei wasn't listening to him. He watched her walk away, wandering through the cafeteria, visiting more tables, asking for more help, all to the amusement of their fellow Archangels.

Just before the afternoon class bell rang, she stood before a table full of senior girls, who watched silently as she launched into her speech, about the Groughs, about the cigarettes, about her undying gratitude to anyone who could help her.

When she finished, the apparent leader of the group—a perfect girl named Audra Banes, who was petite, curvy, gorgeous, and the epitome of all the grace and beauty St. Mike's had to offer—looked wordlessly to her friends at the table.

Lorelei blew air up at her bangs. She held out her hand. "I should have introduced myself first. . . . My name is Lorelei," she said. "Please, I'm not a bad person. . . ."

"I know who you are," said Audra, adjusting the black-rimmed glasses she wore to give herself that aura of nerdy-girl chic. "You're the one my boyfriend chose as Miss St. Mike's."

At the start of final period, Davidek hid in the bathroom, waiting for the halls to clear so he could sneak away. Green would have to cover for him with Mrs. Tunns. He hoped it worked.

When Davidek stepped out into the empty corridor, the weight of his book bag felt more solid, as if gravity had suddenly increased. His bag's back pocket sagged with loose change.

"What are you doing?" a voice said from behind him. Davidek was fabricating a lie as he turned, but it wasn't a teacher or the principal who had caught him. It was the red-haired girl from the third floor, the one who had once touched his cheek and called him "adorable."

"I'm skipping class," he told her.

She smiled. "Me, too. Calculus."

Joy bloomed in Davidek's heart. He fidgeted with the clip-on tie, drawing attention to it by trying to obscure it. "Actually, I could use your help. I need to get to a store."

The redhead seemed amused. "Skipping class to go . . . shopping?" she asked. "Must be something important."

Davidek hefted his book bag, feeling the money in it tinkling in small avalanches as he shifted his weight from one foot to the other. "It is," he promised.

Lorelei walked out the side entrance at the end of the day and found the Groughs in their usual spot behind the bushes. "You get what we want?" asked Mary, but before Lorelei could answer, Audra Banes, the student council president, lead singer in the choir, head cheerleader, and all-around senior St. Mike's power player, stepped into the shade of the smoking bushes, her perfect hair flouncing with each fearsome step.

"What is it exactly that you wanted?" she asked as the Groughs recoiled, but there was nowhere for them to go. Around the other bushes, a coterie of Audra's senior girl-squad stepped forward: Allissa Hardawicky, Sandra Burk, Amy Hispioli. The Groughs were surrounded, speechless—and frightened.

"From this point on, you don't talk to the freshmen, you don't look at the freshmen, and you don't let your stinking, fat-ass carcasses bother *this* freshman in particular," Audra said, throwing her arm around Lorelei's shoulder and squeezing her close, which stung around the younger girl's hidden bruise, but felt good all the same.

The Grough sisters backed away, like vampires confronted with garlic and crucifixes. Audra jabbed her index finger in Mary's plump belly. "St. Michael's hazing tradition is about having fun and bonding with the new students—not threatening them, and not forcing them to acquire addictive and illegal products. Do you understand me?"

"I'm sorry," Mary mumbled over her shoulder. The three burly girls scuttled away, and Audra's girlfriends followed, chanting a singsong cry of "Sasquatch! Sasquatch!"

Lorelei thanked Audra, again and again, until the older girl told her to stop it. She winked at Lorelei and said: "We Miss St. Mike's winners need to stick together, don't we?"

Davidek found Lorelei in the parking lot, where she was waiting for her dad to pick her up. He had leaped out of a Jeep driven by a red-haired older girl and ran over to Lorelei, smiling crazily, his short brown hair standing up in little spikes. His clip-on tie hung crooked on his open collar. He opened a plastic shopping bag. Inside was a brand-new carton of Alpaca cigarettes.

Lorelei stared at it. She didn't move.

"It's for you," he said, and held it out to her, shaking the carton like she was a shy pet he wanted to do a trick.

Lorelei put her hands on the box, stepping forward, her face close to his. He could smell her lip gloss, the fruit-flavored shampoo of her hair. "Why?"

He shrugged. "Because you needed it."

"Do you know how expensive this is?" she asked.

Davidek laughed, a little out of breath, "I do now."

She demanded to know how he paid for it, and how he got a store to sell it to him.

"Let's say I found the money. And a guardian angel. Claudia—that red-haired girl, back in the Jeep. She's eighteen! She has a locker up near mine on the third floor and she's really cool and I told her and asked if she would buy them for me." He was talking too fast, excited by it all.

Lorelei stared at the cigarette carton silently. "So let's *give* it to them," Davidek said, pulling Lorelei toward the hidden spot behind the yew shrubs. She let him take her.

When they found the space empty, she explained to Davidek what had happened. He looked disappointed, but a little hopeful, too. "The seniors actually helped you?" he said.

"Sounds like one of them helped you, too," Lorelei answered, and Davidek sort of nodded.

"I guess so, yeah." Maybe things weren't so bad after all.

Lorelei put her hands around his, holding the cigarette carton between them. "So what do we do with these now?" she asked. Their eyes locked, and both knew what the other was thinking. Davidek's hands fumbled at the box, peeling back the plastic cover and lifting open the flaps. He took out a pack and opened it, drawing out one cigarette. The clerk at the convenience store had thrown matches into the bag with the purchase. Davidek struck one.

"Everything they tell you about cigarettes is a lie," Davidek said, watching the white smoke drift out of Lorelei's lips. "They say it doesn't feel good. But this feels great. And they say you don't look cool smoking, but you look very cool, Lorelei. Beautiful, actually . . ."

Her eyes glittered at him. He was surprised by his own boldness. She passed the cigarette back to him and he drew in. When it was almost finished, Lorelei said, "But there's a third thing they tell you about cigarettes, and it's absolutely true. . . ." She dropped their shared smoke on the ground, snubbing it under her penny loafer. "This stuff will kill you dead."

She dropped the rest of the cartoon back into the plastic bag, twisting it shut, then pushed her palms together to crush the carton. "I just saved your life," she said. "At least . . . thirty years from now."

Neither of them knew what to say next. She reached up and brushed his cheek, their faces leaning close—hers serene, his stunned. Their lips were just a few inches apart, and drawing closer. "Thank you," she said, and closed her eyes.

There was a blast of a horn, and Davidek looked between the shrubs to see his school bus pulling out of the parking lot and into the street. A bunch of kids were hanging out the windows, calling his name. "That you?" Lorelei asked.

Davidek's head swiveled back and forth between her and the bus. He still had time to catch it, but . . . but . . . "Better go," Lorelei said.

Davidek waved as he ran off to the yellow school bus, which stopped at the corner, waiting for a red light. "Thanks for saving my life," he said.

Lorelei watched him go. He looked different to her somehow. "Same to you," she said.

TEN

There's going to be trouble today," the pudgy sophomore told them. "You should be a smart guy, not a tough guy. Stay out of sight. Don't give anybody an excuse."

His name was Carl LeRose. ("You know . . . Carl LeRose?" he had said, introducing himself to Davidek at Stein's locker, and looking hurt when that hadn't seemed to mean much to the two freshman boys.) He was only a year older, but had the aura of an unhealthy middle-aged man—thickset, with a slump to his shoulders and a paunch that bulged taut against the bottom of his white shirt, raising his blue-and-red striped tie away from his belt. A watch that might have cost a few months' salary for most people in the Valley dangled around his wrist. His blue blazer was a little too small for him.

"Are you threatening us?" Stein asked, and LeRose sputtered, "No, no . . . why would I . . . Don't you . . . don't you guys *know* me?"

The freshmen looked at each other. They had seen LeRose around, here and there, always on the periphery of things, too low to matter much, too hungry for attention to keep to himself. This was the first he'd ever spoken to them, though.

LeRose blinked at the two boys. "Mom and Dad said you would know me."

Stein shrugged. "I guess *Mom and Dad* overestimated their little boy's popularity."

LeRose shook his chunky face in frustration, then bent in half, aiming the top of his head at them and digging thick fingers through his heavily moussed hair until he exposed a bare split of bright white scar, roughly an inch long, shaped like a jagged half moon. Stein began snapping his fingers excitedly, his eyes wide. "Holy shit! Davidek, it's the kid from the parking lot! This is the kid who got his brains knocked out!"

LeRose turned his face sideways. "Were you there?" he asked, and Stein immediately mellowed.

"Yeah, I was there. Sort of."

"Stein doesn't like to kiss and tell," Davidek said, expecting a laugh from his friend, but it made Stein shoot him a serious look.

LeRose's face lit up. "Kiss and tell? Are you—are you the one who planted one on Bromine? I heard that rumor, but . . . was that for real?"

Stein shook his head and said, "No, that wasn't . . . That didn't happen." *One trick to getting away with something,* Stein explained to Davidek later, *was to know that bragging equals confessing.*

LeRose's face sank in disappointment. He looked to Davidek to see what was true and what wasn't. Davidek followed Stein's lead. "Nah, urban legend, man. Sorry." He stuck his hand out and the sophomore shook it. "Nice to meet you," Davidek said. "I guess the first time, we didn't really *meet* meet."

LeRose nodded gravely. "I'd have come around and introduced myself sooner, but Dad said I should wait a couple weeks to talk to you."

"Your dad tells you who you can talk to?" Stein asked, his face wrinkled.

"*No,*" LeRose shot back. "He wants me to help you out, but . . . it doesn't look so good for a sophomore to buddy-up right away to a freshman, you know?" LeRose lowered his voice and leaned close. "So keep quiet about what I tell you guys, all right?" he said, reluctantly including Stein in the confidentiality. "The seniors are planning this *thing.* . . . I don't know how it'll go down, but it's getting tense around here. A lot of people are getting in trouble, getting yelled at and stuff. Stupid things, you know? Holding hands with their girlfriends gets them detention. You believe that?"

"Criminal," Stein said.

"Everything we do is under a goddamned microscope these days. So, okay—all those little shoves in the hall and shit? It's going to get a lot worse. Just lie low. Word to the wise."

"How bad does all this initiation stuff get over the year?" Davidek asked him.

LeRose rolled his hunched shoulders back and forth. "It can get ugly, I won't lie—but you live. I can be your eyes and ears, okay? Just don't tell anyone where you hear stuff from."

With that, LeRose started to slip off, but Davidek reached out and took his sleeve. "Can I ask you something else . . . about that day? The kid on the roof?" Stein rolled his eyes.

LeRose said, "Yeah?"

"Whatever happened to that guy?"

"Hopefully he's somebody's prison bitch right now," LeRose said. "But he's probably just undergoing bullshit 'mental therapy' or something, eating pills and finding butterflies in inkblots all day."

"So why was the story in the newspaper all watered down?" Davidek asked.

LeRose's face was a mix of awkwardness and pride. "That would be my dad," he said. "Dad's got influence, you know. He's tight with the cops, tight with the church, tight with the city page editor, too. A story like that was bad for the school. So Dad . . . *fixed* it." LeRose's fat fingers twinkled in the air like it was a magic trick. "Dad loves this school. . . . One of those 'Glory Days' kind of things, I guess."

"Glory hole?" Stein asked, but before it could register on their new friend, Davidek said: "Thanks for filling us in, Carl."

LeRose gave a nod as he backed away. "Remember, keep a low profile today. My advice: Be cool, go along with all the goofy stuff—and try to make nice."

"That'll work?" Davidek called after him.

"It worked for me," LeRose said, drifting away amid the flow of other students. "And I'm somebody you're glad to know, right?"

LeRose's warning came true that afternoon.

Restlessness had been brewing among the upperclassmen. Michael Crawford, the handsome senior who had overseen the Miss St. Mike's pageant, began spreading word through his friends that there would be some punishment doled out to the freshmen during lunch, to let off a little steam. Yeah, the faculty was busting balls, but what kind of legacy would their oppressed senior class leave if nobody did any goddamned *initiating*?

Audra Banes intended to personally supervise the stunt they had planned. As student council president, she didn't want anything getting out of hand, and had been warned by Sister Maria that church elders were taking careful note of aberrant behavior. Any unsavoriness would reflect badly on class officers when it came time to write college scholarship recommendations. Also, Crawford was her boyfriend and he had assured her there would be nothing to worry about. She trusted him, and she was an excellent judge of character.

Audra got Lorelei to tell the freshmen not to panic, that things weren't going to be bad. "This'll be fun," Audra said. And Lorelei believed her.

"They're just trying to trick us. Why should we listen to you?" asked Zari, one of many classmates Lorelei tried to persuade to ignore the fear-mongers and venture out of the safety of the cafeteria and into the parking lot during recess. Zari's resentment for Lorelei had become difficult to hide. With all the attention Lorelei received from the popular seniors and the other boys in the class, why was she still toying with Stein? Zari was ready to make her move on him, if only this preppy girl with the odd eyebrows would get out of the way.

"From what I've been told, it's just a big game. And I was assured by Audra Banes, who is the senior class president, and who is also my friend," Lorelei responded, with more pride than she intended.

"Sounds like you're one of them," Zari said, but the others trusted Lorelei, so she did, too.

In the parking lot during lunch break, Michael Crawford grinned his game show–host smile and declared into his girlfriend's cheerleader megaphone: "Good afternoon, ladies and gentlemen, and welcome to St. Michael's Best in Show competition!"

The older boys who were in the know clapped and pumped their fists in the air while making *woof-woof* dog barking sounds, while the rest of the school closed in around the freshmen like the iris of a camera lens.

Stein found his way over to Davidek and Green, who had come out from the cafeteria only to placate Lorelei. "You guys see her?" Stein asked, but Lorelei was over with Audra and the other seniors—outside the pack of surrounded freshmen.

"You!" Michael Crawford shouted, pointing at Davidek, Green, and Stein. Davidek backed away, but Green stepped forward voluntarily. Stein tried to pull him back, but Green smiled fearlessly as he was pulled into the middle of the jeering crowd.

Crawford slapped a hand on Green's meaty back and asked into the megaphone: "So, what kind of dog are you?"

Green just laughed; then he leaned over to the mouthpiece of the megaphone and declared, "I'm a *horn*-dog!" Even though his skin was as dark as coffee, Green was blushing and the whole crowd was laughing along with him.

"And how does a horn-dog go?" Crawford asked, and Green gave a long, high howl. When he was finished, the seniors held his arms in the air like he was a prizefighter.

"Doesn't seem so bad," Davidek said to Stein, who remained unconvinced.

That's when Richard Mullen, aka Asshole Face, and his buddy Frank Simms, got into the act.

Stein's little nickname for Mullen had caught on over the past few weeks, dispelling most of the sympathy he had received as one of the main victims of The Boy on the Roof. When the insolent freshman had called him Asshole Face—without repercussion—Mullen's fame as a survivor became a laughingstock. He knew what a bad nickname could do. People had always called Mullen's best friend Simms "Sandmouth," due to his ever-deteriorating, tan-colored horse teeth. They were a sorry pair, Asshole Face and Sandmouth—the lowest of the upperclassmen, which meant they had a lot to prove.

Mullen and Simms grabbed a pair of freshmen—the wannabe graffiti artist JayArr Picklin and a chubby moonfaced boy named Justin Teemo, and ordered one to sniff the other's butt. Audra freaked when she saw this, and ordered Crawford to break it up just as a gang of raging upperclassmen joined in to shove JayArr and Teemo toward each other.

Other older kids started grabbing newbies at random and ordering them to do tricks. If they liked the freshman, it was "scratch behind your ear," or "shake hands and speak." If they didn't, it was "Roll over!" on the gritty asphalt, or "Fetch!" as they hurled a stolen wallet or purse across the parking lot.

A couple of senior girls had brought cookies from the cafeteria and were making freshmen girls get on their knees and beg for them. Seven-Eighths was refusing, wrapping her arms around herself as the older girls pressed on her shoulders until she knelt. They began mashing cookies against her closed lips, and when she finally opened her mouth, one of the seniors stuffed a piece of chalk in there instead. Seven-Eighths crushed it in her teeth without knowing any better and doubled over, spitting up milky strands of saliva.

With the organizers distracted and feuding, it devolved into a free-for-all. Stein noticed the blue-eyed boy Smitty pushing an escape path through the mob, and he and Davidek followed.

Smitty was big enough to shove through, but Davidek and Stein were intercepted at the edge of the mob by a group of seniors—big guys, basketball players—Alexander Prager and Dan Strebovich, joined by their stubby friend, a fellow named Bilbo Tomch, who was the team's honorary student manager (a glorified title for "towel boy"). He was a *Dungeons & Dragons* kind of kid, always reading sword-and-sorcery books, and he really did look like a fat little hobbit beside his two lanky and athletic friends.

Prager and Strebovich blocked Stein and Davidek's escape while Bilbo informed them their presence was requested in the Best in Show parade. Back in the center of the crowd, a line of freshman boys were being forced to scamper around on all fours with their ties spun around backwards, being held by older students like leashes. Those who resisted were being dragged across the asphalt, grasping at their tie loops to keep from being strangled.

Prager said, "Holy shit, lookit!" and flipped Davidek's clip-on tie into the freshman's face. "I thought you were *a myth*, Clip-On Boy!"

Bilbo hopped around excitedly, enhancing his goblinesque appearance as Prager kept flipping the tie up into Davidek's face, asking: "How we gonna leash you, huh? How we gonna do that to Clip-On Baby, huh? Huh?"

"I gotta go get Crawford and the others. They gotta see this," Bilbo said, and he ran off while Strebovich and Prager kept watch over the two freshman captives.

Stein pushed in front of Davidek, shielding him, and huddled face-to-face with his friend. "Take this, and give me yours," Stein said, popping up his shirt collar and lifting the loop of his tie over his head. He wedged it down over Davidek and snatched off the clip-on, clasping it to the throat of his own shirt. "Now fix it," Stein said, and Davidek began to tighten and straighten Stein's tie around his own neck.

"Hey, what are you—?" Prager shouted, and Strebovich grabbed Stein by the shoulders. "Awwright, Scarface," Strebovich said, looking down at the clip-on. "So now *you're* the faggot baby?"

"Nah," Stein said. "That's just what your pals on the basketball team nicknamed your dick." Strebovich's mouth dropped open as Stein's arms blasted out and smashed the senior in the chest, knocking him back—but not far enough. Strebovich swung a clenched fist into Stein's face, dropping him to the ground as Prager started kicking him. Davidek tried to dive on top of his friend to protect him, but now the parking lot was swarming with teachers.

Mr. Mankowski wedged himself between Davidek and Stein and the two senior boys, who had been joined by Bilbo and a phalanx of friends, all exhaling hot breath in unison, edging each other forward, not really caring that the bald-headed teacher was in their midst.

Davidek pulled up Stein, who was bleeding from the mouth and adjusting his new clip-on tie with a grotesque red smile.

Mankowski said, "That's enough, boys," but Strebovitch stepped up to him, looking through Mankowski instead of at him, his eyes flaring at the freshmen over the horizon of Mankowski's fleshy scalp.

The teacher stepped backwards. The older boys started laughing at him, unafraid, and Mankowski screamed: "Don't you dare disrespect me. Don't you *dare!*"

That stopped the seniors—but only because Mr. Mankowski had delivered his high-pitched scolding not to them, but straight into the faces of Davidek and Stein. "You want to ruin a little innocent fun out here and bother these upperclassmen?" Mankowski said to the two stunned freshmen. "You make me sick. And now you're coming with me. . . ."

As he led them away, Davidek assumed it was a ploy, that Mankowski had felt that pulse of rage from the older boys, knew he couldn't hold them off, and cleverly figured out a way to save them all. But Mankowski's grip didn't ease on their collars as they got near the entrance. "You *will* respect me," he kept saying, like a little kid running out of breath after a tantrum. "You *will* . . ."

The teacher still could have let them go at that point, but that would have meant admitting he had been afraid, been gutless, and it was probably not the first time the teacher had let that happen when confronted by St. Mike's bruiser upperclassmen. Mankowski's anger toward Davidek and Stein had to become real, so he wouldn't have to feel ashamed. Sometimes only a lie can absolve the things a person can't stand to see forgiven.

Bromine stood in the main doorway as Mankowski marched his two prize captives up to her. "These two started it," Mankowski told her in a boastful voice. "*I'm* the one who caught them."

"Nice work," she said coolly, looking over him to where the other teachers were breaking up the larger ruckus. Bromine dismissed the boys with a flick of her wrist: "One week of in-school suspension for our two favorite troublemakers."

Davidek and Stein were the only ones to get that punishment.

ELEVEN

Monday came. Davidek and Stein served their suspension together in the solitude of the school library, a subterranean tomb with a vaulted ceiling hung with clusters of white orbs on brass chains. They sat at opposite sides of a banquet-sized reading table, with books stacked up beside them to hide their whispers. It helped that the ancient Sister Antonia, who monitored them most of the week because she taught only four French classes, could barely hear anyway. She sat at the librarian's desk, reading a *Newsweek*, but never turned any pages.

"Think she's dead?" Stein asked at one point. Then Sister Antonia heaved a deep sigh.

"Maybe sleeping with her eyes open?" Davidek shrugged.

Stein smiled. "Now *that's* something she could teach us." He was still wearing the clip-on tie, which made Davidek feel ashamed every time he saw it. Finally, he began to unfasten the knot of the one Stein had given him. "I think you should have this back—"

Stein put a hand out like a crossing guard. "Stop right there."

"I'm grateful, but . . . you know . . . I could have handled it," Davidek said.

"I know. But I saw you handle it, and handle it, and *handle it* for weeks.

And I know you said your mom kept forgetting, but at some point, you shouldn't have to handle it alone. We're friends. And a friend sometimes takes the bullet for you. Know where I learned that?"

Davidek shook his head.

"From a guy who bought Lorelei a bunch of cigarettes instead of a new tie for himself."

Davidek hadn't realized Stein knew about that. He wasn't sure what to say.

Stein slid down in his chair as if the conversation were starting to bore him. "Anyway, I've got two or three red ties at home I could wear, but I *choose* to wear this one. Everybody wears a tie here, so the fuckers of St. Mike's look for somebody who's got a slightly different one, and they try to string him up by it. And why? Because it makes them feel like they belong somewhere, making another guy the outsider. They hate what's different because they're all so fucking alike."

"What about Green?" Davidek asked. "Green's *black*. That's pretty different. They seem to like him okay."

Stein screwed up his face. "That's because being a bigot is out of style. Everybody wants to beat up a freshman, but nobody wants to be a fucking *racist*. Of course everybody's going to show how wonderfully tolerant and open-minded they are by kissing up to Green. Plus, he plays their game. You saw him up there, goofing along, howling like a wolf."

"He was having fun," Davidek argued. "I didn't see anyone pushing him around. He seemed to be making friends."

"What word do you suppose his 'pals' will call him the nanosecond he crosses them? I'll give you a hint—it starts with N, and it ain't *nipple, Norwegian,* or *nymphomaniac*."

"That's really wrong," Davidek said.

"I'm not saying it's right," Stein replied. "But it'll be a way to hurt him when they want to. That's what I'm talking about, Davidek. *Excuses*. Maybe it's the way you talk, or the color of your skin, or the color of your underwear, or whether you've got a clip-on around your neck. Assholes will find a reason to fuck with you. So I'm going to wear your clip-on proudly. Let them mess with me. The way I see it, this tie is a shithead detector."

. . .

The next day, the boys found themselves overloaded with books and papers—busywork from their classes to frustrate their confinement. They did the work lazily, or at least Davidek did. "You know, Stein, I never hated school before. I was never one of those kids. But I hate *this* school. I hate every minute of being here."

Stein scratched at the long scar by his eye. "Don't say that kind of thing," Stein told him in a voice that was low and serious and devoid of his usual ranting bravado. "It's unfair here, but it's unfair everywhere. That's life all over the place. But if I didn't come to this school, I wouldn't know you. And we're best friends."

"What are you *talking* about? You fight back more than anybody!" Davidek was loud enough to make Sister Antonia shush them from across the room.

Both boys hunched behind their stacked books. "I'm not saying not to fight back," Stein whispered. "I'm saying when they kick you, thank God because they just gave you a license to kick their asses back, and kicking asses is fun!" He flipped through the pages of a notebook. "This is your school, Davidek. Your life, your place in the world—a bunch of blank pages. You got to fill it up with what you want. So they say, 'Do all this homework, you're in suspension.' But what do I do?" He slid the notebook across the table, and Davidek looked at the pages Stein had been scribbling in all morning.

It was a collection of crude cartoons—Bromine eating a plate of turds, Bromine having sexual intercourse with a giraffe, Bromine snipping off Mankowski's penis with a pair of scissors. "Your problem," Stein told him, "is you don't know how to be happy with your unhappiness."

"So are you mad about the cigarettes?" It was day three of suspension, and it had taken Davidek that long to ask.

"Yeah, kind of," Stein said. "Mad at myself, though. I should have done something like that." This dislodged something Davidek had been trying to find a way to ask: "So what exactly is going on with you and Lorelei?"

Stein looked up at him. "I guess I'd call it fate," he said. "It feels like something that's *meant* to happen, like it's all planned out ahead of time.

That's how I felt when I saw Lorelei. She's a perfect fit—like we're puzzle pieces. It's, like, destiny."

Davidek laughed. "Okay, Darth Vader," he said, sucking in breath and making his voice deep. "'Join me, Lorelei! It is your *dessss-tah-nee!*'"

But Stein wasn't laughing. "Maybe that sounds silly, but . . . it doesn't to me. When I'm with her, she makes me feel like the bad stuff around us isn't so bad. The world still sucks, but it's better with her in it. Those first days of class, she kept asking if I knew any disabled students. She wanted to help somebody. That's someone with a good heart. It's easy to love."

"Love, Stein? You guys haven't even gone out to the movies yet. Do you really think you 'love' this girl?"

Stein looked at him blankly. "Don't you?"

Davidek's leg jiggled beneath the table. "No . . . ," he said. "I mean she's cool and all. But we're just friends. I've got my eye on someone else. Claudia."

Stein nodded. "Right. The pretty redhead senior."

"Yeah, I know it's a long shot, but—"

"A guy's got to have ambition," Stein said flatly. "I wish you luck. There's nobody better than you, if she's smart enough to figure that out."

The boys were quiet for most of the rest of that day. Mr. Mankowski came to fill in for Sister Antonia, so they couldn't talk as easily. Davidek kept stealing looks at the clip-on attached to Stein's collar. In the silence of the library, he resolved that Lorelei would be Stein's girl from now on, and that was the end of it. He would never interfere—no matter how sappy Stein got with his theories of fate, destiny, missing puzzle pieces, and true love.

It made Davidek a little sad to surrender the crush, especially before it even got started, but there was something about the sacrifice that made him feel good, made him feel right. He guessed that was what Stein had meant by being happy about your unhappiness.

On the fourth day of suspension, Stein said to Davidek: "You know, I've been hanging around with you for two months, and you've never invited me over to your house."

Davidek wasn't sure what to say, so he told the truth. "Even *I* don't like going to my house. It's not really fun over there. And my mom . . . she's not the best about picking me up and driving friends around." Davidek told Stein about his brother—the secret family shame—and described his mom and dad as "not really what you'd call happy people to begin with."

Stein said, "Sometimes you gotta find your own family."

"You mean turn my brother in for the reward?" Davidek joked, and Stein laughed loud enough to make Sister Antonia take notice and hush them again.

Later that afternoon, while they were eating lunch—again in the solitude of the library—Stein said, "You know, you never asked me about my story."

Davidek said, "What's your story?"

Stein laughed. "You don't care what my story is, or else you would have asked it already. But there is something you do want to know. So far, you haven't had the balls."

Davidek mumbled through a mouthful of grilled cheese, "What do I want to know?"

"Go ahead and ask," Stein said, drawing a finger from his eye to his cheek, tracing the pink mark. "Everybody always wants to know, but nobody ever asks."

"Maybe they think it's rude," Davidek said.

"It'd be rude to say, 'Ugh, God! That scar is hideous! You poor disfigured creature, may the Lord have mercy on your soul!' But there's nothing rude in asking how I got it."

"All right, so how'd you get it?"

"It happened at Vacation Bible Camp," Stein told him. "This was in Texas, four years ago, before we moved here. You go away for two weeks and hang out with the bugs and spiders and mosquitoes while a bunch of loser counselors tell you how bad *Jesus* had it, nailed to the cross and what-not, or wandering the desert. It's supposed to be fun, but it's not. They give you endless shit about when to eat, when to do some dumb craft, when to go to bed. *Don't go into this part of the woods, don't talk back.* Everybody gets so fed up. There are a million other kids at the campground, and all of them are idiots. Each troop has its own camp, although they all get together oc-casionally for sing-alongs and Sunday church services.

"Anyway, there was this rivalry between us and these kids from Fort Worth, who had started it all by TP'ing our tents, so we went back the next day while they were at the lake and stole all of the toilet paper from their outhouses and burned it in a bonfire." He laughed. "They had to go around begging to other troops because they had nothing to wipe their sorry asses with!

"So the Fort Worth kids retaliated by pelting our group with rocks while we were harmlessly sitting around the toilet paper bonfire, telling ghost stories. Freaking rocks! Can you believe it? Coulda killed us.

"The next night, we snuck over with water guns and sprayed the Fort Worthers while they were cooking dinner. They just walked right up to us, laughing," Stein said. "'It's just water,' one of them told the others. So I walked out of the bushes, toward that guy, just letting him have it in the face with a squirt gun. 'Wait'll you taste that water,' I said."

Davidek scrunched his face. "So, what'd it taste like?"

Stein shrugged. "Beats me. *I've* never tasted piss." He leaned back in his chair, grinning. "Well . . . they went insane. And this one kid from the Fort Worth troop, who was a total dick, lunges at me. Piss-covered, teeth bared, nails out, running full speed. So I step to the side and trip him. *Poof!* He hits the ground in a big dust cloud. But—it was dumb of me because he landed right near the campfire. That's when this kid, this dick, grabbed the un-burned end of one of the logs sticking out of the fire, and clobbered me with it. *Wham!* Right in the side of the face. Well, I guess he won that round. Some of the other kids said you could see strings of my skin on the log when I fell away, like melted plastic. So that's how it happened."

Stein knocked his knuckles against the scar. "All better now, though. But I got kicked out of camp for good. . . . I'm not saying the pee-water thing was the *right* thing to do, but at least it washes off. I'm stuck with this for life."

Davidek didn't know what to say.

Stein just shrugged. "I figured since you told me about your family, I'd tell you about the mark." But Davidek thought it was strange that Stein didn't just tell him about his own family, and he wondered why.

On the last day, it rained and the boys were temporarily released from the library to help Mr. Saducci mop up crimson leaks in the third-floor hall.

They hung their blazers on pegs in the boys' bathroom, rolled up their white sleeves, and opened their collars wide as they worked. Mr. Saducci kept telling them they weren't going fast enough, but he was glad for the help, and equally glad to tell a couple of punks what to do and see them do it instead of laugh and ignore him.

A booming voice fractured the silence in the hallway behind them: "So you two are the big troublemakers?" Davidek and Stein turned to see Father Mercedes, clad in a sweeping black topcoat, striding toward them from the stairwell, his eyes shadowed by the brim of a charcoal Borsalino hat.

"Woody, I'd like a private moment with the boys, if you don't mind," the priest said. He lifted the dark hat and ran a palm over his head, streaking back the moist gray hairs.

The janitor wrinkled his face and pointed at the dribbling ceiling. "We got work here. Can't yinz talk later, Fawdder?"

The priest's narrow eyes suggested they could not. "They'll be waiting here when you get back," the priest said, and Saducci looked at the two boys and muttered to himself, walking away and opening the stairway door with an extra hard push. It would have been easy for the priest to ask Stein and Davidek to join him privately in an empty classroom, but just like the janitor, Father Mercedes was the kind of man who enjoyed seeing others follow orders.

The priest smiled at the boys, a shark's smile. "I hear you are the two rabble-rousers who triggered all the trouble last week. . . ." He trailed off, staring them down intently. "But I look at you and, well, find that . . . difficult to believe."

All the machinery in Davidek's chest was working at double speed, so he could only clutch his mop handle and stare. Stein stepped forward and pronounced, "We didn't do *anything* except get pushed around."

The priest managed a half smile, partway charmed. He leaned down with his hands on his knees and made his most serious face. "Do tell . . . ," he said.

The boys—mostly Stein—spilled out exactly what had happened during St. Mike's now-infamous Dog Collar fiasco, and the priest listened with a kind of delight. They couldn't figure out why he was enjoying it so much, unless maybe the priest was just kind of cool and thought they were funny. It made the boys take a liking to Father Mercedes right away.

"If what you say is true, you two fellows have been scapegoated," the priest said when they were finished. "Who's responsible for your punishment this week?"

The boys looked at each other. "Mr. Mankowski, I guess," Stein said, while Davidek volunteered: "And Ms. Bromine."

"Sister Maria, too?" the priest suggested. The boys nodded, and that made him smile. "You two have any character witnesses?" Father Mercedes asked. "Maybe I know your family priests. Which parishes do you belong to?"

"I'm from St. Joe's," Davidek said.

"In Natrona?" the priest asked.

"No," Davidek said. "Over in New Kensington."

"Ah, Father Higgins." The priest nodded. "And you?" He looked at Stein.

"First Evangelical, out near the movie theater in Sarver," Stein answered.

Father Mercedes made a sour face. "That's a Protestant church."

"My family are born-agains, actually," Stein said.

The priest asked, "So what are you doing in a Catholic school?"

"Well, what am I doing at an Evangelical church with a name like Noah Stein?" the boy answered, smiling even wider. "And what was I doing at a bar mitzvah two years ago with one Born-Again sister and an atheist dad?"

"Bar . . . mitzvah?" the priest repeated, like it was a punch line he didn't get.

"My mom, she always wanted me to experience our Jewish heritage—well, my *dad's* Jewish heritage. She was born Lutheran."

"So what are you exactly?" the priest asked in a tone that suggested he felt distinctly bullshitted. Davidek had that feeling, too.

"My family is all sorts of things, Father," Stein said. His face was steady, full of serious intention, and not joking in the least. "My mom, she . . . I guess she worried a lot. We learned a lot about a lot of religions, I guess as a kind of insurance policy. She believed in angels, in heaven, in God—but she had a lot of doubt in her heart, too. None of us knows what's waiting on the other side, but . . . my mom, I guess, she wanted all the bases covered."

The priest didn't know how to respond. The good humor seemed to have drained from him. "Don't try to make an ass out of me, boy," he said, pointing his index finger in their faces. Around the finger was a thick gold ring capped with a fat ruby, surrounded by what looked like diamonds.

The two freshmen inched back, and the priest looked up at the dripping ceiling, which had made a thin pool for them all to stand in. He lifted one shoe, then the other, then found a drier place to stand. "That's all for now," he said. "You better get back to soaking up this filth." He walked away, leaving wet footprints, and they could hear the clack of his shiny black shoes descending the stairwell.

"You think he's still on our side?" Stein asked as the footsteps faded away.

"It depends. Was all that stuff true? About all the religions and stuff you belong to?"

Stein said it was.

Davidek laughed. "I'd like to meet your mom, man. She sounds like a nut." And then, realizing that sounded wrong, sputtered: "I just mean— she sounds weird, but, like *cool*-weird."

"I know," Stein said. "I knew how you meant it. . . . I think you'd like her."

They went back to mopping, waiting for Saducci to come back, but after a while Stein stopped suddenly. "Davidek, I should have told you right away. . . . My mom's not around anymore. She died." Davidek began to gush an apology, but Stein cut him off. "I know you didn't mean anything bad. And that's why I wasn't going to say anything."

Davidek said, "When . . . ?" And Stein just said, "A while ago." Then he went back to mopping, and Davidek understood. That was all his friend wanted to say about it, though there was clearly more to tell.

TWELVE

I n their monthly faculty meeting, the teachers sat around the same polished mahogany library table where Davidek and Stein had passed the previous week, and lowered their eyes as Father Mercedes paced around them.

The priest was berating them over the uproar in the parking lot the week before, an incident he called "a seeping black eye on the institution," and insisted that something needed "to be done immediately." Sister Maria explained that the week-old incident was just some roughhousing and didn't seem like a major catastrophe. The priest said perceptions like that "are exactly the problem."

"We've got a cancer at St. Mike's," he said. "Who's going to cut it out? And don't go telling me it was all the fault of those two boys you stuck in suspension. I've spoken to them myself, and clearly they're just too dumb to defend themselves from the blame."

Ms. Bromine piped up, "They *were* causing problems, Father Mercedes, I can *vouch* for that." Mr. Mankowski half rose from his chair, eager to claim credit for the collar, but Father Mercedes was grimacing and waving them both away like nagging children.

"What I'm saying is that it's *Sister Maria's* fault we don't have thirty *more* students in suspension with them," the priest said, and paused to let that soak in.

Mr. Zimmer looked across the table at Sister Maria, who sat with her eyes lowered to her clasped hands. He kept trying to catch her attention, to prod her into reacting, but she wouldn't look up, even though she knew he was there. *Especially* because she knew he was there.

Zimmer had known Sister Maria ever since he was a student at St. Mike's, more than a decade and a half ago, when he was a lonely beanpole with the big crops of red acne eating his cheeks and she was a mathematics teacher, not yet saddled with the responsibility of being principal, and with just a touch of the wiry gray that dominated her hair today. She knew the other students could be vicious to him—his nickname was Señor Gargoyle (it originated in Spanish class)—but she admired the way he accepted the teasing with a kind of resigned valor, never getting angry, never fighting back. She got the sense that there wasn't much love directed at him from home, but he had nonetheless, somehow, turned into a gentle young man, even as a teenager, who seemed to understand that time would free him from this place of peevishness and someday reward his bigheartedness.

Once she became principal, she had been the one to hire him ten years ago, straight out of college, and it was a joy to see her young friend return to St. Mike's as an instructor, though she once told him she feared that had been a mistake. Perhaps he could have gone on to something greater, rather than return to a place that had treated him so coldly. But he was glad to be home.

Sister Maria had always looked out for him. If she wasn't going to defend herself, Mr. Zimmer would do it for her.

"Here's *the fact*," Father Mercedes was concluding. "I'm demanding the Parish Council investigate this 'Dog' brawl or whatever it was—and any other violent episodes that may follow. If we find a pattern of failure in the leadership here, St. Michael the Archangel High School will—I promise you—be *closed* at the end of this year."

After the meeting, the other teachers scurried away to fret and worry over Father Mercedes's threat, but Zimmer lingered in the library and, once it was clear, put one of his big claw hands on the priest's shoulder. "Father, I was wondering. . . . You ever hear about how Sister Maria got picked to be the principal?"

The priest looked at the hand, but not at the teacher it belonged to.

Zimmer spoke softly: "It was a long time ago, a couple years before you came on as pastor. Not a lot of people know this story, but there was this kid, an okay student, not great, not failing. He wasn't popular. Wasn't good at sports, but he was a good kid.

"Gradewise, he got a lot of A's, and had a couple B's, but only one C-minus. One day when the kid was a sophomore, his dad started to get fanatical. He *insisted* the boy get *perfect* grades—'Straight A's, or I'm pulling you out of that expensive school.'"

The priest was looking at him now, and the teacher kept his hand on him.

"So the kid worked hard, got some extra credit—and lo and behold, pretty soon he was scoring straight A's. And the father says to his son, 'You're not in any activities. What kind of school only focuses on grades?' So the kid joins the yearbook committee and volunteers to help organize the prom. Then the dad says, 'Anybody can do that.' So the kid gets involved in basketball, but the dad says, 'This team loses half the time. What's the point?'"

"What *is* the point?" Father Mercedes said.

Zimmer's pockmarked cheeks stretched back in a sad smile. "The point is, the kid's dad was setting impossible standards. But . . . why? It turns out the old man had lost his job, but nobody knew. The family was short on money, but the dad was afraid to tell his wife and son. He *wanted* the boy to fail because the tuition was eating him alive, and all he wanted was an excuse to pull the kid out of St. Mike's."

The priest said, "Whatever you're trying to say—"

Zimmer cut him off. "It wasn't about the money. He could have withdrawn his son at any time. It was *pride*."

A silence passed, and Zimmer waited for the priest to reply. When Father Mercedes didn't, Mr. Zimmer sighed. "So, these threats about investigating the school . . . shutting it down. Why do I get the feeling you are *trying* to make us fail, Father?"

The priest pushed Zimmer's hand off his shoulder. "I assure you that's not the case."

Zimmer nodded. "You know something? Eventually the truth came out—about the unemployed father, I mean," he said. "The wife found out her husband wasn't working. They had to pull the kid out anyway. You know what Sister Maria did, what made Sister Victor put her in line to be her successor? Sister Maria convinced a group of parishioners to give the kid a tuition scholarship." Zimmer laughed. "He finished out his last two years, no problem. Graduated right up there near the top of his class. Straight A's and B's."

"How sweet," Father Mercedes said.

Zimmer bobbed his head. "The dad wouldn't come to the graduation. How about that?"

"You can stop accusing me in metaphors, Mr. Zimmer," the priest said. "My intentions here are pure. St. Michael's simply *must* begin to function in a way that conforms to basic Christian values."

Zimmer shrugged. "All right, Father. No hard feelings."

The two shook hands, hard. Both of them smiling, neither of them meaning it.

After the meeting, Father Mercedes walked outside, where the autumn winds tugged at his black topcoat and flicked his thin gray hair. His feet carried him along the edge of the parking lot until he stood at the far end of the empty church lot, looking back over the yawning emerald lawn toward the school, a solitary figure with his satchel in one hand and a smoldering cigarette in the other.

Father Harold Mercedes didn't think of himself as a warm man, but he knew he was not cruel. He didn't wish for others to suffer, or to torment those who didn't deserve it. But he had decided more than a year ago—been *forced* to decide—that St. Michael the Archangel parish could no longer support a high school as part of its normal operations.

The question he feared above all was the obvious one: Why?

None of them would understand. Because nobody truly knew him. Not one of them.

The people of St. Mike's knew his name, of course, knew his background—with a dozen years under his belt, he was the parish's longest-serving pastor. The people here knew it was his childhood church, that he had been a student at the school long ago. They knew his birthday, knew he had a dog who died three years ago, which broke his heart, and some of them even knew his parents, though they had been deceased for close to twenty years.

The people of St. Mike's knew many little facts, but facts aren't a person. They didn't know his heart or what he thought, or what he felt, what his philosophies were, what his ambition was. Least of all, they did not know the pressures he faced.

Pressure, that was it. Let Andrew Zimmer stand there in the hallway and rattle off tearjerker anecdotes to make him feel guilty. Let Sister Maria try to put a happy face on every degenerate act that happened in her halls. Let them call him the villain. They didn't understand the forces converging from all sides. After the church fire, St. Michael the Archangel had borrowed heavily, at crushing interest rates, when the insurance settlement was contested and less than expected. Meanwhile, the diocese had increased funding requirements across the board, and parishes that couldn't adequately pay to support the larger church were dissolved, folded into stronger neighboring parishes that could. The diocese was nailing boards over the windows of St. Mike–sized churches all over Pittsburgh, cannibalizing whatever assets were left behind.

If St. Mike's fell prey to weakness, what would the diocese's accountants find in St. Michael's financial holdings?

They would find Father Mercedes's sins.

Everyone in the Valley knew his family as wealthy, but only because his father had lied, claiming they were distant relatives of the German automotive engineering family, and still major stockholders. *Yes, the Mercedes-Benz family*, they bragged. (Never mind that around 1910, more than a decade before the priest would be born, his father had simply switched their surname from the too-Woppish sounding Marcedi.)

The lie about his heritage helped explain Father Mercedes's enjoyment of cars, watches, jewelry, and travel—luxuries he couldn't possibly afford as a humble parish priest. The churchgoers assumed he had inherited immense personal wealth, and Father Mercedes encouraged people to believe that.

Except there was never enough money in the church coffers. Bake sales, pledge drives, in memoriam donations from fat Last Wills and Testaments.

Where did it go? Father Mercedes had become good at making excuses. *There are new wheelchairs in the vestibule! We spend more than you can imagine on electricity and water! Pipe organ repairs don't come cheap.* . . . .

But those weren't the real reasons St. Mike's languished in perpetual debt. The real reason, which nobody knew . . . was quite simple.

Father Mercedes had been stealing.

Not technically stealing, of course—borrowing. He always repaid it. Always. Except for when he didn't. Or couldn't.

The weekly collection plate came directly to him, but not all those neatly sealed envelopes and wads of loose bills made it into the parish accounts. Father Mercedes had dedicated himself to God, to the Holy Roman Church, to serving the people of this parish in their brightest and darkest moments. He pledged his celibacy, his independence, his freedom—his life. Didn't he deserve some temporal pleasures in exchange? He drove a nice automobile, but it was just a Benz. The parishioner who quibbled with him about the furnace repairs was a lawyer who drove a silver Porsche. Did the priest have to get to and fro on a bicycle, like the ascetic Father Henne from St. Joe's, pedaling around like a fool in the hardscrabble neighborhoods of lower Natrona? And whose business was it if he had filet mignon in his refrigerator? He ate alone most nights—did it have to be bread and water for him, too?

Meanwhile, the parishioners had become ceaseless nags: When would St. Mike's finally rebuild its church and move out of that horrible gymnasium?

Father Mercedes had sinned . . . as all men sin. And some of the sins he wouldn't admit, not even to himself, were deeply grave. But he hadn't harmed any person. He had never done *that*. But he had done damnable things.

Father Mercedes's worst flaw was one he had learned from his father: gambling—a thrill like lighter fluid in your veins, the rush of *winning*. Harness racing at the Meadows in Washington County. A few hundred, or a thousand, placed on the Steelers at the Crow Bar in downtown New Kensington, or just playing the numbers at that little barbershop across from the water authority. High-rolling vacations to Atlantic City, Vegas . . . When the good times spiraled, Father Mercedes was a hard loser, and hard losers kept trying and trying. That's how they convinced themselves they'd become winners.

He had lost a great deal of money that didn't belong to him. He wasn't doing it anymore, but it had happened. And when he couldn't repay, he covered it up with a single, shameful, drastic measure. But he intended to fix that, too. A man could sin, but he could also be absolved. If he turned something like the school, which *cost* money, into something else, like a nursing home or a hospice, which *made* money, he might be able to fix the woes of this parish, the ones he had created through his own weakness. He had to make people hate the school. Then they would want it gone. But first he had to take out its protector—the naïve and gutless Sister Maria, who really had allowed the high school to become a festering embarrassment.

When Father Hal Mercedes came to the end of his days, he intended to face his maker and say: *Yes, I have sinned, and sinned terribly. But I made it right. . . .*

Fuck Andrew Zimmer, the know-it-all teacher. And fuck his insinuations.

Father Mercedes stood alone, staring across the shaggy green grass of the church field, which felt like a great void, yawning open, eager to swallow him.

He raised his cigarette to his lips and took a deep drag, but the ember had long gone out.

PART III

Hannah

THIRTEEN

The day after Father Mercedes issued his threats, Sister Maria instituted the Brother–Sister Code. "The hazing tradition can go on," she told an assembly of students in Palisade Hall. "But seniors may no longer indiscriminately terrorize any given freshman. Each individual senior has four weeks to choose one freshman to adopt as a little brother or little sister, which will last until the Hazing Day picnic. You can have your fun, and good-natured teasing is acceptable, but from that point forward, you will be a mentor—not just a tor*mentor*." After some initial grumbling, the upperclassmen seemed to accept it, though Sister Maria worried when she overheard some of them referring to it as the new "Master and Slave" program.

Afterwards, Mr. Zimmer expressed doubt they could successfully tamp down unrest in the school by "turning the freshmen into pets."

"The idea is to transform potential abusers into protectors," Sister Maria said. "It's one thing for large groups of seniors to pick on large groups of freshmen, but if they can see each other as individuals—"

"Do we have a fail-safe if an especially cruel senior chooses an especially weak freshman to be a personal punching bag?" Zimmer asked.

"Then we intercede," she said. "But in the meantime, at least he will have only *one* punching bag."

. . .

Carl LeRose was furious. He pulled Davidek and Stein into one of the
stairwells leading down to the lunchroom and slid his feet from side to
side, like someone trying to figure out how to dance. "What's with you
guys?" LeRose snapped. "Ain't you got no *brains*? Father Mercedes told the
parish council you two told him the whole story about the parking lot
fight. So he has the council members calling parents, telling them to question their kids about what really went on. The teachers got bitched out the
other day. My dad is on the council. He's pissed."

"Fuck your dad," Stein said, and outrage flared on LeRose's face.

"When the teachers start cracking down even harder on us, everybody
will blame *you* two dipshits."

"Yeah, but they can't hurt us if we're somebody's 'little brother,' right?"
Davidek said.

LeRose chewed on a fingernail. "Okay, smart guy. How'd you like to
end up with Hannah Kraut as your big sister? That's what'll happen if
everyone else in the senior class freezes you dumb-asses out."

"Who's Hannah Kraut?" Davidek asked.

LeRose closed his eyes in a prayer for patience. "You've never heard
anyone talk about Hannah Kraut?"

"We're not exactly on anyone's need-to-know list," Stein said.

LeRose ran thick fingers over his face. "Let's just say if you got a mentor
who beat the crap out of you every day, life would be bad for the next few
months. But if you get Hannah . . . Jesus, man, I don't know what to say.
Life's gonna be bad for you *permanently*."

Stein asked, "She one of those Sasquatch-looking girls hassling Lorelei
for cigarettes?"

"She doesn't, uh, hang with a group," LeRose said. "She's nobody, you
know? . . . She's *nothing*. She's a *void*. She's fucking *antimatter*. Do you get
what I mean?"

Davidek nodded obediently, although he had no idea. Stein was more
direct: "That's nice poetry, fat boy. Can you translate what the hell you're
talking about?"

LeRose looked around nervously. "Hannah has this thing she does. . . ."

She's a listener. An eavesdropper." The sophomore lowered his voice, like she might be hearing them right now. "She's been doing it for years. You're standing there talking with your friends, or your girlfriend or something, and all the sudden you realize she's been hovering around and picked up the whole conversation."

"Oh, *I* know who you mean," Stein said, snapping his fingers. "She was in that movie *Predator* with Arnold Schwarzenegger, right? Turns invisible, hangs out in trees. Laughs like this—*mwaah, ahh, ahh, ahh. . . .*"

LeRose squinted. "Let's see if you're laughing when she walks up to a group of your friends and just blurts out some horrible secret thing about you. She's done it before. That's why you don't mess with Hannah—you avoid her. And you definitely don't talk about anything important if she's around. Shit, there are people in her class who won't tell you what *time* it is if Hannah Kraut's in the room."

Stein's smart-ass smile faded a little, which made Davidek nervous.

"This is her final year," LeRose said. "Everyone's scared about what she'll do now that she's saying 'fuck off' to this place forever. You worry about some big guy shoving you around? Try having Hannah spread sick, stupid stories about you for the rest of the year. Doesn't even matter if they're true. By the time you're a senior, even the visiting grade-school kids will be making fun of you."

"So what does she look like?" Davidek asked. "How do we avoid her?"

"I dunno. . . . She's a goddamned *shape-shifter.* Always switching her hair and shit. She doesn't have a single friend in this school, so I can't even tell you who she'd be hanging around with. But one thing about her—?" LeRose shook his head like even *he* didn't believe this part. "She has one blue eye, and one green eye," he said, laughing nervously. "I shit you not. She's fucking *hell spawn,* man."

LeRose was right about most of it, but wrong about one thing: Hannah Kraut wasn't *completely* friendless at St. Mike's. The mysterious and loathed girl did have *one* confidant, though LeRose didn't know this. No one did.

Mr. Zimmer had noticed her right away when she was just a knobby-kneed freshman with electrostatic waves of curly black hair hanging around her head. The other freshmen said she looked like a Halloween decoration, the first of many insults. As they absorbed their share of torment from the seniors, they dumped it back on Hannah, who accepted it meekly, as if it confirmed something ugly about herself she'd always suspected. As if she deserved it.

Zimmer admired her grace, while secretly longing to see her haul off and sucker-punch one of those little jerks. He knew from a decade of teaching that you can't protect a vulnerable student all the time, but you could extend your own friendship. Zimmer tried to talk to her about her hobbies, which she didn't have, and movies or books or music she liked, but she wasn't really into any of that either. "Living doesn't seem to be your thing," he joked to her once, immediately regretting the words. But that had actually brought out a little half smile, and her dour eyes brightened a little. It was only then that Mr. Zimmer noticed that odd little defect, if you could call it that—her one blue eye, and one green eye.

"It's genetic," she told him. "Not even that rare. You'd be surprised."

Just when things were supposed to get a lot better for Hannah Kraut, they got a lot worse. At the end of her freshman year, during the Hazing Picnic, she had been spared any of the ritual humiliation that befell the other freshmen. A senior named Cliff Onasik, a genial burnout, had ended up with Hannah by default when the seniors divvied up freshmen for the picnic's "talent show," the event freshmen feared all year long. While her other classmates were paraded up to the park's band stage as targets for ridicule—in one case literally, as five freshmen were pelted with eggs and tomatoes from the audience—neither Hannah nor Onasik could be found when it was her turn up on the stage.

No one could figure out how that was possible until a rumor began circulating, one far more vile than lame old jokes about her Wooly Willy hairdo. It wasn't until Hannah came back as a sophomore that the ridicule reached an intensity even a teacher could detect. Zimmer pieced together the story from fragments of overheard conversations, though he wasn't sure he believed it. That didn't matter. The kids did.

"Hey, Hannah, how was the hot dog–eating contest?" they'd ask her in the hall.

Hannah didn't seem to know what they were talking about, though the teasing got much more direct as time went on. "How long did Cliffy Onasik make you blow him before letting you off the hook, anyway?" Bilbo Tomch said one day in the lunch line. (He had asked her out on a date some weeks before, but she had said no. Bilbo didn't take the rejection like a gentleman.)

"She wasn't 'off the hook,' man! She was sucking on his worm!" laughed one of Bilbo's pals, maybe Prager, as the boys high-fived. Hannah slouched away when Mr. Zimmer came over to ask what the problem was.

It didn't make any sense, Zimmer thought. Why would she do *that* rather than just appear onstage for the lame song-and-dance teasing all the other kids got at the Hazing Picnic? Cliffy Onasik wasn't around anymore to confirm or deny. The rumor became that Hannah hadn't been coerced—she had offered.

Zimmer couldn't bear to think about the name they called her in the hall, right to her face, whispering it as they shoved past her. He'd handed out at least two dozen detentions, though that hadn't killed it. The upperclassmen told the new freshmen, too green and scared to know better, to walk up to Hannah and bark it at her before running away. Zimmer couldn't even think the word without feeling his jaw tighten:

Fuckslut.

　　Fuckslut.

　　　　Fuckslut.

That poor girl with the wild black hair. The one who couldn't bring herself to look people in the eye or answer their questions with more than a mumble. That was the name she carried with her down the hallways, shorthand for a scummy little sex rumor that would never let her go. *Fuckslut.*

Zimmer never asked her if it was true. He didn't care, and didn't want to know, really. Like any high school, St. Mike's had seen its share of girls with slutty reputations, and most were sad, lonesome cases, filling a self-esteem void with attention from sleazeball boys like Cliffy. All Zimmer could do was try to be kind to Hannah, and protect her when he could, which wasn't often enough. Hannah appreciated his help, and a friendship blossomed between them. She began asking for after-school tutoring, even on subjects Zimmer didn't teach. That was okay by him. He liked Hannah, and he knew what it felt like to be her.

Sister Maria had been one of his only friends when he was student, and in many ways she still was. After school sometimes, they'd hit the Capri restaurant down the street, sharing a pizza and a pitcher of beer, and in the summer they'd catch a movie or Pirates game down in Pittsburgh. Not long ago, Sister Maria asked why he didn't find a nice girl to share such times. Zimmer hated that question. If the answer wasn't obvious, he didn't want to say it out loud. "I guess they're not interested," he told her, but Sister Maria said she doubted that. "Come on, Sister, I can't even date blind girls," Zimmer said, running a hand across his pockmarked cheeks. "In braille, this face says: 'Danger—Keep Away.'"

Zimmer had gotten used to solitude, what Stein might have called being happy with his unhappiness. He had been an ill child, prone to lung and vision problems, thanks to a genetic disorder called Marfan syndrome. It also accounted for his stretched appearance and long limbs. Though Andy Zimmer grew tall, his father still thought of him as a weakling.

Both his parents—heavy smokers, bad eaters, high-stress personalities—had died while he was in college, just two years apart. Their family home was now his alone. He used their old silverware, their dishes, their towels and bedsheets. The TV was new; the couch was not. The little white Subaru was his mother's last car, and his first.

He lived daily with their ghosts, but it was a lot easier to miss them than it was to live with them. They had been hard on their quiet, bookish boy— and unlike Sister Maria, their questions about girls weren't so easily side-tracked by jokes. His father, a failed cop who found sporadic work as a security guard after alcoholism cost him that job, just assumed his son was queer, and after he died, Zimmer's mother decided to finally ask him directly, which he knew was very painful for her. It was painful for him, too, so he hoped a blunt answer would make her never ask again: "No, Mama," he said. "I'm just ugly."

In the spring and summer, students often saw Mr. Zimmer out at the old St. Joseph cemetery, on the edge of town where the shops and parking lots of Natrona Heights gave way to farmland. He would go there to cut the grass around his mother and father's plots because St. Joe's had recently been closed by the diocese, and no one maintained the grounds anymore except the families of the buried. It wasn't a sad chore for him. He enjoyed being out there—the birds heckling him from the tall weeds around the unkept graves, the smell of the cut grass and the way it stained his tennis shoes green. It was peaceful there, and most of all, he enjoyed talking to his mom and dad, freely, about anything at all. And now they listened without hounding or judging him.

"Do you know they call you The Grave Robber?" Hannah had told him once.

"That's a new one," he said. He knew Hannah was good at making herself small and going unnoticed, which made her an excellent spy. "Back in high school, they used to call me The Skeleton," he told her. "They would've considered a cemetery to be my natural habitat."

"I thought they called you Señor Gargoyle," she said.

Zimmer sighed. "That was mainly Spanish class." Hannah laughed at that, and it coaxed a smile out of him, too. Let the kids call him names. What teacher could escape *that* fate? Hannah reminded him how nice it was to talk to the living. He hoped he did the same for her.

The next few years were vicious ones for Hannah. And after any particularly rough time, she would appear at school with a different hair color—blond, black, brunette—as if she hoped to go unrecognized. Her small, pudgy face was always the same, pinched, suffering, dogged by that word, that horrible nickname. The one Zimmer couldn't bear to hear or repeat.

Then a strange thing happened near the end of Hannah's junior year: It all just stopped. The teasing, the name-calling, the torment—it simply ceased. When Hannah moved through the halls, the other kids shifted away from her, like a negative pulse pushing them aside. Zimmer had no idea what happened, but he doubted they had all grown souls overnight. Hannah had done something. She had frightened them somehow. Hannah had *forced* them to stop.

He asked her once what had changed. "I have no idea," she answered, but the lie was heavy in those mismatched eyes.

On the last day of that year, with the floors polished, the chalkboards wiped clean, and the textbooks packed away for the summer, Hannah had found him shutting down the computers in his otherwise empty classroom.

"I came to say good-bye," she told him, and in her hand was a sheet of paper folded in thirds. "And to give you this."

Zimmer opened the page, smiling at her. He'd gotten these kinds of letters before: "Thank you, Mr. Zimmer. You really inspired me." Etcetera, etcetera, etcetera. They were all the same, and priceless, too. He saved every one.

But on this creased sheet of paper there were just three words: *Don't be mad.*

When Mr. Zimmer looked up, Hannah Kraut stepped forward, placing her left hand against the teacher's cratered cheek. She tipped up on her toes and placed her open lips against his.

When he saw her again, another summer had passed, and it was the start of her senior year. He hadn't told anyone about the kiss, not Sister Maria, and not even his parents, who were now good at keeping secrets.

He knew he had done nothing wrong, but still felt guilty. When Hannah had kissed him, he pulled away, staring everywhere but directly at her. But what could he do then—report her? Send her for counseling? Disrupt her already difficult life even more, just as it was turning around? "Hannah . . . I . . . You *really* shouldn't have done that. . . ."

"I know," she said. And as she left the room, she looked back one more time. "And I know you have to say that."

There had been another metamorphosis in Hannah over the summer—a deep, dramatic, and lovely one. She had dyed her hair again, but it now hung smoothly around her shoulders, and a season of heavy exercise had transformed her previous squat awkwardness into a lean, girlish litheness. Her face was more serene, no longer furrowed and angry. She truly did look like a different person, and Zimmer almost didn't recognize her.

She assumed they would return to their regular after-school study sessions again, but Zimmer said he couldn't. "Is it because of The Note?" she asked.

He countered the intimacy of her code language by feigning ignorance. "Note? No. No, I just have nightly commitments now that I can't break. I'm working almost every evening on a special project for the school." He hated to sound mysterious; that made it seem like a lie. "I wish I could tell you, but . . . it's kind of a private matter."

"Secret agent man," Hannah smirked. She didn't believe him. But whatever.

Hannah took out a disposable camera. "Do you mind?" she asked. "To commemorate the first day of my last year?"

Zimmer looked at the open door leading to the hallway. "Sure," he said.

He leaned against the edge of his desk and Hannah squeezed in close, standing on the tips of her toes again to get her face beside his. "Someday we'll look at this picture, and it will seem strange that it was so long ago," she said, holding the camera at arm's length. Her head rested against his shoulder. There was no flash, just a click of the shutter.

They both smiled, though Mr. Zimmer's was a little awkward.

Not that anyone would have found that unusual.

FOURTEEN

I t's a notebook," Green said, standing in biology class while fastening a dull gray apron around his waist. "That's what this Hannah chick's got that has everybody freaked."

He and Davidek stood by the stainless steel sink in the back of the room, dumping little tins of liquefied grape Jell-O and pineapple slices into the garbage disposal. Mrs. Horgen had the lab learning about the substrate-enzyme complex, with the acidic fruit dissolving the collagen cells in the gelatin. The experiment was also delicious, the class agreed.

Davidek was grateful to Green for the news. Since LeRose first warned him about Hannah Kraut, rumors of this most dangerous of senior mentors had trickled through the freshman class, and intelligence on her was at a premium. Not everybody knew an upperclassman well enough to get information, but Green had made friends in high places.

"She's been keeping a diary or something, all these years," Green told him. "They say she's got a whole book full of embarrassing things written down about everybody. And that's why nobody messes with her. The guys"—the guys were the seniors Green had befriended—"say she's been dropping hints that she's gonna make her freshman read it out loud at the big Hazing Day picnic thing."

"So what'll that prove?" Davidek asked.

Green shrugged. "All I know is, she's outta here at the end of the year, but we've got three more to go," Green said. "If she's lighting up an inferno, I don't want to be the match."

Davidek knew Green had a lot less to worry about than he did. Someone safe would choose him as a little brother. Green had ingratiated himself by being a good sport, which made the upperclassmen want to pick on him less. Sometimes, he even volunteered himself for hazing.

One afternoon, a group of upperclassmen were forcing freshman boys to march in formation through the halls singing old-time songs of woe— their favorite was "Swing Low, Sweet Chariot," which the freshmen chanted in creaky mock baritones.

"Hey, fellas, how come you didn't pick me?" he asked Michael Crawford, who was leading the cluster of freshman captives. Crawford looked at his friends, who had nothing.

"You know that song they're singing, 'Swing Low, Sweet Chariot'? That song is what they call a Negro spiritual," Green said. "It's a religious song that black folks would sing when they were picking cotton or doing group labor during the slave times."

"Aww, jeez . . . ," Bilbo groaned, looking like he'd rather die than have this conversation. "It's got nuthin' to do with Negro anything—oh, ah—I mean *black* people anything. It's, uh, an Eric Clapton song. I have it on my dad's CD to prove it!"

Green became very animated. "Eric Clapton?" he said. "Are you kidding me?" Crawford, Bilbo, and the other seniors looked scared, like they'd accidentally inflamed a one-man race war with the school's lone minority. It took a second for them to realize Green wasn't angry; he was excited. "My dad has that album, too!" Green said. "And I learned to play some of the chords to that song by listening to the Clapton version."

The seniors gaped at him. Green said, "You know . . . *guitar?*" and mimed strumming in the air. "I went through a really intense Clapton phase last summer. I love that his version of 'Chariot' has a kind of reggae thing going on."

The seniors were perplexed. "Soooo, it's not racist to make them sing it . . . right?" Prager asked. The freshman boys lined up behind him were wide-eyed, waiting to see how this played out.

Green shrugged. "It's just singing. You're not treating these guys like slaves, right?"

"No!" Crawford said. "No, no no. No." The freshmen behind him shared subtle expressions of doubt.

"It is a good song," Green said. "So you should sing it right. Like Clapton did. It's an old work song, but it deserves some respect."

Some pink color returned to Bilbo's blanched, sweating face. "I'm kind of into guitar, too, you know," Bilbo told Green. "Well, I'm trying to learn . . . *was* trying."

Green looked at the silent freshman singers, who were still awaiting further instruction. "You're singing it like it's torture. You got to sing it *sweet*. It is '*sweet* chariot,' you know? Don't make it a dirge." And Green walked in among his classmates and sang a bit of the verse and showed them what a harmony was. Green's voice wasn't perfect, but he hit actual notes instead of chanting in monotone like the other boys. They got so good at it that Green helped organize the hazing singsong marches all through the week. Even some upperclassmen joined in.

"Just don't leave me out next time," Green had told Bilbo. "If you're into music, maybe we could hang out sometime. I'm always looking for someone to play with." Strebovich stepped forward to tell Green he used to play drums, and Prager said he also always wanted to learn guitar.

"You into rap?" Prager asked, and Green shrugged.

"I'm mostly into guitar stuff," Green said. "I'm in a real nostalgia phase. Lotsa '70s stuff. I'm into, like, Pearl Jam, too, and Tom Waits. You know him?"

"You know who I like?" Bilbo said eagerly. "Hendrix."

Green bobbed his head. "Hendrix is God."

"And, umm, that guy B.B. King," Prager added.

Green said, "B.B. King is also God."

Strebovich snapped his fingers, trying to jog something loose in his brain. "Who is that other, uh, bl—uh *guy* in a rock band . . . uh, whatshisname? Living Colour."

Green's face soured a little. "I like white musicians, too, guys. The Who, The Doors, Pink Floyd. Dylan. U2. Neil Young . . ."

The senior boys stared at him blankly. "How about Prince?" Prager asked hopefully.

Green rolled his eyes. "Yeah," he said. "Sure." Pretty soon, they were meeting up on weekends, and Green was welcomed into the mysterious group of seniors who gathered every day at the bottom of the south stairs, drinking Coke in that open space at the bottom and laughing at their private joke. Davidek couldn't figure out why they hung out there.

One time he asked, but that made Green suck air between his teeth. "You know, I can tell you a lot of stuff, but that one . . . I can't. The guys would kill me."

Green was one of two freshmen considered to be honorary seniors. Lorelei was the other.

In the weeks since Davidek and Stein were released from suspension, she had spent most of her time with Audra Banes, who—after saving her from the Groughs—had already announced she was choosing Lorelei as her little sister, even though the sign-up sheet wouldn't be posted for another month. Lorelei was welcomed into the coterie of sophomore, junior, and senior girls who worshipped Student Council President Banes (when they weren't secretly deriding her thickening legs and deliberately nerdy black-rimmed glasses).

When Lorelei visited the freshman lunch tables, it was like a congressional representative visiting the home district, reassuring them that they had nothing to fear from the upcoming Brother–Sister initiative, and basking in the adoration most of her classmates had for her. The one who had none was Zari, who still resented the attention Lorelei received from Stein.

One late October afternoon, as a harsh wind outside turned the leaves into a flame-colored shower, she sat beside Zari in study hall and asked, "Do you still have those fortune-telling cards?"

Her lanky, black-haired classmate raised her head sharply, jangling her long earings. "*Tarot* cards," Zari corrected.

"Tarot, right, right," Lorelei said, adding with a whisper. "Can the cards, like, help me figure out what to do about a boy?"

"Which boy? Stein?" Zari said—loudly.

Lorelei looked around her, over to where the boys were sitting. They hadn't heard. "No," she said. "Peter Davidek. I think he's . . . cute."

Zari opened her purse and began shuffling the ornate deck. Inside, her heart did a little happy dance. The first card had a young couple beneath a flowery bow; the second was a dead man lying on the ground with ten swords sticking out of his back. "That can't be good," Lorelei said, and Zari shushed her.

"No," Zari said, thinking for a moment. "That means you should definitely go for it."

The next day, Lorelei asked Davidek if he was going to the Halloween dance. She didn't ask him to go with her, or if he would dance with her, or anything like that. Just: Are you going? And Davidek, who was hoping to go, told her he wasn't.

"I don't really care about dances and crap like that," he said, though he wanted to say yes. Still, he had made a decision: Stein was in love with Lorelei, so he wouldn't get in the way anymore.

"What's going on with you lately?" Lorelei asked.

Davidek didn't answer as he stepped past her in the otherwise empty stairwell and descended out of sight.

Later that day, Stein not only asked Lorelei to be his date for the Halloween dance, but also suggested that they coordinate costumes. He wanted to go as Casanova, and hoped Lorelei would go as whoever it was Casanova was in love with. But still stinging from her rebuke by Davidek, Lorelei told Stein just as bluntly: "I doubt I'll even go."

When the Halloween dance finally arrived, none of them went.

It was early November, and Lorelei was walking out the front double doors when she heard a voice behind her. "Can I walk you outside?" It was Stein, standing against the trophy case beneath the white-eyed Jesus statue. "I thought maybe we could talk," he said.

Hurrying students brushed past Lorelei, opening and closing the main doors as they flowed outside to their rides home. Her father would be out there, tapping his fingers on his steering wheel. "Why do you want to talk?" she asked.

Stein shrugged. "I don't know. Because."

Lorelei laughed at him. "*Because?* The answer you give is *because?*"

Stein's face was serious. "Because . . . I don't know. I thought we were friends, but you seem like you'd rather be alone most of the time now."

Lorelei shifted her book bag on her shoulder. *Alone.* "I never said I wanted that," she said.

They left through the side entrance so her father wouldn't see. He'd be angry his daughter kept him waiting, but he *would* wait—unlike her mother—at least for a while.

Lorelei and Stein walked down the street in front of the priest's rectory and the nuns' convent, the red-stone walls of St. Mike's rising behind those homes. The trees lining the street cascaded autumn leaves around them, like ruby embers floating down from a bonfire. Stein reached out to hold Lorelei's hand, but she pulled it away. "I like you, Noah, but you just don't get it, do you?" she said. "You're cute. But we're just *friends,* okay?"

Stein smiled and opened his arms: "But I *am* cute?"

Lorelei took a few more steps, then looked back. The wind played with his short hair; the clip-on tie was a little crooked. He bunched his hands in the pockets of his blazer. "I owe you an apology," he told her. "When you needed help, with the Groughs and the cigarettes, I wasn't much. That was lame. I suck. And I'm sorry."

"Why do you care about *me* so much?" Lorelei said, walking again. "You've got other girls who like you, who'd make out with you in a heartbeat. Maybe even *more* than make out."

Stein caught up to her and said, "Because . . . well, *because,*" and Lorelei laughed at him.

"That answer again—you sound like you're five. My mom won't let me date, Stein," she said. "That's the end of it."

"So?" He shrugged. "No candlelit dinners, I guess. But that doesn't mean we can't *sorta* date anyway, here at school." Lorelei lowered her head. That was exactly what she had hoped for with Davidek, before he started being a jerk.

They were rounding the back of the gymnasium church, crossing through the grass along the pine shrubs and bare azalea bushes. Another turn, and they'd be headed back into St. Mike's parking lot. Stein stopped walking again. No one else was around, and he wanted it to stay that way, just a little while longer.

"The other freshmen are always talking about their old friends, and their old school, and their old lives when they were top-of-the-food-chain eighth graders, and not just peons here at St. Mike's. But I never hear you mention any of that, any of your old life. How come?"

Lorelei was getting impatient. "You don't either," she said.

"That's right," Stein told her. "And it makes me think we're both from places that didn't really like having us around. My guess is, you know what it's like to hurt, Lorelei. And I don't think anyone can truly be happy unless they know what it's like to, to . . . *not* be. That's why I like you. That's why I'm kind of . . . in love with you."

Love? Jesus. Lorelei started walking again, faster. But Stein didn't follow this time.

Lorelei wheeled on him. "You think you can just throw those words around?" Her voice echoed along the brick wall of the gymnasium church.

Stein inhaled, tilted his neck back, and stared up into the tree branches. "The only thing I've ever wanted to hear someone say is: No matter what, I will *never* abandon you," Stein said. He looked back down and locked his eyes with hers. "So I'm saying that to you."

"You're an asshole," Lorelei said, and started walking away again. Stein looked down at the ground, hands sinking into his blazer pockets again.

Then Lorelei was charging back at him, dropping her book bag on the ground, her face full of fury. Stein began to babble another apology, but she shoved him up against the wall of the church and pressed her mouth against his, softly, deeply, until they were both out of breath.

She stepped back. One hand reached down to pick up the shoulder strap of her bag; the other brushed her lips lightly, as if to make sure they were still there.

Stein's face was a jumble of confusion. "Why did you do *that*?" he asked.

As Lorelei disappeared around the corner of the church, all she said was: "Because."

FIFTEEN

Stein didn't try so hard to make anyone else like him.

He was never the go-along type, resisting even the harmless bits of senior hijinks, like the dumb hallway sing-alongs that had made Green so popular. At first, Stein's defiance provoked the older kids into directing ever more brutal treatment toward him, and the more they tried to make him suffer, the more he pushed back. Stein's unrelenting combativeness succeeded in making most of the seniors avoid him. He was more hassle than he was worth, though they all were eager for someone else to humble the hostile little brat. There is always some fringe-dweller, some perpetual loser with lots to prove who moves in where others have failed, desperate to make a reputation.

And that's how Stein crossed paths with Asshole Face and Sandmouth.

Mullen, who had once tangled with Clink's mysterious book bag and got a pen through his face to remember it by, had been waiting weeks to get revenge on Stein for bestowing him with that unpleasant little nickname. The white starburst of scars on Mullen's cheek had healed over, but his pride took the beating now. Sandmouth Simms, was his eager toady, reminding him that torturing Stein would make them heroes to their fellow seniors. They needed something to elevate them from their bottom-feeder status.

Life in general had never been good for Mullen. His family's income was slight, barely able to keep up with the school's tuition, but his parents were convinced a private education would get their boy into a decent college. His father was on disability from the farm-supply outlet, undergoing chemotherapy for a thyroid cancer they suspected was caused by longtime exposure to the pesticides they sold. They had plans for a lawsuit if doctors could prove the connection—one hell of a retirement plan, if the old man lived to see it.

Frank "Sandmouth" Simms came from a similarly desperate financial situation. His parents were Catholic traditionalists who lived along Bull Creek, in a cramped wooden home that was shedding paint like dandruff—even though his father worked as a housepainter. Having their only child receive an education steeped in the teachings of Christ was a luxury they afforded by forgoing medical insurance. The trade-off was their son's horribly maladjusted teeth, which were browning from some type of dental disease—undiagnosed, of course.

Simms was the kind of guy Mullen would have loved to torture, if only Mullen had been able to make other friends. Every time he looked at Simms's big smile, with those furry teeth, and heard his jackass laugh, he felt a secret hatred for his only companion.

Ever since their time as seniors started, Simms had been nagging Mullen about getting in on the freshman hazing. "Man, we got to find something really good to do to 'em. Really fucking *good*, you know?"

Mullen agreed, but the "Asshole Face" nickname had cowed him. Mullen was no longer sure he'd even *get* a freshman slave of his own when the Brother–Sister sign-up sheet was posted. There were about half the number of freshmen as seniors, so some upperclassmen would have to share. Others might get shut out completely.

"We'll double up right away and pick one together, okay?" Simms said. "That way we won't get left with *nothin'*, right?" Mullen reluctantly agreed, once again unhappy to find his fate locked with Simms's.

In the days before Thanksgiving, the senior class introduced a new hazing task for the freshmen—Butler Duty, which required freshman boys and girls to act as servants for the upperclassmen during lunch. They would carry food trays, polish the cafeteria seats before the seniors would sit down, and clean up when the meal was finished. It even had Sister Maria's blessing, since she saw it as a harmless way to initiate the newcomers, and might even create a bond among the freshmen—which, after all, was the entire justification for the St. Mike's hazing ritual.

Davidek spent the entire time trying to spot Hannah Kraut, just to get a look at the dread monster. But LeRose said she always left school grounds for lunch, a privilege afforded the upperclassmen, but not the freshmen. "Nobody wants to eat with her anyway," LeRose said.

While the senior boys were caveman-ish, deliberately spilling their sodas and slopping their food on the table, and testing the patience of guys like Smitty by dropping their silverware and making him fetch new forks and spoons, the senior girls were more orderly and polite—albeit just as demanding. Lorelei, working alongside Zari and Seven-Eighths, even received polite "please's" and "thank you's" as she served Audra and her friends.

Only one freshman refused to participate in Butler Duty.

Stein sat alone at the freshman table, waiting for his friends to finish their work and join him. He smiled at the upperclassmen barking at him to get up and help. Still, no one felt like tackling the infinite hassle of Noah Stein—until Asshole Face and Sandmouth sidled up to the lone figure in the freshman section.

"Listen to me, fuckstick," whispered Mullen, leaning down over Stein's shoulder until his lips were in his ear. "You're going to get up, get over to the food line, and bring me and my friend Frank, here, our lunch."

Simms opened his jack-o'-lantern mouth. "On your feet, faggot," he said.

The sophomores and juniors at the surrounding tables got quiet, watching the confrontation. Stein devoted unusual focus to his peanut butter and jelly sandwich, nibbling tiny bites, while Mullen and Simms looked at each other helplessly. Then Mullen grabbed a metal fork off Stein's tray and stabbed it under the freshman's left armpit as Simms pulled Stein up out of his chair. Mullen dug the fork harder, shoving Stein toward the lunch counter.

"You win, guys," Stein said, wincing as he rubbed his side. He looked over at his classmates, acting as maids and butlers to the older kids. "All you had to do was ask *nice*," he said.

Mullen and Simms shared a brief, surprised glance; then Mullen put the fork back on the table. Stein asked them for their money, and Mullen said: "This one's on you."

"If you say so," Stein said. He grabbed two azure plastic trays and waited his turn in the lunch line for double helpings of pot roast and rice with gravy, two dishes of creamed corn, and two cubes of wriggling green Jell-O. Stein paid with a fistful of wrinkled bills that emptied his wallet.

He gripped a tray in each hand, holding them high at shoulder level as he maneuvered through the crowded aisle toward the senior tables. "Over here!" Simms called, waving his hand from one of the far rows. Mullen plopped down beside his friend, boasting to the other guys at the table about how they had scared the shit out of that scar-faced little prick.

"He's even buying our lunch!" Simms said.

"It's true," Stein said, standing behind them, still holding the trays aloft. "But on second thought, maybe this should be on you guys."

As Mullen and Simms turned to look at him, Stein rotated his hands, dumping the plates full of hot meat and gravy over the tops of their heads. Mullen shrieked, pawing steamy corn away from his eyes, while Simms, wearing a little square of green Jell-O on his head, sprang from the table to slap the scalding pot roast off his lap.

Stein didn't run. He stood still and straight, savoring their agony. When Simms seized him by his shirt and threw him down against the table, a group of teachers, led by Mr. Zimmer, were already there to stop the fight.

"He spilled *piping hot fucking* food *on us!*" Mullen screeched in a high voice. His shoulders steamed with gravy while his shirt and tie dripped brown fluid.

Stein feigned a nervous apology. "No, no!" he cried. "I was just saying I didn't think they should make me pay for their lunch, and that guy—" he pointed at Mullen "—pushed back in his chair and knocked me over!"

"Fucking liar!" Mullen cried, lunging at the freshman.

"Watch your mouth, Richard," Zimmer said, holding him back without much effort. "Did you boys really make him pay for your meal?" Mullen and Simms were dumbstruck. The other boys at their table had just listened to them brag about that.

Zimmer scratched his face and looked around the circle of irate upperclassmen surrounding the lone, seemingly apologetic freshman. Mrs. Tunns and Mrs. Horgen were there, keeping the peace, along with Mr. Mankowski, who looked unsure of himself, as always. Bromine, thankfully, had already gone back to her classroom.

Zimmer thought of Father Mercedes, looking for excuses to attack Sister Maria's oversight of the school. This incident could only feed that, if he allowed it. But an accident was just an accident, after all.

"You're a mess, but are you *hurt?*" Zimmer asked, and Mullen and Simms stared at him. "I got gravy in my ear," Mullen said, which made some of the surrounding students chuckle.

"Why don't you go upstairs to the bathroom and clean up?"

"What happens to *him?* Nothing?" Simms snapped.

Zimmer turned to Stein. "Maybe everybody here needs to apologize to each other," he said, and forced the three boys to shake hands. Stein's hand came away wet with gravy. "This isn't over," Mullen growled as he and Simms wandered upstairs to find warm water and paper towels. A little ripple of laughter followed their retreat through the lunchroom, along with low, foghorn murmurs of "Asssssss-holeface . . ."

Butler Duty was supposed to happen all week, but from that point forward, it was canceled. The seniors were pissed that Stein's behavior had ruined it, though some feared other freshmen might follow his example if they continued. No one wanted to end up like Asshole Face and Sandmouth, wearing their lunch the rest of the day.

SIXTEEN

Carl LeRose's face looked like it was full of red wine. "Jesus, can't you two guys back off? *Christ,*" the sophomore said, pacing in front of Davidek and Stein between classes. "I'm taking a risk trying to help you guys. Goddamnit, if my dad didn't make me promise to look out for you, I swear—"

"You and your *dad . . . ,*" Stein said, rolling his eyes to white.

"Come on, Stein," Davidek said. "He's been looking out for us. Who else is doing that?"

"I look out for myself," Stein said.

"Don't you idiots see?" the lumpy sophomore told them. "This is when the seniors start losing interest in all this initiation crap. Instead, you're pissing 'em off more. They're miserable. Father Mercedes is up Sister Maria's ass, and she's up the students' asses even further."

"You're up your own ass," Stein said.

LeRose's face turned a darker shade of red. "We're going to take it out directly on *you.* Not just you freshmen—*you two guys.*"

"*We?*" Davidek asked.

LeRose shook his head. "*They.*"

"They can bite me," Stein said.

LeRose insisted: "They will."

• • •

"I'm not saying you have to make friends out of the seniors, but do you have to turn them all into enemies?" Lorelei asked.

"Who needs them? As long as I got you," Stein said, smiling crookedly. Ever since their kiss behind the church, they'd been spending their lunch breaks in an isolated spot along the brick wall separating the school grounds from the nuns' convent and the priests' rectory. Making out with Stein behind the school as the wind tossed leaves in spirals made it easy for Lorelei to forget about Davidek—and provided a chance to reason with her boyfriend.

"Just remember Hannah," Lorelei warned, and Stein shot back: "Hannah, Hannah, Hannah . . . You sound like Davidek. She's just a boogeyman they're using to scare us. 'Be nice, or Hannah'll getcha!'" Stein made his hands like claws. Lorelei reached up and laced her fingers through his, bringing his hands back down and placing them on her hips.

"You're trying to change the subject," he said, planting a small kiss on her lips.

"I just want you to be quiet," she said, pulling his face in closer.

They thought they were sneaking away unobserved, but at least one student at St. Mike's took note of their little getaway each day. Zari didn't need second sight to know what they were doing, but she wasn't sure what she could do about it. There were no answers to be found in her deck of well-worn tarot cards.

Girls like Lorelei lived in the future, projecting years ahead of themselves to map out the arcs of their lives, from college to career to marriage and kids. Others like Zari fixated on very basic wishes for the present: just one boy to like, who might like her back.

Every person, someday, tempers wild aspirations with reality. It's those small dreamers, like Zari, who abandon their hopes the hardest.

JayArr Picklin and another freshman named Charlie Karsimen got tossed into the school Dumpster about three days later. The upperclassmen who did it latched the lids shut, so they had to stay in there for about half an hour, until others heard them pounding and crying for help.

A group of freshman girls, including Zari, had their makeup cases confisticated by some senior girls during the changeover for gym class, and were forced to walk out onto the field with their faces painted like clown-whores.

It was no secret. The upperclassmen were terrorizing the freshmen even harder as revenge for what Stein had done to Mullen and Simms. His behavior could *not* be tolerated, and could *not* be allowed to spread. But the scar-faced boy himself was never bothered. It was a tactical maneuver by the seniors, designed to turn Stein's own classmates against him, one by one, until he was isolated. And it was working.

Davidek was spared attack only because of the lobbying efforts of Green and LeRose, but that wouldn't hold out forever, and Lorelei was asked by Audra to reconsider her associations.

Then Audra smiled, a motherly smile. "Of course I'm already planning to pick you to be my little sister, but it would certainly make me look a lot better to the other seniors if you weren't hanging around with that . . . pest."

Lorelei was torn between wanting to cheer and wanting to cry. She would be protected, but the boy who had promised her the same might not—and was becoming a liability for her.

"Don't think that being my little sister means I'm going to let you off the hook at the Hazing Picnic," Audra warned playfully. "Let's just say you better brush up on your Motown."

Most of the freshmen feared the upperclassman attacks would just get worse, so they never accused anyone, although the parents of the victims had no problem calling Father Mercedes to complain. The priest continued terrifying the parish council with news that no one perpetrating these dangerous pranks had been caught or punished. "Can you believe Sister Maria can't stop this?" he asked.

As teachers became more vigilant, a group of senior, junior, and sophomore boys decided a grand gesture was needed—aimed directly at the source of their problem. Stein would need to be punished, along with every other would-be tough guy in the freshman class.

School was ending for the day when a senior girl cried out in the parking lot with sinister glee: "It's a pile-on!"

Davidek was walking from one of the side entrances along with Stein and a cluster of other freshmen when he saw the horde of upperclassmen charging. Their shirttails fluttered and book bags swung in face-crushing arcs as they ran bellowing toward the freshmen. Smitty was just a few feet ahead and turned his cool blue eyes on Stein, like he was considering tripping him so the seniors could pounce as he made his own getaway.

He didn't have to. Stein dropped his bag and said, "To hell with it, I'm fighting these assholes." Smitty, who knew there was no escape, straightened his shoulders and flared his eyes as a pendulous book bag collided with his jaw, smashing the big guy to the ground. Mortinelli, the broad-foreheaded junior who led the Fanboys, leaped onto Smitty's shoulders, while two of Mortinelli's pals flattened themselves against his kicking legs. Davidek dived to the ground as Michael Crawford and his friends closed in, and he was smashed beneath them as they heaved their bodies atop his in crushing pile drivers. A cluster of upperclassman girls were screaming "Pile *on*! Pile *on*!" like psychotic cheerleaders.

Davidek, gasping for air, looked through the tangle of legs and arms and saw three older kids—Bilbo, Prager, and Strebovich—triangulate on Stein, rushing forward and pounding him on the face and back, dropping him to the ground and rolling him back and forth with kicks.

Meanwhile, Mortinelli and some of the Fanboys still clambered over Smitty, who was standing again and swinging them from his arms like King Kong trying to break out of chains.

The guys crushing Davidek were getting bored with his lack of resistance, so they began to peel off and join the crowd around Smitty, the only one with any fight left. It was eleven against one. Smitty's voice was hoarse, and spittle flecked from his mouth as he raised a finger, pointing toward Davidek, who had flattened himself against the wall, trying to find an opening to pull Stein out of his stomping. "Lay offa me," Smitty said. "Let's get *him* instead."

Davidek started to run.

Smitty surged after his fellow freshman, leading the handful of seniors who had just been pulverizing him. They dodged through the parking spaces, weaving between the parked cars and onlookers watching the brawl. Behind them, Stein's attackers had fled to join the chase, and he was staggering to his feet, swinging his arms at nothing, like a man besieged by bees.

Davidek dashed into the school bus, which was where Smitty and the other pursuers stopped, like vampires at the threshold of a church. The driver, a leathery, straw-haired woman with an ashtray voice, told them to clear away from her damned door.

The other kids on the bus were cheering—but for the guys outside. They made *buck-buck* chicken noises at Davidek as he slid into an empty seat.

Smitty smirked as he paced outside the windows of the bus, flanked by his new senior pals. "So they made you their bitch, huh?" Davidek said, his voice muffled by the pane between them.

Smitty laughed and brought his face close enough to steam the glass: "Better to be on top of the pile, I think."

"And bully your own kind?" Davidek spat back.

Smitty's smile broadened as he backed away, his arms raised in a what-are-you-going-to-do shrug. "Everybody is somebody's bully," he said.

Behind Davidek, a sinister-looking upperclassman girl with raven black hair sneered, "Pussy." The freshman peered at her, squinting.

"What are *you* looking at?" she demanded.

Davidek shook his head. "Nothing." Her eyes were both the same color.

Smitty walked back to get his bag and saw Stein wandering away from the site of his beat down, his blazer ripped at the shoulder, his clip-on tie torn off and hanging in the fist of his right hand. He had black grit stamped into his face and a couple bleeding scratches on his forehead. He sat on the sidewalk curb, waiting for his sister to arrive and pick him up.

Smitty loomed over him, his white shirtsleeves rolled up to show off bulging arms. "You sure you got what it takes to finish all the fights you start?"

"Yeah," Stein said, wiping his mouth. "So, you one of *them* now?"

Smitty shrugged. "Guess so."

Stein nodded. "Then I'll finish you, too."

SEVENTEEN

On the last day before Thanksgiving vacation, classes were always suspended for the Turkey Bowl, an annual touch-football game held out on the old church field with the seniors and juniors facing off against the sophomores and freshmen. It wasn't part of the hazing ritual, but this year, those hostilities had infected everything. Mankowski and Zimmer were the referees and had been instructed to eject anyone who got too violent. Sister Maria herself was watching from the sidelines, along with most of the rest of the school. Father Mercedes wasn't around, but Ms. Bromine was, and she planned to report back to him.

Davidek was useless at sports—particularly football—but he showed up to play because LeRose said it would be a good way to ingratiate himself. Green warned Stein not to come, since he'd heard the older kids were hungry for an excuse to "accidentally" smash him into the semi-frozen ground. Stein had said maybe he'd show up anyway if they wanted a fight, then didn't even come to school that morning.

At least two hundred spectators lined the field under a linty sky that made the sun a dim silver dollar. LeRose watched the game perched on the hood of his Mustang—he'd just gotten his license that weekend, and he wore a lemon yellow nylon workout suit with a Pittsburgh Steelers emblem stitched onto the back.

Davidek had changed into a pair of gray sweatpants and a blue SEMPER FI T-shirt his brother had once sent to him. Davidek liked wearing it, remembering Charlie, though it annoyed his parents, who said it just drew attention to what a coward he was. But no one at St. Mike's ever mentioned Davidek's brother, which made him feel sorry for Charlie. The world forgets easily, and then forgets that it forgot.

Davidek found himself on the sidelines most of the time. Smitty stood beside him, scratching his cheek. Breaking the silence, Davidek asked, "So, now that you hang around with the older kids, do you know Hannah Kraut?"

Smitty's blue eyes never wavered from the field, but something in them intensified. "Why are you asking *me* about her?"

Davidek said, "I'm asking everybody."

Smitty looked out into the field. "Don't ask me again."

"I just meant that—"

Smitty grabbed him by the neck, hard. "I said don't ask me again." And Davidek didn't.

While the games went on in the field, there was another play taking place among the spectators. Leaning on the mirrored grille of her boyfriend Michael Crawford's shiny black 4Runner, Audra Banes was buried in a big brown parka, standing beside her friends Amy Hispioli, Sandra Burk, and Allissa Hardawicky and shouting encouragement as her boyfriend gathered mud and torn grass on his clothes out in the field, quarterbacking for the team that always won this contest. Audra didn't notice the dark-haired girl Zari and her jangly jewelry move up beside her.

Zari's eyes focused across the field—not on the game, but on the trio of figures standing on the opposite sideline: Mary Grough; her little sister, Theresa; and their friend Anne-Marie Thomas. They were watching Zari right back.

"Where's Lorelei?" Zari asked, making Audra jump a little.

Audra pulled back the furry hood of her coat. "Oh, God, I didn't see you there. . . ."

"I'm Zari," Zari said. "Lorelei's friend. Remember?"

"Lorelei's over there," Audra said, pointing to the far end of the field, where there was a table set up with cups and a portable water cooler. "I put her in charge of keeping the boys hydrated."

"Oh, right," Zari said. Then, after a moment: "That your boyfriend out there?" Crawford had just thrown a spectacular pass and was pounding the backs of his teammates, sweat dripping down through his hair.

"Yeah, he's going to need a bath," Audra said, and Zari laughed loudly. Too loudly.

Across the field, the Grough sisters were like vultures waiting for something to drop dead. Zari wished they would stop staring at her.

"Lorelei's right about him," Zari said. "He's cute." Audra took a while to respond. She found her smile before she spoke.

"He *is* cute," Audra said proudly.

Zari waited. That's what the Groughs said to do: *Wait. Don't rush in and start blabbing. Draw her out. Got it?*

"Lorelei thinks he's *really* cute. Man, she just goes on and on. The rest of us are, like, 'Whoa, talk about something else, please!'" Zari said, laughing, which made Audra's smile falter just a little. "I'll bet you're sick of it, too, right? Just blah, blah, blah!" She made a squawking gesture with her hand.

"Actually, Lorelei never mentions him," Audra told her. "I'm sure Michael will be flattered, though."

Zari groaned. "Not if he knew the other things she said! Or maybe he *would*!" The dark-haired girl laughed again, but Audra didn't.

Audra moved Zari away from her other friends. "What . . . *other* things?"

That was the hook. The Grough sisters said: *You'll just chat her up, very casual. . . . Then out of the blue, she's going to want to know more. And that's when you say . . .*

"Nothing," Zari said, her face solemn. "I just meant . . . you know, the details and all, of how she likes him. It's nothing. I'm sorry, I didn't mean to—"

Audra put a hand on Zari's shoulder and looked down the row to where Lorelei was handing out paper cups of water. "What else has she been saying about Michael?"

Zari feigned distress. "Look, I wanted to tell you, because even though Lorelei and I are friends, I don't think what she's doing is cool. It's just . . . not right."

Audra was in Zari's face, voice low. "What exactly is she doing that *isn't right*?"

Zari hesitated again, like the Groughs had told her. "At first I just thought it was a crush, but then . . . after he picked her to be Miss St. Mike's in that dumb beauty pageant, and after she's been hanging around with him while hanging around with *you* . . . She says she wants to do stuff to him, you know? Stuff she says you *won't* do for him. Or can't."

"How does she know *what* I can and can't do for him?" Audra asked, though she didn't want that answered.

"If it makes you feel better, I don't think he even notices her."

"He *doesn't* notice her," Audra snapped. "He has me." Then, regaining her composure, "This is too weird."

Zari pleaded: "*Please*, don't tell her, *please*." Audra grabbed her elbow and said, "Let's go talk to Lorelei right now. This doesn't sound right."

Zari dug in her heels as the student council president pulled her arm. "If Lorelei knows you heard this from me, I won't be able to find out any more."

Audra eased her grip on Zari. She walked back against the 4Runner, lifting her furry hood around her head. Zari stayed to watch the rest of the game but was careful not to go over to where the Groughs were standing. They had told her to avoid contact until later. Afterwards, when no one was paying attention, Zari slipped into Anne-Marie's beat-up Ford Taurus.

"It's done," the freshman said. "Just make sure you sign up for me next week like you promised. And if you do anything horrible to me, I swear I'll rat you out."

"So you think she believed you?" Mary asked.

"Probably," Zari said. "I can't read minds."

When the game was over, Audra and her friends piled into Michael Crawford's tanklike vehicle to celebrate the victory at Kings Restaurant on the other side of the river in New Ken. Lorelei was about to get into the 4Runner when Audra signaled Amy Hispioli to close the door.

"Oh, sorry, Lorelei," Audra said, rolling down the passenger window—partway. "Can you call your mom to get you?"

When Lorelei left for school that day, her mother had been passed out drunk on the couch, a cigarette smoldering in the clamp of her prosthetic.

"She's not home today," Lorelei said. "You told me you would give me a ride."

It didn't make a difference to Audra. "Great. Well, see you later. . . ." And then, "Oh, hey . . . Do you know a girl named Zari? Is she a friend of yours?"

Lorelei nodded, still trying to hide her crushing disappointment. "Yeah, she's nice. A little weird, but yeah . . . she's cool. Why?"

"She was just hanging around during the game. Some of the other girls are wondering which freshmen to pick next week. If you say she's cool . . ."

"Yeah, yeah. She's nice."

Audra nodded, as if that concluded things.

"Have a happy Thanksgiving," Lorelei said as the 4Runner pulled away, but her guardian angel had already rolled up the window.

EIGHTEEN

O kay, this is bad," Green said. The boys were standing together in the library. It was Monday, just after Thanksgiving break, and the Brother–Sister sign-up sheet had been posted in history teacher Mrs. Arnarelli's homeroom that morning.

Half the freshmen were already taken. Green had been chosen by Bilbo, Zari had been selected by Mary Grough, and half a dozen others were also chosen by seniors they'd befriended. The upperclassmen looking for someone to hate on were taking more time.

Stein and Davidek had been deemed off-limits to everyone—the seniors of St. Michael's were leaving them as bait for Hannah Kraut. That was Green's bad news. "I'm sorry," Green said to Davidek. "I tried to talk one of Bilbo's guys into choosing you, but they all remember you being a pain in the ass during that Dog Collar Day thing . . . and you running and hiding in that bus didn't exactly earn anyone's respect."

Shit.

Davidek asked Green if he had any idea what was in this book of secrets.

"It's just vague rumors right now," Green said. "Bilbo and the guys think she knows about a senior girl—no one's sure who—who's had abortions. That's abortions with an *S*—plural. And apparently some sophomores are worried she knows about them breaking into cars last summer to steal stereos. I overheard some girls say Hannah knows about a junior—a junior *guy*—who's been secretly snapping naked photos of dudes on the basketball team in the locker room."

"How could she *know* that?" Davidek said.

Stein was looking at a book about medieval torture, and acting like he didn't care what they were talking about. "She wants to make someone read that at the Hazing Picnic?" he said absently. "Damn, I may just volunteer. I'd love to stick it to those seniors."

"It's about more than just the seniors," Green said. "Good luck next year—and the year after that—facing all the sophomores and juniors you humiliate."

"Bullshit. The teachers'll never let anyone read that stuff anyway," Stein said. "They'll cut the mic the minute anyone tries."

Green shook his jowly cheeks. "They can't, remember? It's not an official school event. They've had people get up there at the Hazing Picnic and do all kinds of deranged stuff that makes the school mad. The teachers aren't able to stop anything."

Stein scoffed. "If you're so worried, just refuse to read it if she picks you. Tell her to roll that notebook up and shove it up her ass."

"And what if she knows something about *you*?" Green asked.

Davidek smiled. For the first time, the threat seemed to lift. "Shit, *we* never had any abortions! What's to know about us?"

Green shrugged. Stein riffled the pages of his torture book. "I've had a few," he said.

Davidek figured if he found Hannah Kraut first, she wouldn't find him.

If he could ID her, he could avoid her. If he knew where she went for lunch, which hallway her locker was in, and when her classes were, he could theoretically stay out of her way. And if she didn't know *him*, she wouldn't pick him. But after three days scanning the halls, he never spotted anyone with two different-colored eyes.

On the bookshelves in the library, Davidek, Green, and Stein found a yearbook from the previous year with a grainy, black-and-white photo of Hannah Kraut, and he instantly recognized her frizzy blond hair. When

The Boy on the Roof had been bombarding everyone in the parking lot, she was the one Ms. Bromine snagged by her pigtail as kids were fleeing across the street. There was nothing the three freshmen could gather from her face, however. It had been scratched away to the rough, white paper beneath.

Davidek found three other copies of the yearbook on the shelf. Each one had her face scraped away, and they found other listings of her name throughout the books. Not one image remained intact. They found the yearbooks from her freshmen and sophomore years, too, but already knew what they'd find. Every photo of her had its face scratched away.

"I know everybody hates her, but who would do this?" Davidek asked.

Green got the answer a few days later, after asking his senior friends from the stairwell gang. "*She* did it," Green said, showing them a copy of Bilbo's junior yearbook. "When they came in, they all passed each other's books around, getting everyone to sign them. This is what Hannah did to each one." Just like in the others, Hannah Kraut's face was scratched off in every photo. Underneath her defaced portrait, she had written in bold, black marker: *YOU COULDN'T REMEMBER ME IF YOU TRIED.*

Lorelei was panicking. "Audra, Audra—!" Lorelei said, running up behind the student council president in the crowded hallway. Audra adjusted her black-rimmed glasses as if the girl before her were out of focus. "Yesss . . . ?" she said, like air hissing from a tire.

Lorelei could hardly speak. Her lips worked, and her eyes pooled as she struggled to get the words out. "It's been a week, and I've been very patient, but I just saw the Brother–Sister sign-up sheet, and . . ."

"And . . . ," Audra said, crossing her arms over her books.

"It says you signed up for Justin Teemo. Justin Teemo?"

Audra shrugged. "Michael—my *boyfriend*—told me he was a nice kid. We're going to have the other girls dress up in poodle skirts and sing 'My Guy' to him onstage."

"You said you'd pick me," Lorelei whispered, unable to hold back the tears dripping down her cheeks. "Please. *Please* change it back. . . . Or could you make someone else pick me?"

Audra rolled her eyes as she walked away. "I know who I *hope* picks you."

. . .

Davidek found Lorelei hugging Stein in an empty stairwell. They stood below the stained glass window of St. Francis of Assisi holding a bird on his extended finger and keeping the peace between the sheep and rabbits and ducks and wolves. Davidek couldn't see Lorelei's face. It was pressed into Stein's shoulder.

Lorelei's body squirmed against Stein's arms. She was murmuring, "Your fault . . . your fault . . . ," and gripping him in something that looked less like an embrace and more like an effort to inflict pain. When she finally pulled away, the skin beneath her eyes was swollen and purple and wet. "They hate me because of *you*," she said. "I *knew* it! I *warned* you!"

Stein was trying to find out who? What? How did this happen? But Lorelei wasn't interested in him understanding. As he tried to pull her close again, she snapped. "Keep the hell away from me."

Stein's face was a mask of shock and sorrow. Davidek couldn't look at it, and he backed up the steps without either of them noticing him.

The next morning, Stein found Davidek beside his locker. Word had spread all through the school that Lorelei's connection with Stein had poisoned her relationship with Audra, and Audra allowed that rumor to continue rather than admit she was afraid a freshman was trying to steal her boyfriend.

"You've been a good friend to me, all this time. Never ditched me even when it would have made you a local hero," Stein told Davidek, his voice drained of that usual dangerous enthusiasm.

Davidek tried to make a joke. "I keep you around because you make me look like the nice one."

Stein didn't laugh. "You *are* the nice one. You've got friends. You've got Green telling you stuff, and LeRose coaching you. You even have friends among the seniors . . . that redhead girl, what's-her-name—Claudia—who helped you with the cigarettes? Why don't you go talk to her? Ask her to pick you."

"The truth is, I don't know her that well," Davidek said.

"Well, *get* to know her. I don't want you to worry about who I end up with, because I honestly don't care," Stein said. "We're brothers no matter what."

Brothers.

"Thanks, Stein," Davidek said. He wanted to say more, but he just said, "Thanks, Stein," again.

Davidek found Claudia the next morning in the third-floor hallway, kneeling beside her locker as she separated a pile of loose papers. "Hey, how's it going, Marlboro Man?" she said, zipping shut her denim bag and slinging it over her shoulder as she stood. "Haven't seen you lately. How'd that cigarette thing turn out, anyway?"

"Good," Davidek said lamely, trying to figure out how to ask what he needed. He found himself distracted by the light freckles on her chest, curving down her breasts to the edge of her green bra, which he could just see the outline of through her white uniform shirt.

"—the second floor?"

Davidek snapped back to reality. "What?"

"I said, 'How's life on the second floor?' That's where your locker is, right?"

Davidek blurted "—so, can I be your freshman?"

The girl laughed, errant flame-colored hairs falling forward in her face. "You're a bold one, aren't you! I thought seniors were supposed to choose, not have freshmen volunteer."

Davidek tried to explain but couldn't. He tried to breathe, but that wasn't working either. "I'm sorry, actually. . . . I'm just a bit desperate, so . . . I'm . . . sorry, I'm gonna go."

"Relax," the girl said, putting a steadying hand on his shoulder. "So, all you want is for *me* to sign up as your big sister?"

Davidek nodded, blood pulsing in his cheeks.

"My own little freshman," the girl said. "To be honest, I was thinking about choosing you anyway. You're sweet. What you did for your friend with the smokes. It was . . . sweet."

Davidek beamed, delirious with relief: "Man, *thanks*, Claudia. I was afraid the other seniors would hav—"

"Claudia?" the girl asked. Davidek blinked at her. A nervous and embarrassed smile bloomed on her face, and she drew back her fallen bangs and rubbed at her neck. "Right . . . I told you that, didn't I. . . ."

Davidek bobbed his head, perplexed. "Yeah, back when you—" His eyes fixed on hers, shimmering and smiling at the corners. One was blue. The other was green.

"I was in kind of a weird state that day," she said. "I'm a little bit unpopular around here with some people, and—well, I was testing you when you asked me for help. To see if you knew I was bullshiting you, or if . . . well . . . sorry about that."

She reached out to shake his hand, which he accepted absently. "My name is Hannah Kraut," she said. "You're Peter, right? Peter . . . ?"

"Davidek," he said, his voice a whisper from another dimension.

The redhead nodded and repeated it to herself: "Peter Davidek," she said, smiling. If he had been capable of rational thought at that instant he would have loved how the words looked on her lips.

"You look so serious," she said. "Is there something else you wanted to say?"

Davidek's hand slid away from hers. He let it fall, and for all he knew, it hit the floor. "You changed your hair," he said.

PART IV

Winter

NINETEEN

Seven-Eighths knew everyone called her Seven-Eighths. No one made a secret of it anymore. They said it right to her face, like it wasn't even an insult anymore, like it was just her name. Some of them probably didn't even *know* her real name.

Sarah Matusch struggled not to let it bother her. At her old school, they called her "Hatchet Face," which she was sickened to find listed in the dictionary. Sarah could live with the name as long as it was something created by morons, but not when the *Oxford English Dictionary* seemed to taunt her, too.

Her parents were fundamentalist Catholics, lifelong parishoners at St. Mike's who had met at the high school when they were both freshmen, and Sarah and her little brother, Clarence, were raised to worship not just the Father, the Son, and the Holy Ghost, but also Father Hal Mercedes and Pope John Paul II—in that order. (The pope lost points for not reversing the liberal changes of Vatican II.) Father Mercedes knew the Matusch family all too well. He considered them zealots, and found them tiresome.

They were strict and humorless—blindly, pathologically devoted to what they considered the "traditional" teachings of the Roman Catholic Church. They hated, for instance, that the Mass was now in English instead of Latin, though that change had been made almost thirty years ago.

The Matusch family was also aghast when they complained to him about the textbooks in Sarah's biology class and discovered that the Vatican had long ago accepted evolution as a true scientific phenomenon.

During the family's weekly confessions each Saturday, the mother would drone on about her frustrations with the leadership in Rome, the leadership in Washington, and the failures of the other mothers and wives she knew. When it was her husband's turn, he would just grunt terse apologies for swearing, or slapping his kids—end of confession. The boy, Clarence, was only eleven, but was the family member with the most disturbing misdeeds to confess. He complained about feeling rejected and isolated in his parents' house and considered setting fire to the home several times, though the daydreams made him feel angry at himself and ashamed. Father Mercedes tried to tell his parents about this, but they were more upset that the priest would consider breaking the Seal of the Confessional, the vow of secrecy priests took never to reveal what they hear during the sacrament of forgiveness. Father Mercedes merely suggested they take him to see a child psychiatrist to discuss his aggression issues. "If I ever catch him playing with matches, he'll be going to see a doctor, all right—but not a head-shrinker," Mr. Matusch said.

Although they treated Father Mercedes like a demigod in most other instances, the priest felt only tired contempt for the Matusch family. Father Mercedes, who took such pleasure out of the richness and risk of life, was annoyed by their intolerance of it. They were the fringe of his parish, and Sarah was their dim-witted, hopeless spawn. He would have pitied her if she hadn't made his weekly confession schedule so monotonous.

Sarah always went on the longest of anyone in her family, whining about her lonely life at St. Mike's and the agony of being called Seven-Eighths as the priest yearned for a cigarette and tried not to sigh or drum his fingers on the screen between them. No one who came to confession ever had anything interesting to say anymore. Father Mercedes missed those early years of his priesthood, when people still feared for their immortal souls enough to beg forgiveness for all kinds of crazy bullshit. He missed the young unmarried women, going on at length about their impure thoughts and actions. Those were the days.

He always thought that what Sarah "Seven-Eighths" Matusch really needed was a dose of *real* sin in her life. She confessed to things like look-ing too long at a shirtless man in the underwear section of a JCPenney catalog, and wanting to see a *Teenage Mutant Ninja Turtles* movie.

The priest only wished the girl were more popular at school. Maybe then she could help him collect the ammunition he needed to expose Sis-ter Maria Hest and the fallacy of noble old St. Michael the Archangel High School.

That's when an idea occurred to him.

"Who are the ones causing you this grief, Sarah?" he asked.

"The boys in my class mostly," she said. "And the girls, too. Except for my friend, Linnie. But they make fun of her because she's fat. She's actu-ally *really* fat."

A kind of annoyed energy was building inside the priest. "Please be more specific, Sarah. Who upsets you the most with this hurtful name-calling?"

Her voice rose. "Lots of people, Father. There's this guy Smitty, who makes fun of me a lot. Sometimes, though . . . I almost don't mind because he's cute." A heavy silence followed. "At least he's talking to me. Even if it's just to tease."

Smitty. The priest thought. He asked her for his full name, and said he would check that with the school secretary.

"Sarah, for your penance this week, I'm not going to assign you any Hail Marys or Our Fathers. No prayers at all. I just want you to do some-thing for me. Do you understand?"

Through the screen, he could see the lips on her fishy face tighten. "Like what, Father?"

"I want you to take note of these boys and girls who call you such hurt-ful names. Observe them. Watch the things they do, and listen to the things they say. Can you do that?"

She took a long time to answer. "Do you want me to be more like them?"

The priest rocked his head back and forth, considering. "I want you to do whatever it takes to get close to them, then come back here and tell me what you learn."

"You want me to tattle?"

The priest laughed. "Sarah, those boys and girls aren't like you. They don't come to confession and ask forgiveness for the wrongs they do. I want you to confess for them. I want you to use your position as one of St. Michael's truly decent pupils to tell me things that the school's principal and teachers cannot see for themselves. Together, we can help cleanse this temple of ours. Can you promise me you'll do this?"

"Y-yes, Father," she said, then . . . "Can I also say some regular prayers as part of my penance? They make me feel better."

Whatever, Seven-Eighths, the priest thought. *Knock yourself out.*

Father Mercedes was no stranger to sin himself, though he preferred to keep his own private. There had been times of deep doubt and panic when he considered unburdening his soul to a sympathetic colleague, but he knew any reasonable priest would not just absolve him—he would be given the penance of turning himself in. That was Confession 101 for any minister who had a crime revealed to him. Father Mercedes would be forgiven by God, but only if he went public with his theft, his gambling, his greed, and asked for mercy. Father Mercedes preferred to make it right instead.

If he succeeded in eliminating the school, he could remove a steep cost from the parish's budget while simultaneously converting that empty structure into a revenue generator—a nursing home for the elderly (and preferably wealthy) parishioners of St. Michael's parish. Such a windfall would help balance his grossly misaligned financial books, and that's where he would find absolution—not in some byzantine religious ritual. Confession was for the Seven-Eighths of the world, the superstitious, the weak-minded.

But first the school had to go, and since it had always been a source of pride for the parish, Father Mercedes would have to change that perception. Seven-Eighths was a critical part of making that happen, though it certainly took her long enough.

"What about the other boys and girls at school?" the priest would ask each Saturday. "How are they treating you? Remember—I asked you to keep an eye open for me. . . ." Since he assigned her this mission in the early fall, there had been zero progress.

As a spy, she offered him so little scandal and so much repetitive complaining about her nickname, her classmates' use of swearwords, and other low-grade misdeeds that he found himself punishing her with unnecessary—and spiteful—amounts of penance. It started with fifty Our Fathers and fifty Hail Marys. The next week, when she still produced no useful intelligence, the penance doubled. Sarah spent hours on her knees, murmuring prayers.

Ourfatherwhoartinheavenhallowedbethyname

She recited them so much and so often that the words lost all meaning after a while, and her mind became a jumble of syllables that vacuumed up her entire consciousness. Her parents, naturally, were grateful to the priest for inspiring such piety in their daughter, although they secretly wondered what sins she had committed to deserve such harsh penance.

With the first snow drifting down one Saturday in December, Sarah stepped into the confessional with her eyes glazed and her lips moving soundlessly:

Ourfatherwhoartinheavenhallowedbethynamethykingdom

The girl wavered on her knees. "Forgive me, Father. . . . Forgive me, for I have sinned . . . ," she began.

Father Mercedes put his hand on the screen. "Sarah, Sarah," he said, feeling sincere pangs of regret. "Let's cut it out with these prayers. Just tell me what I need to know about the kids at St. Mike's."

"It's wicked there," the girl said.

"Wicked," he repeated. *Sure. Whatever.* "Yes. What do you know that is wicked?"

The girl was just a ghost behind the confessional screen, and the priest's patience was short. He rattled off examples like a grocery list: Which girl is sleeping with which boy? Which are on drugs? Who's cheating on tests? Where can he find out—?

Seven-Eighths began crying, little tears streaming down her freakishly narrow face. "I can tell you," she said. "But please stop these *prayers*, please. They're in my head. They won't turn *off*. . . ."

"Yes, Sarah," he said, his voice low and tender, reassuring. "Of course. You can stop them. I'm telling you that you can stop."

But first . . .

"There's this girl," Seven-Eighths said. "And they say she has a notebook. . . ."

TWENTY

That's a neat trick, setting yourself on fire like that," Green said, placing a reassuring hand on Davidek's shoulder. Stein was leaning against the vending machine behind them, rolling his eyes. He'd been the first to hear about Davidek volunteering to be Hannah's freshman. Green and LeRose were the second and third.

LeRose was pacing around them, puffing out his cheeks as he exhaled. "Jesus, I never thought I'd see a guy fuck *himself* up his own ass."

"I guess your dad is holding back on some of his tricks," said Stein. He had been an even bigger bastard than usual since Lorelei dumped him.

Davidek put his hands over his face. "*Guys* . . . please."

"Sorry," Stein said, a rare apology. "Just kidding around."

LeRose flipped him the middle finger and turned back to Davidek. "Why was I wasting my time looking out for you?" he said. "Wish I'd known you were just going to kamikaze yourself."

Me, too, Davidek thought. Only Stein knew it had been an accident, and he advised Davidek to play it off like a deliberate choice. "Better to be a badass than a dumb-ass," he'd said. So that's what Davidek was doing.

"Maybe she'll take mercy on you," Green said, trying to find the bright side. "Maybe she'll be glad you're not afraid of her, like everyone else."

LeRose scratched at the scar on the back of his head, which always itched when he got nervous. "You just keep telling yourself that, girls."

For now Davidek was untouchable. The seniors had backed off when Hannah scribbled his name next to hers on the Brother–Sister sign-up sheet, as if he had contracted an incurable—and possibly contagious—disease. Although, in a way, they were relieved.

When they had all been trying to nudge Hannah toward Stein, it was because they expected her to inflict some heinous torture on the punk, but when word spread about her diary, and plans to make her freshman reveal its contents to everyone . . . that sounded more like heinous torture aimed at them. Stein might even be a willing participant in something like that. Suddenly, steering anyone to Hannah seemed like a horrible idea, but mobs have never been especially good at considering unintended consequences.

When Davidek volunteered himself as Hannah's "little brother," LeRose and Green convinced their upperclassman friends that this was the best possible outcome. Davidek wasn't an asshole like Stein, and could be persuaded to look out for them. Plus, he didn't seem to be afraid of Hannah, which might disarm her. Better for them all to be nice to him—at least for now—and not tap-dance on the land mine.

"You know how we all thought Hannah would be the worst thing to happen to a freshman? It's starting to look like the *best* thing—at least for you," Green told him. "This is a chance for you to show who you are."

"That means you're going to have to talk to her some more," LeRose said. "And keep us in the loop."

Davidek still didn't see Hannah very often. No one did, except in class. She kept away from everyone, gliding from room to room without lingering in the halls. She had perfected her sense of stealth.

Since she left school every single day for lunch, Davidek waited for her outside during the start of break one day, and caught her walking to her car with an armload of SAT prep manuals. "Taking the test soon?" he asked, a little too chipper. He could tell she sensed an ulterior motive.

"Yeah, this Saturday, over in Freeport," she said. Bruised rings of lost sleep hung below her eyes, and light-colored roots were peeking through the windblown tangle of her fiery hair.

"Once you're done, I guess you can get back to picking on me," he suggested jokingly.

"I never picked on you," she answered.

"I know. . . . I just meant, like . . . They said you had something bad planned for spring. At this Hazing Picnic thing . . . ?"

Hannah dropped her books onto the passenger seat of her Jeep. "You heard all that, and you still chose me. I'm eternally honored."

Davidek gritted his shoe against the ground. "To tell the truth, I didn't know you were *you* . . . 'Claudia.'"

Hannah considered this. "Believe it or not, that actually makes me happy. You were running from the mean Hannah, but maybe you found the nice one."

Davidek's face brightened. "So all this crap about a diary, and embarrassing secrets, and making your freshman read it at the Hazing Picnic . . . none of that's true?"

Hannah slid into her seat and fired the Jeep's engine. Blue smoke belched into the frozen air. "Oh, it's true, all right," she said, slamming the driver's door. "We're going to pull the pants off this place, you and me."

Davidek walked up to the window. "You think there's a chance we could . . . *not* . . . do that?"

She turned off the engine and rolled down her window. "You're sweet, Peter, but do you understand why everyone at this school is so fucking miserable?"

He shrugged. "Tough times, I guess . . ."

"Tough times," she repeated. "Actually, it's because the church is putting pressure on Father Mercedes, he's kicking Sister Maria's ass, she's beating up on the teachers, and the teachers are coming down as hard as they can on the students, who are shoving it back on each other. Everybody's pissed off and wants to fucking hit somebody, but this whole system has only one rule: You can't hurt anyone who can hurt you back. So Sister Maria can't clock Father Mercedes, the teachers can't tell Sister Maria to fuck off, and the students can't punch out the teachers. They have to take it out on someone else. That's you and me. We're at the bottom of the pyramid—or, at least, we used to be."

"Maybe the thing to do here is just . . . turn the other cheek. You know?" Davidek suggested. "Be nice and see if people—"

Hannah hopped out of her Jeep and raised her fist to punch him in the face. He winced, drawing back, and she hit him on the shoulder, twice. "Two for flinching," she said, getting back behind the wheel.

"You see what happened there," she said, slamming the door again. "You thought I was going to deck you, so you backed off. That's what we're doing right now with this notebook. Except in the end, we're *really* going to knock them out. *Hard.* Remember how I said we were at the bottom of the pyramid? Well, we have the chance to make the whole fucking thing crumble."

The Jeep's engine roared to life. "Now, step back, Peter, and turn the other cheek over on the sidewalk," she advised, blowing him a kiss. "I don't want to run you over."

Mrs. Arnarelli took down the Brother–Sister sign-up sheet after a few weeks. She felt sorry for Lorelei, who walked by every day to see if her name had been written down by anyone. There were lots of seniors who weren't attached to a freshman yet, but nobody was interested in her. Audra had not only refused to pick Lorelei, but ordered that no one else protect her either. "Let the Fanboys shove her through the blades," Audra's friend, Allissa Hardawicky, had joked.

Stein was the only other unselected freshman. No one had picked him, because no one could figure out what to do with the combative little prick. He couldn't have cared less, agonizing in ways they couldn't see as he pined over Lorelei—who refused to speak to him. "She won't even let me apologize for whatever I did. I thought we had this connection, and understood things about each other without even having to say them. I need her."

Davidek guessed Stein just needed *someone,* and agitated his friend by saying things like, "This is not some cosmic romance. It's ninth grade."

"You don't know what it's like to lose something you love," Stein said, and Davidek resisted the urge to tell him how wrong he was. They both spent their days missing the same girl.

As Christmas neared, the early winter evenings fell like ax blades, cutting every day short. Every tree was a cold, brown skeleton, electrified each morning with a blue frost. No one at St. Mike's went outside during the lunch break anymore. The upperclassmen either left school grounds entirely, or they remained packed in the cafeteria, gossiping and threatening one another. The freshmen had no choice. They were stuck.

Lorelei could never find a place to sit. After Audra abandoned her, Lorelei had tried going back to her old table, taking a seat beside Zari and the other girls, asking if anyone could figure out the Spanish extra-credit assignment. It wasn't long before a handful of seniors walked by, mentors to some of the girls at the table. They whispered briefly to their freshmen, eyes on Lorelei. One by one, the freshman girls would dab their mouths, pick up their trays, and follow their orders to move elsewhere.

With Audra's protection gone, the Grough sisters returned to harrasing Lorelei. Anne-Marie Thomas snatched her midterm Spanish paper—a partial translation of *Don Quixote*—and passed it off to little Theresa Grough, who rushed into the bathroom and dunked it in a toilet. Lorelei fished it out, but the handwritten ten-page paper was worthless, the blue ink running and illegible. She tried to turn it in, but Mrs. Tunns wouldn't accept it. "I know the trick of turning in ruined chickenscratch and claiming the dog ate your homework," the teacher said.

Twice the Groughs snuck by with scissors and snipped away a lock of her hair. "Didn't ya hear? Symmetry is so yesterday. . . ." They giggled. To protect herself, she would walk the halls with her free arm looped up over her head. People started imitating the walk.

At lunch on the final day before Christmas break, she slid her tray of food down at a table full of boys. Not one with Stein, but other boys from her class. She assumed they would be less likely to care about who was shunning her, but no seniors even needed to visit the table. After a while, the boys cleared away and squeezed in with friends at other tables, leaving her alone.

Only one person stayed behind.

Blue-eyed Smitty was so much taller and sturdier-looking than the other freshman boys. His face had a chiseled look, with caved cheeks and those pale eyes. There was something about his calm face, his slow way of talking, that she found hypnotic.

"I heard you like older guys. That true?" he said. The rumor that she'd been after Audra's boyfriend was making the rounds, but Lorelei still didn't know that.

Lorelei looked at her plate of uneaten pizza. "I don't like anybody," she said.

Smitty slid down the row to sit across from her, and his heavy weight made that end of the table bend a little. "Suppose I told you that I was older . . . ," he said, those blue eyes burning white-hot across her body, making her squirm.

Lorelei stood from the table. "Suppose I said you had a lot of growing up to do!"

Smitty laughed, and banged the table raucously, making her tray and silverware jump. "You know what else they call you?" he said as she walked away. "Hannah Two!"

She'd heard that before. Variations on the nickname had already passed around her in barely concealed whispers: *Hannah 2. Little Kraut. The Second Coming of Fuckslut.*

Lorelei had faced this kind of isolation before. She had felt her carefully assembled life fall apart. But it couldn't be allowed to happen again.

There must be another senior who would still protect her, who knew what it was like to be the outcast, the one treated cruelly. Lorelei's eyes got wet. She smeared them with the sleeve of her sweater. *Stop it,* she thought, and did.

Audra had been an accidental discovery, but as Lorelei walked through the aisles this time, she knew exactly who she was looking for. The voices rose around her, upperclassmen on all sides.

It didn't take long to find what she needed.

TWENTY-ONE

F irst-semester report cards came out just before the holiday break, and Davidek's dismal grades made Christmas an un-jolly time in his house. "How do you get an F in Religion?" his mother said. "Seriously. Explain this. . . . Do I need to repeat the question again?" Davidek told her the teacher hated him, and his father asked if all the other ones did, too. D's in Algebra and Biology, a C-plus in English, C's in French and Phys Ed, and B's—the high points—in History and computer class. "You spend so much time at that school with all your detentions, I assumed you'd learn something just by accident," his father said.

Davidek's trouble with his schoolwork came from fretting so much over Hannah Kraut, who was the only subject that consumed Davidek. And he wasn't alone.

Father Mercedes had been dwelling on the rumor of Hannah Kraut's notebook all through Advent, but hadn't discussed the diary in any of his weekly evaluations of Sister Maria's disciplinary shortcomings. He didn't have enough information from Seven-Eighths, and for that he had ordered her some fresh penance—four rosaries each morning, four each night—but no prayers during schooltime. That's when she was supposed to be *listening*.

If this diary did exist, documenting true crimes and debauchery from

the halls of St. Mike's, it would serve his cause to have those embarrass-
ments revealed publicly. But he was haunted by one question: What if it
contained suspicions about *him*? He had no idea if a teenage girl would
bother herself with gossip about the parish priest, but couldn't risk silly
rumors turning into serious questions.

In the snowy first weeks of January, he decided to seek help from someone in authority at St. Mike's who was *not* loyal to Sister Maria. Someone
close to the children, but mistrustful of them. Someone who could be
clever enough to gather information, but not clever enough to figure out
his motives.

"Ms. Bromine!" he said, greeting the guidance counselor at his door. "I
get too few visits from you! Is your New Year going well so far?"

"Two weeks down," she said. "Fifty more to go."

"God willing." He smiled, opening the storm door as she walked inside
from the crackling ice on his front porch.

They ate chipped ham sandwiches in his kitchen, though Ms. Bromine
would much rather have sat at the priest's antique walnut table in the rectory's ornate dining room, surrounded by those gorgeous cabinets full of
carnival glassware and holy relics. Compared to that finery, the Formica
table and fluorescent bulbs of the kitchen were a letdown.

"We're of a like mind, Ms. Bromine," Father Mercedes said. "I can
tell. . . ."

She chewed her ham sandwich. "How's that, Father?"

"You've come to me with concerns in the past," he explained. "About the
school's, uh . . . leadership deficit. Now I come to you, as a fellow believer
that increased vigilance is necessary. St. Mike's seems to be plagued with
students we know to be troubled, prone to disobedience—"

"In the faculty, we call them jerk-offs," Ms. Bromine said. "I do keep
watch on them, Father. I do. I even have a list of the no-good ones. . . . I
could show you."

The priest said, "Is a girl named Hannah Kraut on that list?"

Ms. Bromine nodded, chewing a mouthful quickly so she could tell him
all about it. The priest settled back into his chair. "I want you to be mind-
ful of her. These self-destructive types . . . Sometimes they can hurt others
on their way down."

The guidance counselor nodded, still chewing, and the priest smiled again.

"Tell me, whatever became of those two boys who were bedeviling you?" he said. "The quiet one, and the preacher boy I met."

"Preacher boy?" she asked, dabbing her mouth.

The priest groaned. "The one with the scarred face. He was mouthing off about how many religions his family has devoted themselves to over the years. Most likely fiction. Must be interesting for you to teach religion to the only born-again Buddhist Jew in Catholic school."

He laughed, but Bromine didn't. "He's a godless little liar," she said. "I'll prove it someday."

Bromine only wished that Father Mercedes had told her about this sooner. She would happily shred the braggadocious little shit on the pastor's behalf.

She got her chance the next time Stein spoke up insolently in the middle of her lecture—this time on the subject of comparative religions: "Sorry, but Jehovah's Witnesses are different from Mormons," he said. "They're different religions."

Bromine stopped writing on her chalkboard in the middle of MORM. "I didn't say they were the same. I said they were *related,*" she said. "They both go door to door." She extended her chalk. "Would you like to teach the class?"

Stein shifted in his seat. "It's just that . . . my parents were both Witnesses, but only for a little while." Some of the kids laughed. Only Davidek knew Stein wasn't joking.

"It was before I was born," he said. "In our basement, we still have some of the old *Watchtower* magazines those guys give out. My parents met some missionaries in Seattle when they lived there. Dad says my mom would've kept studying, but when she found out they were serious about no Halloween or birthday parties, it was over for her."

"Are you telling me your parents are polytheists?" Bromine said, though the other kids had no idea what that meant. "*Pagans?*" she asked, playing to the room.

Stein shook his head. "My dad's an atheist. My sister is an Evangelical. She wants us both to be born-again, but . . . like I said, Dad's an atheist now."

Bromine snorted. "What's your mother? A leprechaun?" This lame sarcasm actually got a laugh from the class, Bromine's first in a long time. She basked in it.

Davidek slouched in his chair, smiling. Bromine was done for. She had no idea Stein's mother had died. Let her make a few more snide cracks. When he dropped that bombshell, she would melt into the floor like the witch in *The Wizard of Oz*.

"My mom was always looking for something to believe in," Stein said. "She studied Hinduism, Buddhism . . . When we lived in Los Angeles, she got in with Scientology a little. We moved to Florida and she got me to study Judaism, 'cause my dad's parents are Jewish. She wanted me to be bar mitzvah-ized."

"I think you're lying," Bromine said, coming on a little too strong. "I won't be lied to in my classroom."

Stein blinked at her. "I'm not lying," he said.

The teacher stalked to a bookshelf in the back of the room that was stacked with religious texts, including a dozen variations on the Bible, a Book of Mormon, three Korans, and a paperback of *When Bad Things Happen to Good People*.

"I'm holding the book of Jewish scripture, can you tell me what it is?" she asked, hiding the volume behind her back.

Stein shrugged. "Sorry, Jews lose their mind-reading powers after we're circumcised."

Bromine's face flushed. "A real Jew would know the answer."

"There are lots of Jewish texts," Stein said, then made a guess: "The Talmud."

Bromine put the Talmud back on the shelf, seething. "So what exactly is your religion now?"

"My sister's the only religious one," Stein said. "She's born-again. Like my mom."

Who's dead! Davidek's mind screamed. *Just say it.* Destroy *her.* But Stein didn't.

"Born *again* . . ." Bromine sniffed. "Is that for people who mess it up the first time? I'd like to talk to your mother, and see if this is all true."

"You could," Stein said. "Except for one thing."

Davidek's smile bit into his pencil. *Here it comes.* . . .

"What's that, Mr. Stein?" Bromine asked.

"She would just quote Proverbs 12:23 to you."

The other students began riffling the pages of their Bibles, stopping on the correct verse. The kids knew they shouldn't laugh, which made it unstoppable. The snickers and sputters from faces hidden behind upright textbooks gave way to an avalanche. "What does it say, Lorelei?" Ms. Bromine asked.

Lorelei sighed as she read: "'Smart people keep quiet about what they know, but stupid people advertise their ignorance.'"

That was the end of the discussion. Bromine went to her desk and began writing out detention slips—two for Stein's "backtalk" and "lying," and one for everyone in the classroom who had laughed with him.

Davidek, for once, wasn't one of them.

Stein's father picked him up from school that day. Usually it was Stein's older sister, Margie, who worked at Sears in the mornings and attended nursing school at night, but some pipes had burst at the condo complex where Larry Stein was working, giving him and the other electricians the afternoon off. He volunteered to get Noah this time, looking forward to a little father–son time, though the boy wasn't very talkative at first.

Oh well. Larry couldn't make the kid be chatty, so he turned up the radio and sang along with the Eagles about the importance of taking it easy.

The work truck looped along the frozen country road, which twisted toward their little house in Sarver Township. Snow blasted the windshield as the wipers worked in time to the music. Stein's dad kept singing until his son said to the window, "A teacher asked me about Mom today."

Neither of them spoke for a while. Then his father turned off the radio and reached over to jostle the boy's knee. "We were in Religion class and the teacher was arguing with me about, you know, all the faiths and stuff Mom got us into," Stein said.

"Your mom liked to believe in things," his father said. "Everything she could . . . Heck, she believed in a loser like *me* enough to say 'I do.'"

Larry Stein's fingers fidgeted around the wedding band he still wore. He wanted to stop this conversation, though he couldn't. Shouldn't. "If you think this is one of those stages you go through, maybe we could go see a doctor again," he said. "I can talk to Margie about it and—"

"Doctors always want to talk," Stein said. "I don't even like *thinking* about what happened."

His father said, "Then don't . . . just think of other times. Not the end times."

His son just stared out the window. Larry didn't know what to say, so he said nothing.

The driveway to their small wooden house curled up from a country road lined with jumbles of pine trees, which hid the home from their distant neighbors. Larry turned off the ignition and watched the snowflakes settle and dissolve on the warm windshield. His son's face was still turned toward the glass, his eyes closed. Larry reached out to touch him, then didn't. He listened to the boy's soft snores.

Noah looked so helpless sometimes, his father couldn't believe the heartache he had caused.

Larry had been working in Cocoa Beach, Florida, when it happened. Those had been boom times for an electrician, thanks to a rash of housing development. Sun, fun, and sand—it seemed like a bright place for the family to settle after hopscotching around the country so often, following odd jobs and Daphne Stein's increasingly disturbed moods, which could cause more havoc than her widowed husband liked to remember.

One Friday night, Larry stopped at the Mai Tiki Bar on the Cocoa Beach pier for drinks with some of the guys from his crew. The warm ocean wind had drifted through the windows of the same truck he still drove through the Pennsylvania snow, only then it had been shinier, sturdier, more reliable. So had he.

He was avoiding the apartment. It had been a bad time for Daphne, and when they weren't at war, he was trying to stop her from crying, like a boy trying to plug a leaky dam. His whole life was for her—caring for her, consoling her, talking her back through the anxieties that had refracted darkness through every thought she had. None of it made any sense— least of all to him. Larry felt he had earned a few drinks alongside the other flannel-and-jeans guys, telling dirty jokes and ogling the surfer girls on the beach.

Margie was a senior in high school and would be home already. Daphne was better when it was just the kids around. Her emotions were more steady around Noah, her little Ark Boy, as she called him. Noah had been ten.

Cruising back home late that night, one arm leaning out the window and gliding on the current of warm ocean air, Larry Stein had turned up his street and saw dazed faces in robes and sleepwear wandering the warm asphalt, the tall palm trees around the corner pulsing with flashing red and white light, the low clouds overhead tinged with an unnatural orange glow. Mesmerized, he swerved to dodge a screaming ambulance that had appeared in front of him. Black water churned down the gutters, and frenzied firefighters scurried over tangles of turgid hoses. In the background, his apartment building coughed charcoal smoke into the sky.

His wife was in that smoke. His wife. "My beautiful Daphne . . . ," he said out loud, and closed his eyes against the Pennsylvania snowstorm.

Their daughter hadn't been home. She had gone over to a friend's place after cheerleader practice at school, writing college admission essays together. But Noah had been in the apartment. He had been inside, trapped, and so had Daphne. They had rescued Larry Stein's boy, but not his wife. Not her.

Then came the accusations . . . and that was as far as Larry would let himself remember.

As his son got older, he made up ways to explain the burns on his face that didn't require telling the truth. Larry had heard the fictional campfire fight story countless times.

After several years, the legal questions were resolved and the family began looking for a new place to start over. Margie made it all happen. Larry had never seen his daughter cry, and Margie wouldn't tolerate it from him or Noah either. Though she was only eighteen at the time, she became mother to them both. She had handled the move to Pennsylvania while enrolling in nursing school at the University of Pittsburgh. She had helped her father find a steady job, even filled out a lot of the union paperwork, and got him to stop relying so much on booze to wash over the things he didn't want to think about. She had stayed awake countless nights, rocking her little brother as the boy wailed in his sleep.

It was Margie who had suggested St. Mike's.

Last spring, the vice-principal of Sarver Township's junior high wrote a letter to the school board, advising them not to accept Noah Stein into the public high school. "He doesn't so much fight with his classmates as *war* with them," the vice-principal wrote.

Each week brought a new bruise, a blackened eye, teeth marks on his forearm. Once he showed Margie some red skin beneath his fingernails— which belonged to a boy who had made a "Yo momma's so fat" joke at his expense. Noah had screamed like an animal as a teacher ripped him free of the boy. The school administrators hadn't understood the overreaction, and Stein's father chose not to explain beyond saying the boy was sensitive about his mother, who had died.

Stein's most notorious schoolyard feud involved Jim Frankin, the leader of a group of twelve-year-olds who made up a song about Stein to the tune of George Harrison's "Got My Mind Set on You," which they crooned to him in the hallways. "I got my face . . . *Set* . . . On . . . *Fire!* I got my face . . . *set* on *fire!*"

A gym class ended with Stein and Frankin grappling on the ground. Some of the girls said Stein started it, but the larger Frankin scored all the major blows, thrashing Stein around like an empty pillowcase. At lunch the next day, Stein walked up and spit in Frankin's food—then in Frankin's face. The larger boy knocked him to the ground and beat him until he couldn't walk.

On day three, Stein stalked Frankin home after school and surprised him with a kick to the back. Frankin landed on his porch's concrete steps, bruising his ribs. He fell on Stein and choked him until his eyes bulged. A woman with a baby stroller stopped Frankin from murdering him.

After that, both boys had been called to the school district office with their parents, where they were told to quit fighting, or be expelled. Frankin said he would. Stein agreed to nothing. "I'll stop when everyone else stops singing that song."

The next day, a chorus broke out at lunch. Stein tackled Frankin on the stairs and threw three hard punches into his balls. Frankin howled

and cried. He hadn't even been in the cafeteria. Stein was expelled immediately.

Private school was the only option available to them, although tuition
would place a terrible burden on their family. But Margie considered it a
blessing. "He would never have stopped," she said.

Her father knew it was true.

Tap tap tap.

Larry opened his eyes. White snow blanketed his windshield. The air
in the truck was freezing. "Daddy?" a woman's voice said.

He rolled down the window, dropping a sheath of ice to the ground.
Noah was still sleeping, curled against the passenger door. Margie, who
was thickset and wrapped in an even thicker vinyl parka with the hood
pulled up around her head of curls, stood outside his car, holding some
grocery bags. "What's going on, Dad?"

Larry yawned. "Guess we fell asleep, talking old times. . . ."

She pulled back from the window, her mouth twisted. "Old times" was
a subject Margie Stein preferred to avoid. "You should come inside now. I'll
make dinner." Big sister hustled her father and sleepy brother into the
house, and as she cooked, she lectured them about the dangers of hypo-
thermia. Larry had his back to her, and was making goofy faces to get a
laugh out of his son, but the boy had his head down, and wouldn't look at
him.

TWENTY-TWO

A re you going to the Valentine's Day dance?"

Stein just blinked. He was looking at Lorelei, but she hadn't spoken to him in a month.

"I, uh, I think so," he said.

Lorelei smiled, almost a little sadly. She clutched her books tighter against her chest. "I am," she said. "Maybe I'll see you there." And then she walked away.

Davidek wasn't sure how to explain it. "Did she ever get picked by one of the seniors?"

"I haven't," Stein said. "And they took down the sign-up sheet. Maybe she realizes that it was no big deal after all." Even Green and LeRose didn't know for sure, though LeRose thought one of the Groughs had tried to choose her and was told she was taken.

Stein couldn't control his enthusiasm. For the first time in a long time, he couldn't stop smiling.

The night of the dance, a fast-falling snowstorm draped the roads and fields and buildings of the Valley in a foot of frozen whiteness. There was no wind, and the fat snowflakes fell straight and soft, like little dying moths. Headlights cut through the dim wall of falling snow as cars throbbing with music steered into the school lot. Girls and boys wrapped in thick coats and scarves and knit caps huddled close as they tromped through the drifts, making their way into Palisade Hall, which had been festooned with pink and red heart balloons for the occasion.

Some junior girls were selling carnations at the door to raise money for the prom. On the small bingo stage, the twenty-year-old DJ was getting yelled at by some chaperones for playing Bell Biv DeVoe's "Do Me!" He switched it to Steve Winwood's "Roll with It," which no one danced to.

Outside, Ms. Bromine stood alone, bundled against the frozen air on the front steps of the school. She didn't shiver. Her ankle-length black coat made her a shadow against the snow. Ms. Bromine had suggested canceling the dance due to the blizzard, but Sister Maria refused to listen to her—as usual.

Bromine watched another wave of students pile out of a van and head toward the school, laughing to each other, maybe laughing at her. She knew that sound well. She'd heard it a lot.

It was strange to face hostility from the cliques she once led. Year after year, Bromine saw her own face grow older, saw gray strands snake into her hair, saw her body thicken and slow, while the students all stayed fresh, and beautiful, and immortal.

Ms. Bromine had stood on these same steps exactly nineteen years earlier, before any current student at St. Mike's was even born. Gretchen Bromine had been dazzling perfection then, a smooth-skinned teenage beauty with a lithe body that fit tightly in all the right places of her school uniform. All the boys of St. Mike's longed for her then, though most were too intimidated to approach her. She liked it that way. The bad boys hungered as she passed them in the hall, and she delighted in denying their attention.

On the night of her own Valentine's dance in 1968, the seventeen-year-old had stood in bare legs shivering against the cold in her candy apple dress and short fox-fur coat that had been her mother's, her calves flexing in sky-high white pumps—bad for walking in snow, but excellent for dancing. She had arrived with some girlfriends but was waiting for Sam Kudznicki, the school's basketball captain and student council president, who had asked her to be his date.

After escorting her into the dance and gliding across the balloon-strewn floor to romantic songs all evening, Sam proved himself to be just as disgusting as the other boys she ignored—kissing her too deeply when the teachers weren't looking, his fingers tracing the edge of her bra, his hard-on pressed against her hip as he held her close. When they left the dance, he proposed they drive somewhere and park, and she responded by slapping him—hard—not just once but half a dozen times, pounding his face as he stumbled backwards in the snow, calling her a bitch, telling her to find her own way home.

Had she known then that her adult life would be so lonely, that she would go unnoticed and untouched for so long, maybe she would have let those boys like him go a little further. . . .

Davidek and Stein were among the last students to arrive at the dance. They walked inside, stepping in the flattened snow prints of the students who had come before them.

They didn't notice Bromine noticing them. She blended in with the other stony figures lining the walls of the school in perpetuity.

Davidek's parents had agreed to drive the two boys to the dance, and Stein's dad was supposed to pick them up, but when the night arrived, Davidek's mother refused to go anywhere in the snow and his father just said, "It's Friday night," as if the weekend negated all parental responsibility.

June Davidek turned up the volume on the television to drown out her son's protests. "I'm not driving all over creation on treacherous roads so you can *dance*," she said.

"You promised you would!" he said. That didn't matter.

"I said no," his mother said, resorting to that aggravating old question of hers: *"Do I need to repeat it for you?"*

When the battered white pickup truck belonging to Stein's father pulled up in front of the Davidek house, they were already an hour late. "I'm sorry my parents flaked, Mr. Stein," Davidek said when he slipped into the dark cab.

Larry Stein just shrugged. "Roads are bad, but we'll make it," was all he said.

"Sorry," Davidek said again.

Stein was pissed. Lorelei seemed to be undergoing a complete turn-around from her previous standoffishness and moodiness, and he was standing her up. "This is my only time outside of school with her. She can't date. Can't talk on the phone unless she sneaks. This is *one* thing her parents let her do. . . . Tell your mom thanks for me."

"Sorry," Davidek said for a third time, turning toward the window, more ashamed than ever.

Stein mulled the silence, looking at the back of his friend's head. He smacked Davidek's leg. "Listen. No big deal. It's good to make her wait. Absence makes the heart grow fonder, right?" He laughed, and put an arm around Davidek's shoulder, shaking it until Davidek smiled. Larry Stein was a silent chauffeur, but he was smiling, too.

Inside the toasty cavern of Palisade Hall, Lorelei Paskal lingered near the entrance. When Stein came through, she slid up close to him, and Davidek said, "I'm going to get some cookies," and made himself scarce to give them some space.

When they were alone, Stein closed his arms in an embrace around Lorelei's shoulders. "I missed you," he said.

Lorelei scrunched up her face. "Just since this afternoon?"

He tightened the embrace gently, feeling her warm cheek against his frigid neck. "It's been a lot longer than that, and you know it."

When she pulled back, he admired the bulky brown sport coat tilting across her shoulders. "Interesting look," he said.

"It's Mr. Mankowski's. He made me wear it," she said, sticking out her tongue. She peeked over Stein's shoulder to make sure the girls selling carnations nearby weren't looking, then drew open the buttoned jacket to show off tight jeans clinging low on her hips, and a lacy white camisole embroidered with a spectrum of flowers stopping just above her belly button, which was like a little swirl in a smooth curve of cream.

"I wore a big sweater to get out of the house, but I couldn't get past Mankowski. Not 'Catholic school' enough for him," she said, gesturing toward the bald-headed chaperone standing in the center of the dance floor, policing the romance. "The worst part is, it smells like him."

"You make a musty old jacket look very hot," Stein told her. She didn't say anything back, though she held his gaze a long time.

I do care about you, Noah Stein, she thought, *no matter what happens now.*

He draped his arm across the back of the jacket and they walked to the dance floor as the writhing students there slowed for a power ballad—Cinderella singing "Don't Know What You You Got (Till It's Gone)." Lorelei and Stein placed their arms in comfortable spots and began to sway. He leaned his face beside hers, smelling the sweet, candy scent of her hair spray and perfume and makeup.

They didn't leave the dance floor the rest of the night.

Later, he noticed two familiar faces staring at them from the garden of wallflowers: Asshole Face and Sandmouth. Lorelei turned away as Stein taunted them: "Why don't you two ladies have a dance. You look beautiful together."

Lorelei whispered, "Please, don't . . ."

Stein looked at her, then back to the two seniors, who flipped him off as they walked away.

Davidek spent most of the night beside Green, who spent most of the night schooling him on recent music history, triggered by the random songs on the DJ's playlist. He heard all about the New Wave movement and the first song featured in a video on MTV (something about the radio killing someone). A Police song launched him into a lecture on reggae and rock fusion, which concluded with Green doing the robot as he sang along in staccato to "Don't Stand So Close to Me."

Good advice, Davidek thought. Near the end of the dance, Hannah Kraut surprised everyone simply by showing up. "Have you seen Mr. Zimmer?" she asked Davidek. "I thought maybe he would be chaperoning tonight."

"I think I heard some of the parents saying his car was snowed in," Davidek said. Hannah seemed disappointed by that.

Later, he saw Hannah in the corner engaged in an intense conversation with Smitty, of all people. Smitty looked nervous, like he didn't want to be seen with her.

Hey, if she pisses him *off, she can't be all bad,* Davidek thought.

. . .

Stein and Lorelei were face-to-face, lips almost touching, eyes locked. Sinead O'Connor was singing a sad song about eating her dinner in a fancy rest-AHRR-aunt, and Stein's hand moved inside Mankowski's monster-sized jacket until the tips of his fingers brushed the firm, bare skin of Lorelei's hip, hidden in the shadow of the cloak.

"I wish I could kiss you again," Stein said. "Like we did before, outside the church."

Lorelei's eyes wouldn't meet his. Their bodies turned with the music. His touch had made her breathless.

"Let's just take things slow . . . ," she said, and her hand slipped down to stop his caress. "Maybe if—" But before she could finish, he touched his lips to hers.

That's when Ms. Bromine pulled them apart.

The guidance counselor had been wandering the dance floor for the past hour, placing balloons between girls and boys she deemed to be dancing too intimately. "Make room for the Holy Spirit," she said flatly, wedging a pink balloon between him and Lorelei.

Stein smiled at Ms. Bromine, and responded by pulling Lorelei to him so quickly that the thin, pink-rubber bubble of air flattened, then burst. He turned to the guidance counselor. "Something tells me no boy ever popped anything on you."

Lorelei covered her mouth and stepped back, but Ms. Bromine didn't do anything for a long moment. "What did you just say to me?" she asked.

Stein leaned in, raising his voice over the music. "Nothing. You must be hearing th—" But Ms. Bromine grabbed his wrist before he could finish, bending his arm back. Her nails sank into his skin. Tears blurred her eyes, flickering in the spinning lights of the DJ's disco ball. "What did you say to me?" she said softly. Stein tried to pull his arm away, but she kept twisting it, repeating, "What . . . did you . . . say?"

The music kept playing, but everyone around them had stopped dancing.

TWENTY-THREE

Davidek was standing in the exterior stairwell leading up to the parking lot. He'd come out here following Hannah and Smitty, but they disappeared into the snow—maybe together; he didn't know. Stein's dad was already waiting in the parking lot, standing around in front of his headlights with some other parents, singing old songs from their own high school dance days.

A lot of kids were already leaving. He watched Mullen and Simms bumble past him, looking giddy and reeking of Kmart cologne. He was watching them go when he felt a hand on his shoulder. Lorelei.

"Hey," Davidek said.

She was pulling on the bulky sweater she'd hidden upstairs in her locker. "Hey, yourself," she said.

Davidek patted his hands against his sides because he didn't know what else to do with them. "So . . . that's cool you and Stein are back together."

"He just mouthed off to Bromine again," she said. "Nice of him to drag me back into trouble right away. I didn't stick around for it this time."

"He really cares about you."

"You dance with anybody?" Lorelei asked.

"I can't dance." Davidek shrugged. "I just came to hang out."

Lorelei nodded, still standing there, though they were fresh out of things to say. "I bet you could have if you'd wanted to," she said, and began walking up the stairs. At the top, she turned around. "I want you to know . . . how things are turning out . . . this isn't what I wanted."

Davidek looked up at her from the bottom. "It's okay," he said. "I'm glad things are this way. I mean it." And he did.

A pained look crossed Lorelei's face, as if there was something he didn't understand, or couldn't. When she was gone, Davidek kept staring at the empty space she had left.

Mr. Mankowski wrapped his hands around Bromine's wrist. "Gretchen," he said. "Gretchen, it's okay." He loosened her grip on Stein, and she released the boy into the crowd of faces looking at her, *noticing* her.

Mankowski walked the guidance counselor to the corridor behind the bingo stage, and as soon as they were out of sight, the tears gathering in her eyes began to stream down her face. Her heart raced with terror at what she'd just done. What she had *almost* done. "These little shits can really push the limits," Mankowski said. "Don't let him get to you." He tried to put an arm around her, but his shoulder didn't work very well ever since he dislocated it during the incident with The Boy on the Roof.

Bromine closed her eyes, and imagined the clumsy embrace was from somebody else, one of those boys who used to want to kiss her—not the kind who would do it for a joke, and then laugh and lie about it.

Once he was free from Bromine, Stein didn't wait around for one of the chaperones to grab him for more questioning. He shot toward the exit, where he found Davidek standing alone on the outside stairs. "You see Lorelei?"

Davidek pointed upward, lamely. "She took off."

Stein kicked over a blue recycling bin full of empty soda cans, which jangled and scattered out across the bottom of the concrete stairwell. The side of the bin read: PROM FUND.

Davidek stood it upright and began gathering the cans back into it. "You know, you've got three more years here with Lorelei," he said. "You don't have to Romeo-and-Juliet yourself because one night ended badly."

Stein snorted. "You know a whole lot about romance for a guy who spent the night standing alone by the trash."

They got into Larry Stein's truck and rode home in silence. Halfway to the Tarentum Bridge, cars were backed up more than a mile and some police cruisers swept by, followed by an ambulance.

Larry looked at the boys. "You want to sleep over tonight, Pete? I can turn around here, and just take you home in the morning."

When they got back to the little white house in the woods, the phone was ringing in the dark kitchen. Larry answered it, then handed it to his son.

"Hey . . . ," Lorelei's voice said, sounding tired.

"It's her," Stein whispered to Davidek.

"Who?" Davidek asked.

"Her," Stein's father intoned from the kitchen, making his hand flutter against his chest.

"I thought you couldn't call from home?" Stein whispered into the phone as he stretched the cord out to his bedroom and closed the door. Lorelei explained she had gotten a ride home with some friends, and they were at Eat'n Park to grab some french fries. She was calling from a pay phone, and only had a few minutes.

"Who'd you go with?" Stein asked, knowing she wasn't on the best terms with any of the girls in their class. "And why'd you ditch me?" He started ranting about Bromine, how he was sick of her picking fights with him, how she had looked like she really might lose it tonight—

"I love you," Lorelei cut in. "That's what I called to tell you. I was afraid to say it in person, I guess. I love you."

Every thought in Stein's head evaporated. Lorelei breathed on the line. "Just . . . I want to go slow. Okay?"

"Okay," he said. *Okay, yes, anything.*

She was silent. Then, a small voice, almost a whisper. "I liked kissing you." There was a muffled sound, the clatter of the phone on her end. Then she said, "And you're handsome."

"I agree," he said. And when she didn't laugh, he added, "And *arrogant.*"

There was a pause. "So we'll go out again?" she asked.

"The two of us?"

"Maybe with Davidek or somebody else?" she said. There was commotion again on the line; she was covering the phone and saying something.

"Is somebody else there?" Stein asked, and Lorelei responded, "Yeah, just . . . I'm gonna go now."

"But—" Stein heard the click of her line, but held the phone to his face for a long time afterwards.

Outside in the living room, Davidek sat beside Stein's father, watching a late-night rerun of a sitcom about a family who lived with a smart-ass alien. Stein's sister, Margie, bleary-eyed and stumbling around without her contact lenses in, had emerged from her bedroom to ask them to please turn that crap down because the laugh track was giving her a migraine. Now that the phone was free, Davidek got up to tell his parents he was staying the night. As Stein sat down on the couch, his dad noticed the huge smile on his face. "Well, *somebody's* glad to be watching *Alf*," he said.

Inside the Eat'n Park restaurant, groups of old couples dressed in colorful square dancing costumes were pestering the waitresses for more decaf, while teenagers from the public school were making a ruckus and ruining the salad bar. No one else from St. Mike's was around. *Thank God*, Lorelei thought.

She was sitting in the glass corridor between the restaurant lobby and the exit, where the pay phone and cigarette machine were. She spun around as she hung up the phone. "You idiots!" she said. "You tell me, 'Say he's handsome'? He could've *heard* you!"

Mullen and Simms, old Asshole Face and Sandmouth, were leaning on opposite sides of the cigarette machine. Simms shrugged. "My voice was low enough."

"Because I covered the phone!" she exclaimed.

"We did what we had to," Mullen said. "Now, let's get out of here before somebody sees us together."

They led Lorelei outside and she slumped in the front seat of Mullen's 1982 Plymouth Volare—a forest-colored piece of shit known to other students as the Pea Green Love Machine. Mullen got behind the wheel and Simms crawled into the backseat, gnawing on a Smiley Cookie from the restaurant's bakery. "You want a bite?" he asked, extending the half with the eyes to her.

She had no one to blame but herself for this. Lorelei had sought them out as protectors that day in the cafeteria just before Christmas. She had been desperate, and they had promised to make the others leave her alone—all she had to do was help them in return. They wanted to hurt Stein. Badly. But that was okay. At the time, so did she.

At the time.

She wasn't even sure what the plan was. Mullen and Simms wanted her to stay with Stein just long enough to humiliate him, maybe by simply dumping his sorry ass again. They wanted to really get to him, to hit him in a way that would hurt a lot worse than any kick or punch. By devastating the untouchable Stein, they would prove their worth to the other upperclassmen—and Lorelei would do the same.

Out there on the dance floor, feeling his fingertips brush her midriff, Lorelei began to doubt what she was doing. But then Stein had gone and pissed off Bromine for about the seven hundreth time, almost dragging Lorelei into that mess again, too.

Maybe the son of a bitch did deserve this.

As they drove her home, Simms said from the backseat, "You sure you don't want to come back here with me? I like that little shirt of yours. You have a cute belly."

Lorelei pressed her face against the cool glass of the passenger window, feeling her skin crawl. She said to Mullen, "If your creep friend comes on to me again, I'm going to barf in your car."

Mullen laughed. Protecting her from that idiot was easy. Protecting her from the other seniors? . . . That was nothing he could promise, though she apparently didn't know that. Only through pleading with Audra and menacing the Grough sisters had the boys secured her a bit of peace in the month since she approached them. They didn't intend to keep that up forever. When they were done with Lorelei, she was on her own. Nobody in the school liked Stein, but they didn't like her either. Let the bitch and the fucker destroy each other.

"No more flirting with Lorelei, Simms. She's off-limits," Mullen said, grinning in the blue glow of the dashboard lights. "Remember—she's our little sister now, you pervert."

TWENTY-FOUR

A list was circulating. Nothing written, just rumors of names—people Hannah Kraut was singling out for special treatment in her notebook. LeRose heard he was on the list. So did a lot of other people. No one knew if the list changed as word of it passed from room to room, collecting new names the way a bee gathers pollen. No one wanted to talk about why they might be on the list, but everyone was eager to theorize why others could be.

After a long détente, Hannah found herself the object of open hatred once again. In a rare lunchtime appearance, Hannah had been sitting at an empty table in the center of the cavernous, lime-colored cafeteria, one hand carrying the occasional french fry to her mouth, with the other splaying a paperback of Tom Wolfe's *Electric Kool-Aid Acid Test.*

"*Fuuuuuuucckkssssslllluuuuuuttttt!!!*"

The call came from far away, some anonymous drone who bellowed it and hid his face before anyone could spot him. Davidek thought it came from the junior section.

Hannah looked up from her book and turned toward the yell. Then, from the other end of the room, a girl's voice snapped out the word loudly, like a sneeze: *Fkslt!!!*

JayArr Picklin and Charlie Karsimen, two freshmen too crazed to know they should hide themselves, tried to join the bandwagon by chanting "Fuck-*slut*! Fuck-*slut*!" as they thumped on the table.

Davidek could hear the word murmured now by other voices, low, swirling around the cafeteria . . . *fuckslutfuckslutfuckslut*, underlined by hidden giggles.

Davidek watched his beautiful redhead senior stand up and place one shoe on her chair, stepping up onto the lunch table, her mismatched eyes gazing around the room. "You think I don't see you," she said softly. "You think you're hidden."

Her voice silenced the whispers like a knife slicing a throat.

She pointed in the direction of the juniors, toward a guy with a thick neck and a handsome all-American-boy face that was perpetually smeared with a smirk. "John Hannidy," she said.

Hannidy shouted back in protest: "I didn't say anything!" He glared at another boy at his table, one who had been calling out the name.

If Hannah realized this, she didn't care. "Go ahead and lie, but I know what you've done, Turkey Baster. Did you think the people who knew would lie for you? Did you, John?"

Hannah turned toward the senior tables, where the *fkslt!!* sneeze had originated.

"Nora Dalmolin," Hannah said, as the girl turned to her best friend, Beth Weitz, asking what the hell Hannah was doing. "Beth Weitz," Hannah said, still pointing. She lingered before turning again. All she had said were their names.

But a panicked Beth and Nora began babbling at each other in a pitch like dolphins trying to talk their way out of a fishing net.

"Who wants to be next?" Hannah said, spreading her arms wide to the faces staring up at her. "Who wants to be singled out?"

Ms. Bromine strode over toward Hannah's stump speech, flanked by Mr. Mankowski and Mrs. Tunns. They were approaching cautiously, unsure what was happening.

LeRose stood up from his table, hair falling down in his face as he shouted: "We don't have to *take* this. We can crush her if we all stay together. Don't—"

"Carl LeRose," Hannah said, silencing him. "How's Daddy?"

LeRose sank into his seat, jaw clenched, sweat boiling on his forehead. "You're not allowed to say anything about my father," LeRose said flatly.

"Hannah Kraut, step down from that table immediately," Ms. Bromine said, looking at her fellow teachers for justification. "It's . . . unsafe."

Hannah, still holding her hands out, nodded once. But before she stepped down, she scanned the faces of the room one more time. "EVERY. SINGLE. ONE OF YOU," Hannah said. "Don't you dare doubt it."

No one knew for sure what she meant, but no one was saying a word. Hannah walked out of the hushed room with the unmistakable feeling of triumph.

Let them hate me, but in silence.

If it was possible to become more radioactive, Hannah accomplished it. People fled from her, moved away from doorways if she walked near, and didn't speak if she was around—mostly out of fear she'd imagine them talking about her, even if they weren't.

The students of St. Mike's focused their unhappiness on Davidek. They only wanted his help, but there was menace in their outreach.

"Davidek, what do you suppose Hannah meant when she mentioned my dad?" LeRose asked, sidling up to him in the lunch line the next day. LeRose had a saggy, sad look in his eyes and offered to buy Davidek's lunch if they could sit and talk. Davidek said he didn't have to pay but stopped objecting when LeRose opened his billfold for the clerk, revealing a seam of green like coal strata in a mountainside.

They found an empty table, but soon Green and then Stein came and sat with them. Neither liked each other very much anymore, but they both liked Davidek when the other wasn't around. "This is a private conversation," LeRose told them. Stein said, "You can go talk about your privates somewhere else. This is a freshman table."

"It's okay, LeRose, these guys are friends. You can trust them," Davidek said.

"Plus, he's just going to tell us everything you said later," Green added.

LeRose laid his arms open on the table, mulling his words. "You know my dad's a big deal, right?"

Davidek chewed. "So you keep saying . . ."

"Well, he's a *really* big deal."

Green said cautiously: "Isn't he a funeral director?"

"Creepy," Stein said. "Dead bodies and all that?"

"He's a town selectman," LeRose said. "And a member of the parish council. He owns apartments and commercial real estate all over this valley, and—yes—we also own the LeRose funeral home, which my father inherited from an uncle. We do not involve ourselves with the bodies, for your information. Okay?"

"You don't get involved?" Stein said. "So it's more of a one-night-stand kind of thing for you and the bodies."

LeRose blurted, "Does Hannah say anything about my dad in her little *book*?"

"How do I know?" Davidek asked.

"Well, has she shown you any of it? Or told you about it? People have seen you two talking, and you don't exactly look like you're standing up to her or anything."

"What's he supposed to do?" Stein demanded. "Piss her off, like you did yesterday?"

LeRose kept his eyes fixed on Davidek. "You're her freshman—but you can use that position to look out for your friends. Protect us."

Davidek's throat felt tight.

"Even if you don't fight her, let us know what she's got," LeRose said. "It's probably lies, but I want to know. All of us—*we* want to know. To prepare ourselves."

"What's there to know about your dad?" Green asked. "What does he care about what a high school girl thinks of him?"

"Nothing. Nothing in the least," LeRose said, leaning back in his chair. "But as with any successful businessman, people like to spread lies about him."

"Like what?" Davidek asked.

"I'd prefer not to say. . . ."

"I doubt Hannah even knows who he is," Davidek said. "I mean, your old man is just another nobody, like all our dads."

"A nobody?" the sophomore laughed. Carl LeRose was not the kind of person who could control an emotion like pride. "My father is a good, hardworking man, and he has always done the right thing," he said. "But the *right* thing, and the *legal* thing . . . sometimes aren't the same. He's got some enemies."

"Your dad? The church councilman? Now he's Don Corleone?" Stein said. "I like you, LeRose, but seriously . . ."

LeRose's beefy neck bulged against his collar. "You want to laugh? Let me tell you about this guy, a patrolman with the Tarentum police. A few years ago they get a call—house alarm. Lots of crime over there since the—" he shot a barely perceptible glance at Green "—since a lot of *poorer* people started moving in."

"*I* live in Tarentum. Haven't *poorer* people always lived there?" Green said.

LeRose ignored him: "This happened five years ago," he said. "So the house alarm goes off, and the cop shows up. There's this guy out on the front lawn. It's dark, the lights are off in the house, the guy's in shadows. He's waving his arms. . . . The officer is the first one there, but he hears sirens off in the distance. His backup is coming, but it's not there yet. He says, 'Hands up, get down on the ground!' The guy keeps walking over to him, so the officer says it again, but the guy doesn't stop. Finally, the officer draws his gun. *Now* all the sudden the guy wants to cooperate, but when the cop goes to cuff him, he starts getting all panicky again and 'What the fuck is going on here?' and all that shit. The guy starts struggling. The cop draws his gun again. *Stop!* But the guy doesn't stop. Then suddenly, *Pow!* The gun goes off, right across the side of the perp's head."

LeRose paused, letting it sink in for the boys around him.

Davidek said, "Are you going to tell us the cop shot your dad in the head, and that's why you're rich today?" Green and Stein laughed out loud.

"No, stupid . . . ," LeRose said, his dramatic pause ruined. "My dad wasn't anywhere near there. The twist is—the dude the cop shot was the homeowner. He'd come back from vacation and his wife opened the door, sent the kids in, then he came out to unload the car—forgetting to turn off the alarm.

"So when the cop arrived, the guy was just trying to explain—false alarm, right? And when he started getting arrested, he freaked out, didn't follow orders—and *that's* what got him shot."

"So what's this got to do with your dad?" Green asked. "Or Hannah's notebook?"

"Well, you can imagine—the cop was royally screwed, right? Career in ruins? *Wrong.* First, the dude didn't die, but he had part of his skull sheared off. Minor brain damage and disfigurement. Then my dad steps in. This isn't just bad for the cop, who happens to be my dad's friend—he's got a lot of cop friends—but it's going to cost the city a fortune, too. Dad talks to the police chief and gives the department access to my dad's private lawyers. This homeowner who got popped, he had some drunk driving arrests, an assault charge in his past. He's no saint. He managed a shoe store over in Lower Burrell, which was in a strip mall my dad had a partnership in. . . . So my dad comes up with a plan: The cops charge the guy who got shot. Disorderly conduct. Resisting arrest. Soon as he gets out of the hospital, he's going to the slammer. Then the lawyers search for—and find—some irregularities in the lease the shoe store signed. Rent's going up. You can't stay in business here? Oh, sorry. Maybe you need to lay off some staff. . . .

"So jail time looming, the employer is cutting him loose, legal and medical bills mounting . . . The guy's wife decides to strike a deal. They settle the lawsuit against the city for cheap, no charges against the cop. Misdemeanor disorderly conduct for the victim—suspended sentence. The city covers medical expenses, and the shoe store rent goes back to normal. The family didn't stay. They moved elsewhere. The cop *did* stay, and he got promoted. Officer Bellows was his name. Now he's a captain in the department. And all because of my dad."

"When does your old man pick up the Nobel Prize?" Davidek asked.

LeRose stood from the table. "I like you, Dav, but you don't get it sometimes. The point of this story is, it's important to have *friends*. When you *don't* have friends, you end up losing your job at the fucking shoe store. You get me? There are other stories about my dad . . . things I wouldn't exactly want announced to a crowd. . . . So just check with Hannah, all right? See what she's got. Lemme know. I'd appreciate it." He extended his hand to Davidek. "Okay, friend?"

TWENTY-FIVE

Bilbo grabbed Davidek's sleeve as he walked up the steps. The usual cluster of senior boys was standing at the base of the stairwell, joined by Green, who usually didn't say much to Davidek when his older buddies were around. Like always, they were sipping Cokes and laughing to each other as they loitered in the open space at the bottom of the stairs.

"We want to know something," Bilbo said. His face had the same hopefulness as LeRose's last week. Davidek could almost predict the words as they fell out of Bilbo's mouth. He'd heard them a lot lately: *Hannah doesn't know . . .*

". . . about the hidden porno stash in the library, does she?" Bilbo asked. That was a new one. Davidek had no idea.

He also didn't know if Hannah knew about the junior guy who'd been selling date-rape drugs on the side. Everybody who asked him about that was certain who it was, though they all believed it was somebody different.

And he didn't know about the rumor that two sophomore guys on the golf team were seen making out behind the pro shop one weekend. Dan Foster and Pat Trombolla fumbled over their reason for bringing it up, saying they were asking on behalf of the actual boys—not that they were the ones themselves, of course.

Davidek pleaded ignorance—and that was the truth. But after people approached him with their questions, they tended to turn belligerent—fearing he'd tip Hannah to something new. He seemed to make new enemies every time somebody asked him to be their friend.

Only Bilbo was forthright. "That stash of porno was here when I was a freshman," he said. "Hell, some of those beat-up stroke mags were probably here when my *old man* was a freshman. . . . It's important for it to stay there—for tradition's sake."

Bilbo sounded almost patriotic. Davidek said he sympathized.

As he walked away, Davidek turned back to the stairwell sanctuary and asked, "So why are you guys always standing around here, drinking pop? Why here?"

A wide smile spread on Green's face, "Dude, it's a secret. . . ." And then he tipped his head back and took a long swig. One of the seniors slapped the can out of his hand. "Don't even hint around at it, dumb-ass," Prager said.

Green looked helplessly from Davidek down to his own reflection in the fading fizz of the spilled soda. "Sorry," he said.

Davidek was waiting in the snow at Hannah's Jeep again. Hannah brushed her bangs from her eyes as she took out her car keys. "They're hassling *you* about the notebook, aren't they?"

"They're asking," he said.

"Asking you or threatening you?"

Davidek hesitated. "Which one *are* you doing?"

When Hannah Kraut smiled for real, she only half smiled, like one side of her face couldn't shake its unhappiness. That's how she smiled now. "You're sweet," she said, ruffling his hair. "You're a good kid, Petey. . . . And I've been pretty easy on you so far. Reading this thing at the end of the year won't be too much to ask. So don't worry about it."

Davidek's heart hammered in his chest. "People are going to hate me!"

Hannah slid into the driver's seat of the Jeep, and a thought occurred to her. "You'll be tempted to comfort people at the school, to tell them they're not included in my little Secret History. You'll want to make them feel better," she said. "But when that turns out not to be true, when they *are* in there—that would be very bad for you. They'll feel like you lied to them."

"Some of those people are my friends," Davidek said, and Hannah's eyes slid closed.

"No one is your friend at that school," she said. "Not a single person. Everyone you think you care about will disappoint you. They'll all hurt you in the end."

"You, too?" he said.

Hannah just stared at him. Then that little half smile appeared again. "Little old me?" she said. "I wouldn't hurt a fly."

John Hannidy's eyes pulsed in their sockets. His all-American smile was a snarl, and swatches of his black hair fell down into his eyes. The junior had a little American flag pinned to the lapel of his blue blazer, located just below a gold pin for the Holy Name Society. Both adornments jostled up and down as he slammed Davidek against his locker.

"Why'd she say my name?" Hannidy asked. "Why'd she point at me? What's she going to do?" Before he was strong enough to lift people up and swing them back and forth, Hannidy used to be known by the nickname "Turkey Baster." Some people thought he'd been a test-tube baby because his parents looked like grandparents. Others said it was because his dick was thin enough to fit in one. Either way, Hannidy didn't want the name coming back.

Hannidy's friend, Raymond Lee, a short, blubbery kid with the thick neck of a sea lion, tried to hold him back. They served on the student council together, and had plans for Hannidy to be president next year. Raymond wasn't worried about nicknames—he was worried Hannah knew they'd been skimming money out of the student activities fund that the council oversaw. Hannidy, as usual, was fixated only on the bullshit.

Green was waiting to help Davidek up when the juniors left him. "Maybe it's time we turn to someone new for help," he said.

As they stood outside Mr. Zimmer's classroom, Davidek said: "*This* is it? Your idea of helping me is to *tell?*"

Green pulled his hand away from the doorknob. "Mr. Zimmer told me a long time ago that I could come to him if I had any problems with the seniors. You can trust him."

Mr. Zimmer was overseeing a study hall, and his room was full of kids from various grades, most of them working on projects for the school's upcoming International Day celebration, an afternoon of foreign foods, shoddy-looking dioramas, and stage skits presented by the language classes.

"Hey, Green!" the lanky teacher called out, rising from his desk. "What can I do for you guys?" He clapped Green on the shoulder, and Davidek felt a pang of jealousy that he wasn't pals with the teacher, too.

"We need help with something," Green said. "And it's kind of *serious*."

"*Very* serious," Davidek emphasized.

Zimmer look from boy to boy. "*Very* serious. Okay. Well, let's talk."

"Not here," Davidek said, eyeing the senior Spanish students, who were arguing whether the "Murder of Gonzago" scene from *Hamlet* was too complicated to translate in time for their International Day show. Mullen and Simms were among the unfriendlies. "Up here, then . . . ," Zimmer said, and he walked with them toward his desk.

Davidek was relieved to see only freshmen sitting nearby. He was safe. "You know Hannah Kraut, right, Mr. Zimmer?" he asked.

The teacher looked at him steadily. After Davidek explained about the notebook, and her plans to have her freshman—him—read it at the Hazing Picnic, all Mr. Zimmer had to say was: "Hannah has been treated very badly here."

"Not by me," Davidek said.

Zimmer cocked his head toward the older kids in the back of the room. "By them," he said. "She's not the monster you think she is."

"Then why is she doing this to a freshman who never did anything to her?" Green said.

"Will you talk to her?" Davidek asked. "Get her to back off?"

Zimmer thought about it, then nodded. "Someday when you two are seniors, desperate freshmen are going to tremble in your shadows. When that day comes, remember how you felt coming to ask for this favor. Okay?"

Davidek and Green walked to the door, and Zimmer called out: "One more thing . . ."

They stopped, and he waited for them to walk back to him. "Just wondering. She say anything about the teachers in this notebook?" Zimmer asked.

Davidek thought before answering. He had no idea. But maybe it would be good if Mr. Zimmer and the rest of the faculty felt invested in stopping this notebook from coming to light. "Yeah," Davidek said. "Teachers. The principal. Father Mercedes. She's got something on everybody."

After they left, Zimmer looked over to the spot where Hannah had once stood on her tiptoes and ambushed him with a kiss.

In front of his desk, Seven-Eighths sat as still as a statue behind her computer screen. Davidek and Green hadn't noticed her as they talked to Mr. Zimmer. No one ever did.

She felt a swell of pride after school, as she walked over to the rectory and knocked on Father Mercedes's front door. "You were right, Father," Seven-Eighths told him. "That girl *is* going to try to hurt you."

The next day, Sister Maria sat behind her desk as Father Mercedes stood behind her, and Ms. Bromine paced the floor of the small principal's office. The priest said he had recently learned about Hannah's notebook, and felt Sister Maria needed to take immediate action to ensure this irresponsible young girl did not needlessly damage the reputations of good people in the St. Mike's community.

Hannah Kraut kept her hands folded on her lap as they questioned her. She said she had no idea what they talking about, and kept repeating that for nearly an hour as she was interrogated, scolded, threatened. . . .

"I'd like to know exactly where this so-called information you have collected is being kept right now," Father Mercedes demanded.

A silence followed. Hannah opened her mouth, then closed it. "I can only tell you again," she said finally. "There is no diary or notebook or whatever."

"Hannah . . . ," Sister Maria moaned. "Can we please stop playing games here?" The nun's heart wasn't in this—Hannah could tell. But the priest was furious, and Ms. Bromine seemed gleeful.

"Where'd you hear these things anyway?" Hannah asked. "Rumors are almost never true, you know." She cocked a little half smile. "Not that I keep track."

Ms. Bromine slammed her palm on the principal's desk. "I was there when you stood on the table in the lunchroom, threatening people," she said. "What was that all about?"

Hannah raised her eyebrows. "I was pointing out the people who were calling me a disgusting name. Why were *you* just standing there, watching me? I could have used your help."

The priest folded his hands. "I'm sorry to see it come to this." That was true. He had hoped the girl's little notebook would work in his favor as a nice smack across the face to St. Mike's, proof that the high school was better amputated than saved. But he simply couldn't risk himself being listed among the implicated.

"Who exactly is accusing me of having this notebook?" Hannah asked.

"Teachers," Father Mercedes said, not wanting to reveal his real source. Not even Sister Maria and Ms. Bromine knew about his little freshman mole.

Teachers? Hannah thought.

Ms. Bromine's lips pursed into a thin smile. "That name they were calling you, Hannah. It refers to something, doesn't it? You have a reputation for being—let's say—*loose* with your favors. Isn't that so?" The guidance counselor's eyes were bright, knowing. They said, *fuckslut.*

"Maybe you'd like to enlighten us as to her history, Ms. Bromine?" the priest asked.

"That's enough," Sister Maria said.

Ms. Bromine ignored her, drudging up all the old slurs and rumors. Sister Maria looked away during most of it, but Hannah did not. At the end, the girl just said, "None of that is true either."

"You're applying to Penn State, right?" Bromine asked. "Who's writing your letter of recommendation—Mr. Zimmer?"

Hannah didn't answer.

"That's enough," Sister Maria said again.

"You know, it's not unheard of for a letter to be rescinded," Bromine said. "Even a state school might not admit a student if St. Mike's sends the proper warning."

"I said enough! *Enough!*" the nun shouted, rising from her desk.

Father Mercedes finally acknowledged the nun. "Why is it only 'enough' when we're trying to enact some discipline around here?"

The principal turned to Hannah. "You are excused," she said. "For now."

As Hannah walked out, Bromine came to the door, closing it on her until there was only space for their faces. "We'll find out about this notebook—with or *without* your help."

"You'll be sorry if you do," Hannah said.

Bromine smirked as the principal's door clicked shut. Father Mercedes's muffled voice from the other side said, "Just one more wreck of a student, Sister Maria."

TWENTY-SIX

A day later, Hannah knelt in the hall, digging her gym shoes out of the bottom of her locker. A pair of long legs in khaki pants walked up beside her.

"Ready to bowl a three hundred?" Zimmer asked.

Ever since the church fire led to the school's gymnasium being transformed into a chapel, the school had made an arrangement with the bowling alley in a neighboring shopping mall. It was walking distance for the students, even in the snow, and two hours of pin smashing fulfilled the state-mandated physical requirement during the winter months.

"Maybe you could walk with me to the Lanes today, Hannah," Zimmer said. "I think we need to talk." The gangly teacher crouched down, and Hannah gazed into the older man's face, the bruised half moons beneath his eyes, the long teeth in his smile. There was nothing beautiful about him, but she still wanted to pull him close.

Outside, the class moved ahead of Hannah and Mr. Zimmer in a thin column led by Mr. Mankowski, pressing forward across the icy parking lot of the shopping center. With Hannah's hood pulled up over her head like a monk's cassock, she and Mr. Zimmer passed along the shopfronts—the CardVark greeting card store, the Little Professor Book Nook, the Jo-Ann Fabric outlet, a Christian music store called: Christian Music.

"What do you want to talk about?" she asked, certain she already knew the answer. Who had tipped off Bromine, Sister Maria, and Father Mercedes? *Teachers*, the priest had said. Hannah guessed it was actually only one.

Zimmer crinkled his brow. "I've just heard some stuff, Hannah. About a . . . notebook?"

"What about it?"

"It's how you made them stop teasing you, isn't it? Gathering up everyone's worst secrets to throw back at them. Kind of ingenius, really. My little Madame Defarge, always sitting, waiting, listening. . . . Maybe it's time you should let it go, though."

Before you lose something more.

Hannah closed her eyes so she wouldn't have to look at him. She thought of her visit to the office—Ms. Bromine leaning into her face, detailing all the old horror stories about Hannah the "fuckslut" for Father Mercedes and Sister Maria. "You know how they treated me, Mr. Zimmer? You know the things they said about me?"

"Yeah, but these new kids aren't the ones who treated you badly," Zimmer responded, assuming she was talking about the students who had bullied her all these years. "Please don't take this out on some innocent freshman who never did anything to hurt you."

Hannah stopped. "Wait. What are we talking about here?"

The teacher watched the rest of the Phys Ed class move ahead. "We're talking about you, Hannah," he said, kicking at the ice on the sidewalk. "That scared little freshman who came asking me for help—you should have seen him. He's not so different from how you were once."

That scared little freshman . . . She hadn't thought Davidek would be nervy enough to alert the school administrators. The kid had some surprises in him.

Zimmer put his arm around Hannah, and got her walking again. "You know, out of all the students I've ever seen at St. Mike's, you're the one I like the most," he said. "And you're the only one I wish never came here."

She looked up into Zimmer's battered and scarred face. She understood now: Bromine's source had been Zimmer, and Davidek had started it all.

After years spent isolating herself, she had forgotten: Only the people you trust the most can hurt you the worst.

They stopped in front of the bowling alley's swinging glass doors, which belched out the oily smell of wooden lanes, rented shoes, and lightbulb-toasted pizza. A couple of senior guys inside were playing the Big Choice claw game by the jukebox—the St. Mike's equivalent of Phys Ed extra credit.

"I'm surprised Davidek waited so long to start crying for help," Hannah said.

Zimmer shrugged. "He seemed to think a lot of people already knew."

"A lot," she agreed flatly. "But no one else ran to the teachers. . . ."

"Until it went too far," the teacher reminded her, and Hannah tightened her fists inside the sleeves of her coat.

"You like to let people off the hook, don't you, Mr. Zimmer?" *All except me*, she thought. *You didn't look the other way with me. Not this time.*

The teacher opened the door for her. "I like to think I see the best in people," he said. "You included." Hannah's white teeth pressed together between her soft, peachblood lips. Zimmer thought she was smiling at him. But she wasn't.

She was trying not to hate him.

The sun made a cameo appearance one day in late February, turning the white winter landscape into a giant gray Slurpee for a day. After school, a familiar Jeep pulled up in front of Davidek as he trudged through the parking lot slush toward his bus. "Hey, little boy, want a ride?" Hannah asked, tipping down her sunglasses.

"Uh, maybe another time," Davidek said, walking around the Jeep, but Hannah revved the engine and blocked his away again.

"I've been rotten to you. I'm sorry," she said. "Why don't you get in the car. I'd like to start over, if we can."

Davidek was tired and pissed off. He had gotten bitched out by the ancient Sister Antonia last period because he was the only one in French class who hadn't yet volunteered to bring a food dish to the International Day festivities, even though they were more than three weeks away. In the Jeep, Hannah had a scrunchie in her teeth and was pulling her scarlet hair back into a ponytail. He looked from her to his bus, then opened the Jeep door. Her back wheels sprayed a fan of gray ice as they pulled out into the street.

Hannah was bouncy, and more chipper and cheerful than he'd seen her. "I need to pick out a dress for prom. You want to come to the store and help me?"

Davidek made a face like someone discovering that milk has gone sour. "Isn't that kind of a *girly* thing to do?"

"I want a guy's opinion," she said, and nudged his shoulder. "You are a guy, aren't you? *Aren't* you?"

He acknowledged, yes, he was a guy, but not one who felt like dress shopping. Hannah's enthusiasm faded. "Fine," she said. "I'll just take you home. *Boring.*"

They rolled down Butler Road with the windows down and the warm air tossing their hair and St. Mike's growing small in the distance. "Remember when you first saw me and thought I was somebody else?" she asked. "Imagine my surprise when you turned out to be somebody different than I thought, too."

Davidek shrugged. "All right."

She stopped at a red light and lowered her sunglasses. "I didn't think you were the type to run and cry to Sister Maria, Ms. Bromine, and Mr. Zimmer."

Davidek sat forward in his seat. "I didn't do that." He was a bad liar. "Well, not Ms. Bromine, or—"

"It's okay," Hannah said. "I'm not *mad* at you. I've been thinking about it, and . . . you're right. I did put you in a bad spot."

Davidek's heart leaped. "Wait. So you're *not* going to make me read that stuff at the picnic?"

"Oh no," she said. "You're going to read it. That's not changing."

Goddamnit. Davidek looked out the back window of the Jeep. He could jump out now and walk back to school, but his bus would already be gone.

Fuck it. This had to stop. And this was as good a time to make a stand as any. "Hannah, you should know I'm never gonna read those things. I don't care what you say or what you do. I'm not going to be your shield, and do your dirty work, and make everybody hate me for the next four years just so you can get a little payback out of this stupid hazing ritual bullshit. I'm just *not* going to do it. End of story."

As the Jeep rolled toward the great blue span of the Tarentum Bridge, linking the two sides of the Allegheny Valley, the Jeep took a turn instead of crossing the bridge into New Kensington, where Davidek lived.

"Where are we going?" he asked.

"To see if I can change your mind," Hannah said.

The Jeep bounced down a ramp that deposited them on a narrow street running below the bridge and alongside the river. Battered row houses stretched off down the road, as still as gravestones. Hannah turned on a driveway under the bridge, leading to a ramp that sloped down into the frozen river—a boat launch for the spring and summer seasons.

Hannah pulled her Jeep beside the bridge's colossal concrete leg, hiding it from everything except the river, shuffling its dissolving sugar-plates of broken ice toward Pittsburgh. High above them, the bridge span blocked out the sun and sent down thunder from the rumbling, unseen traffic.

Hannah turned off the Jeep's engine and slid one leg up beneath her plaid skirt to sit a little taller. "Do you have any secrets?" she asked, taking off her sunglasses and tossing them on top of the dashboard.

Davidek guffawed. "What—are you going to blackmail me?"

"I was thinking about it," she said.

The concrete leg of the bridge rumbled beside the Jeep—a convoy of trucks hauling large rolls of steel from the Kees-Northson mill, probably. It drowned out Davidek's laugh.

"You telling me you don't have *any* secrets?" Hannah asked, laughing along with him—just for the hell of it.

Davidek's disbelief was irrepressible. "Oh no, I've got lots!" he said. "Let's see. . . . I guess you know about my abortion? My *six* abortions. What else? . . . Oh, I killed JFK. And Elvis. And I'm a porno star who goes by the name Pat McGroin. All the skeletons in my closet are your hostages, Hannah!"

Hannah picked at her skirt idly, not looking at him. "What about your brother, the draft-dodger?"

That made Davidek crack up. "Actually, he went AWOL. He was already enlisted. There isn't any draft."

"You're not embarrassed?"

"That one's only good for pissing off my mom and dad. They spend their lives hiding from it. I have immunity from family embarrassment—one of the advantages of being the kid they don't care about."

The bridge column beside them groaned as another heavy vehicle trundled across the top. Hannah's hands fell to her skirt, plucking at the fabric again, drawing it up on her thighs. "When you were little, did you ever pick on a girl? Like a girl in your class? They say boys always pick on the one they like, to get her attention. . . ."

She took one of Davidek's hands and placed it on her bare knee. She leaned close enough for him to smell the scent of soap and water on her neck. "Yeah, you know . . . ," Davidek said, reaching for the door handle. "Fake flirting with me, that'll work. Thanks."

Hannah stared through the windshield, out to the empty river, the distant shore. "Want to hear one of my secrets, Peter? . . . Sometimes when a girl asks you to look at dresses with her, she doesn't really want you to look at the *dresses*."

Her mismatched eyes met his as one hand went to her shirt and undid a button. Then another. Then all of them. Davidek tried to say something but never got beyond the first syllable of any word.

"I really did like the way you looked at me . . . ," Hannah said. "When you thought I was someone else." She let her blouse fall open and leaned forward. Her breath smelled like cherry Starbursts. "I like how you're looking at me now, too."

She pushed him back as she kissed him, her tongue probing his mouth as she laced her fingers with his, pressing his hands down against her bare, warm thighs.

It was impossible to tell how long the kiss lasted. Time and space ceased to exist as Davidek's brain scrambled to memorize every scent, every touch, every sound. He had kissed a girl before, but only once—Tara Frank, a girl he had crushed hard on throughout eighth grade. She had agreed to kiss him at the class Christmas party. A smooch under the mistletoe. It had been incredible. And nothing like this.

Hannah pulled away, sliding back up against the driver's door. Davidek gasped, "What's wrong?"

"Nothing," she said, flashing an evil little smile as her fingertips traced the tops of her breasts. "We're alone."

Hannah was still sitting on her left leg, but she extended her right leg and used the gearshift between the seats to pop off her white canvas shoe. She put her toes against Davidek's chest, nudging him backwards.

He said, "I'm sorry. I'm not very experienced."

Hannah put a dagger in his heart. "I know. But it's okay." She arched her back and pushed her bra-covered chest up into the air, hands clawing behind her back.

"Hannah . . . !" Davidek turned his head nervously toward each window.

"Yes . . . ?" she said, part ecstasy, part annoyance as her bra clasp sprang loose.

"Hannah, I . . ." He stopped speaking, watching her twist and draw her arms into her blouse sleeves, one at a time, shimmying as she removed the bra without removing the shirt. She held it out to him with one hand—a simple B-cup with lace trim. She clasped her uniform blouse with the other hand, and through the thin fabric, Davidek could see the threat of every fantasy he could imagine.

"Take it," she laughed, jiggling the bra, and he did, holding it like it might snake-bite him.

Her bare foot slipped down into his lap and Davidek jumped. "You're hard," she said. "But you're not thinking about her now, are you?"

Davidek squirmed. "Who?"

"That girl we bought the cigarettes for."

"Let's just . . . go somewhere."

"We *are* somewhere," she said.

"Somewhere alone."

"You are alone."

"We're *outside*, Hannah. . . ."

A tube of glittery lip gloss appeared in her hand from beneath the seat. She began to ice her mouth heavily. "You know what they say about me, right? The stories they tell? . . ."

Davidek bobbled his head.

"Not all rumors are false," she said. "Do you think I'm bad?"

"*No*," Davidek said emphatically.

"You're always telling me no," she said. Her foot brushed his hard-on again. "Would you like to make *me* excited?" Hannah released the blouse, letting it fall open. "Don't say no this time."

Cool air from the icy riverside had begun to seep into the Jeep, but pinpricks of sweat beaded all over Davidek's body anyway.

"The things I like—they're not what other girls like. They *are* bad." She leaned forward, picking up the fallen bra, and began smearing his mouth with a kiss. He groped at her breasts, but she grabbed his hands, pushing the bra straps over his arms and sliding the garment up onto his chest. He pulled away, his face shining with sparkling lip gloss. "What th—?"

She collapsed back, biting her index finger seductively.

"Shh . . . Shh . . . Peter . . . ," Hannah said, and Davidek lost his words. The bra was stretched across his chest, bunching his tie up against his glittery chin. He looked insane, but didn't care. He *was* insane.

"Can you show me?" she asked, inching up her skirt to reveal a white snug of panties.

"Show you what?" Davidek sputtered.

"Show me . . . *you*," Hannah said.

Davidek knelt in the seat, towering over her, the loose bra straps dangling around his shoulders as he drew down his zipper. At the moment he reached inside to free himself, Hannah said: "Peter—look at me."

He did.

She was holding a yellow disposable camera.

There was no flash. Just a click.

"That one's for the yearbook cover," she said, winding the film. The camera clicked again as he lunged at her, one hand still stuck inside his fly. He toppled onto the steering wheel, honking the horn, and Hannah brought her knee up into his side, knocking him back into the passenger seat. He pulled his hand free, his fly hanging open, the white underwear sticking out like a mocking tongue.

She snapped another shot, winding the film to the next frame as fast as she could. He scrambled to rip the bra off his chest. "Ooh, good," she said. "Action shot!"

When he grabbed once more at the camera, Hannah finally touched him where he had always wanted—but with a swift punch.

Davidek collapsed, his mouth a little circle of pain, still smeared with secondhand lip gloss.

"Don't try to take it again," she warned, tucking the camera safely under her seat. She began to rebutton her shirt as the freshman, still clutching his aching groin, grasped the door handle and tumbled out onto the snow-crusted ground.

Hannah adjusted her mirrors and fired the Jeep's engine. "You can find your own way home, right? I know it's a long way, but . . . You understand." She reached over and tossed his book bag out the open door, then pulled it shut. And locked it.

Davidek gasped in enough air to wheeze out: "Fuck you."

"Almost," she laughed. "But it didn't quite happen. . . . Here's what *will* happen, though. We're going through with my hazing plan. You'll read the notebook when I *tell* you to read the notebook. Got it? . . . No more crybaby running to Bromine or Zimmer or your parents or anyone else. Not unless you want to be the next *Playgirl* centerfold."

Davidek shambled to his feet, glowering at her.

"I'll keep the camera under wraps and give it to you later—undeveloped," she said, putting on her sunglasses. "But I promise, you'll see those pretty pictures stuck to every locker in the school if you ever forget. So *don't* forget."

"Forget what?" he said, scowling.

She smiled. That little half smile. Her true smile. "Now you *do* have a secret."

TWENTY-SEVEN

W hy did he kill the albatross?"

Davidek was staring out the window. He didn't notice Mr. McClerk walk over and stand in front of him, holding his book open, and he didn't hear the English teacher's question until the second time he asked it. By then, the other kids in the class were already giggling.

"Mr. Davidek, why did he kill the bird?"

Davidek's mind was still in a Jeep underneath the Tarentum Bridge. He couldn't think of a thing to say except, "Who?"

Mr. McClerk snapped his book shut with one hand. "The protagonist in Coleridge's *Rime of the Ancient Mariner*. Did you read it this weekend?"

"Of course." He hadn't.

"Then please tell me why he killed the bird."

Davidek looked at Stein, who shrugged. He hadn't read it either. "Umm," Davidek said. "Because the bird was evil?"

Mr. McClerk removed his glasses and wiped his forehead with his jacket sleeve. "Mr. Davidek, I rarely say any interpretation of literature is flatly wrong—but that's a very, very *stupid* answer."

Davidek sucked on his top lip and stared at the desk. Across the room, Seven-Eighth's hand shot up. "He killed the bird because it was a Christ figure," she said. Davidek winced for not thinking of this. Everything was *always* a Christ figure with Mr. McClerk.

The English teacher confirmed this by triumphantly pointing his glasses at Seven-Eighths. "Yes, that's *one* answer. But is there something more to it? Something universal to all of us that would motivate self-destruction?" No one answered him, so he walked to the chalkboard and wrote: IMP OF THE PERVERSE.

"Mr. Davidek, do you remember this from our reading of Poe last fall?"

Davidek thought he had read that story, but right now he could remember only one thing, and it involved a yellow disposable camera. "Um, yeah," he said.

Mr. McClerk put his glasses on. "Then please remind us from our readings of 'The Black Cat' and 'The Tell-Tale Heart': What did Poe mean by the term 'Imp of the Perverse'?"

Davidek took a deep breath.

Stein was still laughing at lunch as he imitated Davidek's answer: "'Is it, like, *a perverted midget?*'" he said, falling against Lorelei, who was cracking up, too.

They were standing out in the parking lot, though Davidek had left his winter coat inside and was freezing in just his blazer. "I couldn't remember!" he said, opening his arms to the cold. "I thought the imp was maybe the dude who got buried under the floor."

March had struck the Valley, and the weather turned schizophrenic: sunny one day, freezing the next. The daffodils and tulips in the school's gardens were fooled. Lured by the spring sun, they popped their heads from the earth only to have them bitten off by frost.

When the day was warm, and students who hadn't left to eat off-campus gathered again in the parking lot, Stein and Lorelei stayed inside the basement cafeteria. When it was bitter cold, and everyone was huddled indoors, they bundled into their winter wear and lingered outside. Davidek hadn't told them about Hannah and the Jeep. He prayed to God no one ever found out about that, even his friends. Especially his friends.

It was getting harder for Davidek to hang around with Stein and Lorelei. Sometimes he felt lonelier with them than he did by himself. Even wrapped in their heavy coats, the couple couldn't keep their hands off each other. They were always leaning into one another or nudging each other or kind of still-dancing with his hands on her hips and her arms over his shoulders. The snow-frosted statue of the Virgin Mary looked down at them with her hands out, like, *What is this shit?* Davidek felt the same way.

Something moved in the window of one of the upstairs classrooms and Davidek looked up to see Mullen and Simms duck away from the glass.

Lorelei noticed them, too, but before Davidek could say anything, Lorelei exclaimed: "My hands are cold!" And she pressed them against Stein's cheeks.

"Now my cheeks are cold," Stein said, and Lorelei leaned in and kissed each one.

"Now tell her your crotch is cold!" Davidek joked, and Stein grabbed a chunk of ice off the Virgin Mary and tossed it at him. "Get outta here, you perverted midget. . . ."

"We have to be careful," Lorelei said. She wasn't allowed to have long telephone calls with boys, but after her mom went to sleep—or passed out—and her father sank into some late-night cable movies and a six-pack, she was able to sneak the cordless phone into her bedroom and call Stein. It was still a risk she didn't like taking. It amazed her that Stein's family didn't object to these midnight calls, but his father and sister had stopped even answering the phone when it rang that late. They knew it was for Noah. His secret girlfriend.

She would call him only a few times a week, though he wanted to talk every day, and sometimes rang her house against Lorelei's wishes, which made her mother suspicious. "It's just homework questions," Lorelei explained to her parents. "He's my study partner in Biology."

"Maybe I should call his mom and tell her he needs to start his homework earlier in the night," Miranda Paskal had threatened, and Lorelei derailed her anger by saying. "His mother is dead."

"Dead?" Lorelei's mom didn't like to be trumped in tragedy. "How'd that happen?"

"I don't know," Lorelei said, which was the truth.

Stein wasn't the world's greatest conversationalist in their late-night talks. Mostly he just told her how much he wished he was beside her in her bed instead of separated by miles of wire. God help Lorelei if her mother ever picked up the phone and heard a boy say something like that to her daughter.

"Being around you is the only time I can stand being around myself," Stein said. Lorelei didn't like hearing that—for a lot of reasons. But such flattery was nice in its way. The more time she spent pretending to like Stein, the more she actually did.

They still snuck away to make out during school, though that space outside along the rectory and convent hedges was now packed with snow. "Let's find somewhere warmer," she had suggested, and they began skipping class to find hideaways in St. Mike's many basement stairwells and corridors. Lorelei thought kissing Stein under false pretenses would be weird, but Stein was a great kisser—not pushy or slobbery, the way she imagined other boys to be. He was gentle, and careful—for a change.

Sometimes they'd just sit on the stairs facing each other, their legs tangled across the length of a step. He talked about strange things, like whether you could love someone without knowing the worst thing about them. Stein could be morose, but she saw it as typical teenage moodiness, and when it got too weird, she would just kiss him again and he'd be his old self.

Even when it was all over, she could never know for sure what she truly felt about Noah Stein. Lately, she wondered if the only ones she was fooling were Mullen and Simms.

Life at St. Michael's had finally become what she wanted. She had a boyfriend in Stein, and she also had a best friend—of sorts—in Davidek, someone she could confide in, who cared enough to rescue her from trouble. The other freshman girls no longer objected to her sitting at their table from time to time, and even Audra Banes and her other former acquaintances in the senior class no longer actively tried to attack her—she had, after all, been somewhat pitied when word began to spread that she'd gotten Asshole Face and Sandmouth as her seniors.

Maybe she could escape this trap she'd set up. Just tell Stein the truth, warn him what Mullen and Simms were planning, and he could protect her from whatever fallout came after.

· · ·

There was no way Lorelei's mother would let her go out on a date, but she was permitted to meet Stein at the Peoples Library in New Kensington—a long way for Stein's sister to drive, but walking distance for Lorelei. They were translating a passage of *Don Quixote* for International Day, which was coming up a week after Easter break. Freshmen, still struggling with the rudimentary aspects of their new language classes, were only required to write papers for the festival and bring a dish for the big potluck lunch. Davidek had been working on an essay about French bread, and methods for making it—further isolating him from the Español students Stein and Lorelei.

"I think this story is sad. He's so lost," Lorelei said as they copied passages from an English translation, getting just enough of it wrong in their papers to make it seem like they translated it themselves. Stein disagreed. "He's seeing what he wants to see . . . and it makes him happy. He's forgetting the bad stuff from his past."

"The bad stuff is what makes us who we are," she said.

Stein was quiet. "You really believe that?"

Lorelei looked up at him, smiling. "I don't know. . . . I was just talking."

There was something Stein wanted to tell her. He'd been waiting a long time to tell anybody. In the night-darkened picture windows of the library, his reflection spoke while hers listened, and neither one moved until he was finished.

Mullen and Simms had lost.

Defeat was familiar territory, so they saw it coming. Lorelei had been brushing them off for weeks as they pressed her for information, and they were powerless to change it. No one respected Asshole Face and Sandmouth, and when Lorelei began ignoring them, no one was surprised they couldn't even control a little freshman girl.

Richard Mullen's and Frank Simms's undistinguished careers at St. Michael the Archangel High School were fizzling to an inauspicious end. They'd be ejected with a diploma and the lowest possible grade-point average. No one would remember, except maybe that Mullen was the dude who got stabbed with a pen. Simms would just become whatsisname. If they truly wanted to humiliate Stein, maybe they should have thought through their plan a little more.

Now it was over. They knew it.

So just before Easter break, when Mullen and Simms heard their freshman "little sister" was looking for them, they knew what was coming. The Big Tell-Off, when even Lorelei Paskal, once one of the most helpless of all St. Mike's students, would instruct them to go and eat shit.

That night after Stein's confession in the library, Lorelei had parted with him on the street and whispered, "I love you," after kissing him good-bye. This time she meant it. Even later, she believed that though that made the rest only more unfathomable, even to her.

Lorelei asked around for Mullen and Simms, but got only shrugs. Between classes, she passed silently through the crowded hallways of chattering students—searching. No one spoke to her, but that was okay. Maybe that would change.

When she found them by the vending machines, they were ready for the end.

What she actually said, she said freely. Unforced. Unafraid. Aware. If the motive baffled her, maybe she didn't want to know the real reason. Easier to believe it simply made no sense.

Lorelei told them, "Would you like to know how he *really* got that scar on his face? . . ."

PART V

La Verdad y Nada

TWENTY-EIGHT

Sister Maria stood at the podium on the Palisade Hall bingo stage and announced to the assembled students: "*Buenos dias. Bonjour. Wilkommen.* And—*welcome*—to St. Michael's International Day!"

There was mild applause, and then the hundreds of kids sitting in their school uniforms ignored the rest of her speech about what a long-standing tradition this event was at St. Mike's, blah, blah, blah. They just wanted the free food.

Freshmen had already turned in their papers. Davidek got a C+ on French bread; Lorelei and Stein fared an A- on their plagiarized *Don Quixote* passages. The day's festivities belonged to the upperclassmen, and each class had separate duties.

Everyone brought some kind of dish, but the sophomores supplied the main courses for the afternoon-long festival. LeRose bragged to everybody who would listen that he pumped intestine-scorching levels of Vietnamese hot pepper juice into his chimichangas. "Give 'em a try, man. You'll shit a jet of blue flame!" But that was a bad sales pitch. His ripening little prank coagulated untouched at the end of the long buffet, while the students devoured crepes and baguettes from the French classes, sauerkraut and weiners from the German students, and a dump truck of spaghetti cooked by the handful of seniors participating in a special college-level Latin course.

Juniors were responsible for decorating Palisade Hall, mostly poster-board displays with facts about French impressionist painting or Germany's autobahn freeway, but there were always a few enterprising kids who tried to build miniature Spanish galleons out of Legos or a Popsicle-stick Eiffel Tower.

The seniors supplied the entertainment by writing, directing, and acting out skits on the auditorium stage, with most of the dialogue panto-mimed so that everyone could understand the foreign-language action. In between the little plays were some song-and-dance numbers. The French class *always* lip-synched to an old record—"Aux Champs-Élysées"—while twirling parasols, and the teachers always acted surprised when the students would pull them up onstage to dance with them.

The day had an unusual sense of joy about it. Davidek laughed along with some seniors when they saw Mr. Mankowski enter the proceedings dressed in the puffy white shirt and emerald green leiderhosen of an Okto-berfest dancer—and Mankowski laughed along with them, giving his be-socked legs a twist and a tap for their amusement, in on the joke for once.

Zari floated around the periphery, snapping pictures for the year-book—a duty she had been pressed into by her mentors, the Groughs, who gave her specific instructions of whom *not* to photograph. She didn't care, and just shot whatever she wanted.

Hannah Kraut was one of the French students, and before the "Aux Champs-Élysées" number, she sat on one end of the stage with her feet dangling over the side, her downy blue cancan skirt drooping like a giant predatory flower choking on a pair of legs. She saw Davidek and winked at him. "Hey, Playgirl," she said, making him look away.

"Come on, Stein, let's go sit in the back," Davidek said, weaving through the crowd.

"I need to find Lorelei first . . . ," Stein told him.

He spotted her in the corridor leading backstage, where the Spanish seniors were gathering for their performance. She seemed to be arguing with Mullen, who was holding a giant piñata shaped like an airplane.

"If that guy is giving her shit, I'll bust that piñata right over his fucking face," Stein said, and Davidek held him back as Lorelei pushed through the crowd toward them. "I'm not feeling well. Can you take me upstairs?"

"What's wrong?" Stein asked.

She shook her head, frustrated, as if he wasn't listening. "I don't *feel* well. Will you please take me upstairs?"

"Sure, sure thing . . ."

But Ms. Bromine had been watching them and stepped forward as Lorelei's hand slipped into Stein's. "No touching on school grounds!" Bromine barked.

"She's sick," Stein said. "I'm taking her up—"

"Are you the school nurse now?" Bromine said. "I'll take care of it."

Davidek put a hand on Stein's shoulder. "Come on, man."

Bromine smacked his fingers, a little hard. "No touching, Mr. Davidek," she said as she led Lorelei away.

The Spanish teacher, Mrs. Tunns, was bitter over having to once again follow Sister Antonia's terrible dance number, and hurried the French students offstage as she scowled at the slow-moving Spanish students hauling their props. This year's Spanish show was whipped together at the last minute, and she was worried it would be a mess. She had wanted a translation of Hamlet's "Murder of Gonzago" scene, but some of her lowest-watt students, Mullen and his pal Simms, had persuaded the other kids to do a stupid, slapsticky public service skit instead.

The stage was set to look like a room with a table and chairs and a bed. On one chair, they placed a bulging white sack with an oversized plastic nozzle affixed to the end. PEGAMENTO LOCO, its label read in fat, hand-drawn letters.

"What's that mean?" Davidek asked, peering around heads from where they sat in the middle of the audience.

"Uh . . . *loco* means 'crazy.' I don't know what the other word means," Stein said.

"I think it means 'glue.' It's Krazy Glue," LeRose spoke up from the row behind them.

"Ha, ha," Davidek said flatly. "Hi-larious."

The Spanish teacher took the microphone at center stage and ran a

hand across her goatish head to smooth any loose hairs. "St. Michael's senior Spanish students would like to present: a public service announce-
ment. *Parada, Gota y Rodillo* or, in English: 'Stop, Drop, and Roll.' The skit
will be performed with an English translation."

As Mrs. Tunns walked off, the actors marched into formation onstage,
led by a girl in a shawl who wore an enormous brown wig that looked like
a lot of small animals sewn together. Behind her came the infamous and
revolting Mark Carney, one of those scumbag types who rarely bathed and
thought pulling down his pants to light farts at parties was a good way to
impress girls. Now he stood before the whole school, sucking his thumb
and stretching the life out of a pair of Winnie-the-Pooh footie pajamas. He
waggled his tongue at the audience as he bent over, pointing at his ass, and
asked, "Where's the hatch on this thing? I gotta poop!" which drew furious
laughter from the crowd, but made Mrs. Tunns jab a finger at him from the
wings of the stage and snap "Non *español!*"

"It's weird," Davidek said. "The seniors are up onstage doing the kind of
dumb stuff we're all terrified of at the Hazing Picnic. And they love it."

Stein shrugged. "It's different when you choose to be the idiot."

The show's translators walked out to the podium: Asshole Face Mullen
and a stout, disgruntled-looking girl named Beth Bartolski, each wearing a
birthday sombrero from Chi-Chi's restaurant. Beside them, Carney's little-
boy character plopped down on a pillow and pulled a blanket over himself.
"*¡Mamasita! ¡Mamasita!*" he called out to the actress with the critter wig
and shawl, who sat beside him, knitting.

"Mommy. Mommy," Mullen translated from the podium, a satisfied
smile on his lips as he faced the audience.

"*¿Sí, mi hijo?*" the girl playing the mother responded.

"Yes, my son," Beth Bartolski translated in monotone.

Carney wobbled forward on his knees—his way of playing a little kid.
"*No soy sonoliento,*" he said.

"It is bedtime, but I'm not sleepy," Mullen echoed in English.

*You have too much energy. You must be in bed before your father returns
home,* the mama said, and the little boy began to wail and throw himself
around the stage in a comical fit. "*¡Déjeme acabar mi piñata!*" the boy
shouted. *I want to finish building my piñata!*

The girl playing the mother pretended to look to the audience for parenting advice. "Let him play!" a girl shouted, followed by a round of applause. "Spank him!" another voice yelled, this time to bigger applause.

"This is kind of hilarious," Davidek whispered over his shoulder to LeRose, who nodded enthusiastically. Davidek elbowed a smile out of Stein, who was sitting quietly. "Yeah, it's funny," Stein agreed.

Onstage, the mother agreed to let the boy finish his airplane piñata, and Carney's bizarre man-child grabbed the gigantic, fake tube of glue and held it over his head triumphantly as the crowd cheered. The mother warned him in Spanish: *Be careful! That glue is very flammable and very dangerous.*

Then, as Carney continued to cavort with the glue and piñata, the girl playing the mother laid herself down on the make-believe bed and closed her eyes. *Oh, I am so tired from caring for this little monster!* she said

Carney stage-whispered to the crowd: *This piñata needs more glue!*

Then he huffed, and puffed, and squeezed the cardboard bottle until his face turned crimson, the whole time barking: *"¡Más pegamento!"* The audience began to chant it along with him. *More glue! More glue!*

But the little boy was out of glue. *"¡No más! No más!"* he cried, and began hunting around the stage for more, opening the drawer of a dresser and finding a cartoonishly large book of matches made out of cardboard and red construction paper.

Carney made his mouth into a devilish little *o* and flashed his eyebrows at the hooting audience, who cheered as he raised one of the big matches into the air and swiped it across the floor, touching it to the imaginary trail of flammable glue.

A rush of wind threw a flurry of orange and red plastic shreds into the air. It was a neat special effect for fire—designed by Simms—made from a window fan filled with red confetti and hidden behind the bed.

Carney backed away on his knees as two students dressed in orange jumpsuits draped in red, yellow, and orange ribbons leaped onstage toward him. "Raarrh!" one of them said, throwing a fistful of red confetti at Carney, who slapped both hands to his face and vented a howl of distress. "Oh, no!" Mullen translated, his glimmering eyes scanning the audience. "The glue is on my face! I am burning!"

"¡Fuego! ¡Fuego!" the flame-people cackled as they shoved the boy back and forth. Just then, a siren wailed, and boys and girls dressed as firefighters rushed onstage, throwing buckets of blue confetti to simulate water. They scooped up the boy to rescue him, but he reached back, crying: "¡Mamasita! ¡Mamasita!"

The mother awoke from her slumber just in time for the students playing the fire-folk to attack her. "¡Estoy muriendo! ¡Donde está usted, mi hijo!" she cried.

"I am dying," Beth Bartolski translated tonelessly. "Where are you, my son! Why? Why!"

The firefighters began a clumsily choreographed kung fu fight with the flame-people, and it all ended with the spray of an actual fire extinguisher, burying the stage in a low-floating white cloud. When the air cleared, the flame characters were heaped atop one another, groaning like comic-strip thugs who'd had their lights knocked out.

Carney's little-boy character sat on the edge of the stage, rubbing his eyes and sobbing melodramatically. Half his face was now painted with red marker to indicate burns. A firefighter girl walked up to him carrying a plastic, glow-in-the-dark Halloween skeleton. "Your mamasita es muerta!" she declared, waving the skeleton mournfully at the son, who hugged it and cried out "BOO HOO! BOO HOO!" as the firefighters shook their heads. (Inexplicably, the skeleton had a rubber snake slithering out of one eye socket.)

Let this be a reminder to everyone . . . , Mullen translated as all the actors onstage said in unison: "¡No juegan con el fuego, o usted será quemado!"

"Do not play with fire, or you will be burned!"

The Spanish stars took turns bowing before the whooping crowd. Carney even brought out the skeleton with him for a curtsy. Davidek looked at Stein—who wasn't applauding, who wasn't doing anything except sitting still and staring at the stage with blank eyes. At the foot of the stage, a relieved Mrs. Tunns was congratulating Mullen and Simms for authoring the show, proud for once that her two worst slackers had accomplished something worthwhile.

Stein stood from his seat, not hearing anything around him—certainly not Davidek saying his name again and again.

He brushed through the crowd, moving up the aisle. Davidek tried to follow, but Stein went too fast, shoving people as he began to walk faster and faster.

Mullen and Simms whispered at each other, grinning as they peered through the audience. By the time they saw Stein he was already upon them. "Bring back some memories, you fucking firebug?" Mullen asked. Simms was even less delicate: "So when they found your mama, was she Extra Crispy or Original Recipe?"

Stein smashed his fist into Simm's tombstone buck teeth, staggering the senior back against Mrs. Tunns, toppling both of them over. Mullen flailed his hands in front of his face, so Stein launched a foot into his balls instead, dropping him to his knees, where he kicked him in the center of his chest. Mrs. Tunns was crawling out from under a howling Simms, whose green teeth were dripping red, when Mullen fell on her, too. "For chrissakes, stop him!" Mrs. Tunns shrieked as the closest students, teachers, and even a few parents who had come to help out for the day snapped out of their paralysis in unison.

Stein loomed over the fallen seniors, his shoulders squared against the panels of the hall's cheap dropped ceiling, heaving breath, hungry for more. Blurred figures rose behind him, pressing forward as if through heavy water. The freshman did not turn toward them and did not resist as they struck, their arms blossoming around his body, swallowing him, dragging him down.

TWENTY-NINE

Lorelei heard the International Day performances unspool from the secretary's office—the raucous French music, the tepid applause, the muffled foreign babble and laughter rising up through the hardened arteries of St. Mike's basement corridors to its sunny front office.

After she had feigned illness downstairs, Ms. Bromine dragged her up to sit on the couch beside the school secretary, Mrs. Corde, a tall, boxy woman with carrot-colored hair, who typed with only her index fingers, jabbing them down against each key like someone playing a miniature game of Whac-A-Mole.

Bromine left the door open when she departed, and the sounds of International Day continued wafting up from the basement. Lorelei picked up on Mrs. Tunns's muffled introduction to the Spanish performance and strained to hear, then strained not to. She heard applause when the Spanish program ended, and there was a brief moment of silence.

Then—an eruption.

Mrs. Corde perked up from her typewriter like a woodland creature detecting distant danger. She turned to Lorelei, as if to verify the commotion, and the sound grew louder, drawing closer, a thunder of movement. "Is that part of the show?" the secretary asked.

Lorelei's lifelessness evaporated. She sprang from her seat as twin doors banged open in the hallway and what sounded like a beast made of many bodies thundered against a row of lockers. Feet scuffled and squeaked on the tile, and voices shouted desperate, contradictory instructions as the rumble dragged nearer.

Lorelei closed the door of the office and pressed her finger against the brass button in the center of the knob, but the click of the lock felt useless as backs and arms and faces slammed up against the narrow window of the door, like bodies swirling in floodwaters. Mr. Mankowski was orbiting the melee in his ridiculous lederhosen and bright green cap, barking orders at the uniformed boys, all grappling with one struggling figure: Noah Stein, with at least three boys on each arm, pulling them out straight as his flushed neck strained like a clutch of cherry licorice whips, ready to snap.

Stein finally saw Lorelei when his attackers shoved him against the office door. His eyes held her, deep pools of questioning grief, crisscrossed by the wires embedded in the glass. Then they slipped shut and stayed that way, as if to preserve an image of her that would escape if he opened them again.

The Lorelei he knew was a ghost, fading in and out of view. Just on the other side of a door, but gone from him forever. His racing mind made a bargain with the universe: Return the girl he knew he loved and he would forfeit every kiss, every touch, every word, every sight of her. Take her from him, but just let her exist somewhere, and not only have been a dirty trick.

Lorelei's fingertips brushed the doorknob, but Mrs. Corde grabbed her arm. "Are you crazy? Don't let him in! We're *safe* in here."

When Stein's eyes opened again, Lorelei was backing away, staring at him—hard—ready to absorb whatever hatred he could spew at her, but she exuded no pity, no remorse, and he was stilled by it. He opened his mouth to say her name, but couldn't.

As he was pulled away, the stranger who looked like Lorelei grew small in the window, and Stein closed his eyes again, still trying to preserve the fleeting remnants of that girl from the first day of school, the one with the cockeyed bangs, crooked eyebrows, and big, busted-up heart, which he thought would fit so perfectly with what was left of his.

. . .

Father Mercedes's mouth kept twisting as Sister Maria tried to explain what had happened—again. The priest raised a finger to her. "Enough," he said. "I've heard enough."

He opened the door to the chemistry lab and peered inside. Mullen sat at one corner of the room, and Simms sat at the other. Both boys looked scared, and Simms flashed his icky smile at the priest, who responded by closing the door again. Across the hall in the Spanish classroom, Stein sat at a desk with his head slumped in the nest of his folded arms. One eye, shot with red veins, opened when the priest cleared his throat.

Father Mercedes drew back into the hallway and closed the door, then stared expectantly at the nun. "So he's a matricidal little firebug, eh? I'm sure the parish council will be thrilled."

"What happened was an accident, but—the basics are true. I just spoke with his father," Sister Maria said.

"I guess it was coincidence that these two characters decided to make a mockery out of that sad old story?" the priest said, waving an unlit cigarette like a magic wand toward the room with Mullen and Simms.

"They have a . . . *belligerent* history with the boy," Sister Maria said. "We think the girl tipped them off. They're her freshman mentors, and it's possible they threatened her. Or perhaps she had a falling out with the boy. . . ."

"And *she* says . . . ?"

"She hasn't spoken a word."

The priest scratched at his face. "You can't make a fifteen-year-old girl answer your questions?" When the nun didn't respond, he tucked the cigarette between his lips and lit it. "Another very nice mess, Sister . . . very nice. Now, how do you plan to handle this soap opera?"

"Detention all around. A week of suspension for the Stein boy. What they did was awful, but he turned violent."

The priest snorted at her, smoke rising from his thin, disbelieving smile.

Sister Maria said defensively: "And they're getting a D-minus for the theater project."

Father Mercedes pinched the bridge of his nose as the cigarette ember glowed. "The St. Mike's community will be glad to hear their punishment was the lowest possible passing grade. Another solid reason to keep this illustrious institution going."

"Schools have fights, Father. There are a lot of decent kids in this school, and they had nothing to do w—"

"And they *suffer*, Sister," the priest said, walking away from her. "While you make excuses for the worst of them."

It was dark by the time Stein returned home. Picking him up at school, Larry Stein accepted apologies from the parents of the two other boys, who had been waiting for him to arrive. Stein had been told to apologize to Mullen and Simms in return, but refused, no matter how much threatening and coaxing his father and the principal directed at him.

Margie's dinner was sitting out for them, cold, when they got to the house. Stein's father didn't yell or ask any questions. Margie did, at first hammering her little brother with the usual variations on "Why?" Then her dad took her out onto the porch and closed the door. Their muffled voices rose and fell as Stein sat silently at the kitchen table. He couldn't make out what they were saying, but wasn't trying. Margie cried for a little while. When they came back inside, his sister reheated dinner, and they ate in silence.

"I'm sorry," Noah Stein said in a small voice.

Margie set down her silverware but didn't look up as she chewed. His father did the same, then asked: "For which part?"

"I don't know," the boy told him.

Margie stood from the table, carried her dish to the sink, then walked down the hallway to her room and closed the door.

Stein's father was quiet again, searching for reassuring words, and found none. All he could think was his wife's name: *Daphne . . . Daphne.*

There was no desire for vengefulness in Larry Stein over the accident his son had caused. But in those years after, when his son was still just a little boy and the nightmares would come, followed by loud tears in the night, he often didn't rush to comfort the boy. A part of him wanted his son to never entirely lose the pain he had caused. That little voice bit into Larry's mind, buried deep, but still alive. He even had a name for that feeling, a line he'd heard in a song once—*the rabid child.* It felt like a part of him that was not adult, not rational.

Now their tragic family history had been rediscovered, six years later, and it brought forth that same old feeling. Unforgiving. Animal. Hateful.

Larry and Daphne had never spent more than four years in any one part of the country. They started their romance as nineteen-year-old dropouts in San Antonio, moved on to Seattle for a few years, then began zigzagging America: Tucson, Aspen, Galveston, Boston, Los Angeles . . .

Moving away was merely running away, a distraction from Daphne's restless mind, which tended to spin out of control, ruminating on phantoms. The doctors had called it "the baby blues" after Margie was born, but the spells only deepened as the years passed. When Noah was born, it seemed to stabilize Daphne. Around her baby boy, she was often her old self, bright and passionate, quick-tempered and tough, and almost pathologically energized. But by the time they settled in Florida, her anxieties had returned, more ferocious than ever, the fears more acute and irrational. Larry seldom held a job with medical benefits, so doctors, hospitals, and medication were only last resorts. Her moods spiked and fell so rapidly that Larry was never sure which version of his wife he'd come home to. Often he tried not to come home at all.

That's how it was the night she died. With the teenage Margie away at a friend's house, neighbors had heard the nine-year-old boy screaming from the smoke-filled apartment. They broke in and dragged him free. But not his wife. They never even heard her, or knew she was there. Larry wasn't surprised. Daphne's mood had been bleak that morning, and he left her two sedatives on the kitchen counter (the others he kept with him). But those two pills were enough to knock her into a deep sleep. When the fire his son set while fucking around with model airplane glue finally overtook her, Daphne probably never knew it. That's what her husband hoped, anyway.

The fire marshal and police had expressed pity over the child's carelessness. It didn't happen a lot, but it did happen—a child sets a fire and ends up accidentally killing a family member. Since he was so young, Noah was not detained in a jail, but the courts ordered psychological counseling and medication, which Larry couldn't afford indefinitely. If that meant the boy's emotions sometimes punished him, well . . . maybe that wasn't the worst thing.

But that was the rabid child talking.

Late at night, Larry sometimes sat alone in his locked room, the brass lid of his wife's urn by his side as he sifted the gray powder through his fingers. It was sand, really, not even dust. *Heavy*. He found out later that the remains from a cremation aren't even ashes, but the pulverized bits of bone that were left over. It was, simply, the only thing the fire didn't want.

Larry thought of that as he sat at the kitchen table, the boy's apology for everything and nothing hanging in the silence. He stood and stacked his plate on Margie's in the sink, then kissed his son on the head, brushing the burned side of his face with his thumb. "Sweet dreams, kiddo," his father said, and tried to ignore the part of him that wished otherwise.

THIRTY

Lorelei's body was facedown beneath the kitchen table. A chair was knocked over beside her, and beyond that was the dead socket of a shattered twelve-inch television set, lying upside down near the basement door with a small lightning storm flickering deep inside its electrical guts.

A tang of smoke had risen up to the ceiling, but no one was standing to breathe it. Soon it would trigger a brief squawk from the kitchen smoke detector, and the shrill digital siren would open Lorelei's eyes.

A streak of spaghetti sauce bled down one wall. A dozen small bottles—paprika, thyme, coriander, cayenne—were scattered along the linoleum amid a battlefield of shattered balsawood from a now-obliterated spice rack Lorelei had made in summer camp four years ago. The remains of a flat, yellow telephone handset dangled over the back of one chair with a miniature speaker hanging out of its cracked mouthpiece like a detached eyeball.

The water faucet in the sink gushed a steady crystal stream down the drain, unattended.

Lorelei tried to stand, but something heavy on her back broadcast shriveling pain up her spine. She reached back and felt the spot, trying to knock the weight off, but the heaviness was beneath her skin—a thick rectangular welt. Three of them, actually—each in the shape of that flat telephone handset. It took her a long time to push herself up.

Lorelei hadn't seen Stein after the International Day fiasco. He and Mullen and Simms were sequestered in other rooms, and she left without being part of the big, forced apology when no one could prove what her involvement was. "I don't know," was all she said when they asked her why. She wondered what she'd say if Stein ever asked her.

Her father jiggled his knee as he drove her home. He pressed a knuckle against his lips and shifted his eyes everywhere but at her—twitchy as a junkie missing his fix. "How could you do this, Lorelei?" he asked. "To yourself . . . to me . . . How could you be so stupid?"

Lorelei looked straight at her father, who kept his thin, unshaven face aimed at the road. "We don't have to tell her, you know. You could ground me. Take away TV for a month. A year. Whatever. She doesn't have to know anything. We don't have to involve her."

Her father's defeated eyes sagged with pity, but he still wouldn't look at her. "Who do you think answered the phone when they called the house?" he asked.

When they got home, Lorelei's father hurried into the kitchen. It was already five thirty and he was late getting dinner started.

Lorelei dropped her bag into the corner by the front door. The back of her mother's head was in the center of the couch, a nest of fading orange hair that had once come out of a box labeled RED PENNY. On the television, a silver-bearded attorney was wagging his finger and vowing that if you're injured in an auto accident, he charges NO FEE unless he gets money for *you*. Miranda Paskal's prosthetic hand rose from the couch with a smoldering cigarette in its chrome claw. She dragged in a cloud of smoke, then exhaled it as the clasp lowered again.

"How was school today?" her mother's voice asked.

"Um, fine," Lorelei said, and followed her father into the kitchen.

It took a few minutes, but her mother eventually rose from the couch and appeared in the kitchen after her, dragging one last time on her cigarette before releasing it from the clasp into the sink, where it died with a hiss. In her other hand, the flesh-and-blood one, she carried a giant, sweating *Who*

Framed Roger Rabbit plastic cup from McDonald's—full of ice and Captain Morgan. "Don't give me that 'fine' bullshit," her mother said, blocking out the kitchen light as she loomed over her daughter. "Explain the trouble you caused at that school today."

Lorelei began to babble. She said the altercation was nothing, a misunderstanding, not her fault. A kid at school, some guy . . . he flipped out. He was mad at her.

When she finished, the water on the stove was boiling. Her father dropped in a fat clutch of spaghetti sticks.

"I spoke with a lovely woman from the school—Ms. Bromine, the guidance counselor there," said Lorelei's mother, scratching at her scalp. She set the Roger Rabbit cup on the kitchen table. "We figured out that this boy is the one you've been claiming is your 'study partner.'" She made air quotes with both her fingers and the clasp. "Other students saw you and this boy sneaking away together. Even during school. Skipping class." She clucked her tongue and turned to her husband. "Do you think they were sneaking away to *study*, Tom?"

Tom Paskal was tying the strings of an apron behind his back. "I'd toast some garlic bread, but we're out of bread," he said. Beside him, the untended spaghetti sauce was sputtering in its pan, polka-dotting the white stovetop around the pot.

Lorelei's mother lumbered into her daughter's face, inching her backwards. "Ms. Bromine raised some very good questions: Why am I paying *thousands* of dollars in tuition so my daughter can spend each day slutting around with *some delinquent little shit* in her class?"

"I wasn't, Mom. . . . Jesus."

"And why is my daughter sneaking around with two *other*, even *older* lowlifes at the same time? What exactly did my daughter *do* that made all three of these degenerates decide to go to war over her?"

"Mom, that's not—"

Lorelei's mother grabbed her by the front of her blouse. "Don't *lie* to me. I've lost *everything* . . . had so much *taken away*. . . . And you just *keep taking*, Lorelei. . . ." Tears began to trickle from her rheumy eyes as she jabbed her clasp in the flinching girl's face to punctuate her words. "You are killing me . . . *killing* me, Lorelei. And it's a *joke* to you."

Lorelei pushed away from her mother. "Actually, it's the chain-smoking and the Big Gulps full of booze that are killing you, Mom," she said. "*I'm just the one you take it out on.*"

At first, Lorelei's mother didn't react at all. Then she smashed her daughter across the face with her prosthetic arm.

The teenager fell back against the kitchen table, spilling the plastic Roger Rabbit tumbler full of booze across a stack of unopened PAST DUE mail. Miranda fell on top of her daughter, hooking Lorelei's cheek with the blunt steel clasp, pulling her down like a hooked fish as the girl mewled. "I thought you learned a lesson when I caught you stealing my cigarettes, but you're not a very good learner, are you?"

Lorelei's father dropped his wooden spoon on the floor and began pulling at his wife, like a small dog trying to hump a hippo. "Stop it, Lorelei!" he was yelling, as if his daughter were in control of this. "Stop it right now!"

"You're *still* stealing from me, *begging* me to send you to that school. Spending *my* money—so you can *whore* yourself out . . . ," her mother hissed.

Lorelei began to cry. The chrome hook pulled back her cheek, exposing a skeletal amount of teeth.

"That teacher knows . . . ," her mother's chapped lips said, hovering over Lorelei's eyes. "Everybody *knows* what kind of girl you are now. . . . What you *do* with those boys you rut with. And you want to keep *lying*? . . ."

"I'm *not* . . ." The girl drooled, pinching her eyes shut against the tears, hands hovering delicately around her mother's prosthetic, desperate to pull it away, but afraid that might take part of her jaw with it.

Miranda Paskal yanked up her daughter's skirt with her hand, fingers grasping at the elastic band of the girl's underwear. "Let's prove it, then," her mother said, pluming sour drunken breath into the girl's face. "Let's see if you're lying. Let's see if you're *intact*. . . . Then we'll know what these boys took . . . or what you gave away."

Lorelei's stretched-out mouth moaned as she forced the clasp out of her mouth, and donkey-kicked her mother across the room.

Miranda sprawled backwards against her husband, who slammed into the open pantry door, crushing the spice rack as little bottles clattered around them like an overturned chess set. Lorelei's mother lurched forward as a cylinder of paprika shot out from under one foot, dropping her to the floor as her prosthetic slashed for support against the counter, yanking down her small portable television, which exploded on the floor in a belch of glass.

Lorelei sat up, gasping. Her eyes darted around the room—She lunged for the telephone, crying, and got to 9 and 1 before her mother yanked the drooping, curly pig's-tail cord and the phone vanished from her hands like a magic trick.

Her father had backed against the sink, knocking the faucet on. "Go!" he said, jabbing a finger toward the living room. "Now!" He was about to do the same.

Lorelei turned to run, but her mother was already staggering to her feet, swinging the fallen phone like a mace. For a moment, the flat banana handset was weightless, spinning in the air below the tiny sun of the kitchen light. Then it was shattering against the back of Lorelei's head.

As she collapsed against the stove, her shoulder struck the saucepan handle, catapulting a streak of marinara against the floral wallpaper. She slid to the floor, legs splayed, too blinded by splinters of white light from the back of her head to feel the scorching flecks of sauce on her shoulder and neck. Her mother swung the cracked receiver down onto her back three more times, each one a heavy *whap!* Lorelei's arms pulled her beneath the shelter of the table, and the last thing she saw before passing out was the phone hitting the corner of a chair and disintegrating into a knot of multicolored wires and bits of plastic.

Then the world faded to a blur.

Lorelei didn't know how long she was sprawled beneath the table. Maybe minutes. Maybe hours. When she opened her eyes, the room was still, except for the gushing water faucet.

The kitchen door was open to the night, and her father was nowhere in the house. Lorelei turned the burners off on the stove and went upstairs.

She found her mother passed out on the floor beside her bed, a stain of saliva and blood from her cut lip seeping into the tattered carpet. Lorelei tried to lift her, but couldn't. She unclasped the battered prosthetic from her mother's forearm, like she was unholstering a gun that might still go off, and tucked it beside the sleeping woman like a teddy bear. When her mother woke, she hated to have to search for her arm.

Then Lorelei pulled a blanket from the bed and draped it over her mother, tucking it in around her feet, which were stained on the bottoms with tomato sauce.

Downstairs again, Lorelei walked to the long cupboard by the basement and took out a broom and dustpan. She bent over to begin sweeping up the mess, careful not to let the pain in her battered back show on her face, even though no one was there to notice.

THIRTY-ONE

Stein returned to St. Mike's on a stormy Monday.

His week of suspension passed in silence. Stein spent a lot of that time in the basement, tinkering with his father's old weight set, or sitting in his room with the lights off. Whenever his father or sister would look in to check on him, he pretended like he was sleeping.

On the morning he returned, Noah awoke to a heavy gray rain smattering his window, as if trying to scratch inside. His father sang along to the radio as they drove toward St. Mike's, some idiotic tune about a guy who was too sexy for this or that. "*I'm* . . . too sexy for this coat . . . too sexy for a boat . . . too sexy for my dog . . . too sexy on a log . . ." He nudged his son's leg, trying to make him laugh. "It's kind of like Dr. Suess, isn't it?" But Noah Stein just stared ahead silently, clutching his book bag in his lap.

As they rolled into the school parking lot, the truck's brakes groaned to a stop and the windshield wipers worked triple-time to slap away the downpour. "Try to have a good day," he told his son. It seemed like he should say something more. Noah looked at the dashboard a long time, and then at his father. "You're a good dad," he said, and kissed him on the cheek.

The storm had dragged darkness back into the early morning as great clouds of purple and black spun overhead, dumping waves of white rain

across the earth. Thin waterfalls cascaded down the brick face of the
school, rippling over the windows.

As he drove out of the parking lot, Larry Stein looked back at his son,
walking alone toward the school's front entrance. That night, Larry Stein
would fall on his knees, sobbing, bathed in the sterile glow of the Allegheny
Valley Hospital lobby, and hug Margie's knees as he thought back to that
moment with Noah in the rearview mirror as a last, lost chance to save
him.

As Stein approached St. Mike's, a dark shape lurked under the eave beside
the school's front doors.

It was Davidek, coatless, with his hands jammed under his arms for
warmth, his white shirt dampened by the splashing rain and his shoes
squishy with water as he stepped forward and grabbed Stein's arm. "Come
on. Let's get out of here," Davidek said.

Stein didn't move. "You're out of uniform, Davidek," he said, smiling
faintly. "Don't you know enough to come in out of the rain?"

Davidek wasn't playing along with the big-brother act. He kicked at the
fractal swirls of oil on the wet asphalt because he couldn't quite look his
friend in the face. "You can't go inside, Stein," he said. "They're . . . waiting for you."

"Mullen and Simms?" Stein asked.

"And everybody else, too," Davidek said, pulling at his friend's arm
again. Something solid shifted in Stein's book bag.

"What about Lorelei? She okay?"

Davidek was slack-jawed, shaking his head. "Who gives a *fuck* about her,
dumb-ass? She's the *cause* of this!"

"Is she here today?" Stein asked hopefully.

Davidek paced through the rain. "You know what? . . . No, she's not!!
She hasn't been here since . . . since . . . fucking . . . ! *Fuck!*" He ran both
hands through his dripping hair. "Just listen to me this *one time*. We're
skipping school today."

Stein lifted his eyes toward the shimmering glow of St. Mike's waterfall
windows. When he looked down again, his face dripped with rivulets of
water. "I can't run away," he said. "Anyway, there's nowhere else to go."

"We can go to the bowling alley over at the mall, for Christ's sake," Davidek told him. "Who cares? We'll spend the day in the Dollar Store eating candy from two Halloweens ago."

Stein put a hand on the brass handle of the door. "And what about to-morrow?" he asked. "Transfer to Highlands? I already got kicked out of there. Should my dad move us to a new town? And what happens when they find out there?"

A golden light from inside spread across Davidek's face as the door opened. "I've lived with this thing a long time," Stein said. "But after today, I won't have to anymore."

A warm gust of dry air inhaled Stein, and Davidek lingered in the cold morning darkness. "Fuck," he said to no one, and followed his friend in-side.

Stein hung his head as he pushed through the hall, and Davidek caught up close behind, glowering at the onlookers as they whispered to each other, watching the boy who had once set a fire that took his own mother's life.

In the north staircase, crowds of students were flowing down in gleeful alarm as a red, sandy fluid coursed down the walls from three stories up. Davidek's shoulder brushed the side and came away sticky with decompos-ing brick. "The leaks are getting worse. It wasn't this bad when I went out-side," he said.

The lights flickered off as they pushed their way up the murky stairwell against the crush of descending students. Another freshman, a harmless moonfaced boy named Justin Teemo, slammed into Stein, nearly knocking him backwards. He had been pushed by Morti and the Fanboys. "Look at the face of the guy who hit you!" Morti cackled, but Teemo hurried away with a hand up to his cheek, as if he didn't want Stein to recognize him.

When the lights flickered back on, another figure had appeared behind Davidek and Stein—Smitty, who stopped when they stopped, and started moving again when they did.

Davidek had seen him earlier with Hannah down near the boys' bath-rooms, talking in the awkward, icy way Davidek had seen them conversing at the Valentine's Dance. Smitty hadn't looked happy to be cornered by Hannah. But then, no one ever did.

"You in on this, too?" Davidek snapped at him. He could hear whispers passing up the jammed stairwell: *Here . . . Stein . . . He's here. . . .*

Mark Henson, a skinny freshman who never had much to do with Davidek and Stein, was standing just ahead of them, looking like he was ready to pee his pants. There was a thick streak of red lipstick on his cheek, and two juniors—John "Turkey Baster" Hannidy and his snarling girlfriend, Janey Brucedik—grabbed the quavering Henson by the shoulders and spun him to face Stein, so the big red check on his cheek would be clear.

The lights flickered again briefly. Almost all the faces around them had that thick, red ink mark on their cheeks. The ones who didn't were passing red markers back and forth, hurriedly streaking their faces with the mock scars. The gasoline smell of Sharpie markers wafted through the stifling humidity of the stairwell.

Stein looked from face to face in the hallway ahead—everyone was smiling, or laughing. Davidek was still behind him, getting angry and pushing people away, telling them to fuck off, and launching his shoulder at them to clear a path of escape.

"Do you know what your mother would say if she were here today?" a voice boomed from overhead. Davidek looked up to see a group of snickering sophomores.

"Sssssssss . . . ," came the hissing answer from every face around them, momentarily drowning the sound of pouring water. A lot of kids started jiggling their bodies, like bacon in a frying pan.

SSssssss! SSSSSsssss!!!

Davidek surged higher on the stairs, pulling Stein, whose eyes looked at nothing, whose voice was flat, and hollow. "Where did you say they were?" Stein asked.

"Who?" Davidek demanded.

"Mullen and Simms."

Davidek shook his head. "I'm not looking for *them*, Stein. I'm trying to find some fucking teachers!"

They discovered them all on the third floor—panicking.

Iciness seeped into Davidek's feet as he and Stein reached the third floor. An inch of crimson-colored water was coursing around their shoes.

"Downstairs!" Bromine snapped at the straggling teenagers in the hall, her eyes crazy with alarm. "This is an *e-mer-gen-cy!*" She dragged out the last word as if no one listening would understand English.

Behind her, a chunk of plaster fell loose from the ceiling, plunging to the floor with a comet trail of water behind it.

At least five showers were sprinkling rose-colored water from the arched ceilings of the hall. The floor was a low river in both directions.

Sister Maria stood at the center of the maelstrom, fluffing her drenched blouse to prevent the translucent material from sticking to her bra. Mattings of iron-gray hair hung down in her eyes as she tried to direct a bucket brigade of faculty. Mostly, she fretted. "I told them we needed to replace the entire roof—not these patchwork fixes." No one was listening. Mr. Mankowski, Mr. McClerk, Ms. Marisol from Algebra, and the Spanish and part-time Latin teacher Mrs. Tunns, were stumbling around with wastebaskets, trying to catch as much water as possible before it hit the ground, like contestants in some strange game show.

Davidek tried to tell them about all the kids with scars on their faces, and that they should stop it—but no one was listening to him either.

Students stood all around them, some eager to prove their worth and help out, others just enjoying the sight of this wrath-of-God chaos. Zari was on the periphery, jewelry jangling as she aimed her yearbook camera at the recovery effort, pumping the hallway full of flashes.

Mr. Zimmer, Audra Banes, and half a dozen other kids were at the other end of the hall, trying to forge a dam out of rectangular packages of paper towels, flotillas of plastic-wrapped toilet tissue, and heaps of discarded clothes that Mrs. Horgen and Mrs. Arnarelli dragged up from the church's St. Vincent de Paul charity box.

None of it worked. Deep pools formed behind the absorbent barriers, then easily gushed around them. "You two," Mr. Zimmer said, lifting a dripping finger toward Davidek and Stein. "Either get in here and help or get downstairs."

The two freshman boys hurried past them. Every single student's face turned to watch them—and each had the red mark.

Back in the stairwell, the third-floor flood was pouring off the side in a scarlet gush. Leaning against the stained glass mosaic, watching the indoor waterfall, was Smitty, his blue eyes glittering. "Back off," Davidek said, leading Stein past him.

Smitty bowed, extending his arm. "Homos first," he said. There was a faint smear of rouge on his cheek, but not a fully painted scar like the others. It looked like someone had wiped it off him.

The fight against the flood ended in defeat when the school lost power to all the upper floors. Water was pouring down through the second floor, then into the first, and was soon building up in the storage rooms and sub-basements. School was canceled for the day, and probably would be for a long time.

The hundreds of students were crowded into the cafeteria to await their buses, parents, or other means of evacuation. Those teachers not busy with swamp duty upstairs were escorting kids to the convent so they could call home for rides.

Students who drove themselves to school received permission to leave immediately, but a lot still hung around, mostly so they could savor tormenting Stein. The red pens were still making the rounds, adding fake scars to people's grinning faces.

Davidek and Stein sat together. Stein was still lugging his heavy bag, but all Davidek's belongings had remained upstairs.

Carl LeRose passed by to invite Davidek to join him at the junior tables. "Come on over," he said, whispering so Stein couldn't hear him. "People are already pissed about you not having any guts when it comes to Hannah. You don't need to tie yourself to this guy—"

"I'm staying," Davidek said. Before LeRose left, Davidek grabbed him by his tie, then gently pulled the older boy's head to the side. There was no mark. "Come on, I wouldn't do that . . . ," LeRose said, pulling back and straightening his tie.

"Ssssssss!!!!" came the simultaneous sound from the packed cafeteria tables. Michael Crawford stood on one of the chairs, conducting the whole hissing room in unison.

Hannah stopped and knelt beside Davidek, putting a hand on his knee. "I drove here, so I'm free to go. I can give you a ride," she said. "Your friend, too."

"Buzz off," Stein said, not looking at her.

Davidek leaned close so only she could hear. "I don't think I'll be taking *rides* with you anymore."

Hannah shrugged. There was no scar on her face either, which Davidek was glad to see, although he noticed traces of red ink on her fingers when she blew him a kiss. "Have it your way, Playgirl," she said.

Carney, the carnival geek wannabe who'd played the firebug kid in the Spanish play, came bounding over to their lonesome table swinging a lidless pepper shaker. "I hearby sprinkle the ashes of this deformed loser's mother to the four winds," Carney said, his left cheek painted with a scar roughly the shape of South America. Holding the shaker aloft, Carney dumped the remnants of the pepper on top of Stein's head. Trickles of spice poured through his hair and onto his shoulders.

Zari came over with her yearbook camera. "Say cheese," she said, and snapped their picture.

Stein just sat there, oblivious, watching Mullen and Simms across the cafeteria as they watched him watch them. Although they had driven to school in Mullen's Pea Green Love Machine and could leave at any time, they were trying to savor the havoc they'd helped create. When this was all over, they still expected to be heroes, the vanquishers of the mother-burning freshman prick. Strangely, though, they hadn't been included in the plan to pass around all those red markers. Of course, they'd get the credit eventually. They hoped.

The buses were finally arriving, and Sister Antonia stood at the lunch-lady intercom calling out the routes as a great exodus of students gathered itself and began inching toward the stairs that led up from the cafeteria and out into the dumping rain and wind.

"I'm going to stay with you until you call your dad or sister, all right?" Davidek said, but Stein was gone from his seat. His eyes were still on Mullen and Simms, who were among those closest to the doors. Stein moved after them, the heavy book bag swinging at his side. Something inside made a low sound, hollow and metallic.

Davidek tried to follow but was mired in the crowd as Stein pushed toward the jammed exterior stairwell. Davidek cupped his hands around his mouth and called, "Wait up!" But his friend was already gone.

A hand fell on Davidek's shoulder. "Hey, man, can I help?" asked Green.

Outside the school, kids scattered toward their buses with jackets and bags over their heads. The world was glossy brown and gray beneath the pale shower of the storm. Mullen slowed as he ran toward his car, fishing the keys out of his blazer as Simms hesitated at an ankle-deep puddle pooling below the Pea Green Love Machine's passenger side.

Stein had heard Davidek calling for him, but it was too late to stop now. His feet kicked through the fingerlake streams of water, weaving between the parked cars and crisscrossing classmates. He reached down without breaking pace and opened the zipper on his bag.

Mullen fumbled with his car keys as Simms stood beside him. "I'll get in on your side," he said. Stein's feet splashed fans of water backwards. From his bag, he drew a thick metal bar, about a foot long, threaded at either end, with a corrugated grip in the center. It was a dumbbell pipe from the weight set his father kept in the basement, bloomed with rust.

Stein dropped his book bag, leaving a few pencils hanging out and his Biology book open to the rain.

He would take Mullen first. The slower one, Simms, would be better to hit second, since he probably wouldn't realize what was happening until he saw his own moldy teeth scattering across the parking lot with bits of fleshy gums still attached. By then, Mullen would already be on his knees, collapsing to the ground with the back of his skull cratered in.

"She's the only one I told," Stein said softly, the rain on his lips.

Mullen and Simms turned at the sound of Stein's voice as his arm swung the chrome bar through the rain, slinging a streak of water in an arc as it glided toward Mullen's surprised eyes.

In that instant, a dark hulk exploded through the silver curtain of rain and collided against Stein's back, crushing the air from his lungs and flexing his spine backwards. Stein's feet were in the air and the ground was gliding sideways beneath them. Then he was skidding along the rough, wet blacktop, tumbling side over side until he came to rest in one of the empty parking spaces. The chrome bar rolled after him.

Stein gasped for air and stared up at the purple and black sky as the behemoth who had flattened him stepped into view.

Smitty.

The bruiser freshman stood over the fallen Stein, exhaling steam, hands on his hips, trying to decide what came next.

As Davidek ran toward them, Mullen and Simms hurried into their car. "That the best you can do, pussy?" Simms shrieked toward Stein's unmoving form as the car peeled its tires and carried them away.

Davidek shoved Smitty's chest, which felt like pushing a tree trunk. Smitty smiled and knocked Davidek to the ground, where he soaked up an assfull of rain.

"I did your psycho friend a favor, you little bitch. . . . You oughtta be thanking me."

"You blindsided him, asshole," Davidek said. "I saw it."

"Did you see this, too?" Smitty asked, grabbing the chrome bar off the asphalt.

Sister Maria and the half dozen remaining teachers were hurrying out of the cafeteria, alerted to the brewing trouble by Green. They gathered around Stein, whose eyes were open to the rain, the back of his head lying in a chocolate-colored puddle.

With no one looking, Smitty heaved the chrome bar end over end into the sky, where it vanished on the roof just beside the outstretched arms of St. Thomas Aquinas.

Davidek glared at him. "You're welcome," Smitty said.

"I thought you weren't the do-gooder type."

Smitty looked to a Jeep in the corner of the parking lot, and the small figure behind the windshield, watching him. He shrugged as he walked away. "I'm not."

THIRTY-TWO

All around them, students were halting their retreat to the buses, asking: *What happened? Who saw it? What did we miss?*

"Anyone still here in the next five minutes goes back up to the third floor to push a mop. Now, get moving!" Sister Maria called out through the rain, and the rubberneckers hurried away to their waiting rides.

It was a bogus threat: the school was empty—evacuated by order of the diocese's lawyers. The main halls and classrooms were still flooding, and no students or teachers were permitted to reenter until county building inspectors could verify the structural integrity. Mr. Saducci had already locked the front door. St. Michael's had gone dark. And it would stay that way for a while.

Stein had gotten to his feet, dirty water pouring off his arms and down his face. He said nothing to anyone, and lumbered back toward the school, around the corner to the side entrance—ignoring Sister Maria's calls to him.

"Please go get your friend," she said to Davidek. "I don't have time for this today."

Davidek spread his arms. "You didn't have time to notice the whole school was making fun of him either, did you?" he snapped. The nun's face was puzzled, and Davidek raked an angry scratch down his wet cheek. "The red marks?" he said.

Sister Maria pinched her eyes. In all the chaos, yes, she had seen the painted scars. But was she supposed to stop every single problem at every single moment of the day? "There are worse things in life than a little teasing," she said, unaware of how close St. Mike's had just come to something *far* worse.

Davidek wandered through the storm, gathering up his friend's abandoned schoolbag and chasing the wind-scattered papers. By the time he was finished, the last handful of students still waiting for rides were huddled with Sister Maria beneath the awnings of the gymnasium church doorways. The last of the teachers were departing in their cars.

"Stop stalling, and please go get him," Sister Maria called out, and Davidek walked backwards toward the school, annoyed. "My bus just left, so you know . . . we still need to call his parents—and mine. If you have 'time' for that."

"*I'll* give you a ride back," Sister Maria said. "Just bring him out here."

Davidek gave her the finger when he was out of sight around the corner of the building. He pushed open the side doorway, and an endless blackness opened before him. Rain from his hair trickled down his face as he stepped inside. "Stein!" he called out. There was no answer except his own echo, and thousands of drips from the floors above, ticking into faraway puddles like a collection of ill-timed clocks.

Davidek left Stein's soaking bag by the door and groped for the wall, finding a bank of light switches that his splayed palm clicked up and down. Nothing.

There was a distant shuffling followed by a door banging closed. Davidek began walking toward it, one hand trailing the wall of lockers, peeking through the narrow window of each classroom as he went. He could see out into the parking lot through some. Only two students were left waiting for their rides, still clustered under the gymnasium-church eave with Sister Maria. He wondered if they had red scars painted on their faces.

A faraway explosion of crashing glass wracked the silence, hammering echoes down the corridor. Davidek hurried toward the sound, past the first floor's trophy case to the bathroom, where a million years ago, a crazed and desperate student named Colin "Clink" Vickler emerged to become the infamous Boy on the Roof.

A shadow lurked in the light under the door.

Davidek said, "Everybody's gone, Stein. . . . Can I come in?"

There was no answer. Davidek pried open the door.

The opaque windows cast a dim, gray glow throughout the lime green bathroom, desaturating everything to black and white. Stein sat against the radiator in the shadow below the window with his knees up, his head down, and his arms wedged under the flaps of his blue blazer.

The red clip-on tie drooped over one of the bathroom sinks like a tongue, and the mirror above it was webbed with cracks, with silver fragments of glass littering the floor, each one holding a tiny reflection of the two boys.

"You smash that with your fist?" Davidek asked. Stein didn't respond, so he stepped closer. "Could have hurt yourself."

Stein lifted his head and gave a faint smile, dislodging a few flecks of grit still clinging to his cheeks from the parking lot. "I did," he said, tilting his head toward the trails of red spots beside the sink, like glistening clusters of spider eyes.

"You okay, though?" Davidek asked. Stein nodded, squeezing himself tighter. He lowered his head again.

"I need to tell you what happened," Stein said, his voice dry and aching, like he'd swallowed dust.

"I saw," Davidek said. "Part of me wishes you had nailed those fucking guys, but maybe it's best that you didn't. I mean, shit, man. I think they'll give you more than detention if you put two other students in the ground."

Stein's face looked pained. "Not that," he said, his voice low. "I need to tell you about my mom. About what happened to her."

Davidek sighed, and slid down against one of the bathroom stalls. "I saw the same show as everyone else. You don't have to."

"No," Stein said, and his voice was louder, stronger. "What I told Lorelei, and what she told everybody . . . that's not the real truth. I wanted to tell Lorelei, but . . . I never told anyone what really happened. Not my sister. Not my dad—but now I want to tell you, okay? I have to."

Davidek leaned his head back. He actually *didn't* want to hear it. But Stein kept speaking. So Davidek listened.

"There *was* a fire," Stein said. "And I set it. But it *wasn't* accidental." He looked up. His face gray and empty. An old man's face in the dim light. "I set the fire on purpose, Davidek."

Stein studied his friend for a reaction, and Davidek closed his eyes so he couldn't get one.

"I didn't kill my mom, though," Stein said. "She had already done that herself."

Davidek swallowed and opened his eyes. Stein was still hugging himself under his blazer, like someone freezing to death. He turned his eyes toward Davidek, just dark sockets in the shadows. "That's the secret nobody knows. . . . Nobody until now. Nobody until you."

Stein explained that his mother had attempted it a few times, but her doctors believed those were merely cries for attention. "When you slash your wrist, it makes a mess, but the veins seal up right away. They said people who really want to end things slash *up* their forearms instead of across. Anyway, we didn't have any knives or razors in the house after that. That's when my dad grew his beard." Stein smiled faintly to himself. "And Margie's legs got furry."

Stein shifted, closed his eyes. "Anyway, one day, when I was nine, I walked home from school by myself. Usually she came to get me, but sometimes she didn't. Especially when she had problems—her bad thoughts. Let's just say, I had a key and knew my own way home."

Stein's head had lolled back against the radiator. He didn't speak for a long time, and Davidek thought he might be asleep.

Then Stein said, "The building we lived in was a dump. The superintendent had this big plastic jar of white powder he gave us to sprinkle behind the refrigerator and in the cabinet under the sink to kill ants and cockroaches. Boric acid—I still remember that. Written in big red letters. Anyway, I had gotten home, but didn't see my mom. So I was looking for Oreos when I found the plastic container on the counter—empty—next to a lot of spilled water and a glass that had the powder crusted on it. Her body was on the floor by the couch. There was vomit *everywhere*. Her eyes were open. So was her mouth. She had on a white robe, but no clothes underneath. I covered her up with the blanket from my bed." Stein opened his eyes, even smiled a little. "It had Transformers on it."

Davidek's throat was tight. "She leave a note?"

Stein nodded. "That was the first thing I lit on fire. I don't remember what she wrote. There was a lot, all scribbled out. . . . Mostly, it just said she was sorry. 'Sorry, sorry, sorry . . .' Over and over again. I tried to get her to put her arms around me, but she was cold. And she was stiff. Like a piece of the furniture. I started crying, asking her to wake up. But I was nine— not stupid."

Stein looked over at Davidek. "I told you that my mom used to go to all kinds of churches, remember?"

Davidek nodded. Stein looked back at the floor. "I remember one of the church ministers, talking with my dad about my mom's problems—after she'd been in the hospital a few times. The minister said we had to be really careful because if she killed herself, she wouldn't be allowed into heaven. Do you think that's true?"

Davidek didn't answer. Couldn't. Stein was quiet for a long time again.

"So I set the fire," he said finally, as if hearing that news for the first time himself. "I thought . . . maybe I could *hide* what she'd done. Hide it so good, maybe even God wouldn't know."

Davidek was standing now. He couldn't take any more. "You have to tell your dad. You have to tell people this wasn't your fault."

"I didn't think I'd ever *have* to explain it," Stein said. "I laid down next to my mom after I put that airplane glue all over her and the couch and the drapes. I wanted to go *with* her. I wasn't even afraid. I was more afraid of these *feelings* beating around inside me—this sadness and anger and confusion and craziness. It was like this . . . *screaming* inside my head. I just wanted it to stop." There were big tears in his eyes now—but Stein wasn't letting them fall. "Do you understand? I *still* want it to stop. . . ."

"I do, too," Davidek said. "But you survived for a reason."

Stein looked at his friend like he was missing a much larger point. "That fucking Transformers blanket saved me. When I lit the glue, it didn't burn—it *melted*. Onto my face. I wasn't afraid to die, but I was afraid to hurt. And it hurt *so* bad . . . I thought it would all be over fast, but suddenly I was screaming, and running, and smacking the flames off my skin.

I'm not even sure what happened next. There was smoke everywhere. They found me passed out by the door. The neighbors hit me with it when they busted in. They never got to my mother. The flames were too much. I was glad about that. In the end, it was all just a horrible accident, caused by a very stupid, very sorry kid."

"Your mother was sick," Davidek said, choosing his words cautiously. "That's not your fault. Not hers either. You were just a boy. And you saw something no kid should. It was a mistake, that's all."

Stein nodded, slowly, as if it hardly mattered anymore. "She deserves heaven, I think. Silly as that sounds. I hope she got there. She never hurt anybody. . . ." His voice drifted so low, he was hard to hear. "But *I've* hurt people. . . . I'd have hurt those guys today. All for a girl." He snorted a laugh, but it could have been a cough. "One I couldn't even . . . tell the truth to."

"You can tell everyone the truth now," Davidek said. "It's overdue."

Stein looked up at his friend, his arms still squeezed under his jacket. His voice broke, just a whisper. "You tell them for me . . . Okay?"

Davidek rolled his eyes. "Come on, man," he said, reaching down. But Stein's legs slipped against the floor. There was something beneath him, a darkness, spreading.

"Oh shit," Davidek said. "Oh fuck . . ."

He dropped Stein, whose hands fell out of his jacket and flopped against the tile in great scarlet splatters. The belly of Stein's white shirt, hidden before by his folded arms and dark blazer, was soaked black with blood, seeping into the top of his khaki pants.

Davidek tried to hold the cuts on his wrists closed, but couldn't. The slashes were long jagged streaks reaching all the way up Stein's forearms, glinting with flecks of broken mirror glass.

Davidek didn't realize he was moving. In his mind, he remained rooted to the spot by the door, not cradling his friend, not watching Stein's arms flail against his neck and face as he dragged the boy, screaming for help.

The bathroom grew distant in the dark hallway. Then he was in the rain. Someone was shaking him, grabbing his jaw and turning his face. He stared dumbly up at Sister Maria, whose eyes bulged, as if a giant fist were squeezing her. "Stay here!" she screamed. "Stay here!"

Then the nun appeared in front of him in a little burgundy car. Davidek was looking down through the back window at Stein, sprawled on the backseat, his blood smearing the gray cushions. *I'm sorry . . . sorry . . . sorry,* someone was saying. Maybe Stein. Maybe Davidek. Maybe both.

Then the car was gone, and Davidek was alone. He stood so long in the rain, staring at where his friend had gone, that the water pouring through his bloodsoaked clothes washed him clean.

THIRTY-THREE

It was midnight by the time the storm faded, retreating in threads through a moonless sky. Sister Maria's little red car cut through the low mist on the street outside the convent and jerked to a stop with one tire perched on the curb. The nun got out and closed the door quietly, folding her arms across a blouse that had been white that morning but now bloomed with patches of dark brown, like a garden of dead flowers.

Behind the convent, the lightless monolith of the school cut a black square through the array of stars beyond it. Sister Maria looked next door to the priest's rectory. Father Mercedes's home was also dark, and she watched it in silence.

A window in the shape of a cross in the convent's front door cast a glowing T across the floor as Sister Maria entered and crept upstairs, careful to avoid the steps she knew would creak. Feeling silly, like a teenager—sneaking home after curfew.

The nun felt along the wall of the hallway rather than turn on a light. Her housemate, Sister Antonia, was asleep, tucked neatly beneath the covers in her bedroom. Her white hair, usually hidden by a black habit, flowed out on her pillow, and a rosary was clutched in her hand, like a body laid out in a funeral home. The image filled Sister Maria with sadness. The convent once housed seven nuns, but someday, probably soon, she would be alone here.

In her own bedroom, Sister Maria clicked on the small reading lamp, and the taut pastel sheets over her mattress tempted her to slip between them and close her eyes. As she removed her ruined blouse, dried specks of blood fell from the buttons to the wood floor. She studied herself in the dresser mirror. It wasn't her mirror—everything in the home belonged to the Sisters of Saint Joseph. The mirror had been there when she arrived, and it would remain after she was gone. Only the reflection was hers—this old woman, flesh spotted and gray. Weak. Frightened.

This is who she was, though her faith taught that the body was just temporary. A rental, of sorts. The soul was all we truly owned. Sister Maria got down on her knees, the floor creaking along with her joints, and prayed thanks to God for letting the boy live.

But her work was not finished, and she asked Him to help her with that, too.

The nun crossed the moist grass in the front yard again, now wrapped in a warm, fresh sweater beneath a black peacoat. She passed under the pine trees bordering the priest's home and walked up the rectory steps, where she knocked on the front door and waited. Then she rang the bell and waited some more. Heavy footsteps and groaning complaints descended the stairs inside. Father Mercedes's hands fumbled with the strap of a terry cloth robe as he opened the door. The nun had known him a long, long time, but had never seen his skinny white legs before.

"Did I wake you?" she asked. A stupid question.

The priest pursed his lips, and asked one of his own. "Where the hell've you been?"

Sister Maria felt her pulse quicken, thinking: *This is how guilty students feel when they stand before me trying to lie their way out of trouble in the principal's office.* "We had a terrible tragedy today," she said, then waited to see what he'd say next.

"I'll say you did," the priest told her. He was trying to focus his eyes in the darkness of the porch, but had forgotten his glasses upstairs.

"Did you . . . go inside to see any of it?" the nun asked, praying that he had not.

The priest groaned. "I spent all day in Pittsburgh at the bishop's biannual, explaining why our parish can't match last year's goal in the Vatican Advancement fund this year. You knew that—"

"Did you go *inside* . . . when you got back?" Her voice was small, hopeful.

The priest shook his head. "Saducci said I'd need a wetsuit. And it was late. And I was tired, Sister. Anyway, I can't can't clean up all your messes," he said. "I'll see the damage tomorrow. If I must."

Sister Maria held back a hallelujah. "Thank you, Father. I just wanted to make sure you were properly informed."

The priest began to close the door and she thought that was the end, but he swung it open again for one last dig. "And where were you all day? Saducci and Mrs. Corde spent the afternoon in the church office, making appointments with contractors for tomorrow. Without you. Make sure you're available to meet them. "

"I will, Father," she said. "I just had to manage a small crisis today. The Stein boy." Part of her wanted to say everything, right here and now—confess everything.

"What's he got to do with this?" the priest asked.

Sister Maria backed away. She raised one hand from her coat. "Nothing, Father. We'll talk tomorrow," she said, smiling faintly. "No need to burden you more tonight."

The nun descended into the yard, slipping around the side of her house, where she waited until the rectory lights clicked off again. Then she headed toward the school.

She had made a promise at the hospital, but wasn't sure she could keep it until now.

Orderlies, nurses, and doctors had swarmed the boy as they retreated into the emergency room with his body, which looked like a gruesome doll on the white gurney, shriveled, unmoving. Sister Maria had knelt beside the vending machines, praying the rosary by memory, and at the start of the third set of Hail Marys, the boy's father stormed into the waiting room. The nun gushed apologies, begged forgiveness. When the boy's sister arrived, they all held hands and prayed some more.

Doctors came and went. They gave no predictions, no comfort, certainly no promises. Two police officers entered sometime later. Sister Maria repeated what she knew and answered their questions. *It was self-inflicted, yes? Was there anyone with him?*

Sister Maria thought of the boy—Davidek. *No,* she lied. *No one else.*

The police talked with the family, going over the boy's history, his mother, the fire, his troubles at the school. A psychiatrist was called in to speak with the family about the boy's mental state.

When the police officers departed, Sister Maria walked with them outside. "This will follow him, won't it?" she asked. "All his friends at the school, other people in the town . . . How much time does he have before your report goes public and the newspaper picks it up?"

The police officers seemed embarrassed. They looked at each other and the equipment around their belts jangled restlessly. One said, "We do have to file a report, that's the law." And the other said, "Of course, we've got a lot of work to do." The nun didn't get the insinuation. He smiled at her. "Do you understand, Sister?" the cop asked. "We have a lot of *other* work to do. Real crimes—these personal tragedies . . . those reports go to the bottom of the list. Sometimes they stay there, or get misfiled. Unless something dire happens . . ."

His partner said, "That wouldn't necessarily be a sin, would it, Sister?"

"No," she said, and reached out to touch both their faces. "It's mercy."

Inside the emergency room, she found the boy's father and sister again. They wanted to pray some more, but she had other business to discuss with them. If Noah Stein survived, there was something more they could do to make his life a little easier.

Sister Maria found everything she needed in the janitor's storage room, which Mr. Saducci had left unlocked in all the pandemonium during the flood. That was good. That meant anybody could have gotten ahold of these items, even a student.

In the boys' bathroom, there was more blood streaking the floor than she expected. Her flashlight didn't reveal all of it to her at once, which was probably for the best. She might have stopped right then, overwhelmed, but she had made a pledge. It was time to fulfill it.

She positioned the flashlight on the window ledge and hung her coat on a hook inside the third toilet stall, then rolled up the sleeves on her sweater.

The crowbar from the storage room was almost as long as a golf club, and so thick and heavy, she could hardly raise it. She wondered how Saducci would even use it, but it was so rusted and cobwebby, she guessed he didn't. The nun raised the crowbar high over her head and let gravity do the rest.

The solid steel hook bit into the thick white lip of the sink and shattered it, dropping crumbled pebbles of porcelain like a shattered jaw, gushing a clear drool of water. She turned to the opposite wall and raised the prybar higher this time, turning her face aside as her frail arms pounded the hook against the first urinal, shattering it into ice-white chunks.

She tapped the crowbar against the flush handle a few times, sending a cascade of toilet water across the floor, flooding the bathroom and dissolving the thick trail of blood smeared across the tile, which swirled in a wide, brown galaxy as the brass drain embedded in the floor swallowed it.

Sister Maria closed her eyes and used the blunt end of the hook to crush out the remaining glass in the mirror Stein had punched. That might have been enough, but something in her wouldn't stop. She hammered dents in the metal stalls around the toilets, cracking away round disks of paint, six decades thick. She caved in the towel dispenser, then swung at the plastic soap dispenser like it was a baseball, popping it in a plume of pink ooze.

When Sister Maria finally stopped, her lungs heaved furiously, her peppery hair hung in her eyes, and sweat beaded on her face and back. She leaned against the crowbar like a cane, flexing the numb fingers on her hands. A soreness clawed at her throat. She didn't realize she had been screaming.

This was enough. She left the crowbar standing in one of the toilet bowls. *That's how a vandal would abandon it*, she figured.

In the janitor's closet, she had also found a box of spray paint—all different colors, though black seemed to be the appropriate one. She pulled the canister out of her peacoat pocket and aimed the flashlight toward the wall with the shattered urinal.

Keep it simple, she thought. *Use an old standard.*

FUCK YOU, appeared on the green tile in long, dripping lines. She held the nozzle so close to the wall that black droplets bounced back and stained her fingers.

Sister Maria stood back, admiring the block letters. "Fuck . . . you," she read aloud. It was the first time in her life she'd ever said those words, and it felt disgusting—bitter in her mouth.

She turned to the opposite wall, with the fractured sink and the smashed-out mirror. She needed something different here. How else would a crazed fifteen-year-old unleash his fury on his school? He would attack the people who had driven him to this, but Sister Maria knew she couldn't single out any particular students, however much they deserved it. She raised the spray can and said each letter aloud as she wrote: "Ess . . . Ayy . . . Eye . . . Enn . . ."

Sister Maria stood back to scan the words with her flashlight: SAINT MICHAELS

Then she spritzed an apostrophe between the *L* and *S*. The kid was supposed to be furious, not a moron.

Now what? *Saint Michael's . . . Drop Dead?* Too tame.

It had to sound like a boy, not some fussy old nun. Everyone had to believe the story—a kid with a history of behavior problems had turned violent, trashed a bathroom, cut himself (accidentally) in the process, and was now suspended. The story might have a few little holes, but it would hold together. She just needed it to look legitimate.

SAINT MICHAEL'S . . .

". . . Sucks," she said, and began painting the word, cutting across the mirrors. Kids say that all the time. *This sucks, that sucks, you suck . . .*

Sister Maria raised the paint nozzle once again, but hesitated, hovering in front of the letters. She had already committed to *sucks*. But what sucks? What did that word mean anyway?

The nun thought of the drain, guzzling water, and porcelain chips. That sucked, in the literal sense, but the slang referred to . . . Funny, she had never thought about it.

Penis, she thought. Fine, she had unleashed the word in her mind. But *penis* was too clinical. She had never heard an angry student say, "Suck my penis!"

Pecker? That was good. *Pecker*—she mentally added it to her list of euphemisms, but it felt a little too jaunty. *Wang* or *Ding-dong* seemed too . . . what? Juvenile?

The nun agonized over this longer than was prudent.

Cock. That was a good one, right? *Cock.*

But no. A kid might use that word, but she would not. Too lusty.

Cock. She tried to forget it, but the word kept insinuating itself.

"Dick," she said, and it fit like a puzzle piece. The nun said a quick mental prayer of thanks. Strange to offer an Our Father for a word like that.

SAINT MICHAEL'S SUCKS DICK appeared on the wall.

As she finished spraying the downward line on the *K,* Sister Maria's arm absently let the hand holding the canister fall to her side, her finger still pressing the spray button, which hissed black mist into nothingness until it finally slipped from her shaking hand.

The bathroom door was open, and a shadow stood there, watching her.

Sister Maria's foot clattered the spray can away as she stumbled backwards, grasping for the flashlight on the windowsill. The whiteness of a face stared at her from the darkness as she spun the light toward it.

The nun leaned back against the radiator, clutching a hand to her thundering heart. *Thank you God, thank you, oh God oh God oh God.*

Peter Davidek stepped forward into the dim light, looking ill, his face pale, his hair matted and knotty. The navy blazer hanging over his shoulders seemed too large.

"What the hell are you doing here?" the nun asked, overwhelmed with relief that the person who had discovered her was the one person at St. Mike's she needed to include in the lie anyway.

Davidek looked at the walls, and the runny black curses sprayed across them.

"I guess I could ask you the same question," he said.

The homes of Tarentum were just glowing windows hanging in the mist as Sister Maria's car rolled by in the darkness. Whenever the car passed under the cone of light from a streetlamp, Davidek's eye kept being drawn to the backseat, where streaks of blood were crusting on the gray upholstery.

"So . . . he's alive," Sister Maria said, hoping for some sign of cheer from the boy. "We should be grateful for that."

"How bad?"

She didn't want to answer. She didn't want to upset him. But she didn't want to lie. "You know what you saw," she told him.

Each of the boy's questions seemed to take a long time to arrive. "Will he be okay?"

The nun knew that if she and this boy Davidek were going to fool everyone else, they needed to be honest with each other. So she didn't answer that one.

"You saved your friend's life," Sister Maria said. "But now we need to protect him some more. No one knows about this except us. I'd like to keep it that way."

Davidek kept his face turned toward the nothingness outside his window. "I bet you would," he said.

Sister Maria slowed to a stop for a red light at the Tarentum Bridge. To the right was a ramp leading down to where Hannah had taken Davidek for her little trap with the disposable camera. "The mess in the restroom was camouflage," the nun said. "It will be better for him to be gone from school for that reason, rather than . . ." She didn't finish the thought. The light turned green, and they were rolling again. "We all deserve to lose our mistakes. Maybe have a second chance? This will protect him if—"

"If he lives?" Davidek interrupted.

"If he comes back," the nun said.

Davidek lowered his head. "He's not coming back. Not to St. Mike's."

"That may be true," Sister Maria agreed. "But he'll be somewhere. This doesn't have to follow him."

"And what about the people who caused this?" Davidek asked. "Mullen and Simms? Smitty? *Lorelei?* You act like you're doing Stein a favor, but nothing happens to them. They don't even get to *feel* guilty. You say, 'Oh, I'm protecting Stein. . . .' But you're protecting *them,* too."

The nun's fingers tightened on the steering wheel. "Would hurting them help your friend?"

Davidek sank in his chair. He wasn't wearing a seat belt. "Go past Valley High School, then keep on through the intersection toward Parnassus," he said. When they passed a gas station and a video rental store, Davidek pointed right and she turned down his street.

Every window in his house was aglow. The nun parked at the corner and looked at the dashboard clock. It was 1:53 A.M. "How will you explain being gone to your parents?" she asked.

"They'll just want to yell, not ask questions," he said. "I'll just tell them I was hanging out with Stein and didn't call because I didn't want to come home. That's true, isn't it?"

"Peter, can I count on you to tell the story we've agreed to?"

Davidek got out of her car and reached back to pick up something he'd left on the seat—a red clip-on tie. "Everybody knows the school is falling apart," he said. "The last thing you need is a kid trying to kill himself, right?"

The nun leaned forward so he could see her face in the dome light. "If you're his friend, you'll keep his secret."

Davidek closed the door, then turned back and poked his finger against the glass. "Yeah, I'll keep quiet," he said. "But just remember—it's *your* secret." He looked down at the clip-on in his hands. "Stein wasn't keeping them anymore."

THIRTY-FOUR

The priest settled into the cushioned seat at the head of the main library table. Afternoon sunlight filtered in from the basement windows. The chatter in the cavernous room went silent. The entire faculty settled into their seats along the table, listening, every face grim.

"I'll let Sister Maria explain it," Father Mercedes said. "She's the one responsible for it."

Sister Maria began to speak what everyone already knew from gossip: The Stein boy had gone back into the school during the evacuation and wreaked havoc. Now he was suspended—indefinitely. "It's a sad turn of events," the nun said. "But this is for the best."

The school had been closed for a week, and this was the first faculty meeting since the flood. No one knew whether to be celebratory or serious. Mrs. Arnerelli whispered to Zimmer that they better not extend the school year—she and her husband had already purchased nonrefundable tickets to Vegas for early June.

When Sister Maria finished, Father Mercedes rose from his seat. "You all give out a lot of grades at this school, but now it's time you were graded yourselves." He began to pace, slowly, caressing his hand on the back of each chair as he passed. "I've spoken with the parish council about a new plan: From now until graduation day, we're going to fill the school with parish Monitors. These are regular people, concerned citizens—men and women from St. Mike's who will oversee the behavior problems at this school firsthand. They're going to spend the rest of the year documenting the problems here. And when it's done, we'll find out whether St. Michael the Archangel High School passes—or fails."

There was general unease and shifting among the faculty. "What happens if the council decides we fail?" asked Miss Marisol, the young, first-year Algebra and Trigonometry teacher.

The priest fixed her with a flat expression. "Well," he said. "The school closes."

He stood there awhile and let their panicked chatter build, then shouted over it. "I don't want to see any surprised faces! You know this. You talk about it privately. Parents confront you and you shrug and say, 'I know, we're trying. . . .' That's not good enough any longer. Not for the children you teach. Not for the parishioners who continue paying for your mistakes."

He continued his slow walk around the table. "Another year will pass where I am asked, time and time again, 'When will we rebuild the fallen church?' After all the fund-raisers, all the donations, all the pancake breakfasts and candy sales and solicitations. After so much money is *nearly* raised to begin work on a foundation, I have to tell them, 'Sorry. We gave what little we had . . . to fix the *school*.' But right now, 'the school' is synonymous with 'the embarrassment.'"

The priest flattened his hands on the long table, and his dim reflection in the varnish pressed back against him. "Right now you're thinking, 'It's not *me*. . . . I do *my* best. . . . I show up, teach the lessons, grade the homework. . . . *I* work hard and stay late and sacrifice. . . . I do a good job.' And maybe you do." The priest shrugged. "But if you're not to blame, who is?" He let the question hang there. No one spoke. Most heads around the table were bowed shamefully. Only Bromine kept her face high, eyes locked with Father Mercedes, trying to send him telepathic messages of support.

The priest faced Sister Maria, seated quietly in the chair at the opposite head of the table. "I believe *you* deserve the blame, Sister Maria," he said. "I have told you this privately. Now, regrettably, I'm telling you in public.

Your leadership here has been a shambles, and there's no denying it. Brawls, scandals, and now vandalism. Still, you come with your hand out."

Sister Maria didn't fight back. This was a little dance they did. Father Mercedes would harass her in front of the staff, blame her for the problems at the school, and she would let him. Ultimately, he had to provide the funds needed to repair the water damage and vandalized bathroom. That's all she cared about. Let him menace her. She had faced worse lately.

"Let's hear from you, the teachers," Father Mercedes said. "I'd like to hear your feelings about what's going wrong at this school."

Another long hush fell across the library. Ms. Bromine raised her hand primly, but Mr. Zimmer slid back his chair and ratcheted his frame to stand before she could speak.

"I'm glad you brought this up, Father," Zimmer said. "Responsibility is a good topic to discuss. I don't like the idea of 'blame,' that sounds awfully childish and unproductive, but it's the word you used, so I'll use it, too." Zimmer opened his arms to the priest. "I guess I blame you, Father."

The faculty's collective muscles tightened, and the priest's expression changed from intrigue to heavy-lidded boredom. "Lovely, Mr. Zimmer. By all means, grind your ax later. I believe Ms. Bromine had something to say first—"

Zimmer just kept talking. "You blame Sister Maria, but for a long time now, Father, it's been clear to everyone around this table that you aren't interested in helping this school."

Ms. Bromine boiled over, sputtering, "It's not clear to *me*. You don't speak for everyone in this faculty."

"I speak for the truth," Zimmer told her. "For a while, Father, I thought you just wanted to get rid of Sister Maria," the teacher went on as the priest sank into his chair, sighing heavily. "But now—I think that's just a first step. Get her out of the way. Then you can get St. Mike's out of the way. Right? But I can't figure out: Why?"

"Preposterous," Father Mercedes said, forcing a smile.

"You asked everybody around this table to think about what's wrong with this place," Zimmer said. "But think about this: When there's a problem, who takes the time to say, 'We can do this. We can fix it.' . . . It's Sister Maria. Not you."

Mercedes closed his eyes. He said, "That's enough . . . ," but Zimmer kept talking.

"Who has counseled every teacher around this table about personal issues that had nothing to do with work? I won't mention names—don't worry—but when marriages have been in crisis, or an older relative has been sick or dying, or the simple pressure of teaching becomes overwhelming, who spends hours talking it over in her office? Who stays late *every day* at this school, doing her paperwork at night since she has to spend the day policing the halls, all because some priest has been telling people the school is a haven for delinquents and lost casuses?"

A silence crept back over the proceedings. Zimmer felt deeply uncomfortable standing in front of all these staring eyes.

"You know it's true," Zimmer said, a shake edging into his voice. "You can blame Sister Maria for the fact that we can't afford to rebuild the church, but Sister Maria didn't make it burn. You can tell the parishioners to blame God for that one. Or maybe blame the priest who didn't follow the insurance codes."

"Apologize to me," Mercedes said suddenly.

Zimmer's hands fought not to tremble. His mouth felt like a wad of cotton puffs. He had crossed a line. But it was too late to go back.

"Apologize to me," Father Mercedes repeated. "Apologize, or so help me, you'll regret it."

Zimmer scanned the faces around him. "Sister Maria didn't cause the fire, and she didn't cause the flood either. She has warned you all year long that we need a professional, major overhaul. Roof, walls, ceiling . . . And you've refused, haven't you, Father? You could have spent a couple grand on a permanent fix, but instead we're spending ten times that because *your* decision was to ignore her—and that made it much worse. I don't know why it's the church versus the school. There is no life without a next generation, Father. These kids we're teaching, they *are* St. Mike's."

"Kids who trash bathrooms," Father Mercedes snapped. He was looking at Sister Maria now—his eyes screaming with contempt for not silencing her employee.

"Yeah, kids who trash bathrooms," Zimmer said. His legs were unsteady, so he sat down again. "Maybe those kids matter more than even the good little ones who sit in the front row and try to answer every question."

Father Mercedes rolled his eyes.

"I wish you were a student here," Zimmer told the priest. "You're acting like a bully, Father. You might benefit from a little of the humanity Sister Maria tries to teach."

No one in the room was breathing.

Father Mercedes rose from his chair. "I thought you could be spoken to as adults. Clearly, I was mistaken." He pulled on his coat and fixed his hat, then picked up his valise and walked to the door. "The Monitors will be in place on the first day that school resumes. Be ready."

He walked out of the library and was met in the hall by Ms. Bromine, running to catch up with him, her chest heaving as her legs clattered down the corridor.

"Father, Father!" she called. "Father, I'm sorry for what happened there . . . so sorry . . ." The priest's eyes were cold. He tapped his pack of cigarettes and didn't stop walking.

"Father, you know I'd love to see Sister Maria removed—more than anything. But . . . these people, these parish Monitors . . . You don't *really* want them to close the school? I mean, you *don't*, right? It's just something to scare everyone?"

The priest slowed to a stop. He almost felt pity for this clueless woman.

"Can I do anything to help?" she asked.

The priest considered this. "I'm quite concerned about Mr. Zimmer," he said. "Perhaps you could let me know if he demonstrates any other . . . erratic behavior."

She nodded enthusiastically. "He's weird—and he's nuts. Wants to be one of the students, not one of the grown-ups. You know the type, Father. I'm glad the parish will have people watching us. They'll see for themselves."

"Excellent." He started walking again. Bromine called out: "But to be safe . . . I'd like to suggest we cancel the Hazing Day picnic. There's too much chance it could go bad. And with Hannah Kraut planning her sick little thing . . ."

The priest stopped again, but didn't turn around. Hazing Day getting out of hand? That would work just fine for him. As long as that Hannah girl didn't attack him, why not let her stand as an example of the worst St. Mike's had to offer? He just needed to be sure there were plenty of Parish Monitors to see it. And he also had to be sure he wouldn't be among her targets.

But that was the catch. The gamble. Luckily, he had a way to check the odds. He smiled to himself. "Don't worry. I'd say things are . . . *seven-eighths* in favor of working out just as we hoped."

He put a hand on Ms. Bromine's shoulder, and she smiled, too, even though she had no idea what he was talking about.

THIRTY-FIVE

I t began with looks. That's what Lorelei remembered from years before, when all her old friends fell away from her. When she had felt her existence shrink to nothing. When she had become the strange one, the hated one. When she had stopped mattering. No one said anything. They just stared.

Lorelei counted only a few friends at St. Mike's, and she expected to have none of them left when she returned for the first time since International Day, since betraying the one boy who had shamelessly devoted himself to her.

In some way, perhaps, she had always known this would happen, and had even invited it. A twisted part of Lorelei knew that her mother, that her old friends, that her new enemies all had it right—she was despicable. Deep down in her core. She was a shallow little shit.

And that was the attitude she struck two weeks after the flood shuttered the school, striding down the hallway of the newly reopened St. Mike's—her chin high, those lovingly curled gingerbread locks of hair flowing out behind her, hips tempting with each step in the blue-and-yellow tartan skirt. Lorelei held a thin smile on her face, and refused to let it fall, no matter how terrified she was.

It was her "go fuck yourself" smile.

Those who despised her were the ones looking away, turning inward, staring at the floor as she passed. They busied themselves with books and papers and rearranged lockers or examined coats as she passed, all fully aware of her presence. People stopped their conversations and turned away, at least as far as their peripheral vision would allow.

Lorelei's shoes clicked in the pockets of silence she created.

There were strangers in the hall. Unfamiliar adults. She overheard other students calling them "The Monitors," parishioners who were here to report back on what they saw to the parish council. They traveled in pairs, most of them elderly married couples with nothing better to do than volunteer as hallway cops. They didn't scold or correct misbehavior; they were here to observe, not enforce. Uniform violations, or inappropriate touching, like boyfriends kissing their girlfriends by the lockers, just led to a line in a notebook. They didn't tell stragglers to hurry to class, or order rowdy kids to settle down. They just watched. And took notes. And conferred with each other in grave whispers. They watched the other students watching Lorelei, and she supposed they wondered—who was this girl? What had she done? Maybe somebody would even tell them, and they could write that in their little notepads.

Lorelei gathered the morning's books from her locker. The area around her cleared. She scooped up her bag and pulled her sweater tight. The crowd parted as she passed.

No one said a word. Not until she was gone.

The senior guys were standing at their usual spot under the north corridor stairs when Bilbo's old friend Alexander Prager, the school's star basketball center (and one of the thugs who cornered Stein and Davidek on Dog Collar Day) started a joke: "All right, guys, so who's the only girl in school you *don't* want to fuck you?"

The other fellows shrugged, waiting for the punch line. Green, the only freshman in the group, tipped back his Coke can and wiped his mouth to cover up a burp.

"Lorelei!" Prager declared anticlimactically. There were a few chuckles, and the boy felt compelled to add the postscript: "Because when *she* fucks you, she *really* fucks you!" He punctuated this by pumping his fist in the air and collected some more polite laughter.

After a minute, Bilbo said, "That Stein guy was a prick and a half, but I wonder what he did to piss her off so bad. Blowing the whistle on him killing his mom? . . . Jesus, that's cold. She wanted him to *feel it*."

One of the other guys, Dan Strebovich, said, "She screwed him over hard."

Green sipped his Coke. "Anybody ask Mullen or Simms why she did it? They helped, you know. . . ."

Prager shook his head. "They're tools. They'd love for you to think it was all *their* idea." Everybody laughed for real at that. Asshole Face and Sandmouth—vendetta enforcers. Ha ha.

Then a group of junior girls walked into the stairwell and all the guys took swigs of their sodas in unison.

Lorelei never explained it to anybody. She wasn't sure she understood it herself.

A few older girls, none of them friends, none of them even people she'd spoken to before, brushed by occasionally to say, *So. What was the deal? What'd he do?* And Lorelei always told them the same thing: "Nothing."

You can tell me, the girls would insist. *Total confidence, I won't tell a soul. . . . But I have to know.*

"There's nothing to know," Lorelei would say. This was the point where the conversations always soured. Lorelei knew she could craft an elaborate lie, a tale of justified revenge, and make one or two sorely needed allies out of these busybodies, but she never did.

They always went away annoyed. One girl said to her, "Just because you're a bitch to your boyfriend doesn't mean you have to be a bitch to everybody." A friend of that girl cautioned her later: "If I were you, I wouldn't say stuff like that to Lorelei. You saw what she did to the one guy who was *nice* to her."

On the third floor, plastic sheeting still hung draped from the ceiling, and fresh white lines of cement glowed from between the bricks. The heavy reconstructive work had been completed in a flurry in the canceled two weeks of classes. The rain had held off, which was a blessing because the rooftop was in the process of a quick and dirty re-tarring. That would be at least another week of work, and in the summer, it would need a more thorough job. Meanwhile, at night, a masonry crew came in to reinforce the cracked walls and ceilings. Until they were finished, students would have to maneuver between the scaffolding and drop cloths.

It was there that Lorelei came face-to-face with Davidek for the first time since that afternoon in Palisade Hall. She had seen him distantly in the days since class resumed, often slumped over his desk morosely, isolated from everyone, even his other friend, Green.

Davidek avoided her as much as possible, but amid the construction in that upstairs hallway one morning, they found themselves on opposite sides of a foggy plastic sheet. Lorelei raised one hand, tentatively. "Hi," she said. Davidek's face was unreadable behind the opaque sheet. She waited for him to pass around the other side, but he backed up rather than move closer to her, his face fading away.

She thought of the boy who had once spent every penny he had on a carton of cigarettes to save her from being hurt. "Good-bye," she said to the empty space.

Ever since Audra Banes came to believe Lorelei was trying to steal her boyfriend, the freshman girl with the sometimes-funny hair was a forbidden subject. Then Audra brought up Lorelei herself, while dining at Wendy's after a student council meeting that Friday: "So, why *do* you think she did it?"

The girls around her feigned ignorance. *Who? Did what?*

Audra bit a french fry. "She's all by herself, but she pairs up with this other weird kid, Noah Stein. Then she cuts his throat. In front of everybody. So—why?"

There were a lot of theories, most of them already percolating for weeks. Everyone at the table had only been waiting for Audra to open the door to discussion. Someone suggested Lorelei was trying to curry favor with upperclassmen who hated Stein.

"Then why isn't she bragging about it?" Audra asked.

Allissa Hardawicky raised her palms. "Asshole Face and whatsisname are saying they forced it from her. Threatened her."

"Gross," Audra said. "I can't believe those guys are actually proud of picking on a freshman girl. Weaklings."

"What about the rumor that Lorelei had *volunteered* to be their freshman? Had *begged* them to be her mentors?" asked Sandy Burk, Audra's best friend and consigliere. "She chose them *because* they were at war with her boyfriend."

"He must have done something to her. Hurt her in some way," Allissa suggested.

Audra shook her head. How Machiavellian. "The girl's got ice water," she said, and bit into another fry.

Gym class. Spring had warmed the Valley to a humid sweat, and the trees had just begun to show blooming buds of green.

There was no longer a need for Phys Ed class at the bowling alley. Mr. Mankowski and Mr. Zimmer organized outdoor games in the old church field, which after the heavy rains was the consistency of chocolate pudding beneath the grass. The boys frolicked in the filth as they played football at one end of the lot, while the girls tiptoed through the sludge around the volleyball net, letting the ball plop into the muck if hitting it required anything more than a slight lean. Many of them slipped and fell a couple times anyway, soaking up the clay-stained mud like paintbrushes. The new school Monitors kept asking Mr. Mankowski whether it was necessary or appropriate for the children to have class in these conditions and then penciled in the teacher's dodgy, defensive answer in their notebooks while remaining firmly on the dry asphalt of the parking lot.

After class, in the bathroom, across from the one that was now closed due to Stein's vandalism, there was a line of freshman girls in underwear awaiting their turns at the sinks. Lorelei was the last. She had dressed quietly in the corner at the start of class, but here at the end she was tired and careless, and she peeled off her grimy T-shirt and shorts and slung them to the ground like everybody else.

She didn't stop to think about it.

Meanwhile, the next class—sophomore girls—had also entered the

bathroom to begin changing for their outdoor activities, squawking in protest about the muddy conditions.

It was Theresa Grough, a sophomore, younger sister of the brutish
Anne-Marie, who was the first to notice the marks on Lorelei's back.

Theresa's face was in the mirror over Lorelei's shoulder, her mouth
open. Lorelei didn't realize what the girl was looking at, but she expected a
nasty remark.

The insult didn't come, though. Theresa backed away. She was whispering in the corner now, and those girls were also staring at the freshman.
Lorelei didn't care what they were talking about. Just another insult. She
was getting used to it.

But that wasn't what the girls were doing.

It had been three weeks since the brawl at her house. The shattered
phone had been replaced, the spaghetti sauce stain cleaned. There was no
mention of it between her, her father, or her mother.

But the damage hadn't healed yet, either.

She couldn't see the marks herself, so she didn't know they were still
there—giant seeping bruises blossoming along her spine in clouds of purple and yellow, like fat, toxic clouds.

Lorelei walked back to her bag, trying to ignore the looks. She slid on her
blouse, buttoning it quickly, then pulled up the skirt and slipped into her
shoes, walking out the door with her duffel bag hanging from her hand.
For the first time, the other girls remained silent after she had gone.

"What do you mean, 'What do I think'? I think it's bullshit," Davidek said.

"But that's what people are saying," LeRose told him. "All the girls in my
class. They saw the marks on her back. Everyone says Stein must've done
that to her right before she sold him out."

They were standing near the third-floor exhaust fan, which was loud
enough to keep the conversation private. "Are you sure you'd know if it was
true or not?" LeRose asked.

Davidek ran fingers through his hair. "*Yes*, I'd fucking know. And you
should, too, asshole." LeRose's husky body squirmed as Davidek jabbed his
finger in his chest. "Remember lying facedown out in the parking lot?
Who the hell do you think saved you?"

"You," LeRose said quietly.

"Yeah, well, what about Stein? You think he was just standing there? If he hadn't—"

Davidek swallowed his words. He thought of that infamous kiss, Stein holding Ms. Bromine's stuffed-turkey face between his palms and planting a big wet one on her. Stein never wanted anyone to know it was true. *That's called getting away with it,* he had said.

"Let's just say Stein did his part to help drag your ass clear, got it?"

"Fine," LeRose said without really believing it.

"It's not 'fine,'" Davidek insisted. "Lorelei's a liar and she's trying to make herself look like some kind of I-am-woman-hear-me-roar feminist fucking martyr, but he never laid a finger on her. All he did was talk crazy Hallmark shit about *how he loved her,* and *they were meant for each other* and—"

"I talked to a bunch of girls in your class who saw the bruises," LeRose said.

Davidek closed his eyes. He tried to like LeRose, but sometimes . . . "Stein never hurt her. Never." Then a memory came back to him: Lorelei after stealing her mother's cigarettes, saying she got caught . . . and the marks on her arms.

"It's her mom and dad who made her a punching bag," Davidek said. "They probably did it this time, too."

LeRose squished his chins together doubtfully.

"She's a *liar,* fuckface," Davidek protested. "Quit looking at me like that."

"Well, I'm just telling you what people are saying," LeRose said, then squinted at him and asked, "Are you wearing his clip-on now?"

Davidek's hand shot to the red tie clasped at his throat. "No," he answered. "It's mine."

"Looks goofy," LeRose told him, pulling open the stairway door.

Davidek's hand fiddled with flaps of his blazer, closing them over the tie as much as he could. "Who cares what you think?" he said. But LeRose had already gone.

"What are you ladies doing?" It was Michael Crawford, standing beside the lunch table where his girlfriend, Audra, and her friends from the student council sat huddled around their pizza slices.

"We're talking," Audra said. "About—" She nodded in Lorelei's direction without saying her name.

"Ah, yes," Crawford said, flashing his JCPenney–model smile. "The only girl in school that no boy wants to get screwed by!" He chuckled, but Audra curled her lip in disgust. The other girls looked frightened for Michael's safety.

"That joke's old. And it's not funny anymore," Audra snarled. "If you ever laid a hand on me, I'd do the same thing to you. . . ."

Michael Crawford took a very long, very slow step backwards. "Uhh-hhh," he said. "What . . . are you talking about?"

Minutes later, Crawford walked up to a lonely table, where Mullen and Simms were sitting and looking at a car magazine, lingering on the bikini models spread across the hoods. Crawford had a few friends along with him now—reinforcements. "Hey, Asshole Face," he said, and Mullen and Simms both looked up, though only one of them had been addressed. "Audra wanted me to ask you something. . . ."

Mullen and Simms looked at each other dumbly. Michael Crawford said, "Did you jagoffs know beforehand that Lorelei was getting beat up by that kid?"

Mullen's face spread in a confused, nervous smile as his eyes slid toward Simms. Crawford lifted the edge of the table, spilling the two dweebs' lunches into their laps as they scrambled up from their seats in panic.

"Yeah, you guys are the masterminds, all right," Crawford said, then took an unopened bag of pretzels off Mullen's tray and walked away, sharing them with his friends.

In the same lunchroom, a day later, Lorelei sat alone, as she usually did.

Then a girl from her class sat at the far end of the table. Then two more. Then a whole crowd, and eventually the table was full. It made Lorelei nervous.

Eventually, she would hear bits of the rumors that Stein had abused her, but the stories would never be complete, not in the detail that spread throughout the school behind her back. She would never have the opportunity to truly deny them. And she probably would have.

Zari took the seat beside her and began fluttering a deck of tarot cards on her tray. "You ever had a reading?"

Lorelei looked down at the first card Zari drew: an ominous portrait of crows flying away from a dead tree. "That looks bad. . . ."

"No," Zari said hesitantly, and thought about how to make it seem reassuring. "These crows are together. They travel as one, in a group. The crow card is a sign of friendship."

As she laid out the rest of the cards, Zari's gaze wandered over Lorelei's neck, trying to peek beneath the collar, to see the bruises the whole school was whispering about. If things with her and Stein had gone differently, she wondered whether those bruises might instead be spread across her own back.

Lorlei looked around the table. All the other girls were staring—once again. But now they were also smiling. Sweetly. Sincerely. That was the moment of Lorelei's resurrection.

It began with looks.

PART VI

Prom and Promises

THIRTY-SIX

D avidek was dreaming.

The gritty ground felt hollow beneath him. He was standing in the middle of a flat roof, on top of St. Michael's, and the low brick walls of the ledge surrounded him. The sky was almost radioactive in its glow.

The crazy boy from the roof was here, but Davidek could only sense him, not see him. Davidek kept turning around, but the boy was always right behind him. Then the statues of the saints lining the wall began to turn toward him from their guard posts along the wall. They told Davidek that it didn't matter if he could see The Boy on the Roof—he was here, and he was doing what needed to be done. Davidek could only hear him.

The unseen crazy boy repeatedly shouted *Jump!*, and with each cry, one of the stone saints would leap from the edge of the wall and dive downward like rifle bullets. There were people down there. Davidek couldn't see them, but he could hear them screaming. The dive-bombing saints were shattering the students into shrapnel clouds of stone and bone.

Davidek kept trying to get closer to the edge. He wanted to see it happening, wanted to witness this, to see them destroyed. But the statue of St. Joseph put its hand on his chest. *There is another way down*, the figure said without speaking. Davidek looking up at its unmoving concrete face—and pushed it away.

That's when he woke up.

He had been grounded ever since the day of the flood, the day Stein had slashed himself, the night he hadn't come home until after midnight. His parents demanded, of course, to know exactly where in the hell he had been, but Davidek annoyed them by just shrugging and sitting and listening to them yell. Eventually they got tired. Then, when they'd heard about the vandalism at the school, they demanded to know whether their son was involved. "Is that where you were?" his mother shouted, quaking with fury, her face contorted and red. His dad shoved him when he didn't answer.

"Do I have to repeat it for you?" his mother said. God, that annoying phrase.

That's when he gave in. It was when he always gave in.

Davidek said he didn't do anything. "You can ask Sister Maria," he told them. And they did, and the nun said, "Your son didn't do anything." This surprised them. They were prepared to incinerate their second-born, but Sister Maria said their boy only missed his bus because he was trying to stop the Stein boy. She said she drove him home herself when she found him late at night, trying to do what he could to clean up the destruction. Davidek was impressed by how good a liar the nun was. "Without Peter, I can assure you from the bottom of my heart that things would have turned out much worse." Her eyes met the freshman's. Those were the only honest words spoken during the conference with his parents.

Davidek's parents grounded him anyway. For not telling them the whole story. That was okay. There was nowhere Davidek wanted to go. Green was busy with some little band he was trying to get started with his senior friends. LeRose only nagged him about whether he'd heard anything new about Hannah's secret book. When Hannah came around, all she wanted to talk about was the upcoming prom—as if he cared.

Davidek's parents also took away TV, which was especially bad during the two weeks trapped at home, cut off from everybody, when school was canceled to repair the collapsed roof. Sometimes Davidek would lock his bedroom door, crawl under his blankets, and bury his face in a pillow, where he could cry his eyes out without anyone hearing. It made his head bulge with pressure, and sometimes his eyes itched afterwards. Sometimes he just fell asleep that way, and would wake up the next morning in the same clothes he'd worn the day before.

At night, when his parents were asleep, he began sneaking into the basement where there was an old telephone near the washing machines. From their bedroom upstairs, they wouldn't be able to hear him. He called Allegheny General Hospital each night, trying to find out about Stein. Davidek wasn't part of Stein's family, so the nurses on his floor wouldn't reveal much. Davidek thought about lying—maybe saying he was Stein's brother—but the nurses probably knew if Stein had a brother, and maybe hospitals could trace telephone calls. Davidek had no idea.

The nurse's usual acknowledgment was enough. "I can't tell you anything about that patient." That didn't mean Stein was getting better, but at least he was still being treated. At least Stein still *was,* period.

When school started again, Davidek visited Sister Maria's office each morning, trying to learn more about his friend's status, but she was evasive. "Oh, you know . . . ," she said. ". . . This isn't really the best time."

It was never the best time. He realized soon that Sister Maria was never going to tell him more, that she still wasn't certain he could be trusted—though he already knew enough to be dangerous to her. "Sometimes you have to keep a secret by not acknowledging there *is* a secret," she told him. "And your friend is not a student here anymore. He is indefinitely suspended. So it would look strange to people if I were giving daily updates to his old buddies."

Davidek felt like he deserved more from the nun after the night they had shared.

Indefinitely suspended. What did that mean?

Mr. Mankowski still read Stein's name each morning during homeroom roll call. Mankowski would say: "Stein, Noah . . . ," and wait for the response he knew would never come. Then he'd check the boy absent. On the third day of this, Davidek said loudly, "He's not here, and you know it."

"Did I ask *you* a question?" Mankowski said.

Davidek told him, "No. You were just embarrassing yourself. He's gone, not *invisible*." And then *Davidek* was gone, dispatched to Sister Maria's office for "verbally abusing" his homeroom teacher. The nun sighed when she saw him. "This has to stop," she said. But it didn't.

In the halls throughout the next month, Davidek bristled with violence.

Mullen and Simms moped by the water fountain, and he wanted to slam their heads into the brick wall. "Cocksuckers," he whispered, and one of them called back weakly, "Oh yeah? . . ."

When he saw Lorelei Paskal, he wanted to bellow in her face, but his nerve always disintegrated when she was near. He couldn't stand to see her, mostly because she still looked like the girl he used to know, the one he'd sneaked a cigarette with in another life. She had tossed away the rest of the carton. *I just saved your life,* she had said. And she would have kissed him then if he hadn't flinched. If he hadn't been shy, and afraid.

Most of all, Davidek was tired of seeing Smitty, tired of his ice-cube eyes and his big razor-smile. Davidek drove his shoulder into the bigger boy as he squeezed through the crowded hallway. Smitty wasn't expecting a hit and lost his balance, bumping back against some sophomore girls.

"Watch yourself," Davidek said. The larger boy, stunned, watched Davidek moving away. "How about 'excuse me,' shithead?" Smitty shouted. Davidek turned back, still moving, "Excuse me, shithead," he said.

A pair of elderly Parish Monitors in the hall noticed that, and began scribbling in their notebooks.

Hannah stopped Davidek after school that day, ambushing him beside his bus. "I'd like you to stop picking fights with Smitty."

Davidek shrugged her off. "Or else what? You gonna print up some photos? And why do you care about Smitty? He's a big boy."

She grabbed his arm as he tried to walk way. "What's your problem? Why start something with him? Don't you have enough people out to kick your ass?"

Davidek squinted impatiently. "That day, the rainstorm . . . He fucking rammed Stein from the back. *From the back.* For no reason. Stein had enough shit that day. He didn't need *that.*"

"Smitty had reason," she said.

"Whatever . . . ," Davidek said, and pulled away.

"Stein was gonna do something he'd have regretted, Playgirl!" Hannah shouted after him. "Anyone could see that. Mullen and Simms are dumb-asses, but they didn't deserve what he—"

Davidek turned back on her. "They deserved *worse*. And you weren't even around. What the hell do you know about anything?"

"I knew it before he even walked into school that day. All those people with the red scars. Of course he'd go after the two who caused it. Actually, I thought he might go after his little girlfriend, too. Let's face it—your friend was psycho. Sorry. And Smitty says he showed you the steel bar."

Davidek didn't respond. Hannah said, "What if he'd shot or stabbed them or something?"

"He didn't have a gun," Davidek said, irritated by her implication.

"But he *could* have. So, fine, he had some *iron bar* instead. And Smitty took it off him. Where would your friend be if those two losers were lying brain-dead in the parking lot?"

"I don't know. Couldn't be much worse than where he is now."

"What*ever*," Hannah laughed. "Your angry pal with the big sad story smashes some toilets and gets expelled. At least he's sitting out the school year at home instead of jail, right?"

She paced toward her Jeep, then whirled back at Davidek. "Smitty had reason to go after him. And *I'm* the reason, okay? I'm the one who thought something bad might happen and I *told* Smitty to watch you and Stein, to follow him around that day. To make sure nothing happened that couldn't *un*happen—do you understand? Smitty did you *and* your fucked-up friend a favor. So try thanking him instead of giving him needless shit, okay?"

The bus driver called out to Davidek: "On or off, buddy?"

Davidek shifted his book bag on his shoulder. "So Smitty just does what you tell him?" he asked Hannah. "And why would he do *that*?"

The wind played in Hannah's fiery hair. "Because I know *his* secret, too," she said. Hannah was turning the key in her Jeep's ignition when Davidek opened the door and got in. "Thanks," he said.

"For what?"

"For watching out for Stein when I wasn't," he said. The yellow school bus passed in front of the Jeep's windshield. "And for giving me a ride home," Davidek added. "No detours this time."

"Are you going to come to the prom for me?" Hannah asked as the neighborhoods of Natrona Heights rolled by outside the Jeep.

Davidek said unhappily, "Why, you need a date?"

She laughed, brushing stray hairs away from her face. "I'd take you, Playgirl, I really would. But freshmen can't go as dates. You can volunteer to help out, though—decorate, and clean up and stuff. Lots of underclassmen do that."

"Not interested," Davidek said.

"Then just come and see me," she said. "There's a little photo area and a red carpet and everything. Usually a lot of parents come, but some freshmen do, too. I'll be all by myself, so it would be nice to see a friendly face. Maybe you could snap some pictures of me all dolled up in my dress." She formed the fingers of one hand into a small invisible box and raised it to her face, clicking the nonexistent shutter.

Davidek shrugged. "And if I say no, do you head off to the Fotomat to order double prints of your little trick from under the bridge?"

Hannah looked at him steadily. "No," she said. "I won't do that. Prom is only if you want to, Peter."

He nodded. "All right," he said, not sure if he meant it.

THIRTY-SEVEN

In Biology the next day, Davidek asked Green if he planned to go to the prom. "Sure," Green said, delighted that Davidek was feeling chatty again. "Where else can I see Bilbo Tomch in a tux?"

Davidek said, "You going to work? Like, that volunteer stuff . . . or just go for fun?"

Green shook his head. "I'm volunteering in the kitchen, but I'm also gonna take some pictures for the guys. My dad's got a good camera. Plus, my mom said I should go. She said girls like guys who act interested in proms and stuff."

Davidek said he might go, too. Just to see it. "Want to carpool?"

Green thought for a second and said, "Sure. My mom can come get you, and your mom or dad can pick us up." Green was quiet; then he added, "The guys saw you get in the Jeep with Hannah Kraut yesterday, out by the bus."

"Oh yeah?" Davidek said.

"Yeah," Green replied, fiddling with his fingers. "So we're wondering where you stand with her. Are you just going to do everything she says from now on?"

"She's my senior," Davidek told him. "You're doing what *your* seniors tell you. That's how it goes."

"Yeah, but Hannah . . ." Green trailed off. "Maybe it would be best to make *her* your one big enemy, instead of making a million enemies out of everybody else. All the other students are crapping their pants, wondering what stupid-ass thing they did three years ago that's going to rise up out of her notebook on Hazing Day. And with these old people, these parish Monitors, hanging around, watching everybody like hawks . . . The teachers are going nuts, too. The point is, Hannah's a backstabbing bitch, man. And you have to decide whose side you're on."

"Hers or the rest of the school?"

Green pointed a finger at him. "Her side—or *your* side." Davidek thought of Hannah's little disposable camera, but his mind also drifted to the other things he saw during those moments in the Jeep, the glimpses under her skirt and between her shirt, the smoothness of her legs as she held his hand on her thigh. . . .

"I'm definitely not with the backstabbing bitch," he reassured Green, who put a hand on his shoulder.

"I knew you weren't, man. The guys'll be glad to know it, too. You know, they're not so bad. I think you'd like them. And if the guys believe you're on their side, they'll be a lot nicer."

"Awesome . . . ," Davidek said unenthusiastically. *The guys . . .*

Each morning, Mr. Mankowski still read Stein's name in the homeroom roll call. And each morning, Davidek wondered if that would be the day his friend came back. He kept calling the hospital at night, never learning anything.

Sooner or later, Stein would get better. Then he'd help Davidek figure out what to do about "the guys," Hannah, and everything.

But it never happened.

The next Friday ended early so it could run late.

That was the tradition at St. Mike's before prom night: classes cut off at lunchtime as the upperclassmen hustled home to prepare themselves in the finest and most glamorous attire they could rent. It would be the best they'd look in their young lives—until they were married, or possibly, as

the teachers liked to joke about the less attractive students, until they were
buried.

The prom took place each year in the same location—Veltri's Restaurant, a glass-and-steel box leaning over the bluff atop Coxcomb Hill, overlooking the towns of Springdale and Cheswick, as well as the rocket-sized
orange-and-white smokestack of the Duquesne Light power plant between
them, which belched coal smoke into the orange sunset.

The first people to gather at the prom were the underclassman volunteers, then the paparazzi crowd of family and friends—overeager parents
and grandparents and uncles and aunts and glum younger siblings, all setting off storms of photo flashes as the formally attired teenage couples began arriving to walk the red carpet (donated courtesy of the local Prizzant's
Carpet Warehouse chain, as a sign beside the walkway attested). The
prom-goers smiled and waved for the starstruck relatives, who saw them all
the time, but now acted as if they were looking at Tom Cruise and Nicole
Kidman.

Quite a few freshmen were gathered along the photo line, most of them
girls who cheered for their upperclassmen friends, then snottily pointed
out amongst themselves who had lifted her hairstyle directly from *Prom
Time* magazine instead of the glossy and more respected *Spring Fling*.

The school tried to add a touch of class to the night by having Mr.
Mankowski stand near the entrance and announce each couple through a
microphone wired to a small amplifier at his feet. He was bad at it, and
some guessed deliberately so—although that wasn't true. He tried his best.
He was color-blind, so every dress was described as "light" or "dark." He
also had trouble remembering students' names.

Stretching out in the property adjacent to the restaurant was a gravel
parking lot that crumbled away at the edges to hardpan dirt and grass.
Thick stands of trees rimmed the grounds and swayed to the muted throb
of music coming from inside the building. Parked along the trees in the
shadows, far away from the other vehicles, Hannah sat in her Jeep, watching the festive line of classmates move inside. She had a jean jacket over
her bare shoulders, and the shimmering layers of pink chiffon puffed up
around her midsection, as if she had sunken into a pile of cotton candy.

Since she had no date, Hannah preferred to wait until everyone else was inside so Mankowski wouldn't announce her solo status. Plus, she hadn't seen Mr. Zimmer's car in the lot, and she didn't want to go into the party until she had someone to talk to.

Mr. Zimmer was really the only reason she was there. She was hoping to end this year with one happy memory. A dance with the person she loved. Even if it just looked to everyone else like a lonely student dancing with a sympathetic teacher.

Zimmer arrived around the last of sunset, and he and Mankowski stood outside the doors staring into the horizon over the bluff like old sailors appraising a storm front. They exchanged a few words; then Zimmer bowed his head and vanished into the restaurant without noticing her parked in the distance. Still she waited. Davidek wasn't here, and he had promised he would take a picture as she walked inside. Her mom and dad wouldn't be here. She told them not to come. She didn't want people in the crowd to say anything about her to them.

Hannah was in no hurry to get inside. She was about as welcome among her classmates as a drunk-driving fatality. Before the night was over, though, it would be nice to get one photo of herself, smiling, looking cute in her new dress, which she had saved her own money to buy.

The sun settled into its cradle behind the hills. Hannah Kraut waited awhile longer, wondering where her little freshman could be.

Davidek had been in the basement putting a shirt in the wash before the prom when he picked up the old phone that hung beside the dryer and made one of his routine calls to the hospital. He knew the number by heart, and listened patiently to the recorded intro message, which brightly advised him that if he was having an actual emergency that he should dial 911. Davidek pressed the four-digit extension to the nursing station on Stein's floor.

A man's voice answered—it had always been a woman before—and the man said "Y'ello?" instead of the standard "Allegheny, floor five, station two."

Davidek said, "I'm calling for Noah Stein." The man's voice said, "Uh . . ." And there was the sound of shuffling papers. "Are you family?"

Davidek decided to take a chance on the man's confusion. "I'm his cousin," he said. "How is he?"

More papers shuffled. The man sighed and took a long time to answer. "That patient is *gone*," the voice said at last.

"Gone where?" Davidek said.

"Gone," the man said. "He's just . . . I don't know. He's gone. Look, I'm just an orderly, the nurse asked me to watch the phone. . . ."

"Let me speak to a nurse," Davidek said. He waited a good while. He heard voices conferring on the other end, and then a female voice got on the line: "I'm sorry. We've been asked by the family not to say anything." Then she hung up.

Davidek immediately dialed Stein's house. He didn't call there much anymore. The line had been busy at all hours for two weeks. It didn't go through this time either.

Davidek slammed down the phone. When he rounded the corner by the furnace, his mother stood at the foot of the basement steps. "Were you just calling someone?"

Davidek said, "No. . . . Yes, but it's just—"

His mother jabbed a finger at him. "You're still grounded—and that means no phone, you got that?"

"Yeah, but it's . . . ," Davidek said. He started up the stairs, trying to figure out a lie. "The prom's tonight," he said lamely.

"Grounded means no prom," she said.

"Mom . . . ," Davidek said, his voice shaking. *He's gone.* That's what the hospital worker had said. "It's . . . it's for school. Freshmen *have* to go. I have to volunteer. It's not like I *want* to. . . . Dad knows already. . . ."

"Your father's driving you?" his mother said, grabbing his arm. Davidek told her, "No, he's picking us up. That's what I'm trying to tell you. I was calling my friend, Green . . . his mom is picking us up."

His mother shook her head. "Always an exception for you, isn't there? . . ."

Davidek jerked his arm away. He glanced sideways at the phone. "I have to get ready," he mumbled to the ground, and his mother stepped aside.

"By all means, my prince," June Davidek purred, bowing as she extended a hand up the stairs.

There was a cordless phone in Davidek's parents' room. He waited until his mother wasn't watching him anymore, then grabbed it and slipped outside to the space between their house and the neighbor's.

The sun was almost gone over the hills. Silhouetted birds chattered overhead as they circled the chimneys. Davidek knelt in the balding grass and his thumbs danced over the phone's keypad. The line began to ring, and the voice of Hector Greenwill answered.

"Listen, Green, I need to ask you a favor, okay?"

Green said, "Ooooohhkay," with a doubtful tone.

"Can your mom come over here early—like, right now—and give us a ride out to Stein's house?"

Green groaned. "Stein's house? I thought we were picking you up to go to *prom*."

"We just need to do this first," Davidek said. "I promise, it's *very* important and I'll explain later—well, as much as I can. I need you to trust me."

"So, *what* are you asking?"

Davidek told him again, and Green repeated: "So my mom and me are supposed to come all the way from *our* house in Brackenridge, over the bridge to *your* place, then backtrack all the way over here again and out to the woods to where *Stein* lives? And you can't tell me why?"

"Green, listen—"

"And then what? We go *back* over the bridge toward *your* side of town and head up to Veltri's for the prom? Dude, we'll be two hours late!"

"Forget the prom, Green. I just need you to give me a ride to Stein's. And we need to do it now."

Green laughed in spite of himself. "Bilbo and some of the guys said maybe I could help out a little with the DJ, you know? They said they knew him."

"Green, you can go to the prom later, but I need this favor first. Stein needs us."

"Stein doesn't go to school with us anymore," Green told him flatly.

"You don't know the whole story. . . ."

"Are you trying to sneak him to the prom? Davidek, the guy is a waste. *Forget* him."

"Stein was your friend," Davidek said.

Green broke some news to him: "No, he wasn't. He was *your* friend, and I put up with him. And he gave me endless shit all the time about hanging out with seniors. But guess what? They were nice to me. He wasn't."

"Look, he didn't mean it like th— It's just that you were—"

"Davidek . . ."

"—you were doing whatever they *told* you to do. Their little favorite. And the rest of us are just getting pushed around—"

"Davidek . . ."

"—so just do this, *okay?*"

"Davidek."

"*What?*" the boy cried.

Green informed him: "I'm *not* doing this."

"Just ask your mom. You didn't even *ask!*"

"I don't want to. . . . I want to go to the pr—"

Davidek screamed, "Fuck! Fuck the prom!" and Green fell quiet again. "Some fucking *friend*, Green. If you won't do it for Stein, then do it for *me*."

"I'm not doing anything," Green said. "I want to go to the *prom*. And see my *friends*. And hang out."

Davidek grasped for words, his lips shook, and his skin tightened against his jaw. His pulse surged and roared in his ears. "Goddamnit, Green," he said. "Your *friends?* You think you have *friends?* You want to know what those *friends* say when you're not around? The name they call you?"

Green sighed on the other end of the line. "What name is that, Davidek?"

"You know which one. You haven't heard it, but you *know*."

"No. No, I don't. So enlighten me."

The truth was he'd never heard anyone say that about Green, but the angry part of him, the hurt and desperate part wouldn't let it go. He wanted to wound Green. He wanted to hurt him as badly as he could, as badly as he was hurting. "They're nice to you because they're afraid not to be," Davidek hissed. "And you're too fucking stupid to know it. Too fucking *stupid* to know who's *really* your friend."

"Like you?" Green's voice cracked. "Because you're really showing it now. What name, Davidek?"

"Guess, Green. Take a fucking guess."

"Why don't you say it? It sounds like you might want to."

"Fuck you, Green."

"Say it! You basically already have. Or are you too much of a coward to actually do it?"

The words exploded from him, like a spray of poison. "*Nigger*, Green. Is that what you wanted to hear? That's what they call you, your bullshit upperclassman ass-kissers. Happy?"

Green was silent on the other end of the line. Davidek couldn't even hear his breath anymore. "I always stood up for you, Green. I always said you *weren't*."

But Green didn't respond to that either. "Green, I wasn't . . . Green! Come on, I'm *sorry*. I'm just . . . I need your help, Green. *Green*! . . ."

Davidek kept talking, kept pleading, kept saying he was sorry, even though he knew his friend had already hung up. Eventually he just held the phone out from his face and looked at it, as if it had just bitten him. The sky had faded to dark blue, and the sickly green glow of the telephone keypad was the only light between the houses now.

Stein had once made a prediction about Green: "*What word do you suppose his 'pals' will call him the nanosecond he crosses them? I'll give you a hint—it starts with N, and it ain't* nipple, Norwegian, *or* nymphomaniac." Davidek's heart sank to know he was the one who'd made it come true.

The shrill buzzing of a busy signal squawked from the phone and an insistent electronic voice said, "*If you'd like to make a call, please hang up and try again.*" Davidek hurled the phone against the concrete blocks at the base of the house, where it smashed and fell silent into the tall weeds. As he bent and scrounged for it, he slapped one flat palm against the foundation. Then hit it again. And again. And again, until his skin split.

Bill Davidek turned down the volume on the *Columbo* TV movie he was watching. "What's the matter?" he asked his wife, who was standing in the archway staring at him with her arms crossed.

She pouted. "Peter says you're driving him home later from this silly prom thing he allegedly *has* to do. Do we really *have* to let him go? Does the school *really* make the new kids do *work* there?"

Bill Davidek shrugged. "I didn't last long enough at St. Mike's to make it to prom."

"I can't believe he didn't even ask *me*," she said. "That's because he knew I'd say no. You're too easy on him."

"Jesus Christ . . . ," Bill Davidek said.

They heard the back door open in the kitchen, and June called to her son from the living room: "Peter? . . . Come in here, please. We need to discuss this prom thing."

There was no answer. "Peter—come in here!" his mother said. *"Do I need to repea—?"*

Davidek stepped into the light of the kitchen hallway, and his mother's words broke off. The boy's eyes were red, his lips swollen. He was clammy, and his pale skin looked like a freshly used bar of soap. "I need a favor. A ride," Davidek said. "I need you to take me to my friend's house. Please?"

His mother scoffed. "Your friend's house now?" she said. "We're telling you, you're not going anywhere. Not the prom, and certainly not for a play-date . . ."

Davidek turned to his father, as if his mother didn't exist. "Dad, can you take me? I need to leave now." His father turned up the volume on the television.

"I think you're confused about how things work around here," Davidek's mother said. "We tell you how it's going to be, and you're going to start listening, mister—"

Davidek backed away into the kitchen. They heard the loud spray of the faucet in the stainless steel sink.

"Get back here when I'm talking to you!" his mother screamed. She crossed her arms and said to her husband: "Are you going to let him treat us this way?"

June turned toward the kitchen hallway, and yelled. "Peter!" But her son didn't answer. The two parents listened, but the only response was the steady, angry hiss of the faucet.

"Peter! Get in here!" his father said wearily.

June spotted droplets of blood on the kitchen tile and walked toward them. "What the hell is wrong? Did you cut yourself?" she called. Bill Davidek turned down the volume again, irritated. "What's the problem now?" he asked.

June turned the corner into the kitchen, which was empty. The sink, loaded with dishes, was beginning to overflow with water. Bill Davidek appeared behind his wife as she turned off the faucet with a slap. He looked toward the wide-open back door. "He'll be sorry when he comes back," he said.

June pushed past him. "I'll be damned if he thinks he can just do whatever he wants. I'll chase the little shit down." She reached for her car keys, which usually hung on a little wooden plaque beside the stove that read: KEYS TO THE KINGDOM. The plaque had a picture of Jesus having a chat with some sheep.

But her car keys were gone. So were her husband's.

Bill Davidek walked to the front door and looked outside. His truck was still there, thank goodness. His wife appeared at his side. "Where is my goddamn minivan?" she asked.

THIRTY-EIGHT

Davidek hugged the steering wheel of his mom's Aerostar as the rushing scenery attacked him. He had never controlled a moving vehicle before, though as a little boy—like all kids—he fantasized about it while sitting in the driver's seat with the ignition off and the steering wheel locked in place.

But when he twisted the stolen keys in the ignition outside his house, he wasn't prepared for the fluidity of real-life steering. Each turn seemed to send the wheels beneath him sideways—as if the tires were trying to break free, and then the hulk of the rest of the vehicle would lurch over to grab them back. The white streetlamps were flickering on as he piloted the car down his quiet street, gaining speed as he imagined his mother and father running in furious pursuit behind him.

He swerved out of his neighborhood onto a four-lane strip known as the Bypass, so called because it looped away from New Kensington's downtown business district en route to the Tarentum Bridge and the main freeway leading to Pittsburgh. It was no place for a first driving lesson. Especially one that didn't have a teacher. The terror of driving actually cooled Davidek's other panicked thoughts—of reaching Stein's house, and what he might find there.

Davidek overcorrected on a curve, and the minivan wiggled crazily down

the road, hanging over the dotted center line. Staying in one lane just seemed
too narrow to him. The Bypass cut through a section of woods, which opened
on an intersection with a stand of condominium apartments on one side,
and on the other a brown-brick strip mall with a Kings Family Restaurant and
a real estate office that shared two misspelled words on one sign:

CARMEL APPLE PIE TODAY

MORTGAGE! 5 PRECENT DOWN!

The rapidly approaching traffic light hanging over the road did not stay
green, and Davidek noticed the red too late, holding tight to the wheel and
flattening his foot on the brakes, unleashing a hideous squeal. The minivan
blasted out peals of blue smoke, and Davidek imagined the tires stretching
backwards on the road like soft butter as the car jerked to a stop.

Davidek tapped his fingers on the wheel, trying not to look at the other
drivers, and after several decades, the traffic light finally turned green
again. He pressed his foot softly on the gas and crept past the Giant Eagle
grocery store, rolling out onto the great steel and concrete tongue of the
Tarentum Bridge.

The long, straight blue band, shining off the surface of the river below,
yawned out ahead of him—four lanes of sheer terror, leading to infinite
plunges into watery oblivion. The traffic here was more reckless—cars,
buses, and trucks weaving around him like a slalom. Blasting their horns
at his slow-pokery.

As he drove above it, he wondered absently if any couples were necking
in their cars in that hidden spot below the bridge, where Hannah had once
tempted him so coldly, so deliciously.

Hannah fixed her makeup.

She peered into the rearview mirror of her Jeep and cracked open the
door so the dome light would come on. Hannah didn't wear makeup very
often, so she hoped it looked all right. When she was finished, the Jeep
door swung open, hatching the pink chiffon Hannah into the world like a
fuzzy Easter Peep. The crumbling asphalt made it hard to walk in her high
heels. She balanced awkwardly, fingers tracing the red hair that fell in

curls across her shoulders. She tossed her jean jacket inside the Jeep and slammed the door, then smoothed down the ruffles of her pink-puff dress and composed herself.

The crowd of family and friends had put away their flashing cameras and were beginning to depart. Mr. Mankowski hadn't yet coiled his microphone cord when he spotted Hannah. The bald man cleared his throat and announced: "Here is Hannah Kraut, looking lovely in a light-colored dress." He smiled at her, and didn't point out to those still around to hear that she was alone, which made her smile back.

The thrum of music from inside bulged against the walls of Veltri's Restaurant, like the pulsing of a giant heart, clarifying instantly as the glass doors swung open, revealing a black-tie crowd of teenagers meandering about a semi-elegant habitat of ferns and mirrored columns, more ready to eat than dance, despite the best intentions (and frenetic light display) of the DJ. There were already kids sitting at Hannah's table, watching some freshman volunteers help the restaurant staff deliver plates of food.

Against the far back wall was the long table for teachers and chaperones, but Hannah didn't see Mr. Zimmer. Then she heard his voice behind her. "I thought you skipped on me!" he said, surprising her with a tap on the shoulder. He grinned at her in his pale gray suit.

"Very stylish for a guy who prides himself on being unfashionable," she said.

He frowned playfully. "I don't take pride in *that*."

Tears were gathering in the corner of her eyes as he linked his arm with hers and escorted her into the dance. "Thank you," she said softly, but he didn't know for what. Then, trying to seem casual, she nudged his shoulder with her small fist. "Dance with me later, all right?"

"Right," he said, hands in his pockets.

"You promise?"

Mr. Zimmer smiled and nodded more dramatically, the way students do when they're promising after three warnings not to turn in their papers late anymore. She could tell he was uncomfortable. "You don't want to . . . ," she said.

Zimmer laughed, "Uh, it'll look *strange*," he said, flattening his hands together. "But, no funny business, okay?" He figured he could make it look benign to the others—like she was dancing with him as a joke, because who would ever want to dance with a mug like him. He wanted to say no, but was overwhelmed by sorrow for Hannah, who was so friendless and needy. He'd been there himself. He wanted her to be happy.

"Wait until you see my moves," Zimmer said, ratcheting his arms in exaggerated robotic gestures. "You'll live to regret cutting a rug with me."

Hannah's eyes began to tear again, and she lowered her head against his chest as she hugged him. Mr. Zimmer raised her chin. "I'm kidding, Hannah," he said, trying to get her to smile. "I'm not *that* bad."

Davidek's van was parked crooked on the street in front of the convent. The engine was was ticking as Davidek walked across the lawn.

He decided not to go to Stein's house first. Maybe he was afraid. Anyway, he only knew how to get there by starting from the school, and before he did anything, Davidek wanted to see Sister Maria. She should have told him if Stein was out of the hospital. She could tell him now if Stein was better, or . . . He didn't want to think about the alternative. Stein *had* to be better.

Davidek pounded on the convent door. He kept expecting police sirens to race after him. His mom would certainly be willing to turn him in. His father probably just wanted to go back to watching TV. Davidek felt a thrill at the thought that his parents had no clue where he was or why he had gone—or how to get him back. Let *them* feel helpless now.

He knocked on the convent door again and a tiny head appeared in the cross-shaped window. The prunelike face of Sister Antonia demanded to know who he was.

"Sister, it's . . . Peter Davidek, I'm a student at the school—"

"Who?"

"Peter Davidek . . . I'm a student." He said it louder: "*I'm a student.*"

The nun's eyes regarded him without recognition. "This is a nun's convent," she said.

"I'm looking for Sister Maria," Davidek said. "I have something to ask her. It's something important. I've come a long way and I need her to talk to h—"

The wrinkled face disappeared. Davidek considered knocking again, but Sister Antonia returned again. "I have a piece of paper and a pencil," she said through the glass. "Tell me your name again and spell it. Spell it *right*."

"I'm looking for Sister Maria," he said.

"I *told* you," the nun insisted, even though she hadn't. "Sister Maria's *not here*."

The prom, Davidek thought. *Of course.*

He spelled his name, but had to repeat himself three times before Sister Antonia could finish scrawling it. Then she tapped the pencil against the glass and said, "Now I have your *name*. If you bother me again, I'm going to tell the police!"

"Just call Sister Maria. It's an emergency!" Davidek said, and hurried back to the minivan. The old nun's eyes watched through the cross as he drove away.

At the corner beside the school, along the edge of the field where the church once stood, Davidek stopped to think. Turning left would take him back the way he'd come. The other way led to Stein's house.

Davidek sat there several minutes, then spun the wheel. He even remembered to use his turn signal.

THIRTY-NINE

M s. Bromine was not an official Parish Monitor, but she volunteered her observational services on prom night nonetheless. Note-taking was a job that delighted her. When she had been a student at St. Mike's, she had always been excellent at writing down exactly what was said to her, and as a teacher, she'd been waiting years for the chance to speak her own mind. Now she'd get to do both.

The guidance counselor had never liked proms, even when she was a girl. Her senior year date, Billy Fredickson, had tried to put a hand up her dress on the way home. She hadn't let him. Now she wondered which boys would be trying that tonight, and which girls might let them. The proms she attended as a chaperone seemed to grow more debased every year. Once the meal ended, it was disgusting how quickly bow ties sprang off, shirttails came untucked, and cummerbunds went askew. Girls kicked their high heels under the table and danced with grubby feet. She wondered what else they'd be taking off when they left the prom.

As the other Monitors patrolled the dance, making the occasional note, Ms. Bromine sat alone at one of the abandoned tables and filled the pages of her stenographer's pad while trying to block out the deafening music.

Many of her observations were petty:

7 p.m.—Male student (JAY FRAMALSKI) steps on hem of skirt of female (short black hair, green dress—possible outsider date) while entering prom. She shouts S-word loud enough for everyone to hear.

And

7:35 p.m.—Dinner served buffet style. DJ (professional?) announces order of tables to be served. Sez, "Enjoy your meal, then get your BUTTS on the dance floor." "Butts" = inappropriate language.

Other things weren't wrongdoing at all, though she tried to make them seem that way:

8:01 p.m.—Principal (SISTER MARIA HEST) standing near food, observing crowd, has exchange with students. Senior student MICHAEL CRAWFORD proceeds to touch principal inappropriately = grabs her hands, mockingly dances with her, releases her. Principal laughs (Reinforces LACK of authority!!!)

Bromine noticed Hannah (marked in the notebook as "well-known problem student") approach Mr. Zimmer at 8:10, 9:15, and 9:55 P.M. and wrote "UNUSUAL" in all capital letters beside each instance.

In between were several other low-grade concerns:

8:35 p.m.—Meal is free for monitors, but chicken is undercooked.

AND

9:08 p.m.—Fellow Monitor Mr. August Shristmeyer (spell??) informs me that underclassmen volunteers were seen behind restaurant—SMOKING CIGARETTES.

After Bromine observed a fourth "suspicious" interaction between Hannah and Zimmer, the guidance counselor approached the girl directly and asked if she might be of assistance:

10:00 p.m.—Kraut girl is VERY rude. Approached to ask about nature of conversation with Zimmer. Told to "F- myself." !!!!!!

10:10 p.m.—Approach fellow teacher (Zimmer) to inquire about behavior of Kraut girl. He sez it's "nothing." Keeps blowing me off. NOTE: This is why Zimmer is problematic for school. Proving it tonight again—NOT COOPERATIVE.

10:18 p.m.—Zimmer approaches and apologizes. (SAW me writing in notebook I'll bet!) Sez Kraut girl is having troubles, nothing serious. Sez graduation "weighing heavily" on her. Asks NOT TO WRITE THIS DOWN!! (Too bad!!!)

Around 10:30 P.M., she noticed Sister Maria missing from her seat at the chaperone table. Mrs. Tunns said the principal was called away by a waiter to a phone call. "Who?" Bromine asked.

The Spanish teacher shrugged. She took a sip from a glass of red wine.

"Eleanor, is that alcohol?" Bromine was horrified.

Mrs. Tunns fluttered her eyes. "Do you want to card me?"

Bromine huffed away and immediately wrote about the incident in her notepad, followed by the words: "BAD EXAMPLE."

The call Sister Maria received came from Sister Antonia. "Sorry to bother you, but it's an emergency," the ancient French teacher said after one of the waiters asked Sister Maria to come to the phone in the manager's office. "There was a boy here looking for you."

Sister Maria couldn't imagine who it might be. The elderly nun recited the name as she'd written it: Peter Daffodil.

"What did he want?" the principal asked, but Sister Antonia didn't know.

"The boy said you'd know what it was about."

"Can you put him on?" But Sister Antonia said he had gone away more than an hour ago.

"Then why call me?" the principal asked.

Sister Antonia said, "Because the convent received another telephone call concerning this boy, from an—" a piece of notepaper crinkled beside the receiver "—from a Margie Stein. She said to call you because a boy is outside, bothering their household. I said, 'Who?' And she said this same name—*Daffodil* something."

Sister Maria closed her eyes. Sister Antonia said, "The woman wanted you to come right away. She said the same thing the boy said, 'She'll know why.' Do you understand any of this?"

Sister Maria did not like to tell lies, even little ones, but she had been accumulating a lot of them lately. "No," she said. "I have no idea."

"Who was on the phone?" asked Ms. Bromine as Sister Maria approached the restaurant's cloakroom.

The nun smiled sweetly. "Nothing important, Ms. Bromine. Just Sister Antonia . . . we're out of milk and I'll pick some up on my way home." Ms. Bromine wrote something in her notebook. Sister Maria glanced over the woman's thick arm to peek at it. "You just wrote 'REFUSES TO EXPLAIN ABSENCE,'" the principal said. "But I just *did*."

The guidance counselor clicked her pen. "I know a lie when I hear one."

Sister Maria sighed. "Have a good evening, Ms. Bromine," she said, and turned toward the cloakroom, only to face another Parish Monitor, Mr. Harrison Bellamy—a slight, balding man with rimless glasses and a neat gray suit. He was one of the Valley's top divorce attorneys. "Are you leaving us?" he asked Sister Maria.

The nun smiled at him. She repeated her lie about picking up milk for Sister Antonia. "Poor dear has trouble sleeping without a warm cup before bed," she explained. "I was just telling Ms. Bromine, as a matter of fact. . . ."

Mr. Bellamy nodded. His rimless glasses became white orbs, then human eyes again as they caught and then lost the light overhead. "So the principal is leaving the school's prom—" he checked his watch "—an *hour and a half* before it actually ends?"

"For milk . . . ," Ms. Bromine added.

Sister Maria could see her navy peacoat and crimson scarf on the hangers inside the room behind the two Monitors. "I think these young men and women will survive without me here in the treacherous no-man's-land of Veltri's family restaurant, Mr. Bellamy," she said.

Bellamy raised a pen and notebook and began to write. "Sister, frankly

I'm saddened. *Saddened.* I've been one of your defenders on the parish council, and to be honest—there aren't many of them." He continued to write, then looked up at her.

His silver eyes reflected the light again. "There is real consideration toward closing this school, Sister, a *real* possibility. . . . And seeing you, the highest-ranking figure at St. Michael's, *leave* an event that could turn volatile—"

"Volatile?"

"*Volatile,* Sister," Ms. Bromine echoed. "The high school prom is supposed to be fun, but we know what it has turned into in this age."

Mr. Bellamy painted a more direct portrait. "It's a night of drinking, drugs, premarital sex, car accidents, fights. Girls giving birth to babies in the bathroom and leaving them in Dumpsters and urinals. . . ."

The nun rolled her eyes and tried to move around them. "I'll check the Dumpsters on my way out," she said. "You check the urinals."

Bellamy put a hand on her arm. "I thought you took your job as a supervisor of children seriously," he said. Over his shoulder, Sister Maria saw Bromine trying not to smile.

Someone needed to get over to the Stein house immediately, but Sister Maria knew it couldn't be her. Not now. Not with this scrutiny.

Sister Maria took a step back. "You know . . . I . . . I suppose I lost my head. This loud music and all . . . I'm eager for bed. . . ."

Bellamy smiled uneasily. "So are we all, Sister—"

"Yes," she said, nodding. "Yes, I suppose I was a bit overeager. Best to stay awhile, though. You're right."

"Until it's finished," Bellamy said.

"Yes, yes," the nun agreed, backing away toward the dance floor. "Yes, absolutely. Thank you, Mr. Bellamy."

As they receded from view, Sister Maria gasped like a person who'd just escaped suffocation, and began searching for the one person who could help her.

Across the dance floor, Mr. Zimmer could see Hannah watching him, a small head poking out of a great plume of pink, sipping from a glass of Coke. The reflected images in the great bank of windows overlooking the river were dim ghosts of the slow-moving couples on the parquet dance floor. The song was "Wonderful Tonight" by Eric Clapton, one of Green's favorites. The freshman had finished with his kitchen duty and was over by the DJ, looking through his record collection with Bilbo and Strebovitch.

Zimmer had stood up and was walking over to accept Hannah's repeated requests for a dance when a thin, cold hand pulled at his shoulder.

Sister Maria hovered behind him. She whispered, even though the music was loud enough to mask her words. She couldn't risk anything with the Monitors watching so closely. Zimmer stooped to hear her. "I have something I need to tell you . . . ," the nun said. "And a favor to ask."

It took longer than she would have liked to explain the situation: Noah Stein's gashed wrists, his friend Davidek, the hospital, and what she'd done to the bathroom to hide it all. Zimmer overflowed with questions, but Sister Maria couldn't allow many. "The Davidek boy is there now . . . At their house . . . I can explain all of this more, but *later*. . . ."

Mr. Zimmer closed his eyes and covered one side of his face with his hand. "I know both those boys . . . ," he said. "But if this kid is at their house causing a disturbance, maybe we should just call the police. Or contact Davidek's parents—"

"*Andrew* . . . ," Sister Maria said wearily. "I've tried to keep as much secret as I can—even from the Davidek boy. And all this may be a mistake . . . a huge one. But I've already done it. And I think it can still turn out right. I'd go myself, but it would raise questions with the Monitors." She tucked a note into Zimmer's hand. "I wrote down the address. The house isn't hard to find. I think you'll know the way. . . ." She began describing the route to him, but Mr. Zimmer took her hand.

Standing before her was no longer Mr. Zimmer, the longtime St. Mike's faculty member. It was Andy Zimmer, her heartbreakingly lanky sixteen-year-old Geometry student from decades ago. His face was solemn. She knew this ended it, the whole big lie. Zimmer would tell her enough was enough, that this had to stop, that she had gone too far. He would tell her to admit the truth, however painful, however destructive. It would be a cleansing—and she needed that.

If Zimmer had said those things to her, she would have been proud of him, for his honesty, for his integrity, for his responsibility. But he didn't.

She was proud of him, still.

"I know the way, Sister. I'll take care of it. . . ." His narrow fingers re-folded the note and placed the paper in his jacket. "But can I just have a minute? You see, I promised I'd dance—"

The nun raised her head, her brow creasing. *Dance?* "I need you to go *now.*"

She had her back to Zimmer, and deliberately avoided watching him as he left.

Zimmer put a hand on the exit and looked back at the room, bathed in the swirl of lights. He spotted Hannah across the room. She had been star-ing at him the entire time.

Good-bye, Hannah, he thought. *Not tonight. But someday. On your wed-ding day maybe, I'll be one of the faces in the background, one of the lucky men who will dance with you on that night, and we will celebrate happier times than these.*

As he pushed through the door, he raised a hand to wave. But she looked away.

FORTY

D avidek piloted the minivan down the darkened country road, his mind scrambling to remember directions and landmarks from the few times he'd traveled this way as a passenger. The sulfur-glowing grid of the Allegheny Valley floated away in the blackness as he motored farther into the hills, like some distant galaxy drifting against the void. The road bent along the path of a stream, which kept switching sides beneath small, rusting bridges, and the new green buds of the springtime branches dangling nakedly above the spread of his headlights.

The last time he saw the Stein house, it had been buried in snow. Now the little white structure looked exposed on the hill sloping down from the woods. Two cars were parked in the gravel driveway—Stein's father's truck, and his sister's beat-up Honda. Far away down the empty road, distant neighbors' homes were just specks of light between the forest branches.

Davidek just watched from across the road for the longest time. His mother's minivan sat crooked on the shoulder of the road, pressed in close to the low-hanging pine trees, which swayed their limbs in the wind as if stroking the vehicle like a sleeping pet. The engine of the van ticked as it cooled, but the boy's hands remained clasped to the wheel, as if afraid the vehicle might roar back to life on its own.

Davidek crossed the empty strip of road and slipped toward the back of the house. All he wanted was to catch a view of Stein from afar. Let Mr. Mankowski call out his name every day in homeroom for the next three years. All he wanted to know was that his friend was *somewhere*.

Davidek stayed close to the tree line as he peeked into the back kitchen through the sliding glass door on the rear porch. The dining table beneath a brownish light fixture was piled with mail and unread newspapers. Dirty dishes were heaped in the sink, threatening avalanche with every drip from the faucet. A telephone on the wall had its receiver dangling off the hook—the reason no calls were coming in.

From inside, he heard the muffled voices of a man and woman arguing with each other, then the roar of some machine—a vacuum cleaner. Davidek couldn't see into the living room or the back bedrooms, so he walked around to the other side toward Stein's room—and was heartened to see that light glowed brightly, though the window was too high above the sloping yard for Davidek to see inside. The howl of the vacuum was loudest here, and Davidek leaped and hopped and tried to prop himself in the crook of a too-slim dogwood tree to peer inside—desperate only for that glimpse, a flash of proof, that his friend was okay.

From his low angle, all he could see clearly was the glare of the ceiling light and the tops of the walls. Stein's white bookshelf had been cleared of his comics, *Sports Illustrated* back issues, and old toys. The wall beside it was bare where there once hung a sepia-print poster of a squinting Clint Eastwood, crossing monstrous guns against his chest as in *The Outlaw Josey Wales*.

Davidek dropped back to the ground. For some reason, that made him think of his fallen paper schedule in the school hallway on that afternoon of St. Mike's eighth-grader open house, and the strange, scarred kid who grabbed it for him and helped him to his feet as the rest of the crowd pushed and shoved on all sides. Davidek's mind reeled through whatever memory he could find to keep Stein real, to make him seem *here*.

All this sneaking around would be easier if Stein were with him.

He knew what his friend would suggest: outright provocation. Stein wouldn't have pussyfooted around the house, propping himself into little trees. He would have pounded on the front door and demanded answers.

Davidek's feet scuffed against the front porch steps, breaking loose some of the gray paint still clinging to the boot-softened wood. He could see through the thin curtains of the front window, and the sound of the vacuum from the bedroom cut off. A television blared in the living room—a war movie Davidek had seen years ago, where the Communists invade America and it's up to a bunch of high school kids to give them the heave-ho.

Stein's sister appeared in the living room, holding a sagging plastic garbage bag in one hand. "Dad? . . . Daaa-aad! . . . What happened to my show?" she asked, fists punched against her sizable hips. She glared at Stein's father as he lay on the couch, out of Davidek's sight, just below the window.

Stein's father grumbled her name—"Margie . . ."—in response, and reached forward to the coffee table, his clumsy hand toppling two empty beer bottles into the cushion of an overfilled ashtray as he grabbed at the remote control an instant too late. Margie Stein had already snapped it up, clicking the channel over her shoulder to a Christian basic cable station, where a snowy-haired minister with his pious face turned up to God replaced a Russian soldier who had just collected several arrows in his spine.

". . . was watching that," Stein's father muttered.

"No," Margie replied, stuffing the remote in her back pocket. "No, Dad, I was watching *this,* and you changed it."

"Y'were in the other room!" he said, the words slurring lamely, undercutting his outrage. *"Cleaning up . . ."*

"Right," she said coldly. "Until you feel capable of *helping,* for once, I get to watch what I want! And you'll watch it, too. It's good for you."

"You're *not* watching," her father said.

Margie squeezed her eyes shut in frustration. "I was *listening!*"

Stein's father lurched to his feet. "Well, I can't take preaching from both of you." He didn't sound like the man Davidek remembered, the smart, mellow, cheerful one who had picked them up from the Valentine's Dance, politely accepting the duty Davidek's mother had shirked. Now Stein's father seemed like a bratty little boy, trapped in the slow skin of a withering man. And he was fully, utterly shit-faced.

Margie didn't respond to her father. She had frozen. The loose mouth of her garbage bag drifted sideways to the floor as she stared straight ahead to the curtained window.

"Who's out there?" she called, jerking aside the drapes. Her face was round and red, thick in a matronly way that made her seem much older than her early twenties. "Who the hell are *you*?" Margie barked through the glass.

Davidek had met her before, here at this very house. "It's me. I'm Noah's friend, remember?" he stammered. "I'm here to see him."

Margie's face knotted. She pulled the curtain shut again. "I'm giving you five minutes," her silhouette said. "Then I'm calling the police."

Davidek flattened his hand against the glass and tried to peer inside. "I'm his friend. I just want to know what happened to him! I just want to know if he's all right!"

"*Right* . . . ," Margie scoffed from the hallway. "I'm sure it's a big joke. You got friends waiting down in the car or something? Did you win the bet? Or the dare, or whatever? . . . Just get *out* of here. *Now.*"

"Please . . . the hospital said he wasn't there anymore," Davidek persisted. "I've been calling. No one will tell me anything. . . . I just want to know if he's okay. And when he's coming back?"

Margie marched out and stuck her face back in the window. "He wasn't in any hospital. He just vandalized the place, so they kicked him out. You St. Mike's kids are just bound and determined to start rumors about him. Can't you just let him be?"

"I *know* he was hurt!" Davidek screamed. "I saw him all cut up. I *saw* it. He was talking to me. I carried him out to Sister Maria and the car!"

"What crap . . . ," Margie said, narrowing her eyes. "Sister Maria never said a word about you." Davidek held her gaze; then Margie put a hand over her face. She had given away the lie.

"That's it," she said, storming into the kitchen. "I'm calling the police." She placed the phone back in its cradle to reconnect the line, then took it off again and began dialing.

"No, Margie . . . no attention on this," her father said, still standing in the middle of the living room.

"I'm not going to be harassed at our own house!" she said.

"No *police*, Margie," her father called, following her into the kitchen. He loomed beside her. Margie hesitated, then hung up the phone.

Davidek watched through the curtain as the disheveled older man put his arms around his daughter. They held each other for a long time, the boy outside momentarily forgotten. Finally, Margie broke away and yelled toward the front of the house: "I don't know *what* you think you know, but whatever happened to my brother, whatever put him where he is—it was an *accident*, and that's all."

"What do you mean, 'where he is'?" Davidek asked. "Isn't he here?"

No one answered him. "Is he *here*?" Davidek said, louder this time. He thought of his mother, *Do I need to repeat it for you?* "I swear I won't tell. I just want to *know* . . . ," the boy pleaded.

The front door swung open, and Stein's father stood there. Gray scruff covered his face, and his red eyes rested in big swollen pods of skin. Davidek drew close, believing this to be an invitation, but Stein's father didn't budge. Facing each other, they both struggled to recognize something in the other from long ago. "You . . . ," the older man said finally. "The St. Valentine's Day dance . . ."

Davidek nodded. Stein's father did the same, then grabbed Davidek by the shirt and yanked him forward. "So where were you when my son *needed* a friend?"

Davidek raised his hands in surrender. "Please—I've been calling and nobody answers—"

Stein's father shoved the boy backwards on the porch. "We keep the phone off the hook," he muttered. "We get enough prank calls from you kids."

Margie squeezed in beside her father. "You think it's funny hearing somebody make those damn sizzle noises? . . . They wanted to terrorize my brother—fine. Maybe he deserved it. But she was my *mother*." She covered her mouth, and her drunken father put his arms around her.

"I've been calling here because I'm *worried* about him," Davidek insisted, getting sick of explaining himself. "He's my friend. . . ."

In the hallway behind Stein's father, Davidek spotted a row of cardboard boxes on the floor. Two were filled with Stein's clothes, washed and folded. Another had some stuffed animals, rolled-up posters, and other junk cleared from Stein's bedroom—ready for shipment . . . or to be given away.

Davidek looked to the white garbage bag Margie had dropped on the floor. Some spiral-bound notebooks had spilled out of the lip of the bag, among some other crumpled drawings, candy wrappers, and miscellaneous

garbage. As Davidek rose from the porch floor, he could see Stein's RELI-
GION notebook in the pile. A mad-eyed cartoon of Ms. Bromine with devil
horns and a pitchfork adorned the cover, and the frayed edges of old quizzes stuck out. Davidek pointed at them. "What are you doing? We saved
our quizzes as proof in case Ms. Bromine tries to screw us on the quarterly
grades like last time! . . . Stein *needs* these!"

Margie and her father exchanged an uncertain glance, and Davidek's
words suddenly felt like foolishness. There was some glaringly obvious
truth he was missing. *"Where is he?"* Davidek demanded, and Margie's face
wrinkled, trying to gauge whether the boy's naïveté was real or only an
effort to bait them.

She walked back to the kitchen and picked up the phone again.

"I said no police!" her father hollered over his shoulder.

"I know," she told him boastfully, like a self-satisfied child showing off a
newfound ability to count to ten or tie a shoe. "I'm calling the nun."

By the time Sister Antonia relayed the message, and Sister Maria made
arrangements at the dance to have Zimmer race across three towns to get
there, almost another hour had passed.

Davidek continued peppering Stein's father and sister with questions,
becoming frantic as they ignored him from inside their locked home. A
panic had hit him. If Stein were able, he would have mentioned Davidek
to his family. He would've told his dad and sister about the friend who
helped rescue him when he was hurt. . . . *Or maybe he doesn't trust them,*
the boy thought. Or maybe Stein now blamed Davidek just as much as he
did the others.

He went around to the side yard and climbed higher into the dogwood
tree this time, getting a view straight into Stein's room, with its bare bed
and open, empty dresser drawers. "You can't just throw his stuff out because
he's sick!" Davidek screamed. He went back to the porch and pounded on
the door some more. "Stein! . . . Stein, it's Davidek! If you're here, come
out!"

Stein's father scratched his head and peered at him through the living
room window. "You're talking to nobody," he said.

"I want to see my friend!" the boy said.

The old man just stared at him with his big stewed-tomato eyes and let the curtain fall back.

Eventually, the headlights of Zimmer's rumbling hatchback bathed the Stein house in light as he pulled into the gravel driveway and parked. "Peter . . . Peter, would you come down here, please?" he called from beside the road. "Sister Maria sent me, Peter. I just want to talk to you."

"You come up here," Davidek said.

Zimmer didn't move. "What do you want with these people, Peter?"

Davidek's eyes glinted. "I just want to see if my friend can come out and play."

The tall shadow walked up into the yard and stood at the foot of the porch steps. Margie peeked through the window at the stranger. "We called the *sister*," she said. "You're *not* the sister."

"I'd like you to come with me, Peter," Zimmer said calmly. "I know you have a lot you'd like explained, but go down to my car and wait there. Let me talk with them, and I'll come back to talk to you."

The front door opened and Margie stuck her face out. "Where's the nun?" she asked.

"Where's Stein?" Davidek shot back.

Zimmer walked up to the porch, the wooden steps creaking beneath him. "Sister Maria will be along. The school had its prom tonight. She's delayed there, I'm afraid. She asked me to come in her place."

"Well, she knows us. She's *assured* us," Margie said. "She said the best thing is for everybody to just to *leave my brother alone*. No phone calls, no visitors . . ."

Zimmer raised his palms to her—as though trying to get her to lower a gun. "I'm Andrew Zimmer," he said. "I teach Computer Science and Phys Ed at the school. Is it all right if I come up?"

Margie nodded, then pointed at Davidek. "He can't."

Zimmer agreed and they went inside.

Davidek tried to eavesdrop through the windows, but they didn't talk for long. Zimmer emerged from the front door and put a firm arm around him, steering him toward the steps. "Let's go home, Peter."

"I want to know about Stein."

Zimmer sighed. "I explained to the Steins that, yes, you were a friend of Noah's, and that, yes, you had tried to help, and that Sister Maria trusts you. But your behavior tonight . . . well . . . let's just go now, and we'll talk about it later."

Davidek said, "I'm not leaving unless you tell me *now*."

Zimmer looked up at Margie, whose face registered disgust, then back to Davidek. "His body is recovering, Peter. Doctors have been taking good care of him. They healed the cuts, they stabilized him, but he's not strong yet. He lost quite a lot of blood—and some of the things that are broken in people can't be fixed with just medicine. Do you understand?"

"Don't talk to me like that, like I'm stupid," Davidek said.

Zimmer nodded, and his next words were a slap across the face. "You're not stupid. You're just an idiot. Coming here and screaming at these people? That doesn't help anything. Your friend is gravely ill. He's not altogether there even when he *is* awake—which isn't often. But he's with people who are caring for him. Far from here. And you can't keep bothering his father and sister. . . . You can't keep asking for more. . . ."

Davidek felt the edges of his vision bending away, growing distant. Nausea overtook him. "*Where* is he?" the boy asked.

"At a hospital, and it's out of state. That's all you need to know. You can't see him. Even his family aren't going to be with him, not for a while. They're sending his clothes and some of his things. If he recovers well, and you apologize to them for tonight, maybe in the future, maybe someday they'll . . ." He didn't finish. There was no promise he could make.

As they walked down to the car, the boy looked back up to the porch, where Stein's sister had emerged and was glaring down at him. "You didn't have to clean out his room. Like he never was." He thought of his own brother—the AWOL A-hole, whose many stupid choices had resulted in him being erased from the world.

Margie crossed her arms. Her face was hard. "My little brother is a long list of bad memories that we'd just like to put away for a while. . . . Don't tell me that's wrong."

"It *is* wrong," Davidek said, starting back toward the house. "It's his stuff, and Stein was a good person. Maybe I didn't know him as well as you, but I know that much for *sure*."

"My brother is a volatile, dangerous *burden,*" she said. "He is very unstable, very sad—and he has a lot to be sad about. And thanks to what Noah did to *himself,* the care he needs now . . . the *cost* . . . *I'm* the one who doesn't have nursing school money anymore. We can't pay for both." She shook her head, tears pouring down her cheeks. "So I'm an official *dropout* these days. And maybe I'd have been a *good* nurse. . . . Maybe I'd have *helped* people—"

Her father shuffled forward and put his arm around her, pulling her back to him. Margie made a watery sniff. "He took my *mother* away. He takes *everything* away," she said. "And he just keeps taking. . . ."

Davidek thought of what Stein had told him, lying with his bleeding arms stuffed into his jacket, the secret he didn't want to die with him: a confession. . . . Davidek knew how devoted Margie was to the last religion her mother had clung to, hoping to set her mind right. He wondered if she still believed suicides wouldn't get into heaven.

Zimmer started to pull Davidek away, but Davidek wouldn't go. He wanted to tell them more. Needed to tell them how wrong they were about Stein.

He wanted to tell Margie and her father that the fire had been a frightened little boy's desperate effort to protect his family, to stay in line with their roller-coaster religious bullshit, to protect his mother from sorrow he thought might follow her into another life. Even now, all these years later, Stein had let his sister and father believe the worst in him rather than know the truth.

Davidek pictured his friend on that first afternoon when they were still just visitors at St. Mike's. Stein planting that crazy kiss on the lips of Ms. Bromine, paralyzing her, while Davidek bolted toward the unconscious LeRose . . .

When the seniors had pushed in, jackal-like as they heaped new torment on Davidek, the Clip-On Boy, Stein had loosened his collar, pulled off his own tie, and said, *Take this, and give me yours.*

Stein stepped in front of other people's bullets. He let himself absorb the worst the world threw at the people he cared about. Maybe that did make him strange or crazy; Davidek didn't know anyone else like that.

But what would that matter to his sister now?

Stein had intended to keep the secret about his mother for as long as he lived. Since he still did, Davidek would do the same.

"When you talk to him," Davidek said, "just tell him I'm wearing his clip-on, okay? Tell him that. . . ."

He couldn't read their faces, which was just as well. He didn't need them to understand anymore.

Zimmer led him away, and Davidek slumped in the passenger seat of the teacher's little car. The stolen minivan receded in the darkness. There was still plenty of trouble ahead for him tonight.

Zimmer asked him for directions to his house, and Davidek told him. "Do you feel like you got what you were looking for?" the teacher asked. Davidek mumbled yes, like it was the most tiresome question imaginable.

Zimmer used the long drive to lecture him: *Sister Maria is taking a great risk in trusting you. Blah blah blah . . . There are a lot of people who would use this to hurt St. Mike's. You've disappointed us.*

Davidek said "yeah" a lot, and looked out the window.

Back at his house, the boy had made it in through the front door and almost to his bedroom when his mother grabbed him in the upstairs hallway screaming for her husband, "Bill! Bill! Bill!" like an agitated seagull. Davidek's father bounded out of his bedroom, cornering his son.

Davidek's mother slapped him across the face. When he looked up again, she slapped him a second time. "How dare you?" she said. "How *dare* you?"

They didn't ask Davidek where had gone, or why he had stolen the minivan, or where it was now. That would come later, and Davidek made up as many lies as he needed—he had been trying to run away, got scared, left the car on some random road, and hitchhiked back. It didn't matter if they believed him. That was all they would get.

Davidek didn't need his parents to understand anymore either.

FORTY-ONE

The night whispered around Hannah Kraut.

Hannah sat alone on a ridge of rock jutting over the edge, hidden in the darkness behind the restaurant, away from the buzzing parking-lot lights and the noise of the prom cleanup inside. Her fluffy dress bunched around her. She was a pink spot amid dark blue shadows.

The only light here was the occasional flash from workers going in and out of the back kitchen entrance. She could hear the other prom-goers leaving the premises, tearing away in their cars and sending trails of dust into the air to float over the river valley like a little procession of spirits.

From the kitchen, two sophomore student volunteers came out carrying a clattering stack of dirty dinner plates, which they hauled over to the rocks and began hurling one by one over the cliff, cackling with each distant shatter. They each gave Hannah a cursory "What's up?"—unashamed of their activities. One guy pretended to shoot the flying dishes like skeet while the other explained to Hannah that the restaurant's big dishwasher was full, so the plates had to disappear or else they'd have to wait around for the current load to finish.

Hannah had listened, nodding, smiling thinly. Then the skeet shooter said, "You're not going to tell, are you? You're not going to write this in that . . . uh, book thing, right? And read it at the Hazing Picnic?"

He was trying to sound friendly and goofy, but he was clearly worried. Hannah said, "Maybe you should go now, then," and they did. Quickly.

Hannah knew when Mr. Zimmer left the restaurant that he wasn't coming back, that she wouldn't get her dance, but she made herself wait around anyway, just in case he did return. Of course, he didn't.

Alone now, Hannah unzipped her purse, which matched the cotton candy color of her dress. The only thing wedged inside it was a small framed picture, one she had snapped herself at the beginning of the year, hugging Mr. Zimmer from the side as she held the camera at arm's length. She had intended to give it to him tonight.

Hannah heard footsteps behind her and wedged the photo back into her purse.

A small girl stepped forward to the base of the rocks, looking up at Hannah. "I'm Sarah," she said, though she was already better known to Hannah, and almost everyone else, as Seven-Eighths.

Hannah played with the hem of her dress. "What do you want?"

The girl was crawling up the rocks beside her, wearing the uniform blue pants and white polo shirt of the volunteer underclassman workers. At the top, Seven-Eighths became transfixed by the lights of the valley, not saying anything—but her lips were moving softly. Hannah could barely make out a whisper. She was saying the Our Father prayer to herself.

Hannah considered scaring her off but thought of that nickname— Seven-Eighths—and held back. As far as nicknames went, it was better than Fuckslut, but something in the girl's weird fishface, a strange chiaroscuro of light and blackness in these shadows, made Hannah feel a rare twang of mercy.

"You're sad," the freshman girl said. "I can tell."

"It's just puppy love and heartache and all the stuff you hear about in bad songs," Hannah said. "You'll feel it yourself when you get older. Teenage bullshit. No biggie. I'm glad to be leaving it behind."

A timid smile appeared on Seven-Eighth's beaklike mouth. *Bullshit.* She didn't say words like that. "I saw you sitting here alone. And I saw you sitting alone inside, too," Seven-Eighths said.

Hannah began to wonder how much this girl knew about the notorious

Hannah Kraut, scourge of the senior class, keeper of hideous secrets, cowardly slut, and blackmailing bitch. "Maybe I wanted to be alone," she said.

The girl laughed. "No . . . You're Hannah Kraut. You're the one everyone makes fun of behind your back."

Sometimes, when you are feeling your worst, an extra stab of pain doesn't hurt at all. Hopelessness is a great anesthetic. So Hannah laughed. "Well, they don't do it to my face, now, do they? That's something."

The young girl's scissor jaw clenched. "They say it to *my* face," she said softly. "They say it *about* my face." She looked sideways at Hannah. "But you're very pretty. They should be talking about how lovely you are, but instead they talk about hating you."

"Better to be hated in secret, than hated out in the open," Hannah said. "At least nobody *bothers* me anymore. I stopped all that."

"You have their secrets, don't you? That's why they leave you alone . . . so you'll leave them alone." The girl slid closer to Hannah. "I want to know how to stop people, too."

Hannah regarded the river far below. Maybe her troubles were ending at St. Mike's, but this girl's were just beginning. "Tell you what, Sarah . . . tell me *who* is bothering you, and maybe I can help."

The girl took a very long time to answer. Hannah thought she could guess the response: probably Smitty, who had made up the Seven-Eighths name and still bragged about it. Or maybe it would be one of those bitchy freshman girls, like that Lorelei person. Or the Grough sisters—those boars.

Seven-Eighths surprised her—she said: "Can you help me stop Father Mercedes?"

Hannah's eyebrows turned into two little darts aimed at her nose. "Exactly . . . *what* . . . did Father Mercedes do to you?" she asked, expecting the absolute worst.

Seven-Eighths stared down at the town lights on the other side of the valley. "He makes me pray," she said, the words beginning to flow uncontrollably. "A *lot* . . . I like to pray, but Mother and Father make me do confession every Saturday with my brother, Clarence, and confession is good, but I can't pray like Father Mercedes wants, all the time, every hour . . .

the prayers get stuck . . . Do you know what I mean? They keep saying themselves and I can't shut them off even if I *want* to shut them off. That's a sin and you should never want to *not* pray, and—" She cut herself off, and her mind raced with a soothing:

Hailmaryfullofgracethelordiswiththeeblessedartthou . . .

The girl's insect eyes widened; her jaw quivered. "Can you tell me something about Father, please? Something that will hurt him? Do you have something about him in your book?"

Hannah hung her head for a long time. She searched her memory, honestly . . . and fruitlessly. "I wish I did, Sarah," she said. "But I'm sorry. I never paid much attention to him."

Sarah shrank back from her. "Are you sure? . . . *Please?*"

Hannah said, "Listen, I'd tell you if I did. From what you've said—he's an asshole—but that doesn't really make him stand out in a crowd around here."

The girl said in a small voice, "If you do learn something, will you tell me?"

Hannah raised two fingers in the air. "Scout's honor."

The little freshman drew her knees up to her chin. After a while, she said, "So . . . who's the boy who made *you* sad tonight?"

Hannah laughed. "Nobody makes me *sad*. . . . I'm pissed off."

Seven-Eighths giggled at the profanity again. "Then who made you mad? Who made you come sit out here alone?"

Hannah shook her head. In the darkness, Seven-Eighths was looking at Hannah's purse, where she could see the top of the framed photo sticking out. She cocked her head slightly, studying the faces in the dimness. Hannah didn't even notice.

The girl ventured, "Do you know something that will hurt *him?*"

"Him who?" Hannah asked, then noticed her looking at the photo. Hannah's sad smile vanished. "Maybe you need to mind your own business."

Seven-Eighths smiled grimly and looked down at the purse again. "So you *hate* him, but you don't want to *hurt* him. . . ." Her brain calculated this in silence, temporarily blocking out the constant background noise of prayers.

Hannah pulled the purse close to her hip, hiding the photo. She could guess what the girl was thinking now, and Hannah was tempted to let her imagine whatever she wanted. Why not allow some nasty rumor to spread? It's easy to hate those who don't love you back.

But Hannah didn't really want that.

She leaned in close to the freshman, close enough to kiss. "Get those thoughts out of your weird little skull, Seven-Eighths. They're a fucking *sin. . . .*"

The girl stood abruptly, and Hannah watched her scamper down from the rocks and fast-walk back along the edge of the restaurant. Being mean always made Hannah feel a little better.

The passenger door opened, and the dome light in Father Mercedes's car came on. Then the door closed, and the vehicle was dark again except for the priest's little orange cigarette ember. He started the car and drove out of the restaurant parking lot. It was late. He had been waiting a long time.

He looked over at the girl slumped in the seat beside him. "Well, what did she say?"

Seven-Eighths didn't look up when she answered. She tried never to look at Father Mercedes. It was easier to do the things he asked if she didn't have to face him—if she could just pretend their meetings were confession, in that little room, with a screen between them.

"I did my best, Father," she said. "But you don't need to worry. She said she didn't know anything about you. And I tried hard to get her to tell me. I tried to trick her."

The priest said, "You're certain she's telling the truth? She has nothing?"

Seven-Eighths told him, "Just that you were a . . . *blank*-blank."

The priest rolled his eyes. "Just say the word."

"She called you an '*ass*-hole,'" the girl said, as if it were two words. Then she crossed herself and thought a quick Hail Mary to cleanse.

Father Mercedes laughed, then coughed, breathing smoke through his nose as he smiled. If true, this was hugely comforting. Let Hannah read her toxic scribblings in front of everyone at the Hazing Picnic and scorch the world—as long as nothing could hurt him.

He stuck the cigarette in the corner of his smile and let it hang there as he drove Seven-Eighths back to her home. *This was it. He was safe.* He had been blessed by this type of relief once before, when the peril of discovery had been its strongest, when the anemic financials of St. Michael the Archangel had nearly exposed his petty crimes.

It had seemed like a tragedy to everyone else—the burning of the church—but from those ashes a grand disorder was born, and his misdeeds, his chronic theft, had been obscured by much greater loss. The windfall of insurance funds, though not enough to rebuild, had helped hide what he had taken. Now, he needed to make further amends, to shutter the school, to make St. Michael's chapel rise again on the spot where it had once smoldered.

This blessing, this freedom from exposure in that strange girl's notebook, was the first step. He had faith in that now. God was again watching out for Father Mercedes. He wondered what blessing would come next.

It happened to come immediately.

Father Mercedes drew on his cigarette, a deep, biting lungful, feeling alive. It made Seven-Eighths turn her face toward the door and ask permission to roll down the window slightly. She hated the smoke. It was how she imagined hell would smell, and the stink would be in her hair now when she was trying to get to sleep tonight.

Sarah "Seven-Eighths" Matusch truly did despise Father Mercedes, deep down in her heart. She knew he was cruel and manipulative, and that part of what she'd said to Hannah had been no lie. But sometimes we crave the love of those we're afraid to hate.

"You might want to know one other thing . . . ," the girl said softly.

Father Mercedes grunted. "And what's that?"

The glow of the dashboard cast dismal shadows on the angles of Seven-Eighths' face. "I think Mr. Zimmer is having sex with Hannah Kraut."

PART VII

The Other Way Down

FORTY-TWO

Peter Davidek stood by the classroom window, hands stuffed into his pockets, his blazer swept back at the sides, the red clip-on tie squared at his collar. The morning sky was tropical blue, and a breeze scented with fresh-cut grass swept in and lifted the bangs of his hair. Just next to the Tobinsville shopping center, he could see the yellow insects of earthmoving machines shifting around piles of gray slag from the Kees-Northson steel mill, and green waves of lush, wooded hills floated beyond the river, rolling on toward anywhere-but-here.

Mr. Mankowski was doing the homeroom roll call again. "Dahnzer, Missy," he said, and a girl shaped like a pear with two pencils for legs said, "Present."

The bald teacher looked squarely at Davidek's back and said, "Davidek, Peter . . ." When Davidek didn't answer right away, he said it again, louder.

Davidek replied, "Here."

Mankowski went on and on, name after name, and when he got to "Stein, Noah," he paused, as he always did, and was disappointed that Davidek wasn't facing him. The teacher said it once more, just for the heck of it: "Stein, Noah." But Davidek didn't respond.

Mankowski wrinkled his mouth, then made a mark with his pen and moved on.

. . .

Hannah saw Davidek in the lunchroom, a rare appearance there for the radioactively unpopular girl. "You never came to the prom, Playgirl," she said.

Davidek was holding an empty lunch tray. He told her, "I had trouble getting a ride."

She scrunched her face. "Weren't you coming with that fat kid from your class? I saw him there, hanging around with Bilbo and his buddies. . . ."

Davidek said, "Yeah . . . well, that fell through."

"What happened? I was waiting and—"

Davidek shrugged. "It fell *through,* so you can threaten me or something, and I'll say, 'Sorry, Hannah, sorry . . . It wasn't my fault. Please don't!' And then you'll either do something to me, or you won't."

Hannah cocked her head, studying him. She almost looked hurt. Almost. Then it was gone, and she said, "You on the rag or something, Playgirl?"

Carl LeRose ambled over during study hall in the library, his fingers stuffed in the pages of a decrepit *Advanced Biology* textbook that was swollen with water damage from the flood. "Check it out," the sophomore whispered, bending open the cover. "There's a picture of a naked chick in it."

Davidek looked over at the pages and winced. "She's old," Davidek said. "And what's that on her skin?"

"Uh, some rash . . . ," LeRose said, scanning the caption: "Smallpox."

Davidek pushed the cover of the book closed again as LeRose threw an arm over his back and shook him. "I came over here to cheer you up. Everybody's talking about you these days. The hazing thing is coming up. They need to know—are you gonna help us get Hannah, or are you a pussy asshole coward?" He raised an eyebrow. Davidek looked bored.

LeRose settled into the empty seat beside him. (All the seats were empty around Davidek.) "Hannah has something on you, too, doesn't she?" he whispered. "Just like the rest of us."

"No," Davidek said. "Turns out, I'm just a pussy asshole coward."

LeRose bobbed his head. "I get it. You're feeling a little pressure—okay. But I'm coming over here as your friend. And maybe the folks at this school aren't treating you so nice, because they don't know if they can trust you. I'm spreading the good word about you, though. I just need you to show some goodwill back."

"You guys would just deny what Hannah writes anyway, so who cares what she makes me say?"

LeRose drummed the table. "I *still* don't want her to say it. . . . I could sit here and say your mama's a whore, and what difference would that make? You still don't want to hear it, right? Same way I don't want her talking about me or my dad."

Davidek leaned back in his seat. "I probably said this to you already . . . but does your *dad* really care what some random teenage girl says about him?"

LeRose poked a sausage finger into Davidek's chest. "My dad is clean-cut all the way, but he's coming to the picnic with some other parish Monitors, and some of his old school buddies are going to join him. Maybe my mom will come, too. . . . So I'd thank you very much if you can help me stop Hannah Kraut from throwing shit all over him. . . . You know?"

Davidek looked around the library. A lot of people were watching them. "Well, if your dad is such a fan of the school, he knows that on Hazing Day I don't have much choice. I have to do what my senior tells me."

"Apparently, I'm not being heard," LeRose said, nodding patiently. "You saved my ass once, so I want to help you. I know Hannah's terrorizing you, but what you need to think about are all the *new* Hannah Krauts you're going to make for yourself if you don't stand up against her and be a man. You've got three more years at St. Mike's. Every person you let Hannah hurt is going to remember it. And when the time comes, they'll be happy to hurt you back."

LeRose nodded soberly, his eyes wide and heavy with adolescent gravitas. "They took out your buddy, didn't they? You want to end up like Stein, too?"

Davidek's jaw set. "So what should I do?"

LeRose leaned in close. "See, we've got a plan. But we need your help," he said. "If you can't resist Hannah openly, maybe you can help the rest of us in secret."

Davidek raised his hands in the air. "Yeah. Fine. *How?*"

"Help us stop her *for* you. Fucking *physically!*"

LeRose made Davidek promise to keep quiet before continuing: "Some of the juniors—John Hannidy, Raymond Lee, Janey Brucedik—they got the idea that we use *military intervention,* if that's what it takes. Just like over in Desert Storm. Only this is Fuckslut Storm." The chunky sophomore snorted at the term. "A bunch of seniors are on board now, too. Prager and Strebovich told me they're ready to kick Hannah's ass if that's what it takes. And they're like your buddy Stein—they don't even care about hitting a girl."

Davidek squinted, and LeRose went on: "We're gonna jump her the morning of the picnic. Before she shows up at the park, we're gonna grab that bitch and turn her upside down and shake her until that fucking notebook falls out. Then we take the notebook and fucking destroy it. Nobody at the picnic is the wiser. You get off scot-free. As far as she knows, you had nothing to do with it. Secretly, though, you'll be helping us."

"Again—how?"

"We need you to find out what she has. Not really the secrets and all that, but what it looks like, this notebook: a binder, a bunch of crumpled-up drawings like a crazy guy in a shack would write? Photographs, scribbles . . . *Whatever.* Anything she's going to shove you onstage with. We just want to be sure we take everything she's got. No surprises."

Davidek said, "I have no idea what she has."

"Then find out," LeRose said, standing up. "It'll be good for you."

"What if she tells somebody you ganged up on her?" Davidek asked. "What if she calls the cops or something?"

LeRose laughed and rolled his eyes. "I love you, man, but you're one dense dude. . . . Remember? My dad *knows* the cops. They owe him. And the cops wouldn't like what Hannah's up to anyway. So let her complain. We'll already have the notebook at that point."

"And what if she tells the teachers?"

LeRose said, "Look, that's another thing you just don't get. The people in charge don't want any of her shit. Not with these Parish Monitors around. They want to have a place to fucking work next year. Understand?"

LeRose mussed Davidek's hair. "You worry too much," he said. "This will work. And you're gonna wanna kiss me. Because everybody is going to fucking love you when it's done."

Davidek considered this. It would be nice to feel protected. To be watched out for. For months he'd been fretting over this. Now he finally had a way out.

"Fine," Davidek said.

LeRose messed up his hair again and kissed him on top of the head.

FORTY-THREE

A week went by, but Davidek hadn't delivered anything useful. Everybody seemed willing to give him some time, since Le-Rose assured them he was on their side, but others weren't so sure. Bilbo and his Stairwell Boys were in their usual spot, drinking Cokes, telling jokes, and staring up through the big void stretching three stories above them when talk turned to Davidek. Bilbo mentioned that Green and he were pals.

This piqued the interest of Michael Crawford, who kind of hated the way Bilbo, Alex Prager, and Dan Strebovich had made a pet out of Green. This chubby, black freshman, best friends with seniors? Stupid. But they loved Green. Whatever.

"So how good a friend are you to this Peter Davidek guy?" he asked.

Green's face scrunched, like his soda just turned to sour milk. "We're not what I'd really call friends anymore, guys."

Bilbo said, "But he's a good guy, right?"

Green shook his head. "He's a piece of shit, actually."

This lit a fire in Crawford. Resentment had been building up for months in the handsome, dashing senior as his senior year sputtered out into noth-ingness. The basketball team he captained had sucked. He was graduating without distinction in the middle of his class, while the valedictorian would most likely be his girlfriend, Audra Banes, who was beginning to grow as tired of him as he was of himself. He hated her increasingly thick thighs, and just because she was class president didn't mean she had to wear those damned black-rimmed glasses to make herself look smarter. She was the cheerleading captain, for God's sake. Show some goddamn sex and sass!

Still, he didn't want to lose her, even though that was bound to happen when she moved to Rhode Island in the fall to attend Brown. He was sticking much closer to home—at St. Vincent's in Latrobe, way out in the sticks beyond Pittsburgh. He didn't get into Brown.

Crawford had always been the smartest boy in his class, the most charming . . . the leader. Yet now he felt like nothing was in his control. This Hannah thing felt like a chance to salvage his reputation. "So you think we can trust this Davidek guy—or not?" he asked.

Green just shrugged, and tipped back his Coke. "I wouldn't."

After another week of no progress, Crawford's warnings about Davidek started to spread alarm. John Hannidy pinned Davidek in the corner of the hallway one morning, while his friend Raymond Lee bent the freshman's arm behind his back. "You promised you'd help us, but we're starting to think you're a fucking liar," Lee drawled.

Hannidy's girlfriend, Janey Brucedik, folded her arms over her scrawny chest as she paced behind them, keeping an eye out for Parish Monitors and their ubiquitous little notepads. "I say he's too much of a pussy," she said.

"Why don't you guys just ban her from the picnic?" Davidek's smooshed mouth asked as his lips tasted the metal of the locker. "Or cut the mic when it's her turn?"

"We've already thought of that, genius," Janey said.

"Do you want to be the one to tell her?" Hannidy asked.

"Nobody wanted to step into that line of fire alone," Raymond added.

Of course, that's why they had to stop Hannah as a school, as a collective—dozens of kids, not just the three of them. Hannah couldn't get revenge against everyone. But first they needed Davidek to do his part and tell them what they were looking for.

"Why don't you tell *me* what you're afraid she knows?" Davidek sneered.

The three student council members, who as juniors had spent the year covering up irregularities in the student activities fund they'd been skimming from, shared a worried look. Then Hannidy punched Davidek in the stomach.

Other seniors tried to win him over with kindess.

A few days after Davidek was manhandled by Hannidy, two other juniors named Will Framalski and John Jay came forward and asked Davidek if Hannah knew about their little marijuana-dealing operation. Secretly, they also feared Hannah might know that they'd been supplying Alexander Prager, the onetime basketball team high-scorer, with anabolic steroids. (The drugs had made him not only thick with muscle, but lately quick to violence.) His juicing was one reason for the team's losing season, since the thickening muscle mass that helped in baseball and football only slowed him down on the basketball court, where speed was more precious than mass. The dealers just hoped graduation came before Prager realized this.

Framalski pressed a small plastic bag into Davidek's hands. Inside were three tight joints. "It's a gift," he said. "Just, you know, make sure Hannah ain't gonna say anything about us."

"You help us, we'll keep you stocked. Cool?" John Jay added.

Davidek, fearing immediate arrest, dumped the joints in the second-floor toilet and flushed them.

Days passed, and he hadn't spoken to Hannah once. With the picnic just two weeks away, student after student pestered him, all of them losing patience with his excuses. Then one afternoon during Religion class, the door opened and brutish Mary Grough stuck her face in. "Ms. Bromine, the office sent me up here to get Peter Davidek."

Bromine looked at the boy, sitting quietly in the back row, fiddling with his clip-on. "Well . . . get going!" Bromine said.

Davidek walked outside, and Mary closed the door behind him. A group of other upperclassmen stood silently in the hallway—Bilbo and his stairway pals, Streb and Prager. Morti and his Fanboys. Carl LeRose was with Hannidy, Janey, and their blubbery third wheel Raymond. Mary Grough took her spot beside her sister and their friend Anne-Marie Thomas. Audra Banes was in the center of the group, surrounded by her own coterie—Allissa Hardawicky, Amy Hispioli, and Sandy Burk. Michael Crawford scuffed his foot on the tile, sourly hanging near the back.

Audra put her hand on the door across the hall and opened it. "Please come inside," she said. And Davidek did.

It was Mr. McClerk's English room, but there was no class during this period and the lights were off. In the back, there was an alcove behind a row of bookshelves, and a long table with a pair of computers, which served as the de facto yearbook office. With graduation only two weeks away, the book had gone to print just days ago and would be rushed out just in time. The scattered remains of its frenzied assemblage were still spread out in slivers of layout pages and discarded photos.

In one of the chairs beside the table sat Sister Maria. Audra closed the door to the classroom, leaving only the three of them in the room.

Sister Maria asked Davidek to sit down. "Are we friends, Mr. Davidek?"

Davidek shifted in his seat. He wasn't sure what to say or not say in front of Audra. "Is the welcoming committee in the hall gonna beat me up if I say we're not?"

"I wanted you to see how many of your fellow classmates are concerned about your plan to disrupt the Hazing Picnic," Sister Maria said.

Davidek sat up. "My plan? You're the one who came up with this great Brother–Sister idea."

"Very well, your *senior's* plan," the nun corrected herself. "To use *you*. And your inability to resist her. It's something that can't be allowed. I have no actual control over this picnic, but whatever happens there reflects on me and this school. And we are in a time of extreme volatility at St. Michael's—as you well know."

"Maybe you should talk to Hannah, then," Davidek said.

"I have," the nun said in a clipped, businesslike tone. "But I was unable to persuade her to relent. And I have also been unable to persuade Father Mercedes to cancel the picnic."

"Could he even *do* that?" Davidek asked.

Sister Maria answered without answering. "He says the students of the

school must be able to behave in a civil manner at a public event, and be-
lieves the Hazing Picnic will prove that, one way or the other."

"He's right," Davidek told her.

Sister Maria's fist tightened. She had been so much friendlier two
months ago, when she was smashing up toilets. "I know you to be a cooperative boy, Peter," the nun said. "So why haven't you been able to help
Audra and the other students with this problem?"

"Do you even know what they're planning to do?" Davidek asked. "They
want to beat the shit out of Hannah and take her—" But the nun put a
hand up to silence him.

"*No one* wants to hurt Hannah," she said. "I've been assured of that.
And under normal circumstances, I wouldn't allow any of this. But I happen to trust the students of St. Michael's to do the right thing."

Davidek scoffed. The nun said, "Maybe you won't laugh when you see
this. . . ." She spread a stack of photographs across the table like a deck of
playing cards. They were glossy, eight-by-ten portraits of students, snapped
by Zari on the day of the flood. Dozens of them. All familiar faces—each
smile was accompanied by a fake red scar.

"The yearbook committee wanted to publish some of these," Sister Maria said. "Audra found out, and we forced them to stop."

Audra spoke up from across the room. "We did it as a favor for you. To
reward you for helping us."

Davidek's fingers sifted through the images, then studied one in particular. "Are you sure it wasn't because you put a scar on your face, too?"

Audra opened her mouth. She said, "N . . . no," but hesitated, then
stepped forward and snatched the picture out of his hand.

She wasn't in it at all. But Davidek had the answer he was looking for.

Sister Maria reached out and put her hand on top of Davidek's. "Please,"
she said, her eyes steely. "You, of all people, know what pain is caused when
people have their deepest sorrows exposed as a joke."

Davidek leaned back in his chair, still scanning the images before him.
His eyes met Sister Maria's, then looked away.

After school that day, one of the saints watching from the roof of St.
Mike's would have seen Davidek lingering in the parking lot, trying to

look inconspicuous as he waited for the senior girl with the wispy red hair and mismatched eyes. He stopped her and they talked a while; then they both got into her Jeep and rolled away.

The next afternoon, Davidek met Audra and LeRose in the empty hollow of Palisade Hall. "It's a collection of notes, in a blue binder. About thirty pages," he said.

Audra wanted to know about photographs. Michael Crawford had asked to take a few of her one day last summer, when they had been sunning themselves at her pool. Her parents weren't home. They'd been drinking. She may or may not have taken off her bottoms. She definitely took off her top. She knew they'd be breaking up soon, so she'd asked him recently whatever became of those photos. He claimed to have lost the film. Either he was lying, or someone else had it.

"There are *no* photographs," Davidek said. "And she has only one copy of this book. I think. She didn't want anyone finding the extras and knowing what she has planned. She talks a lot about the 'element of surprise.'"

"What a bitch," LeRose said as Audra placed a sweet-smelling hand on Davidek's shoulder and caressed the back of his neck. "You are awesome, Peter. I mean that."

"So this is going to *work*, right?" LeRose said.

Davidek matched the big, dumb smiles plastered on their faces. "I sure hope so!" he said.

In the Jeep with Hannah the afternoon before, Davidek had been full of questions. Had she ever developed those photos of him? Would she be bringing the disposable camera to the picnic to give to him after he did as he was told? How could he be sure it was the same one unless he developed the images himself?

"Why so nosy all the sudden?" she asked. "Just don't cross me, and you'll be fine."

"I'm not going to cross you, Hannah," he said. "I just want to know what else you have." After a while, he said: "So this notebook . . . is it handwritten? Do you have copies?"

"It's on my computer," she said. "I'll print it out the morning of the picnic.

I'm still adding to it. I can't tell you any more. Element of surprise, and all that . . ."

Davidek said, "How many pages is it?"

Hannah said, "A few—but it's not like you're going to be reading *War and Peace* up there. It's quick, spicy little blurbs. Like Santa's list—only all naughty. I put the juicy stuff up top because they're bound to take you down sooner rather than later."

"But you *can* make multiple copies?"

"I guess," she said. "Why? You want a souvenir?"

The wind blew in Davidek's face. "They're going to try to stop you," he said quietly.

The neighborhood drifted by, all neat houses and cute green lawns. Fresh buds of blue and red petunias bloomed in gardens. Hannah asked, "What are you talking about?"

Davidek named everyone he knew was involved: Audra, Hannidy, Grough, Bilbo, even LeRose and Sister Maria. "They want me to find out about your notebook: what's in it, but mostly what it looks like, whether you've got more copies. Stuff like that. They're planning to trap you, and take it away before you can get to the picnic. So you have to listen to me, okay?"

Hannah seemed amused. Davidek assumed she just didn't believe him. He told her, "Give me an extra copy this week, so I can bring one to the picnic myself."

Hannah lowered her sunglasses. "*Give* you a copy?" She laughed and patted his knee.

"Don't you get it? I *want* this to happen now," he said, pushing her hand away. "I want to fucking *hurt* them—just as badly as you do. Keep a copy for yourself, fine, but they're going to try to take it. So give me a backup. That's all I'm saying."

At the next red light, Hannah looked back and forth between his eyes, as if trying to detect a lie there. "Okay, Playgirl," she said. "I'll trust you."

Davidek looked out the window again. "Just do me a favor, and make sure something about Lorelei is in there. Something horrible. Right at the top."

Another week passed, and Hazing Day arrived.

But Hannah never gave him the book.

FORTY-FOUR

It was 5:38 on Saturday morning. Hazing Day, and Hannah Kraut awoke at the usual time, just before sunrise. The rest of the world remained still.

Their house was gigantic—the largest in their upscale housing development of Roman Oaks, which was full of palatial estates, four-car garages, marble-lined eternity swimming pools, and backyard greenhouses. Surrounding this oasis of affluence were acres of dense woodlands and rolling farmland. Hannah's father, a pharmaceutical executive, had built a putting green in the backyard, and her mother had turned the small guesthouse into a studio where she taught classes in oil painting and stained glass. The Kraut home took up two lots at the end of a cul-de-sac, and had seven bedrooms—which was a lot, considering its only occupants were Hannah, her mother and father, and the ghost of her dead little sister.

Claudia Kraut still took up more room than any of them, eight years after her burial. Two bedrooms remained devoted to the memory of the young girl, who had died just a few weeks before her fourth birthday, when Hannah was nine. Claudia's bedroom was a monument to her brief existence, with her Strawberry Shortcake comforter still arrayed across the bed, dresser drawers still full of her clothes, and a neatly arranged pyramid of stuffed animals, still staring from the corner. The room beside it was a

memorial to her death: large plastic binders full of health insurance information and medical bills, lined up on shelves like sets of encyclopedias; IV
stands and empty drips that once fed into her veins; the small, stainless
steel hospital bed they had always meant to donate to some other needy
child (but never had); and a collection of miniature wigs Claudia had been
given to wear when the leukemia treatments made her hair crumble away
like spun sugar.

Hannah was five when Claudia Kraut was born, and had adored her
little sister like a favorite doll. When she got sick, Claudia fought valiantly,
but withered in her bed, crying herself hoarse, the muscles in her small
frame curling like shreds of old paper. It would have been easier on them if
her death had been something shocking and quick: a car crash or drowning. Instead, Claudia suffered endlessly, and her family did, too.

Hannah took it worst of all, reacting with fits of rage instead of tears
when her little sister finally lost the battle for her short, painful life. Hannah was never one to cry.

One summer afternoon, when Hannah was ten and Claudia was more
than a year gone, she saw some boys from the neighborhood clustered
around a decaying stump at the edge of the woods. There were three of
them, all boys from her class at school. They were passing around a steel
magnifying glass and angling the lens to send lasers of hot sunlight onto
the backs of beetles, centipedes, ants, and spiders crawling along the mossy
insect metropolis. She heard one of them cheer on the other: "Hit 'em with
the *radiation*, John!"

That was a word she knew well. Though she had no idea what it actually
meant.

Hannah watched the bugs scuttle away from the beam of light as they
grew warm (at first) and then hysterical and desperate. Beneath short
threads of smoke, the bugs jiggled and rolled, kicking vainly as their legs
ignited like candle wicks. She thought she heard small screams, but that
was just superheated vapor wheezing out of the tight seams of their exoskel-
etons. No matter how hard they fought, their fate was hopeless. She had
seen that before.

Ten-year-old Hannah didn't ask the boys to stop. She just put her hand
on the biggest one's face, and shoved him to the ground. Another boy

pushed her away, and Hannah kicked him in the balls with her pink-and-white tennis shoe. The third boy grabbed her around the neck with his arm and she bit him, not just to get him off her, but with the intent of removing a hunk of his wrist.

The bitten boy and the other one clenching his groin hustled away toward the sidewalk, but John, the big one she'd shoved in the face, rose to his feet and lunged his shoulders at her menacingly. She didn't flinch.

John followed his friends and threw the magnifying glass at Hannah, which hit her in the chest and landed softly in the crevasse of the stump, where she left it, and where it still rusted to this day.

This time, the tears did come for Hannah. She ran home crying, babbling incoherently for help, as her mother frantically tried to find where her screaming daughter was hurt. "Not me, *them*," she said. "We need to fix them! They have radiation!"

"Who?" her mother asked, and Hannah opened her fists to reveal palmfuls of crisp, blackened insects.

Claudia would be a freshman now, if she'd lived. As Hannah grew older, she imagined her little sister doing the same. But Claudia would be very different from Hannah. Claudia commanded love, drew it to her as easily as the ocean draws sand away from a beach. She would be overrun by friends, while Hannah had none.

Claudia would be a dancer, a poet, a straight-A student. She would win science project contests and speak French. She would be an athlete—maybe a runner, or a swimmer. Fit and elegant and bounding with energy.

Hannah had never been neglected. Her mother and father purchased this cavernous house because they intended to fill it with children, but when Claudia became sick, and then succumbed to that sickness, they poured all the love they had into Hannah instead. They had been through extraordinary loss, but tried to give their daughter an ordinary life. They helped her with homework, attended every parent-teacher conference, and punished her when her marks fell low, as good parents should. They bought her the Jeep for her sixteenth birthday, and last year, when she had asked for it, they built her a small workout room in the basement.

Yet nothing they could do erased the feeling in Hannah that the wrong daughter had died. Claudia would have taken all that love, all that kindness, and magnified it. She would have shared it with others. Hannah felt she had only done the opposite.

Her bedroom had never seen a sleepover, and she had never attended one at another girl's house. When she was little, she quit the Girl Scouts for no good reason. She enjoyed playing basketball alone in her driveway, but was no good on a team. Then came high school, and the promise of starting over, which blew up spectacularly in her face.

They had nicknamed her Fuckslut, but even now, Hannah was a virgin who had never so much as made out with a boy, despite what she had told Davidek that afternoon under the bridge. That image all went back to Cliffy Onasik, the senior stoner who had chosen the frizzy-haired girl as his freshman for the Hazing Day picnic, and wandered off with her into the woods instead of marching her up onto the stage. But Cliffy had done that only because he saw no need to torment her—he had been taunted just as mercilessly when he was a freshman and hated the hazing rituals.

He watched the talent show with disgust: Two girls were forced to compete in a marshmallow-eating contest. The loser received a cream pie in the face, to her horror, and her tears were cutting clean streaks in the whipped cream as Cliffy nudged Hannah and they walked into the woods and down a path along the ridge. Far below was the river, and across the chasm were endless leafy hillsides. Cliffy had a pack of cigarettes with one bumpy, bent, and twisted tube of paper. "It's a joint," he said, sticking it between his lips and lighting it. He exhaled a skunky cloud of burning schwag into her face, then handed it to her.

In the river below, a barge—loaded so heavy with gravel that its sides seemed only inches above the water—groaned along the current.

Back at school in the week before summer break, some of Hannah's freshman classmates approached to ask her if "it" was true. "Is *what* true?" Hannah said.

"About you and Cliffy Onasik," said Mary Grough, then a foot shorter and built like a fire hydrant.

Hannah assumed it was about smoking the joint. "I didn't want to," she said, which only heightened their interest. She denied it emphatically when she realized they were talking about something far nastier, but at that point no one cared about her denials. The rumors spread with increasing giddiness. Hannah didn't feel obliged to confirm or deny anything.

Her "Leave me alone" became "Fuck off." Whispers of "Is it true?" lost the question mark and became, simply: "It *is* true." The rumor percolated all summer long. Those who most delighted in it were Audra Banes's friends—Amy Hispioli and Sandy Burk—who, not coincidentally, had been the girls forced to compete in the humiliating marshmallow-eating contest. They were eager to get people talking about something *else* that happened that day—anything else.

Cliffy disappeared from the Valley that summer, moving to Georgia to live with a cousin. For years, whenever the story of Hannah was retold, few even remembered his name. He was just "her senior, some loser."

The next few years were living hell for Hannah, and if it hadn't been for Mr. Zimmer, she was sure she would have asked to leave St. Mike's. But there was also another reason Hannah stayed. A darker, more uncomfortable one: She felt she deserved it.

This never would have happened to Claudia. She had the grace to handle it properly, to win people over. Hannah just made it worse—lashing out with fury, deepening the hostility among her classmates. She hurled back any embarrassing fact she could, no matter how low, which led to new whispers: Hannah Kraut *knew* things about people. Secret things. About everybody.

But this was a rumor Hannah loved. She enjoyed watching people panic simply because she sat near them at lunch. She began writing in her notebooks when other students were watching, even if it was just scribbles to make them nervous. The attacks on Hannah—all of them—simply stopped midway through her junior year.

Sure, the students of St. Mike's still gossiped about her, but they did it in secret. And they left her alone.

Until now.

On the morning of Hazing Day, Hannah rolled out of bed and dressed in her workout clothes—sweat shorts, a sports bra, and tank top. The dim light of dawn rendered her bare room in hues of pale red. She looked out her window as she slipped on her shoes and saw a pink horizon of clouds but no sun. There were many more vehicles than usual parked on her street, and she could see figures sitting inside them, though she couldn't make out the faces. She recognized all the cars from school, though.

Davidek had been right. But she wasn't scared yet.

Hannah went over to her computer and tapped away . . . soon the printer was humming smoothly, filling its tray with pages. Hannah went into the room filled with her sister's old medical documents and cleared out a blue plastic binder. She also found a three-hole punch and some brass paper fasteners and placed them on her desk.

This is it, she thought. *Almost done.*

No one knew this about Hannah, but The Boy on the Roof had changed her. The only person in her class who suffered as bad as she did was Clink Vickler, and when he self-destructed that way, it had seemed cowardly to Hannah. She wasn't ready to quit, wiping herself out like a pathetic kamikaze. She had one year left, and then St. Mike's was in her rear view. She'd be in college, and life would start over, with new happiness sprouting from the grim remnants she left behind. It was too bad she never got to know Lorelei—since they shared such similar dreams.

As her junior year ended, Hannah began prepping for her metamorphosis. She read all the books she'd only skimmed in English classes, hired a coach for the SATs, and spent weekends at museums and libraries. (Why not? She had no friends to hang with.) She had been a lackluster student up until that point, and had a lot of catching up to do.

Hannah was hurt when Mr. Zimmer said he could no longer tutor her after school, and she knew the kiss she shared with him had been a mistake, scaring him off. Or maybe she simply hadn't enticed him *enough.*

Early that summer, Hannah had examined her short, stubby body in the mirror one night, and picked at her frizzy blond hair. She had changed her look before. It was time to do it again—but do it *right* this time. She pored through fashion magazines, trying to find the most beautiful woman she could imagine before realizing the one she wanted to become couldn't be found in any of them.

For her birthday present, Hannah asked her parents to gut part of the basement and install workout pads, a weight machine, and a treadmill. She dropped fifteen pounds by the start of her senior year. Baby fat tightened into muscle, and her puckish, somewhat sinister face softened into something even she recognized as delicate. Maybe even beautiful.

Her parents welcomed her blossoming transformation. Only one part of it bothered them, and that came just a week before the start of her senior year. Hannah returned home from the hairdresser, her kinky yellow locks straightened and hanging smoothly around her shoulders. That wasn't unusual. She'd changed her hair before. But this time she had asked the beautician to dye it cherry auburn—and came home a redhead.

Just like Claudia.

By the time Hannah finished her workout on the morning of the Hazing Picnic, her parents were up and dressed and already heading out the door. Her father hollered downstairs to her that they were going to the club for breakfast with the Tollersons, and maybe tennis later. He said, "Have fun at your picnic thing, honey!"

Hannah hurried upstairs to watch their black BMW back out of the garage and turn down the crowded cul-de-sac. She opened the front door to wave at them, though it was only for appearance. She just wanted everyone to see she was still in the house so nobody would bother them. The road was jammed with cars now, and Hannah could see all her St. Mike's classmates, waiting patiently for her to come out and play.

How nice.

Up in her bedroom, Hannah's computer printer was still working, clicking and whirring and spitting out freshly inked sheets. She took a long shower, savoring the heat on her back, and took her time drying and brushing her hair, just to tie it back in a ponytail. Nothing fancy.

Hannah bounded down the stairs with a loaded book bag over one shoulder. Her legs were coltish in a pair of tight khaki shorts, and her crimson T-shirt was rolled at the sleeves. She grabbed a banana from the kitchen table. There was a note on the counter: *Have fun! Luv, Mom!* and a hundred-dollar bill.

Against the back wall of the garage, Hannah found a box of heavy-duty black garbage bags on a shelf scattered with tools, and grabbed some wire hangers that were stacked on top of old Halloween decorations. A thick orange extension cord lay coiled on the floor like an exotic snake.

Hannah unzipped her book bag and thought of all the people waiting for her just outside that garage door. She had never felt scared like this before, and for the first time, Hannah was no longer sure she would get away with this.

FORTY-FIVE

Nothing arouses suspicion like good behavior from a trouble-maker.

Davidek had been a saint since his grounding over the mini-van incident. No TV, music, phone calls, visits with friends, or any other contact with the outside world was permitted. If he had liked to read, they would have taken that away, too. His mother kept reminding him how lucky he was they didn't have the police throw him in jail. His father kept reminding him of how lucky he was that child abuse is illegal.

In the weeks that followed, Davidek's angelic new nature annoyed both of them, and his mother especially scrutinized every word and action for fresh outrage. She knew he was plotting something, although he insisted he wasn't—which, of course, was a lie.

He wanted to ensure he could go to the Hazing Day Picnic.

Davidek's good-boy scheme to get the necessary brief reprieve also involved playing on his father's own old memories. He'd been asking him about it all week, and had been surprised by how quickly his father agreed it was a mandatory school activity that the boy should definitely attend.

"Hm, sounds like *fun*," June Davidek said at breakfast that morning in a bitter tone that suggested "fun" was not allowed.

Davidek's father huffed through his nose. "It's not really *fun* for freshmen,

Juney. The seniors do pranks and things on them, kind of like a stage show. My year, I got the shit kicked out of me. Bastards." He set down his spoon and rolled up a sleeve, drawing a finger against the soft white flesh. "Got a gash right here from a guy who hit me with a goddamn rail of fence."

"That's part of a *stage show?*" June asked. "And the teachers allow this?"

"Nooooo . . . ," her husband said, waving a hand at her stupidity. "See, me and Sinawski wouldn't do what those jerks said, get up onstage and dance around in ladies' dresses or some goddamned thing." He looked at his son with a smile that was half pride and half fury. "We told 'em, 'Up your ass.' But as soon as the teachers weren't looking . . . *Whack!*" He slapped his hands together, then scooped up another spoonful of colored Trix. "Fucking sneaks," he said.

June Davidek absorbed this. Then something was crawling across Davidek's fingers, and he looked down to see it was his mother's hand. She wore an expression of deep sympathy. "Maybe Peter shouldn't go. I don't remember Charlie talking about this. . . ."

Bill rolled his eyes. He hated even *hearing* their other son's name. "Probably not, because Charlie is a coward," he said, and his wife and son stared at him. He said, "Peter's going. End of story. He's got to be tough about this. Show them he can take it."

"Why doesn't he just resist?" his wife said. "Isn't resisting what you did?"

Bill frowned. "I didn't run and *hide*. I showed up and told 'em to stick it. That's different."

June wasn't impressed. "So our son should go to the picnic to get whacked with a fence? Genius, Bill. Father of the year, once again."

Davidek spoke up, "No, it's . . . I don't know *what* my senior has planned. But the picnic isn't like that anymore."

"Our child *stole a car*, and you think he should get a *picnic?*" his mother asked.

"No, but I don't want him to be a social cripple for the next three years either," Bill told her. "This thing . . . it's an obligation. It's like church every weekend. You don't *want* to do it . . . but if you don't, well—"

"You're basically going to hell," Davidek added helpfully.

"Maybe that would serve you right," his mother said, and stirred her cereal without eating any.

"He's *going*," Bill Davidek said decisively, adding something that surprised even the boy. "And I'm going with him."

Davidek and his mother looked at him with simultaneous expressions of: *Say what?*

"I got invited." He shrugged. "And I'm gonna make sure he does what he has to, and then I'm bringing him home. Okay?"

"Invited by who?" Davidek asked.

His father snapped, "Invited by *mind-your-own-business*."

Davidek's mother stood from the table and dumped her bowl of uneaten Special K into the sink. "Great! He steals a car and gets a fun little Saturday out of it. He'll never learn, Bill," she cried. "You coddle him! He's sitting there laughing at us!"

They both turned to their son, who wasn't laughing.

At roughly the same time Bill Davidek was revealing his plan to attend the Hazing Day Picnic, Hannah's garage door rumbled open to reveal a scene of panic: The kids languishing on the street, waiting for her appearance, scrambled to get into their cars and veer them into the cul-de-sac as she rolled out in her Jeep.

As she stopped at the blockade, Hannah looked back at her house, relieved that her mom and dad had already left, and wondered what they might think, and what they might do, if they saw this. Stubby little Bilbo and Prager and Strebovich were hustling over to her Jeep. Farther away, Audra stood beside her shiny white convertible Mazda (an early graduation gift from her father) while Michael Crawford drummed his fingers on the dashboard of his 4Runner. Lame old Mullen and Simms had parked the Pea Green Love Machine at the back end of the road, running at top speed to get close to the action.

Hannah put her transmission into park as Morti and some of his Fanboys jerked opened her door and pulled her out into the street. "Hey, Fuckslut, heard you had a surprise for all of us today," Morti said.

"You bet, peckherhead," she told him. "And wait till you—!" He grabbed her face and shoved her head back against the side of the Jeep, while the Fanboys held her arms and shoved her toward Michael Craw-ford's 4Runner, where Prager and Strebovich pulled her into the backseat. Audra was overseeing this, saying, "Make sure you don't hurt her!"

"I'll hurt you," Hannah said. "I'll claw out your fucking eyes!"

Audra slammed the door shut, and Hannah began kicking at the win-dow. Michael Crawford crawled from the driver's side into the backseat, and fell on her, holding her still.

Strebovitch opened the front passenger door. "Maybe she's hiding it on her body," he said, flashing his eyebrows. "Why don't we give her a cavity search?" He reached over the seat to grab Hannah's bare leg, pulling her closer. Hannah squirmed underneath Crawford's weight.

Audra ripped open the back door and slapped her idiot boyfriend on the back of his head. "She's wearing shorts and a T-shirt!" she said. "Where do you think she's going to hide it?"

Alex Prager opened the driver's door, laughing softly. "Maybe she rolled it up and stuck it in her cooch."

Crawford looked back at his girlfriend, still pinning Hannah's wrists against the seat. "You want to try holding her down? Go ahead!"

Over by the Jeep, the concerned citizen students of St. Mike's were scattering Hannah's belongings in the street. Amy Hispioli had Hannah's denim book bag, and she and Allissa Hardawicky had dumped it out on the grass. Bilbo was tossing maps out of the glove box. Hannah strained to get a better view. Hannidy and Lee Raymond were probing around the backseats. Carl LeRose was crawling on his hands and knees, sticking his puffy face under the wheel wells.

"I found it!" It was Mullen. His buddy Simms was helping him take the spare tire off the back hatch, and underneath it, Mullen's hands pulled out a square package wrapped in a black garbage bag, which had been wired back there with a coat hanger.

Mullen tore open the plastic and held the stack of white papers in the air. The brass fasteners glistened in the sun. "I'm motherfucking Sherlock Holmes, you bitch!" he yelled at the imprisoned Hannah.

Hannah tried to bring her knee up into Michael Crawford's balls, but Strebovitch was still holding down her legs.

Audra walked over and took the newly discovered pages from Mullen, flipping through them, marveling at the gray blur of text. "Jesus, every sheet is full."

"Why was it hidden *there?*" Amy Hispioli asked.

Sandy Burk told her not-so-bright friend, "Well, *obviously* she saw us out here."

Hannah's muffled voice shouted from the car: "I didn't think any of you idiots would be smart enough to figure out how a tire iron works!"

Hannidy reached out to take the book from Audra. "Let me have a look at that—" But the student council president held it away from her successor. "No, we agreed—*no one* would look at it. Remember?"

"We need to be sure," Morti said.

"Just look at one page, Audra. Just a glance . . . ," said Amy Hispioli.

Audra bent open the book, turning to a page at random. At the top of the sheet were the words:

> *Audra Banes—A frantic bitch, who hides her reputation as a total*
> *slut behind polite . . .*

Audra snapped shut the pages, but her fingers were still in the book. She opened it again and scanned the long section about her. When she finished, she was braced for murder. Beneath the entry on her was a section about her boyfriend, which began:

> *Michael Crawford—Compulsive masturbator, with a fetish for*
> *chubby girls and . . .*

Audra read the whole thing, her jaw clenching.

"You're supposed to glance at it, not read it!" screamed Prager. Everyone began jeering at Audra, and Bilbo snatched the binder out of her hands long enough to read the first few lines about her before she yanked it back from him. "It's the real deal," he confirmed.

Audra fast-walked to her convertible and tossed Hannah's notorious notebook into the trunk, slamming the lid with a thunderclap. "No one reads it. Not anymore. I'm taking it to the picnic. And we'll all destroy it together—agreed?"

Everybody looked at everybody else. There didn't seem to be a better plan.

The black garbage bag the pages had been wrapped in drifted along the street.

Audra signaled to her boyfriend. "Get the fuck off of her, Michael."

Hannah crawled out from under him, eyes glowing. "You're a whore," Audra said to her. "You know that?"

"Yeah," Hannah said. "I know."

The other students were scattering, wandering away from Hannah's Jeep, leaving the doors open and the spare tire rolling toward the curb, where it bumped and fell on its side.

"I'm going to the picnic anyway," Hannah said, though no one was really listening to her.

"Go ahead," Amy told her. "But if you go back into your house, you should know LeRose and some of the guys are staying behind to slash your tires. No copies for you, Hannah. You've lost."

Most of the cars were pulling away now, and as Mortinelli drove off, LeRose's shiny Mustang pulled in behind Hannah's Jeep, preventing any retreat back into her garage. Mullen and Simms volunteered to stay behind, too, and pulled in beside him.

Hannah gathered up her scattered belongings, tossing them back into the Jeep. She rolled her spare tire back and struggled for a while to hoist it back onto its tailgate pegs. LeRose and Mullen and Simms just watched.

When it was all put back together again—minus the notebook—Hannah gunned the engine of her Jeep. The fight was over.

Hannah drove forward. And her watchmen followed.

FORTY-SIX

Davidek rode silently in the seat beside his father, the minivan coursing down the unlined road like a strip of rainwater curving down a plane of glass. They were weaving through the shaded green woods of Harrison Hills Park, where the annual Hazing Picnic had been held since forever.

The minivan emerged from the trees along a field of shaggy grass freckled with dandelions, where some sophomore guys were drawing lines for football with a chalk spreader. Blue and red balloons struggled to escape from every post of the big wooden pavilion. Senior girls were taping down the corners on a dozen wooden picnic tables draped in white paper, and arranging a big potluck buffet.

Adjacent to the pavilion was a wooden stage, with an arch along the back hanging a thick black curtain. All students who spent their freshman year at St. Mike's knew that stage as the place they once stood to make a public ass out of themselves. A few remembered it with good humor; some tried not to remember it at all. Everyone, sooner or later, showed up to see it happen to someone else.

The Davideks parked on the grass at the end of the road along the edge of a big looping turnaround. There were more trees growing along the bank high above the river, and Davidek's father walked over to look down into the canyon below.

"Don't fall in!" a voice called out to them.

Davidek wheeled around into the wide, flat grin of the stranger he knew as The Big Texan—the man who had convinced his parents that St. Mike's High School was a good place for them to send their son. The man loomed over him, teeth gleaming, and stuck out a meaty hand. The Big Texan looked like someone awaiting praise for a good deed. "How's my second-favorite student? Good to see you, buddy boy."

"I'm good, sir," Davidek said, shaking the man's hand. *Second-favorite?*

Davidek's father came up and stood beside his son. The Big Texan's smile stretched wider. He said to the boy, "Did your dad ever tell you what it was like on our Hazing Day? Hell, it *rained*." He let the last word trail on, as if it still pained him. "We had a good time anyway. . . . Well, maybe not your dad. I guess that day *would* be a better memory for a senior than a freshman—no offense."

Davidek's mind began putting together pieces. "*You* were . . . my dad's senior?"

The Big Texan shook the boy's shoulder. "I was *not*," he laughed. "And good thing, too! My buddy, Lester Branshock, had your dad, but they didn't get along. No, sir. Cats and dogs! Your dad was a fighter!" The Big Texan put up his dukes, jabbed at the air, then laughed again. Davidek's father didn't.

"We were all just boys back then," he said. The Big Texan nodded, as if this grieved him terribly. "Yes, we were," he said, and patted Bill Davidek's shoulder. "Good of you to come, Billy. On the phone I didn't think you would."

Then, winking at the boy, the Big Texan said, "Carl should be here any second. He's taking care of that problem you helped him with."

Davidek thought: *Carl?* And his father pushed in the last piece of the puzzle for him. "Pete, what problem is Mr. LeRose talking about?"

"Just this troubled girl your boy unfortunately got for his senior," The Big Texan said, giving Davidek's father the lowdown on Hannah. Davidek watched them talk, and thought of LeRose lying bloody out in the parking lot, and how he had just run out to save him because he hoped someone would do the same for him. And that good deed was why the fallen boy's father had come to their house, pressuring the now-grown freshman he and his pals once bullied to send his son to the same school.

And Davidek's father had given in.

Davidek's old man finally taught him something worth knowing: The things we surrender to when we're young, we keep surrendering to the rest of our lives.

Just then, a procession of vehicles announced by the fanfare of honking horns and cheers emerged from the woods of Harrison Hills, led by Audra Banes's white convertible and followed by a stream of other cars that had ambushed Hannah Kraut just an hour earlier. Students hung from the windows, cheering as the vehicles roared up onto the grass.

A group of sophomores looked up from where they had been stoking a blaze in a stone fire pit just outside the pavilion. The campfire crackled with a demonic orange glow, and the long branches they had dragged from the woods were sticking out of the blaze, which was slowly gnawing them down. Everyone at the picnic turned toward the caravan of newly arrived cars.

Audra hopped from her convertible and opened the trunk, raising the stack of bound paper in the air like the severed head of an enemy barbarian. The mob of admirers followed her as she walked past Davidek, on her way to the bonfire. "I've got it!" she assured everyone. "It's over."

Davidek closed his eyes. Audra spotted him out on the other side of the fire as she held the notebook over her head. "Oh, hi, Peter," she said. "Thanks, by the way. It all worked out!"

With that, she tossed the binder into the blaze, sending up a column of sparks. Davidek could read just a few words in the center of the page: "Michael Crawford: Compulsive masturbator . . ." before it blackened and the binder folded in on itself. Everyone applauded.

In the distance, Hannah's Jeep was emerging from the woods, followed by LeRose's Mustang, and Mullen and Simms in the Pea Green Love Machine.

When Hannah parked, she walked stiffly toward the swing sets, where she rocked back and forth, her shoes brushing the dust.

Davidek knew then that it was true. He wanted to go talk to her, but all the people he wanted revenge against were crowding around to congratulate him.

Ms. Bromine stood with Father Mercedes by the potluck spread, watching the growing crowd of picnic-goers. "Honestly," she said with a mouthful of taco, "it speaks well for our students that they rose up and stopped her themselves. You should tell that to the parish council."

Father Mercedes grunted. He was watching the Parish Monitors wander the park grounds aimlessly. He was disappointed they wouldn't get to hear what Hannah had collected. Disappointed *he* wouldn't hear it, too. "I don't see anything positive in students acting like vigilantes," he said. "I'm sure the Monitors will make note of that as simply more evidence of the lawlessness here." At least, he hoped so.

Ms. Bromine munched her taco. Sometimes she didn't understand the priest. *Honestly, I wonder whose side you're on, Father.* She thought about saying, but didn't.

Mercedes had shifted his gaze to Mr. Zimmer, who was directing the students who were laying chalk lines in the field for the football game. "Have you ever heard stories about a teacher at this school having inappropriate contact with a student?"

A speck of taco fell out of Ms. Bromine's mouth. She thought about Noah Stein's humiliating kiss last year, but decided that might not be what the priest was talking about. Anyway, Stein was gone for good now. "It draws a lot of TV cameras, doesn't it?" Father Mercedes asked.

"Things like that . . . well . . ." She didn't finish the sentence.

Two of the senior boys tossing the football out near Mr. Zimmer had removed their shirts, and beads of sweat glistened on their chests. Ms. Bromine avoided even glancing at them.

Over by the stage, Davidek saw Green talking with some of the boys who had installed the sound equipment. Green was opening a guitar case for them, and they stood back admiring as he held out the instrument.

"Yeah, Bilbo said I could play a couple songs for my part in the talent show," Green was telling them. "I've always wanted to play in front of people. But I'm a little nervous." He placed the strap around his neck and started strumming. Davidek couldn't hear it very well, but the boys with the sound equipment were bobbing their heads.

The crowd at the picnic wasn't just St. Mike's students, but parents, almost all the teachers, and a lot of kids from other schools who came just to hang with their St. Mike's friends. Davidek saw his dad talking with some older guys who were wearing matching T-shirts saying: ARCHANGEL ALUMNI. There were a lot of those shirts around. And lots of Parish Monitors, too, looking glum as they patrolled the park grounds, writing in their notepads.

After lunch, the first event was the Freshmen–Senior football game. Mr. Zimmer and Mr. Mankowski were referees, but the whole game was a fraud designed to let the seniors trample the underclassmen while breaking as many rules as possible. Davidek spent most of the game trying to avoid being near Green.

When the game ended, the freshmen were defeated, 224 to nothing.

Lorelei watched the game play out while sitting alone at the pavilion, nursing a piece of cake that was too big for her to finish.

On the other end of her picnic table sat another girl from her class, chewing on some gummy bears. Lorelei didn't know her well, but lately she noticed the outcasts more. Now that she wasn't one of them anymore.

The other lonely girl said something, and Lorelei asked, "Sorry, what?"

Seven-Eighths cleared her throat politely. "I said, what is your senior making you do? For the talent show?"

Lorelei shook her head. "I don't think anything." If Mullen and Simms even tried, Lorelei now had enough friends to force *those* two losers out onto the stage instead.

Seven-Eighths was impressed. "I had a senior, but she hasn't really bothered with me since the start of the year. . . . It feels weird to feel *bad* that no one is picking on me."

"Lucky you," Lorelei said.

"Lucky us," Seven-Eighths replied.

• • •

Finally, the moment they all were waiting for . . .

Audra Banes walked to the microphone and raised her arms in the air to the not-so-adoring faces at the foot of the stage, who were whistling and applauding weakly. "Ladies and gentlemen," she said. "We now begin an eight-decade tradition. The long-awaited . . . and much-dreaded . . ."

There were some heavy *oohs* from the audience.

". . . St. Mike's freshman *Talentless* Show!"

A few people chuckled and Audra said, "Oops! I meant *Talent* Show!"

The first act was her own: The freshmen of her friends Allissa, Sandra, and Amy came out crooning "My Guy" to moonfaced Justin Teemo, dressed like super-nerd Alfalfa from the Little Rascals, complete with a cowlick standing up in back. After that came a group of guys in Hawaiian grass skirts, shaking their big balloon boobs to some island drum music. One of the guys was Smitty, who peeled off his shirt and flexed his considerable muscles for the crowd. Sister Maria—all too aware of the Monitors' notetaking—came over to Audra and whispered, "Please, it's not a strip show," and Audra went out and told Smitty to pull the shirt back on.

The show went on for about an hour. Most of it was pretty lame. One group of seniors made their freshmen run around, trying to catch tossed Skittles in their mouths. (The crowd booed.) Mary Grough dressed Zari as a homeless person and wouldn't let her change until she'd begged one full dollar in pennies from the crowd. (The rest of the show went on, in the meantime.)

Near the end, Hannah brushed by Davidek and said, "We're coming up soon on the schedule . . . get ready."

Davidek said, "What are you talking about?" But she was gone, weaving through the crowd toward Smitty, who by then was back in the audience, but was still wearing his grass skirt and straw hat.

Hannah whispered something in his ear, and Smitty argued briefly— then grudgingly followed her. Davidek moved to the edge of the crowd for a better view, and he wasn't alone. More eyes were watching Hannah than the stage.

Hannah reached inside her Jeep and pulled a lever that made the hood of the vehicle cough open. Smitty stood beside her, hanging his head, while Hannah reached under the hood and pulled loose a package strapped to the underside with an orange extension cord.

As they walked back to the crowd, Hannah held the package under her arm like a seminarian with a Bible, and Smitty stayed close beside her as a security guard—a necessary one. Right away, Amy Hispioli ran at Hannah and tried to grab the package, but Smitty tripped her flat on her face and they kept walking.

LeRose broke through the crowd and began cursing at Hannah, a demonstration of courage for his upperclassman friends, but when he got too close, Smitty grabbed his shirt and knocked him out of the way.

He didn't like helping Hannah, but had no choice. John "Smitty" Smith used to live in Hannah's neighborhood. In fact, she had once grabbed him by the face and shoved him to the ground for burning insects with a magnifying glass. The secret she knew about him was that Smitty looked so much older than the other freshmen because he *was*. He was her age, eighteen now—but had been held back several years in grade school. He had been doing whatever Hannah asked to ensure she would never tell. Now, as far as he was concerned, the debt was paid.

Hannah beckoned Davidek to the side of the stage as Smitty left her.

Audra approached the microphone like it was wired to explode. "Next up . . . ," she said, her voice pinched. "Uh, musical presentation, by Danny 'Bilbo' Tomch's freshman. . . ." She was going straight to Green's guitar playing. But Hannah extricated a blue binder from the black plastic wrapping and called out, "I think you're moving out of order. . . . We've got to follow *the rules,* right?"

Audra didn't answer. She looked at the crowd, which stared back at her, baffled. No one wanted to challenge Hannah. Not with that book in her hands.

"No, Hannah," Audra said into the microphone. "No! I'm *not* going to allow this!" She stepped away from the mic and blocked Hannah at the back of the stage along the curtain. She looked ready for war—but then whispered, "I'll let you go—but only if you *swear* not to make him say that thing you wrote about me."

This caught Hannah by surprise. "And . . . what about your boyfriend? And your other friends?"

Audra swallowed, then repeated: "Nothing about . . . *me*."

Hannah poked her tongue into her cheek and cocked her hip. *"Yeah?"* she said, as much a question as an agreement.

Audra stalked back to the microphone looking super-fucking-pissed-off, like she had done everything in her power and the sheer injustice of it all simply galled her. "Ladies and gentlemen, Hannah Kraut's freshman . . . Peter Davidek." Then she marched down the front steps of the stage, and all the onlookers stared around helplessly.

Behind the stage, out of sight of the others, Hannah and Davidek stood alone amid the tables and props discarded from the earlier acts.

"Why didn't you tell me you had a double?" he asked. "I thought they burned—"

"That was a fake," Hannah explained. "Those pages were all just the same page—printed over and over again. Since it was all about Audra and her boyfriend, I knew they wouldn't look long, or let anybody *else* check."

Davidek wondered, "Why didn't you just print out a whole other copy?" But Hannah didn't answer. He'd find out soon enough.

"Are you going to do this thing, or ask a million questions?"

Davidek raised a finger. "Only one more—how'd you get that asshole Smitty to do your bidding?"

"I can't tell his secret any more than I could tell yours," Hannah said, fluttering her eyes.

She placed the binder in Davidek's hands. "Whatever happens, just come talk to me. *Don't worry.* I'll be right back here."

Davidek tapped the binder with two fingers. "I'm not the one who needs to be worried anymore," he said, and walked up the steps through the curtain.

What seemed to be a thousand faces greeted him. Davidek imagined all of them with painted red scars on their cheeks. Time to wipe those away.

Bromine was inching close to the sound board, ready to make the kids there cut his mic the second he said too much, but Davidek would keep reading, no matter what. He would shout until his throat tore apart.

There wasn't a whisper from the crowd. Over in the corner, down by the base of the stage, he could see the Parish Monitors, their notebooks poised.

Mullen and Simms were alone together far in the distance, not a part of the crowd, not a part of anything. Green stood alongside Bilbo and his senior friends, shielding his guitar in the jostling audience. Davidek's father was out there somewhere, too . . . and Lorelei.

Davidek opened the binder, prepared to make it hurt. His mouth moved closer to the microphone as he looked down to begin reading. But the first sheet was pure white.

Empty.

He turned the next page, but that was blank, too.

So was the next one. And the next one.

So were all of them.

FORTY-SEVEN

The next few moments existed in Davidek's mind only as snapshots and scattered sounds. At first it was just white, a total void on all sides. Then the whiteness receded; it was only the blank pages he held, and those were meaningless. Even the breeze flipped them dismissively.

The faces in the crowd below weren't people, just a smattering of color against the lime background of the Harrison Hills fields.

Here was another snapshot: Hannah, her eyebrows forming an angry V, teeth bared. Davidek opened his mouth, and that's when she swung her fist at him. The world went black, but not because she struck him. He had simply closed his eyes, expecting to be hit, but Hannah had merely swatted the microphone, skittering it across the stage. It made a sound over the speakers like a lawn mower digesting silverware.

Davidek's eyes opened again and Hannah was leading him by the arm through the backstage door, like an impatient lover. "It's the wrong notebook," he told her. And she hushed him, taking the useless binder from his hands.

"It's not the wrong notebook, Peter. It's the right notebook. It's the only notebook. There never was a notebook."

These notions all seemed to be at war with each other. He couldn't understand and began peppering her with questions she didn't have time to answer. Hannah insisted: "I'll explain more to you later, but for now— you did great. This all happened the way I hoped it would. There's only one more thing I need you to do."

Davidek listened. She said, "Stand behind me onstage and don't say anything. Okay?"

Then she was moving again, and he followed her through the curtain and back onto the stage, where she picked up the microphone and, like all great public speakers, warmed up the crowd. "Just so you all know . . . St. Mike's is a wretched place on this Earth, and you all plague its halls, wallowing in your sick, cruel little lives." She held the binder aloft. "That doesn't change whether my freshman reads this today or not."

Nearly every breath in front of them halted. Hannah's mouth became a thin smile. "My freshman here has been disobedient," she said. "He tells me now he is *refusing* to read what I have *told* him to read." Hannah looked back at Davidek, and was pleased by the angry and confused expression on his face. It fit quite perfectly with the story she was presenting. She had been right to keep him clueless all this time.

"Maybe Davidek is a little soft on you, a little misguided," she said.

The audience began to jeer and holler at her. Someone threw a chunk of grass that flop-rolled across the stage. Carl LeRose, standing in the front row, raised a middle finger in the air. "Get off the stage, Fuckslut!" he shouted.

Someone else yelled, "Freshmen only!" Another voice: "Cut the mic!"

That sentiment was spreading quickly and the noise was rising. "The thing is . . . I like my freshman. Even if he is a little soft on the rest of you." Hannah tossed the fluttering pages to Davidek. "Their secrets are yours now, tough guy—in case you change your mind."

Hannah lowered her mouth closer to the microphone, peering through the autumn hair hanging over her one blue eye and one green eye, and addressed her classmates one last time: "I suggest you treat him better than you treated me."

The heckling became a wave that pushed Hannah off the stage. The crowd screamed names at her, hurled a few more chunks of grass and half-eaten cookies, and booed and hissed and cursed and laughed as she walked away.

• • •

Hannah hurried back to her Jeep. She wanted to talk with Davidek, but not around the others, and she guessed it would take him a while to catch up. Hopefully, not long. She couldn't afford to linger—not with her protection gone.

At the edge of the crowd stood Mr. Zimmer, his thin head rising high above the others, looking like some separate species. They hadn't spoken since he had fled the prom weeks earlier. He never bothered to explain himself to her, but Hannah had chosen to forgive him anyway. She wasn't angry anymore. Not about anything at all.

As she walked by, Mr. Zimmer said, "You did the right thing."

Hannah looked back at Davidek, who was holding the empty pages and being mobbed with congratulations. "Yeah," she said. "Even if that kid never *did* show up at the prom, like he *promised*." She shrugged. "Nothing to take pictures of anyway."

Zimmer said, "I'm sorry, Hannah. . . . But you and I . . ." She let him struggle with his words. All the teacher came up with was: "Maybe your freshman can take our picture at graduation next week. I'd like one of you in those commencement robes, to remember you by."

"Okay. Graduation, then, Mr. Zimmer," she said. "I'll see you when it's time to say good-bye to this place." Then Hannah hugged him, not knowing that moment would be their actual good-bye.

Davidek caught up to her as she was opening the door to her Jeep. She saw him running across the field—alone, thankfully. Before he could ask it, she tried to answer the obvious question: "I made up the story of the notebook with all the secrets. I made it up a long time ago."

Davidek was still catching his breath. His face was furious. She said, "You want to know why, don't you?"

Davidek said, "Fuck you . . ."

Hannah frowned. "Why don't you try 'Thanks'? The notebook story protected me for two years. It made people afraid. And that made me safe. I brought you in because I wanted to pass that protection to you. You're the hero, Peter. To all those people, you killed the monster. All by yourself."

Davidek wasn't impressed. "I didn't want this. . . ." He shook the empty stack of pages at her, and Hannah said, "Then tell 'em it was all a trick. Tell 'em you *didn't* stand up to me and really wanted to read out all the worst, dirty little things about them. That'll cure all the backslapping you were just getting."

"Why'd you lie about it to me?" he demanded. "Why couldn't you trust me?"

Hannah put a hand on her hip. "Are you really going to stand there and say you wouldn't have warned them? That you wouldn't have told them *months ago* it was all a trick? Back when you were getting Zimmer and Bromine to threaten me? Where would I have been then, Playgirl, if I told you the truth? Helpless. *Defenseless."*

Davidek got right up in her face. "Goddamnit, Hannah, this was supposed to . . . to make it *right!* What about all the stories you said you knew?"

"Do you think I'm the invisible-*fucking*-man?" Hannah said. "I told you—I've heard rumors, sure. And some might have been true—but nobody tells me anything. What everyone *imagined* I knew was the trick that protected me. The best revenge you can get is making people see the worst parts of themselves."

Hannah reached into the pocket of her shorts and withdrew the disposable camera. She stuck it in his free hand. "Here, you can have this back, too."

Davidek squeezed it until his knuckles were white; then he thrust it out at her. "And should I thank you for that, too, the day under the bridge? Did you have to humiliate me like that?"

Hannah was quiet. She didn't want to keep fighting with him. She wanted to leave. "I needed you to stop *resisting.* I needed you to stop taking their side, telling teachers, helping undermine me. Let's face it—the main reason you warned me about the plan to ambush me at my house today was that camera. You were afraid they'd get it. Or that I'd print up the pictures—"

Davidek's jaw clenched. "I warned you because *I* wanted what *you* wanted."

Hannah said, "I just wanted to be left alone."

Davidek's raging eyes almost pitied her. "You wanted to hurt them."

"I used to," Hannah said, and brushed her small, soft hand on his cheek. He closed his eyes and let it cradle his jaw, savoring the warmth, trying to remember the feel of it because he knew it wouldn't last. "What I really wanted was to save the kid who asked me to be his senior—the one who thought I was too nice to be the Hannah Kraut everybody talked about. Can't you see the good in this? Please?" she asked. "I did this to protect you. To make you the good guy. From now on, everybody owes you."

She forced a wry smile that she didn't really feel. "As for our incident under the bridge . . . Don't tell me that wasn't a little bit fun."

Davidek put his arms around her and squeezed her close. "No," he said. "It wasn't."

Then she watched him growing small against the plain of green grass as he walked away. "I'm sorry for you, Playgirl," she said, too soft for him to hear. "You always hold on to the worst of things—and you lose everything else."

Davidek was mobbed by people shoving and hanging on him good-naturedly. "That was brave, man," said John Hannidy. "United we stand!" They were all around him now, his enemies—presenting him with the gift of friendship.

There was a cheer as Hannah's Jeep disappeared down the road. Someone asked Davidek what he planned to do with the notebook—the question came from Mary Grough, and it had the vague tenor of a threat. All eyes were on the binder he clutched to his chest.

He walked to the fire pit, and with a gasp of ash, the binder dropped in and Davidek watched the blaze consume a second helping of useless pages. He reached into his pocket and dropped the disposable camera into the flames after it. The heat turned the plastic into smoldering bubbles, releasing tiny purple ghosts of smoke into the air. Then it was gone, too.

Behind him, Audra stood on the stage, assuring everyone that there was more to come. The crowd was voicing supreme dissatisfaction with the so-called talent show this time around. Everyone had waited all year for this? Faces sagged, legs shifted, eyes searched for somewhere better to be. The juniors huddled around the fire nudged the long branches that hung out into the grass, pushing them closer into the sparking oblivion. They pledged that next year, when they were in charge, they wouldn't wuss out like this class. A couple of singsongy numbers? Some guys in dresses? Lame and a half.

Even Davidek's apparent rebuke of Hannah was something of a disappointment. The crowd had wanted blood to be spilled—even if it had been their own. And they still wanted it.

A group of seniors bickered as the dead-time passed onstage, becoming frantic. What could be done to salvage their reputations as hellraisers?

"Please be patient . . . some technical difficulties here! . . . We've got fun stuff still to come!" Audra squawked over the speakers as a small mob of students began congregating behind the stage, trying to cook up a plan.

Carl LeRose swept by Davidek with a group of other giddy upperclassmen, bound for the food pavilion. "You showed that bitch, buddy boy," LeRose said, sweat running down his face. "Now, grab some of those cookies and come with me!" LeRose tossed half a box of Eat'n Park Smiley Cookies into Davidek's hands and scooped up a cardboard flat of cake. One boy was loading a paper plate with a pyramid of hot dogs spackled with sauerkraut, and another was gathering up an armload of roasted corn on the cob.

"Grab some stuff and get back behind the stage!" yelled Alex Prager, hefting a huge bowl of macaroni salad. Audra was back at the microphone, telling the onlookers to wait just a little longer. "We have the grand finale coming right up!"

With his free hand, LeRose dragged Davidek around the corner to the back of the stage, where the freshman accidentally kicked an open guitar case. A little plastic bag of guitar picks hopped out.

The long table by the backstage curtain, once loaded with lame costumes, now sagged with the weight of cakes, Jell-O desserts, a mountain of cookies, and assorted tubs of barbecued chicken, congealed hamburger patties, pasta dishes, and three partially eaten fruit pies stacked in a gooey column. Mortinelli broke through, waddling bowlegged as he hefted half a watermelon onto the smorgasbord, tumbling some brownies off the table edge. LeRose added his flat of cake and Davidek's box of Smiley Cookies to the heap, and Hannidy threw on a slab of molten ice cream cake.

"What the hell is going on?" Davidek asked as a group of seniors lined up around the overflowing food table, trying to figure a way to lift it up the back stairs and onto the stage.

A chant was starting: *Feed* your *face. . . . Feed* your *face. . . .*

Now they were pushing the victim backstage, too.

It was Green.

The heavyset boy stood cradling his guitar, and his cheeks wobbled as he shook his head back and forth, saying, "No, guys, no . . . ," to the giggling seniors around him who jabbered menacing instructions as they shoved him forward.

Green begged his old friend, "Bilbo, come on . . . ," but that portly little senior just stood off to the side helplessly, studying the grass at his feet. Strebovich and Prager, the freshman's fellow stairwell dwellers and bandmates, couldn't look at Green either.

Green told whoever would listen: "No . . . No . . . Bilbo said I could *play*," and then Mortinelli jerked the guitar out of his hands.

Some girl said, "We don't want you to sing some shitty *song*." It was Missy Dahnzer, a fellow freshman. Little Mortinelli waved the guitar at the sky. "That's right, big boy! If you're gonna sing, you're gonna sing for your goddamned *supper*."

The chant was spreading around the front of the stage: *Feed* your *face. . . . Feed* your *face. . . .*

"Here's the deal," Michael Crawford barked at Green. "We're going to put you onstage, and you've got five minutes to eat *all* this stuff. Whatever you *don't* eat—"

The faces of the conspiring seniors blossomed into sick grins.

"—whatever you *don't* eat, or at least *try* to smash into your face and mouth, gets poured into your guitar. Got it? So . . . *bon appétit!*"

FORTY-EIGHT

Green began naming the boys around him, as if it would bring back the friends he thought he knew. "Bilbo . . . Alex, come on . . . Streb. Streb, man. Please, guys. Please . . . Don't, don't do this. . . ." But none of those guys could look at him. No one was stepping in front of this for everybody's favorite freshman.

The other upperclassmen were all smiles as they played a game of keep-away with Green's guitar. Green chased after it haplessly, telling anyone who would listen, "We had an *agreement*, guys. . . . I was practicing. . . . You said I could just sing some songs! . . ."

The "feed your face" chant had revitalized the waning excitement of the crowd in front of the stage. Even Davidek's father was curious to see the big finale, standing off in the distance by the swing sets, drinking beer and chanting along with other old-timers in their St. Mike's alumni shirts.

Behind the stage, Green's face kept shaking *no, no, no*. Smitty and Simms were pulling him closer to the steps behind the curtain. Davidek watched, but his face displayed no passion one way or the other. His eyes met with Green's. Then Davidek began to walk away.

"Aren't ya gonna watch?" demanded Mortinelli, but Davidek just brushed past him, leaving behind the rest of the backstage crowd.

"FEED YOUR FACE! . . . FEED YOUR FACE!"

Davidek made his way over to the pavilion, where blubber-necked junior Raymond Lee was standing around the smoky fire ring. He asked Davidek, "What's he saying? The black kid?" Davidek shrugged. Lee rubbed the heel of his shoe along one of the thick branches sticking out of the blaze, stirring the embers.

Davidek smiled at the junior, inching closer to him. He looked polite as he invaded the stocky boy's personal space, and Raymond Lee staggered back annoyed, his pelican neck wiggling. Davidek put a hand on the boy's barrel chest and pushed him back farther, then nodded polite thanks as he bent down and took hold of the cool, leafy end of the maple branch. It was about the length and thickness of a well-muscled arm. Davidek drew it out of the fire with a sandy rattle of coals.

He hefted it in one hand, tracing a line of smoke through the air as he walked. The shoots of flame at its crackling end dropped burning specks with each step, and the people behind the stage hurried out of its way as he marched through them.

He passed Green and nodded at him, then swung the burning branch at Smitty, who released his grip on Green and sprang away, swatting the smoky air as he felt the heat of the embers pass his face. Simms didn't see Davidek until it was too late, and the torch singed the hair on his arm as Davidek stabbed it at him, sending him howling as he let go of Green's other arm and stumbled backwards.

Prager, Strebovich, and Michael Crawford were lined up around the table of food, ready to lift it up the stairs and through the backstage curtain, when Crawford saw Davidek and said, "What's—?" But that was all he got out.

Davidek hoisted the branch high above his head. Sparks flickered through the air against the white sky. Then in an arc of blue smoke, the scorching branch cut the air and collided with the table full of food.

The stack of pies detonated. Davidek raised the branch again and could hear the thick, sugary innards of cherry sauce gasping against the cinders, dripping off the end of the branch like cooking blood.

The three guys around the table rushed him, but Davidek held them back with a casual swing of the flaming staff. He slashed it at the table again, sideways this time, and the watermelon splashed open like a point-blank rifle shot to a skull. Cool flecks of juicy red fruit dripped down the back of the black curtain.

Davidek raised the branch again, like a tough guy trying to ring the bell in the strength game at a carnival. Each time it collided with the table, it left a new line of smoke trailing over his head, and there were now rows of them gliding away toward the river. The table exploded with sprays of cookies and blackened flecks of wood, all shooting upward in great fountains of sparks and crumbs. Burning ash bit into the Tupperware of the macaroni salad, raising little tendrils of toxic smoke. Pads of cold cuts absorbed the smacks with flat thumps, but the ceramic platters beneath the lunchmeat slabs split in two, then three, then disintegrated. Davidek swung sideways again, like a major league slugger, showering some of the backstage onlookers with pulverized bits of hamburger. A fragmented dish of rigatoni barfed its contents onto the grass. He whacked now at the bare center of the table, feeling it crack, feeling it give. . . . It coughed splinters into the air, and he hammered it three more times in rapid succession. On the fourth hit, the particleboard cracked in two and the table's folding legs wobbled as it fell in on itself. The one remaining cake, which had bounced up and down repeatedly without being struck, slid down now and squished itself in the table's cracked center. Davidek stabbed it like a buttercream heart, extinguishing the last remnants of his bludgeoning torch.

His lungs heaved as he stood at the center of the spray-radius of ruined food, wiping a thick drip of blueberry filling from one eyebrow. A splotch of marinara sauce seeped into the shoulder of his shirt.

Raising the smoldering, icing-coated branch, Davidek spun around at the gawping faces, many of them flecked with specks of food. Mullen and Simms were in the back of the group, fearing he would begin clobbering them next. They might have been right.

Green was standing free, but his eyes were just as fearful as before. Audra leaned down from the curtain in the back of the stage. "What the fuck happened?" she asked, her voice rising an octave with each word.

No one made a move toward Davidek, which surprised him. The people out front were still chanting: *"FEED YOUR FACE! . . . FEED YOUR FACE! . . ."* waiting for something to come onto the stage and make them laugh.

Davidek extended the branch toward Audra, like Babe Ruth pointing to where he planned to hit his next home run. "Tell everybody the show's over."

Edging around the back of the stage, looking at him with a kind of curious outrage, was Ms. Bromine—a figure in a cobalt blue jacket and skirt, wearing picnic-inappropriate block-heeled shoes and folding her arms in front of her broad chest. Everyone backstage found somewhere else to be as she moved in on Davidek. Green stood still by his side, but Davidek was looking only at the guidance counselor.

Bromine slowed as she neared him, extending one pointed finger. "Drop . . . *the weapon!*" she declared.

Davidek looked at the branch in his hands, as if it had just materialized there. Then he smiled as he sized up Ms. Bromine's head and thought of the satisfying squish of the watermelon he'd just clobbered. Then he dropped the club to the ground.

Bromine rushed forward and seized him by the arm, her nails biting into the flesh. She shoved him backwards to the ground and kicked the branch aside. Then she walked back around the corner of the stage and waved for the team of Parish Monitors to get to work back there. She wanted someone else to document the boy's violent behavior this time.

The Monitors swarmed through the dispersing backstage crowd, pens and paper in hand, but all there was to see was a lot of wasted food heaped around a busted table. They stood around silently, not sure what to do about it.

Bromine turned toward Davidek, but he was gone. She spotted him near the tree line, not running, but not taking his time either. She stomped off after him as Audra Banes picked up the microphone on the stage and announced that she was wrong. What they had promised was not going to happen.

The sturdy chant of *"Feed your face!"* dissolved into disappointed moans.

Davidek passed through rays of sunlight shafting through the trees, realizing he had no idea where this path through the woods would take him. There was a scenic lookout ahead—a clearing with a ring of rectangular stones for benches and a small wooden deck jutting over the cliff. Over the side were steep ridges, carpeted with sweet-smelling brush and fallen trees being slowly digested by moss. Beyond that was a chest-cooling drop into space, ending at the still, flat surface of the Allegheny River's chocolate surface, twinkling silently.

Davidek pushed deeper along the ridge. The canopy of leaves created unlikely darkness in the bright afternoon sun, and odd rocks rose like ancient molars from the earth. There was no path anymore, and the thickening woods hushed the noisy picnic grounds behind him. Bromine surged toward him through the growth, pursuing the freshman alone. She yelled, "Stop!" and struggled over the uneven terrain, her round blond head bent low to avoid eye-poking branches. "You just bought yourself two months of detention!" she said.

The trees were skinnier here, leaning out on a gentle slope of crumbling shale that was thinly carpeted with black dirt. Davidek would never know it, but it was the same spot where Hannah Kraut's senior had once sparked a joint with her.

The sun burned through the canopy, tinting the world yellow. A stream of trickling water cut through the hillside and dropped off the cliff into a deadfall of sharp branches, as white as bleached bones. There was nowhere else for him to go. This was the end.

A meaty hand snagged the back of Davidek's head and jerked him backwards. Ms. Bromine knotted his hair in her fingers as she made him face her. "There's a reason we call kids like you dead-enders," she said.

Every vein in her body throbbed. Her face was nicked with little red scratches from the trees, and she had a smear of caterpillar web stuck in her hair. Sweat beaded up on her pink face and ran down her neck. She pulled Davidek close enough to feel his breath. "When I tell you to 'stop,' you damn well better listen. But you have no respect. And that's why you get none in return."

"It's *Saturday*," he said coolly, prying at the fingers in his hair. "This isn't *school*. You're *nobody* here. I don't have to respect you *anything*—"

Little flecks of spittle hit his face. "I *saw* you destroy that food, buddy boy. Sick. . . . Just for a laugh, right? You make a mess and ruin something that's supposed to be fun. Well, I *saw* it. And I've been waiting a *long time* for you to screw up in front of everybody like this. So they can all see what *I* see."

She pulled at his hair again, trying to make it hurt. Trying to make him cry—the way *she* had cried after he and his rotten little friend Stein had humiliated her in the parking lot that first time she even met them. "You're getting a century of detention, little brat." That seemed like weak menace, so she added: "And I'm going to report you to the Parish Monitors and Father Mercedes. I'm going to get you expelled. How do you like *that*?"

Davidek laughed at her again. "If you expel me . . . how will I serve my, uhh, 'century' of detention?"

Bromine felt her heart having a fit. This wasn't her. This wasn't what she did, how she acted. She felt control slipping away, just as it almost had that night at the Valentine's dance, twisting Noah Stein's arm as she squeezed it in her sharp nails. But this time there was no one around to see her, and no one around to stop her. "You want a *laugh*, huh? Here's what makes me laugh—" Her hand cut across his face.

The boy slid toward the ground, but Bromine still held him by the hair. He stared up at her, his teeth white and glistening. "You're gonna get fired now," he said.

Bromine jerked his head back. Her fingers were beginning to hurt from holding his hair so tightly. "You'd like that," she said. "To humiliate me. But I *know* boys like you. . . ." She felt nauseated, dizzy; the air she gasped felt thick as water. Gretchen Bromine could feel the boy in her arms straining against her, every muscle taut as she pulled him against her. "Your friend with the scarred-up face taught me a little trick. Do you remember? I know *I'll* never forget it. . . . It's called 'Who Would Believe You?'"

Bromine's eyes were watering at Davidek's smile. "Boys like you never cared for this school. Not like *I* did. It was all about *you* . . . what *you* wanted. It used to be a nice place when I was a girl. . . ." She could hardly finish. She began to choke: "Boys like *you*—made *me*—the bad guy. You made *me*—the monster. But it's you. It's *you*."

Her free hand pawed sweat off her face. "You know how to play Who Would Believe You?" she asked, almost sweetly. She looked down into the boy's lean, youthful face—his dark eyes staring up at her, the muscles in his arms braced against her.

She remembered boys like this. But they had once looked at her so differently.

Ms. Bromine pressed her lips against Davidek's, sealing his face against hers, leaving a smacking taste of chips and salsa in his mouth as her tongue probed between his lips. The boy flailed in her grip, then slowed, his hands sliding along her sides, caressing her—until—

Bromine shrieked, rearing back as Davidek pushed up on his legs, squeezing fistfuls of her fleshy breasts and twisting them like he was ripping out twin champagne corks. It was the championship Purple Nurple of all time, a last-resort move he'd learned courtesy of countless beat-downs from his big brother, Charlie. If there was one mark Charlie made on the world, it was now imprinted on Ms. Bromine's chest. The guidance counselor flopped her arms in a panic and sprawled backwards on her ass, her blue blouse making twin tents between his fingers as she fell away from him.

Bromine thudded on her back, kicking her fireplug legs to push herself away through the weeds.

"You're right," Davidek gasped, looming over her. "No one *will* believe this."

"You assaulted me!" Bromine bellowed. "Get away!" Her hand scrabbled through the leafy undergrowth and seized on a chunk of rock—roughly the size of an orange, but sharp. It fit neatly into her hand as she struggled to her feet, ready to swing it at the boy's face.

Behind her, a voice said, "Stop! . . . *Now*."

Bromine's hair dangled with leaves and stuck to the sweat on her face. She sniffed quietly, eyes focused on something standing in the woods behind Davidek. She began to sob, and crystal tears streaked down her face. "He attacked me!" she said. "You saw it!"

The slight figure of Sister Maria stood amid the maple saplings. The nun's mouth was a razor line as she began to walk. "Yes. I did," she answered, moving between them. "It looked like quite a little game."

"*Game?*" Bromine barked. "I wouldn't call it—"

"Yes," Sister Maria interrupted. "I believe that's exactly what I heard you call it. 'A little game called . . . Who-Would-Believe-You?' Isn't that right?"

Bromine's weepy expression hardened, becoming a silent declaration of eternal war.

"Maybe you should leave now, Ms. Bromine," the principal said.

Bromine jabbed an accusatory finger toward Davidek. "*He* did it," she said, her voice breaking. She repeated it again, louder this time, but the claim was useless. "I'm telling the Parish Monitors!" she declared finally, heaving to her feet.

"You'll *shut* your mouth and never open it to contradict me *again,* Gretchen, or I'll do what every teacher wished they could do when you were just a student—and *boot* you out for being a miserable, know-it-all, pain in the ass." The nun squinted at the guidance counselor's dumbstruck expression. "Oh, please. Your mother and father *begged* us to hire you. And all you've done in the years since is prove me wrong, time and again—I used to think even the *rottenest* students could eventually change for the better."

Davidek piled on. "Maybe *I'll* tell the Monitors what you just did to me, you perverted bitch!"

Sister Maria spun on him. There was rage in her eyes—but a pleading neediness, too. "*Nobody* is talking to the Parish Monitors," the nun said. "So let's decide that what happened just now in this clearing—*all of it*— never happened. Understand? If I find out *either* of you spoke about this, I will make certain we speak about *all* of it." She looked squarely at Davidek. "Every last part."

The guidance counselor backed away through the trees, overwhelmed with equal parts fear and fury, shouting that this was wrong, that whatever the boy said, whatever Sister Maria *thought* she saw . . . it was a lie.

But she had no more fight left.

Sister Maria and Davidek watched in silence as Bromine retreated, stumbling and muttering through the trees like a lost bull. When she was gone, consumed by the forest, Davidek turned on the principal. "If you hate her so bad, why are you protecting her?"

Sister Maria started walking away, back toward the picnic—determined to present a smiling face to the Monitors and guests still gathered there. "For the same reason I'm protecting you," she said.

Davidek brushed at the dirt and leaves on his clothes. "Sister!" he called as her figure grew small between the trees. "Sister, tell me again . . . who's looking out for *who?*" Maybe she didn't hear. If she did, she didn't care to answer.

. . .

Davidek sat down on one of the big rectangular stones at the river overlook.

Upstream was a barge loaded with muddy grit and gravel, turning a distant bend between the hills in slow motion. No birds sang. The wind was still.

After a while, Davidek heard footsteps on the path behind him.

Green took a seat beside him on the rock bench. The heavy boy was holding his guitar, cradling it carefully, and his fingers began moving along the strings, strumming a soothing song. Green hummed the lyrics, not singing. Occasionally a word emerged, murmured more to himself than to Davidek. Finally, Green said, "I wrote this song, but I need to work on the lyrics. Maybe it's better I didn't have to sing it today."

Davidek nodded. He said, "Sorry they didn't let you."

Green was still strumming. His chubby face split open in a smile. He hummed a few more lyrics and they watched the barge pass below them, short waves grabbing at its sides.

"I'm sorry about . . . us fighting," Green said. "*You* said some things, *I* said some things . . . but what you did back there . . . just now—"

"Don't say you're sorry to me, Green. Don't ever," Davidek interrupted. "You don't owe me any 'I'm sorry's.' I'm the one who should have said it. Right away. Long ago. I'm sorry, Green. Sorry about what I said. Sorry about all of it."

Green just kept strumming. When people are particularly good at playing guitar, the world around them stops existing for a while. The music carried over the bluff. Far below, the river moved the barge silently away from them.

"I wish *sorry* was a stronger word," Davidek said. "I wish it were as strong as other words, the ones that make you *need* to apologize. Like what I said to you on the phone that night. . . . Because I am, Green. I'm so s—"

"That's the cool thing about being real friends," Green told him. "If you really mean it, you don't have to *keep* saying you're sorry. Once is enough. For good friends, I mean . . . Like us."

The two freshmen sat silhouetted against the sunny river valley, looking down over the cliff at the slow, dark water churning by below.

. . .

Back at the pavilion, most of the students and guests had gone. The sun crept toward an orange horizon, but it was still a couple hours until sunset. Clouds of gnats buzzed over the grass fields. Davidek found his father's car, where the old man was standing with The Big Texan.

Carl LeRose caught up to Davidek as he walked. "Hey, you know, if you were gonna smash all that stuff, you could've at least done it onstage. For a laugh."

Davidek said, "Is that how everybody feels?"

LeRose raised his hands—nonthreatening. "Nobody feels anything, big guy. We're cool. All right?"

"All right," Davidek said, too tired to say anything else.

Davidek's father was pissed. As his son approached, he threw open the passenger door. "Where the hell've *you* been?"

LeRose's father, The Big Texan, laughed too loud and said, "Settle down, Bill! This boy did a helluva brave thing up there today. A helluva thing . . ." At first, Davidek thought he meant the smashed food, but The Big Texan was talking about his apparent refusal to read Hannah's notebook, which now seemed like eons ago. "Your boy stood up for himself today," Mr. LeRose said. "He stood up for all of us at St. Mike's."

Bill Davidek didn't like hearing someone else tell him how to feel about his kid. The Big Texan put out his hand. "Not always easy to stand up to people . . . But you and I know that, don't we?" Bill Davidek hesitated, then shook it, and whatever secret history they shared passed between them.

The Big Texan looked across the car to Davidek. "I want to thank you again, for everything, Peter. For helping my son, here, when he needed it. I believe we need more boys like you at St. Mike's."

Davidek's father got into the car and started the engine.

"You know I wasn't the only one who helped Carl that day," Davidek said. LeRose's father looked at his son, and Carl gave him a hey-I-was-unconscious shrug.

"There was another boy who helped me," Davidek said, feeling nervous and talking a little too fast. "His name was Noah Stein. . . . He never wanted any credit, but Stein is the one who helped me get to Carl. One of the teachers was trying to hold me back, but he stopped her. With a big fat kiss on the mouth."

"Bromine?" Carl asked, his face lighting up. "So that *is* true?"

The Big Texan said, "Okay, well, where is this mystery hero? Let's meet him." He looked expectantly at his son, who may have been an upperclassman suck-up, but had never worn a red scar on his cheek.

"Carl can tell you what happened to Stein . . . and what they did to him. Right, Carl?"

LeRose said, "Yeah. Yeah, of course." He was proud to be of service.

As Davidek's father drove them away, the minivan passed Mullen's boat-sized Pea Green Love Machine, parked along the grass near the football field. Davidek looked out the back window at a curious scene. Carl pointing to Mullen and Simms, who were still hanging out at the swing set, then walking his father toward the old green jalopy. The elder LeRose, The Big Texan, drew a small booklet out of his jacket pocket, studied the rear of the car, and wrote something down.

As the woods rose around them, Davidek's father said, "I never liked that guy."

FORTY-NINE

The parish council's vote on whether to close the school was unanimous.

Father Mercedes paced the hallway outside St. Mike's library as the ten members debated the issue in an upstairs classroom. Most of the seats in the library were still empty, though about two dozen more people were at this monthly council meeting than usual—mostly clusters of concerned school parents amid the twenty or so ancient, shriveled busybodies who spent their final years on Earth obsessing over the minutiae of church matters. They all waited in uncomfortable silence for the public portion of the meeting to begin. But it was starting late.

The priest took that as a good sign.

There was no doubt—St. Mike's would be closed. Everyone knew it, because Father Mercedes wanted it. And Father Mercedes, as the pastor appointed by the Diocese of Pittsburgh, brought five votes to whatever decision the ten members decided. That gave him leverage to overrule any divided issue.

But winning by a slim majority was not enough to keep him safe.

Father Mercedes wanted certainty. If a majority of the council dissented in favor of keeping the school open, it might raise uncomfortable questions if he reversed such a controversial decision all by himself. Resis-

? they had demanded.

ather Mercedes told them, feigning extreme reluctance.

is revelation will not reflect well on the church . . . ," the priest had
We must consider this yet another reason to cut our parish off from
rrupt and damaging relationship with that school."

here were many questions: *How far did the relationship go?* Father Mer-
s wasn't certain. *Was anyone else involved?* The priest said only that he
ed not. *Will the girl come forward?* Unlikely, for we can imagine the
nage this could cause her and her family. *What has the teacher said in his
ense?* Before we confront him, we must think of protecting ourselves.

The priest knew their imaginations would fill in the vacancies. And
ey would crave protection, too, from the same things he feared: the long
nvestigation, a media frenzy, potential lawsuits, public hostility toward
he church leaders, not to mention the humiliation of the diocese.

Fortunately, the priest pointed out, they had an easy solution at their
disposal. Close the school, and the problem of a rogue teacher would evap-
orate entirely.

Satisfied with the shock and bewilderment he created, Father Mercedes
stood in the library and looked at the large oak table at the head of the
room, full of empty chairs, where the council would soon deliver their decision publicly.

He had no doubt. These were the last moments of St. Mike's existence.

Sister Maria came in soon afterwards and sat alone in the back of the
room. Father Mercedes had pledged the parish council members to secrecy
about Mr. Zimmer. Sister Maria had no idea what was coming.

Even Father Mercedes didn't expect a unanimous decision, yet that's exactly what Mr. LeRose, the council's secretary and president, announced as
he called the meeting to order. LeRose was one of the two council members
the priest had *not* approached, since they were steadfastly in favor of keeping
the high school open. It seemed even those two had been won over.

"It is rare that we all come to the same agreement," said the man known
by Davidek as The Big Texan. "We pray that this is the right decision, and
it was undertaken with heavy hearts and great concern for the future of
the parish. There were disagreements on both sides, but ultimately the
vote was unanimous."

tance from a few influential council memb
attention of the diocese. He hadn't worked th
to be undone by a few rebellious . . . *volunteers*.
drag out the potential shuttering of the sch
chance that holes in the parish finances would
time.

He had to make sure that as many of the ten mei
go along with his plan. So as they pored over the sta
Monitor program and debated the finances involved
high school, Father Mercedes had taken action to tilt tl

The priest hadn't wanted to do this. It was a risk. But
had been worthless. It was definitely a strange affair, and
be some rambunctious behavior he didn't understand, but
the catastrophe he hoped the Parish Monitors would wit
Kraut's infamous notebook failed to produce any noticeable st
a shame; he had hoped she would reveal that nasty little rume
and Mr. Zimmer—so the priest could act as surprised as ever
sparing himself the responsibility of you-should-have-known. Bu
picion Seven-Eighths had shared with him remained Father M
fail-safe, a weapon of last resort. On the morning of the vote, ho
push one last panic button with the council, he finally used it.

Mercedes had spent the day visiting five of the council membei
knew to be undecided. (Three others were already leaning in his fav
He explained that he had a greivous piece of new information for the
Something he had just learned. Something that distressed him deeply. Bu
still—it was something they needed to know.

"I learned of this troubling news from a student during the holy Sacrament of Reconciliation, so I cannot divulge her name . . . ," he said repeatedly throughout the day, knocking on doors and settling himself in living
rooms, putting on a performance of deep anguish.

"This student . . . she has confessed to a sexual relationship with one of
our most treasured teachers." It was difficult to say that part with a straight
face. Mr. Zimmer had provoked nothing but resistance against him. He
was the worst of a disobedient faculty. And yet, he would be Father Mercedes's salvation.

Mr. LeRose said, "St. Michael the Archangel High School will remain open."

The priest's lungs felt like two squeezing fists in his chest. He had been standing, and now his back found the wall, the coolness of the stone bleeding through his black coat.

But then the relief in Sister Maria's face was soon extinguished as LeRose revealed the rest of the decision: The council remained alarmed by grave behavioral problems at the school. As such, they would revisit the issue of closure in one year. Until then, there would only be limited funds allocated to repair the roofing problems, the dissolving brick in the hallways, and the school's other infrastructure woes.

One ancient board member spoke up to say, "Above all, we want to rebuild our *church*, and remove our worship of the Lord from the ridiculous venue of a basketball court." Her remarks received applause from the other mummies in the audience.

Mr. LeRose read from his notes unhappily: "There will be other constraints as well, including a sharp drop in the school's operating budget next year. We'll detail those matters in the coming months as we assemble our next fiscal-year budget in July."

Mr. LeRose looked up, finding Sister Maria's stricken face. The school was still alive—but that life was about to get even more difficult.

In the parking lot, Mr. LeRose opened the shimmering door to his sporty silver convertible, the one Davidek had first spotted outside his house nearly a year earlier. Streetlights began to flicker on in the warm night air as the sun set in a blue pool beyond the hills.

Father Mercedes charged at him from across the lot, and the priest's large hand, stinking of nicotine, yanked at The Big Texan's gray suit. "After all you've *seen,* after all you've *read* from the Parish Monitors, after all the things I have *personally told you* concerning one of the teachers at this school—you vote to keep this place alive?"

Mr. LeRose removed Father Mercedes's hand from his collar. "Funny how a convenient little rumor crept up on the day of the vote. Did you really think that would fool us? Do you really think *you* fool us?" Mr. LeRose was shorter than Father Mercedes, but he was backing up the older man. "Thanks to your rumormongering today, even the people who wanted to vote *against* the school changed their minds. They finally saw how desperate you were. Even if they believe the school is troubled, they're not taking only your word alone anymore—"

The priest swayed in front of him. "What if I'm telling the truth?"

"About what? The teacher?" LeRose scanned the parking lot briefly, watching as the last of the meeting attendees waddled to their cars. He said softly, "We've provided for that."

Father Mercedes waited for more, but got none. "You'll get the blame," the priest said, waving a finger in LeRose's face. "I'll tell the bishop you did *nothing.* That you protected a man accused of—"

"But we *have* done something, Father. The teacher won't be a problem anymore."

"What? Are you going to 'investigate'?" The priest sneered. "Drag this parish through that *filth* on the front page of every—?"

"Weren't you listening?" Mr. LeRose told him. "Money is tight. The school is getting a new streamlined budget. St. Mike's will, unfortunately, need to shrink the size of its faculty by exactly one. He's not fired. He simply fell off the edge of a shrinking bottom line. This way, there are no questions. No accusations . . . And if he's innocent, we've done him a favor. He doesn't have to defend himself against the indefensible."

The priest shot back: "There are worse problems at St. Mike's than just him."

"And you're *one* of them—aren't you, Father?" Mr. LeRose's face was cold but smiling. "I know a few contractors who say you've inquired about transforming the school into a nursing home for the elderly. You've been pretty cheap with the initial bids, Father. . . . But then, that would leave more for you, wouldn't it?"

Mercedes slapped the trunk of LeRose's Porsche and stabbed his finger in the man's face again. "Who the *hell* do you think you're talking to?"

"Definitely not an heir to the Mercedes-Benz family, that's for sure," LeRose said, looking at the palm print the priest had made on his car. "I looked into that, too. The family name was originally Marcedi, right? But your father changed that, and played it up to his advantage—as have you. So where does all your money come from, Father? . . . All that cash I hear you drop on the Steelers, and down at the Meadows, picking long shots. Not a parson's wage, I'm sure."

Father Mercedes didn't say anything. Couldn't.

"I'm willing to wait for my answer," LeRose said. "The diocese's lawyers and accountants will find it—eventually." He ran his hand along the curved doorframe of his silver sports car, making a razor line of dust on his forefinger. "For now, you can be happy, because you've lost an enemy. I know Mr. Zimmer was a thorn in your side. But don't be too happy—"

The Big Texan's thick, dry hand patted roughly against Father Mercedes's face, leaving a smear of dust on the priest's jowls.

"—you've just made a *new* enemy," he said.

In Sister Maria Hest's office, nothing moved. Not the stacks of manila files threatening to tilt over onto the cushions of the green leather couch, not the statue of the Virgin Mary gazing dolefully from the shelf across the room, teetering among assorted glass and brass award plaques, most of them decades old.

The twisted black phone cord spilling from the edge of the nun's tank-sized steel desk did not sway, nor did the weeping arms of her spider fern, or the slats of the wooden window blinds, casting the white morning sunlight into neat bars on the floor.

Sister Maria slumped in her swivel chair, hands folded on the empty desk blotter. Father Mercedes stood over in the corner, his elbow resting on a battered filing cabinet, a cigarette perched between his fingers, smoke wreathing his face. They were alone, but not for long.

He had enjoyed telling her about Zimmer.

Sister Maria asked softly, "Is there another way? . . ."

The priest exhaled twin columns of smoke from his nose. "Yes," he said. "There is."

He had been considering that question himself. Despite his overall defeat, there was an opportunity here, even better than removing Mr. Zimmer. Father Mercedes would spare the teacher, tell the parish council that the girl had lied, that the accusations proved to be baseless. Zimmer would be allowed to stay, and perhaps never even know the allegations against him. The priest would be willing to agree to that bargain, but only if it meant eliminating a far worse obstacle.

The priest told Sister Maria, "You could step down instead."

The date on Mr. Zimmer's *Simpsons* calendar showed it was Wednesday. Friday was graduation, and the seniors weren't required to show up this week for regular class, so he had the period to himself. Teaching for the year was finished anyway. Now was the time for the remaining students to clean up and prepare for the next year.

Zimmer had surrounded himself with trash bins as he strip-mined the necessary from the not amid the mountains of paper on his desk.

"Mr. Zimmer . . ."

He looked up at Sister Maria, standing in his classroom doorway. "Yes?" he asked.

Zimmer sat down on the principal's green couch, his hands clasped between his tall knees, being careful not to topple two tall stacks of files on the cushions beside him. By the time Sister Maria finished talking, he felt like his gut had been slit open.

Sister Maria looked down at her desk. Father Mercedes hovered over Zimmer's shoulder in the back corner, silhouetted against the window.

Zimmer couldn't breathe—not since they had mentioned Hannah Kraut's name. The air felt like hardening concrete in his throat. "What do you want me to say?" he asked finally, his voice breaking, though he had tried to sound strong. "It's *not* true." Zimmer could only repeat those words. It was not true. It wasn't. There was nothing else to say.

"It doesn't matter," Mercedes said. "That's not why you're being let go."

Zimmer said, *"Then why?"*

The pastor nudged at the papers stacked on the couch beside the teacher, careful not to let the tower fall—just testing. "We simply need to cut the school's expenses—that's the public reason for your departure. The *official* reason. Consider that a kindness. We'd like to spare you the humiliation of these accusations. If we can."

Zimmer looked back to Sister Maria, his eyes wide and frightened, waiting for her to step in and stop this. "However—if you were to challenge us . . . ," the priest went on. "If you were to *fight* this decision . . ."

"Sister Maria . . . ," Zimmer said, pleading. "Sister . . ."

"You'll find the severance package to be—adequate," the priest said. "Before you get emotional, I'd suggest you think of the school. Think of yourself, even . . . Think of the *girl*."

"The girl?" Zimmer said. "Are you serious? If Hannah's saying these things, it's a lie. Sister . . . She's delusional . . . She's obsessed!"

Father Mercedes said, "So you *do* admit there was a relationship?"

"It's a *lie*!" the teacher shouted, rising out of his seat. He laid his knobby hands on the principal's desk, looming over her, pleading for her help. "Let's get her in here. Right now!"

"I would advise you not to confront the girl about this," Father Mercedes said wearily. "If you challenge her, I will see to it that the police are informed immediately."

"Sister . . . ," Mr. Zimmer said. "Sister, please." The principal turned her face up to him. Andy Zimmer, her old student. Her favorite student. She often wondered what would become of her without St. Mike's, but where would she be without Andrew Zimmer?

She had sent him to nurture Green, the school's only black student at the beginning of the year. He had been dispatched on prom night to the Stein house to quiet Davidek. . . . It had been Zimmer who not only saved The Boy on the Roof, but had also forged the secret compromise that satisfied the boy's family and allowed the school to continue operating.

This . . . was just one more thing she needed from him. The last thing.

Father Mercedes and Sister Maria knew the teacher would lose control and didn't try to quiet him. Mr. Zimmer stood before them like a man drowning in deep water, sinking into darkness, his great long arms cutting the space around him. He yelled, uselessly. He gasped in the stifling silence. Then Mr. Zimmer simply ran out of words. His arms stilled at his sides. His back bent, his eyes probed the floor. He had done nothing wrong, and yet it was over. He couldn't explain the relationship with Hannah. Even the truth would not exonerate him.

Just as Sister Maria and Father Mercedes had allowed Zimmer's noise, they now allowed his defeated silence.

"Isn't there some other way?" Zimmer asked after a long while. But his voice had no strength left. In the end, he took what they were willing to give.

FIFTY

A cheerful anarchy filled the sunny stone halls of St. Michael's. It was Friday, the final day of the school year. The seniors gone, except for their graduation the next evening, the remaining underclassmen enjoyed a day that was more playful than educational. Report cards were handed out that morning. Those who performed well celebrated a job well done, while those who did poorly—Davidek included—merely celebrated the final hours before he'd have to face the disappointed wrath of his parents.

Outside the school library, some sophomores were pushing each other around on the battered steel book carts. The day wore on, scorching hot, so the boys were permitted to remove their blue blazers. Shirts were untucked and skirts were rolled, baring buff teenage arms and raising hems to dangerous places above the knee. Every time the class bells screamed, more students were left lingering in the hallways.

Davidek and Green would have been in study hall, but two days ago, the students were told Mr. Zimmer had a family emergency and wouldn't be present. Ms. Bromine was also mysteriously absent, though in her case, the school was told it was due to illness. With no one watching those classrooms, the freshmen filtered elsewhere, fusing with groups of sophomores and juniors—savoring their soon-to-end status at the bottom of the social food chain.

A white van showed up in the parking lot during lunch and delivered two pallets of yearbooks wrapped in plastic, which the students fell upon and ripped open like a pride of lions savaging a carcass. The books spent the rest of the day circulating from hand to hand, as heartfelt messages of friendship were dispatched into the future via the empty pages of the inside cover. Everybody wanted Davidek to sign their book—he was the Hero of the Hazing Picnic, after all. The guy who stood up to Fuckslut. The guy who watched out for them.

Davidek didn't want to sign. He didn't even want a book of his own. But they were thrust upon him, and he flipped through the pages, thinking of his long-ago search through last year's yearbooks for a photo of Hannah Kraut, and finding only scratched-out faces and the line: *YOU COULDN'T REMEMBER ME IF YOU TRIED.* The yearbook committee obliged her this year—there weren't any photos of Hannah Kraut. Not even her name was mentioned.

As more and more kids handed him their books to autograph, he searched his pockets and found a couple pens, but didn't need those. He had some coins in his pocket, but they were too blunt. Then his hand found his collar, undoing the clip-on tie. He pulled out the metal clasp and ran his finger along its edge. Perfect.

Davidek never got an official school portrait (there was just a black square where it should have been). But in the freshmen section, he did find one snapshot of him, standing between Lorelei and Stein as they leaned against a wood-panel wall in Palisade Hall. He had no idea when it was taken, but probably early in the year. Lorelei had her head on his shoulder, and Stein stood with his arms crossed, smirking.

After wandering away to sign them, Davidek always gave the yearbooks back with a smile. But he never actually wrote anything.

Only later did the owners of the books notice that strange photo of the three freshmen—the ones with the scratched-out faces. So many yearbooks had it, that everyone assumed it was just some strange misprint.

That afternoon, the outgoing freshman class—now incoming sophomores—stood in the hallway filling trash bins with discarded class notebooks, carefully hand-shredding unwanted love notes and tearing down magazine cutouts of dreamboat celebrities from the inside panel of their locker doors.

At the bottom of her own locker, Lorelei found a piece of paper where she'd once written the new rules she intended to follow to make people like her: *Be pretty. . . . Get good grades. . . . Don't be the class clown. . . . Sit in the front of class. . . . Befriend a handicapped person. . . .*

She tried to remember when the page was clean, and uncrumpled. Then she squeezed it into a ball and dropped it in the garbage.

Lorelei was surrounded by her girlfriends, and on days like this, it felt good to matter again. Everyone wanted to be around the beautiful tragic girl. Zari had her camera out and kept trying to get Lorelei to pose for pictures with everybody. "I'll print up the photos and maybe when vacation starts, we can meet up at your house and put them in an album," Zari said. Some of the other girls nodded eagerly, but Lorelei was noncommittal, not wanting to risk any of them meeting her mother.

Lorelei noticed a lonely figure at the other end of the hall, and excused herself from the group. The rumor that she had turned on Stein because he smacked her around still made Lorelei feel a nauseated kind of guilt—but not enough to reveal the truth. She finally felt safe. And if she could use her newfound popularity to reward other lonely girls . . . maybe that would make it all right.

It was like a variation on Rule No. 5 from that squashed-up sheet of paper—"Befriend a crippled person." Only, in this case, the handicap was unpopularity.

"I enjoyed sitting with you at the Hazing Picnic," Lorelei said, which made Seven-Eighths' skinny hatchet face blink. "Maybe we could hang out or something over the summer. Maybe go swimming at the wave pool, or get our nails done or just talk girl stuff, you know?"

Seven-Eighths had been thinking about all the confessions she would still have to do this summer. With school out of session, she had started to worry about whether she'd have anything new to share with Father Mercedes—who was still demanding to know everything he could about the students of St. Mike's.

Her little fish mouth broke into a goofy smile. "I'd love to hang out and girl-talk," she told Lorelei. "And trust me—I'm good at keeping secrets."

Someone had picked the lock on the soda machine in the cafeteria, and one of the lunch ladies noticed it too late. She yelled after the group of raiding students as they scampered away through the basement corridors, arms loaded with cans of pop.

At the time of the robbery, Davidek was upstairs, stuffing his duffel bag to the point of bursting with notebooks, tests, and papers, though he no longer needed them. He hefted the bag over his shoulder, thought for a second, then just emptied it all into the trash. From down the hall, he heard Green call out his name.

The heavy boy jogged forward, the throat of his white shirt gaping. The twin red stripes of his undone uniform tie dangled from each shoulder. Green raised his arms in the air, a can of stolen Coke in each hand. "Come on," Green said, and led Davidek down the hall to the foot of the east stairwell.

Green handed Davidek a can, and they leaned against the steel railing. Since none of the seniors were around anymore, this spot belonged to them now. Green was happy to have traded those friends for Davidek.

Above them, on the midway landing, a stained glass mosaic of the Virgin Mary glowed in the afternoon sun, her arms open and slanting multicolored rays down at the boys. Dust drifting from the hollow space three floors up became fireflies in the light.

"What was the big secret of this spot, anyway?" Davidek asked. "Why did they hang out here all the time?"

Green couldn't contain his proud and sinister grin. "Watch," he said, and snapped open the top of his soda. "But you have to keep it just between us. If too many people know . . ."

Davidek shrugged and opened his can, too. He gulped some of the fizzy pop.

"Patience," Green said, watching the first-floor doors in front of them and listening for footsteps from above.

A pair of junior girls began descending from the second floor, and when they appeared on the riser just above the boys, Green tilted his head back to take a long swig and motioned for Davidek to do the same.

As Davidek leaned back, the soda biting in his throat, he finally saw the appeal of the stairwell as a hangout spot—it provided a perfect view straight up the plaid skirt of the St. Mike's uniform. And drinking soda was just the camouflage.

When the girls were gone, Green laughed and pointed at the grinning, mute Davidek. "I never saw eyes that big!" he said.

Davidek told him, "I never saw underwear that big!" which just made the heavy boy laugh harder.

"She was big, she was big," Green agreed. "The other one was all right, but the hottest one—Penny, I think her name is—too bad she was on the inside. That *always* happens for some reason."

The change-of-class bell rang, but Green and Davidek stayed in that hollow between the stairs, talking about their hopes for the summer— sleeping late into midmorning, staying up until dawn, maybe swimming out at Melwood pool, and getting in some quality time in front of the glowing screen of Green's Super Nintendo. (Davidek didn't have one.)

The door behind them hissed open softly, and Lorelei Paskal came through, trailed by her newfound friend, Seven-Eighths. They carried rolled-up tubes of maps on an errand to one of the upstairs history class-rooms. "Hi, guys," she said, but the boys didn't answer. She let the snub pass. In many ways, she didn't blame them. She understood why they didn't like her. Lorelei didn't like herself very much anymore either. "I hope you have a nice summer, Davidek. And you, too, Green. I'll miss you until next year." Then she began to climb the steps.

Neither boy responded.

She tried to smile at Davidek, but it made her feel sad that he wouldn't look back. As she passed by the stained glass window, Davidek took a long, slow slip. Head tilted back, eyes calm, he followed the grace of her ascension; the elegant curve of her calf, and the line of muscle in her thigh as she moved higher. He hated Lorelei like no one else in the world, but couldn't keep his eyes away. Her legs circled above him like a daydream, the hem of her skirt stirring the shadows beneath.

Green understood the harsh feelings there, and tried to join in Davidek's disdain. "She's the devil," he grumbled softly.

"Yeah . . . ," Davidek said, wiping his mouth as his eyes still followed her. "But the devil sure tempts."

EPILOGUE

Davidek was ironing a white shirt and khaki pants for graduation night. The ceremony took place on Saturday evening at the gymnasium chapel, and since there was a Mass associated with it, the school needed altar boy volunteers. That's how the still-grounded Davidek tricked his parents into letting him go. "It's a mandatory school event," he explained, fearing that excuse had worn out its welcome. In addition to being true, however, this time he had documentation: a printed list of duties during the ceremony. "I'm a candle-bearer!"

His parents fought over who should drive him to the church, and his mother lost this time. She had hoped to go to the movies with her friends that night—the one where Whoopi Goldberg played a singing nun had just opened—but instead she was pissed about spending her night in church watching other people's children accept diplomas. "This came in the mail," she said, throwing an envelope down on his bed as he ironed his shirt. Davidek's name and address were printed in block letters. There was a stamp, postmarked Idaho. Nothing else.

She waited for him to open it.

Inside was a single sheet of paper with a fringe along the edge where it was torn from a notebook. The words were nonsense that made perfect sense to him.

I don't know who I am, what I am, where I am half the time. The other half, I know but don't want to. They sent me far away to bring my brain closer to home. Good thing I left a forwarding address. Sorry I can't give you one. Doctor's orders. I'm sneaking this out, but there's no sneaking in.

My thoughts are returning one by one. I will too. Then, my friend, compared to a nutcase like you—I will no longer be "the crazy guy."

Give Bromine a kiss for me.

Davidek's mother read it over his shoulder. "Who's that from?"

Her son lied, holding the page for her to see. "I don't know . . . it's not signed."

Mr. Zimmer spent the morning at the graveyard, drawing the lawn mower around his family plot, using scissors to snip crabgrass and clover away from his mother and father's tombstone. It wasn't even fully summertime yet, and the graves that went untended by family members were already as ragged as meadows.

Zimmer sat against his parents' tombstone, his T-shirt wet with sweat, admiring his work. Now unemployed, perhaps he could open a landscaping business. He liked being outside, using his body, tending his garden at home. It was spare work he did for elderly neighbors during the off-school summer season anyway.

The thought had appeal. *Maybe. But somewhere else.*

What happened to him at St. Mike's sickened him. He kept trying to busy his hands, moving old stones by his house, trimming trees, or clipping the grass out here by the graves. Otherwise, those hands shook.

He didn't want to attend graduation that night, and the school administration didn't expect him to go either. In fact, he was probably unwelcome. But he had promised someone else he would be there. The two of them would show up in secret. Hopefully, they wouldn't even be noticed.

There would be a sign—FOR SALE—in front of Mr. Zimmer's house in the next month. He had few friends left in the Valley apart from his faculty acquaintances at St. Mike's, and they all believed he was leaving to care for a distant ailing relative. Maybe they would hear ugly rumors about him next year. Or maybe they'd actually believe their old colleague was simply the innocent victim of cost-cutting. He would be far away, regardless. "I'm sorry, Mom . . . Dad . . . ," he said to the emptiness around him. "From now on, your grass is gonna grow wild."

Graduation was already crowded, so Davidek's mom found a seat at the end of an aisle near the back. "Don't dilly-dally when it's over," she told her son as he parted company to join the other altar boys getting ready in the sacristy (formerly the girl's locker room, when the church was a gym). "We're leaving right after. I have friends to meet, and we're going to try to catch the nine-ten showing."

The graduating seniors lined up in the school hallway leading to the gymnasium church, shimmering in blue robes and angular mortarboard caps, debating over which side the little gold tassel should hang.

The pews filled with parents, grandparents, brothers and sisters, uncles, aunts and cousins. There were girlfriends and boyfriends from other schools. Most of the freshmen, sophomores, and juniors from St. Mike's also crushed in to see their schoolmates graduate. Davidek saw Lorelei in one of the back rows. Seven-Eighths sat beside her in silence, listening to Lorelei, who was chatting away with her new friend.

Green was with the school choir on the other side of the church, sitting in what were once bleachers when this had been a basketball court.

During the ceremony, Hannah spent most of the time peeking over the shoulders of her taller classmates, trying to get Davidek's attention. But he kept missing her waves.

His eyes seemed to be fixed on the loft in the back of the church, a balcony where scorekeepers used to monitor the basketball games or stagehands wielded spotlights when the gym was sometimes converted to a theater for school plays. Now, organ pipes rose there like an explosion of fearsome plumbing—so deafening that no one ever attended Mass in the benches up there.

That's why the figure up in the loft caught his attention. It was a boy, sitting alone.

Davidek stood at the altar, clutching his candelabra alongside Carl

LeRose—who held a tall brass cross. Father Mercedes stood at the lectern, reading from Psalms about times to live, times to die, times to reap, and times to sow. Davidek wasn't listening. He was studying the boy, but couldn't make out the face from so far away. Still, he was familiar.

The boy's hair was shorn close, his face was drawn and white—ghostly. His arms and legs were thin in a white button-down shirt and black pants. He held hands folded in prayer in front of his nose, further obscuring his face.

The boy looked ill, like he had been sick for a long time. And that's when it occurred to Davidek.

Stein.

LeRose nudged him with his elbow. "Davidek, hey . . . ," he whispered as Father Mercedes droned on from the lectern. "I meant to tell you . . . I told my dad all about your friend, and all that business with the seniors." LeRose traced a finger down his cheek to indicate the fake scars.

Davidek nodded. "Do you see him, too?"

LeRose just blinked, "See who?" And Davidek said, "No—nothing," not wanting to draw attention.

LeRose smiled slyly and said, "Dad thought what Rich Mullen and Frank Simms did was pretty fucked up and horrible. If you'd told me sooner about how Stein helped me that day in the parking lot, maybe I could have jumped in to protect him, you know?"

Davidek looked back up at the gaunt figure in the loft. LeRose smiled knowingly. He said, "I just wanted you to know that," and winked at him. "You're picking up what I'm putting down, right?"

"Right," Davidek said, having no idea.

LeRose said, "Cool . . . let's just keep it between us."

Davidek was very confused now. *Did LeRose see Stein in the loft or not?*

But the older boy was trying to get Davidek to notice something else entirely: the two empty seats amid the rows of graduating seniors.

Mullen and Simms had not enjoyed happy lives at St. Mike's, but they had found some happiness together.

On graduation day, the two boys sat on Mullen's front porch in West Tarentum, leaning their feet against the wooden railing and tipping back on white plastic chairs. It was their final night as St. Mike's students, and they tried to reminisce about some of the better times. There weren't many. All they really had was the vanquishing of Noah Stein, and no one else gave them credit for that.

"You think you'll ever go to college?" asked Mullen, who was moving to West Virginia in two weeks to start summer school at Wheeling Jesuit University. His parents would only pay for a religious school, and the school would only accept him if he took early remedial classes to account for his lackluster SAT scores.

Simms shrugged. "Naw . . . Maybe if I ever wanted to know about medieval times or something, I'd take a class or two." He already had a part-time job as a bagger at Shop N Save in New Kensington. That paid okay for now, but he was still living at home. "Maybe it'll lead to something more. Got grocery stores all over, in every town. I could go a lot of places," he said.

Mullen nodded, his finger absently brushing the button-scar on his face. *Asshole Face.* That was a name he hoped never to hear again. He raised a can of Iron City, stolen from his father's basement refrigerator, and the two boys clinked their beers together. In college, Mullen would join a fraternity, his grades would be above average, and he'd meet a lot of new people who didn't automatically know him as a loser. He'd tell stories about his days at St. Mike's, about the various ways he and his buddy Simms outfoxed the Powers That Were. As the years passed, on return visits home, Mullen would see very little of his old buddy. Someday, Mullen and Simms would each wonder what had become of the other. But Mullen could already tell that day would come. He knew it on the porch that night. Simms didn't. But that was okay.

A black-and-white police car rolled by on the street, and they hid the beer bottles below their chairs. When it was gone, they finished drinking and debated stealing a couple more, but it was getting late, and the graduation ceremony at the church would start soon.

They drove there in Mullen's Pea Green Love Machine, the windows down and their blue robes fluttering on hangers in the backseat. The same police car that passed Mullen's house pulled up behind them. It had circled his block a few times, and here it was again—so Mullen was extra careful, halting fully at every stop sign instead of gliding through.

"What's with all the po-pos cruising around today?" Simms asked.

Just then, the squad car's red and white lights came on and the cruiser gave a single yelp of its siren. Mullen pulled over to the side of the road, the Tarentum Bridge looming just ahead of them. They were about half-way to the school.

A figure in a black uniform emerged from the police cruiser, and Mullen fumbled for his wallet, ordering Simms to find the registration in the glove compartment because they were already running late.

The cop barked: "Hands on the wheel!"

Both boys instinctively threw their palms against the car's roof.

The police officer's belt filled the driver's-side window, fitted with Mace, handcuffs, a nightstick, and a dull gray .38 pistol with the clasp unhooked. A curly black cord ran up his chest to a squawking radio receiver.

"Saw yinz run a stop sign back there," the faceless cop said.

"Nuh-uh, we didn't run no stop sign!" Simms protested, and Mullen shushed him. He didn't think he had run one either, but his dad always said apologize right away to a cop and beg to get off with a warning.

"Sorry, Officer," Mullen says. "See, we're going to graduation, and I guess I didn't realize I was hurrying. It won't happen again." He held his license out, although the cop hadn't asked to see it yet.

Then the cop asked to see Simms's ID.

Simms balked, "I ain't driving," but Mullen motioned for him to just do as he was fucking told.

The cop peered at the documents and said their names out loud. "Richard Charles Mullen and Frank John Simms," he said. "You boys are from St. Mike's, right?"

They both said yes, and nodded politely with nervous, wide smiles.

The cop said, "I know a guy who has a kid at St. Mike's. Nice guy. Good to the city. A Good Samaritan, you know? He certainly has looked out for me in the past. . . . He actually warned me there might be some trouble-makers on the road today, celebrating a little."

Mullen gestured to the robes hanging in the back. "Not us," he said. "Just going to the church."

The cop stood silently his face still unseen. He said, "You boys been drinking." It wasn't a question.

Mullen's color drained. He said, "No, no . . ."

The cop leaned down and sniffed deeply, then coughed. He said, "You boys been smoking some illegal substances today, too?"

"NO," they said emphatically, their words falling over one another. *"No, no way. Uh-uh."* The cop sniffed again, looking from one boy's face to the other.

The cop was in his forties, with a thick, tight mustache and eyes hidden behind silver shades. It was going to be a long night for the boys.

Photos and fingerprints would be taken, and their parents would need to come down to the station, their mothers crying, their fathers cursing in their sons' faces. The charges would be misdemeanors—traffic offenses and resisting an officer's orders. They had low blood-alcohol levels, but there was some in their system. They'd get the lesser "driving while impaired" charge, but that was enough to haul both of them in. Plus they were underage. Fines would be levied; a little community service would be ordered by a judge in two months, and then the matter would be logged in their records, complicating school and employment matters for a few years to come. Mullen wouldn't be starting at Wheeling Jesuit for a while.

Simms, his hands already cuffed, began to cry and laid his face against the roof of the Pea Green Love Machine. "Please," Mullen said as the cop locked the silver restraints around his wrists. "Look, Officer, what did I do? . . . I don't understand! Can't we . . . Please, *Officer!*"

The cop grabbed at his badge and shoved it in Mullen's ear. A little tag pinned just below it read: CPT. BELLOWS. "I'm not an officer, Asshole Face," he said. "Show some goddamned respect."

The mysterious boy in the church loft knelt there for the entire service, just a pair of eyes behind the back of a high pew.

When he couldn't stand the curiosity anymore, Davidek handed his wooden staff with the swinging red candle to Justin Teemo, the other candle-bearer. "Hang on to this for me," he said, his robes swishing as he crossed the altar and disappeared into the changing room, where he pulled the black-and-white altar robes off his street clothes and ducked out the back entrance.

Davidek ran around the side of the building to the main doorways, where he slipped inside the church's hushed back vestibule. An older man and woman were standing at the interior doorway, their backs to him, looking in at the service. Mr. Zimmer was standing with them.

Davidek crept along the back wall and dashed up the steps leading to the loft. His footsteps caught the worried attention of the old couple.

There was another door leading out into the loft, and it groaned as Davidek shoved it open.

There he came face-to-face with the boy—but it was not Stein. This person was older, taller—he had no scar on his cheek and his hair was dark, but cut so close to the white scalp that it looked gray, translucent. Davidek had seen him before, but they had never met. He knew the face only from a distance, and from photographs in old yearbooks.

It was Colin Vickler. Clink. The Boy on the Roof.

Back then, he had been flabby, but was skeletal now, his face loose with skin and dark lines, the long greasy black hair shorn away to nothing. His eyes watered when he saw Davidek, and his head began whipping around in search of an exit that didn't involve a thirty-foot free fall.

Davidek said, "I didn't . . . ," but before he could finish, the door behind him burst open again, knocking him hard in the back.

Mr. Zimmer was standing there, motioning to Clink—*come here*—and the boy did as he was told, dashing past Davidek and down the steps as Zimmer followed with a hand on his shoulder.

No one in the church below heard the clamor. They were giving out the diplomas now, and each one brought a rise of steady applause as the organ blasted a deafening rendition of "Panis Angelicus" up in the loft.

Davidek looked down to where the boy had been sitting, and picked up a folded piece of white paper. On it was a crayon drawing of an empty jar, with the lid off, tilted against its side.

He raced down the steps and saw the giant church doors sliding shut, cutting off a beam of golden sun. Davidek reached for the door, when he felt a hand grab his arm and pull him back. His mother bit at her lower lip. "Altar boy, my ass," she said. "I knew you were using this as an excuse to sneak around. The whole church saw you ditch your post at the altar."

"Let *go*, Mom," Davidek said, shaking off her grip. "I gotta get outside."

"Yeah? And just why is that?" his mother asked, her voice rising.

"Because I *have* to," Davidek told her, and when she lashed out to grab him with her other hand, he seized her wrist—and held it there.

June Davidek's son glared hard into her eyes. "Do I have to repeat it for you?" he asked.

When Davidek finally pushed through the doors, Zimmer was shepherding the older man and woman into their car. The frail boy was already in the backseat, and the gray-haired woman was bitching about how she knew this was a *mistake, mistake, mistake* as Zimmer closed the door of their blue sedan on her.

Zimmer pointed at Davidek and told him to keep away as the car backed out of its parking space, then pulled into the street. In the back window, the boy known as Clink turned around and watched St. Mike's grow small. Then the car was gone.

"I didn't know who it was," Davidek said. "I thought it was—"

Zimmer gripped the shoulder of Davidek's shirt. "You're pretty goddamn nosy, aren't you? Don't you think that kid maybe deserved a minute's peace to watch his own graduation?"

Davidek said, "No, look—I'm sorry!" as Zimmer released him and paced away, as if he couldn't stand the sight of the freshman. "He's alone," Zimmer finally said. "He's suffered a lot. He's very—he's had a *very* difficult year, as you can imagine."

Zimmer told Davidek he was sorry for grabbing him. Davidek said it was all right. Zimmer apologized again, and Davidek said, "So . . . What did you mean *his* graduation?"

Zimmer clawed through his hair. He'd kept this secret all year, but now a part of him was desperate to explain it, especially since he would be gone soon. At least someone would know, besides himself—and Sister Maria.

"It was part of the deal to prevent the Vicklers from suing the school. And it was a way to try to make things right," Zimmer said. "Ever since he got out of the hospital last summer, I've been spending time with him in the evenings—home lessons, helping him toward a diploma. He's medicated, and going through heavy therapy. . . . But this way he still gets to, kind of . . . *move on* with his life. He'll get his diploma—and then he can start thinking about the next step." Zimmer looked down the road to where the car had gone. "One last chance deserves another."

Zimmer turned back to the freshman. "I thought it would be nice for him to see tonight—even though he's not a part of it. Everyone in their robes . . . His mother wanted to keep him home, but—eventually you have to face things. You know? You have to face the worst things in your life, or maybe you *become* one of those things."

Davidek said he understood. The teacher nodded quickly, as if it didn't matter. "You won't be helping if you tell people what you saw." Zimmer was tempted to add: *Just like I never told anyone about your night on the Steins' front porch.* But he didn't. Sometimes you had to confront things, as he said, and sometimes you had to let them go.

Davidek held out the paper with the empty jar drawing. "He left this. Do you have any idea what it is?"

Zimmer opened the page, turning it over in his hand before folding it again and stuffing it in his pocket. "I honestly have no idea," Zimmer said. "He draws these all the time."

Inside the gymnasium church, the organ began to gush the smooth swells of "Pomp and Circumstance." Davidek looked back to see his mother watching him from the doorway, but soon beaming graduates began to flow out of the church around her. Cameras flashed and hugs were exchanged. Father Mercedes and his two remaining altar boys led the procession out, with Justin Teemo, the lone candle-bearer, awkwardly balancing the two glowing staffs.

Sister Maria stood at the head of the teacher's row, clapping her hands excitedly, smiling at the passing graduates. Audra Banes broke from the line and hugged her, losing her graduation cap and having to chase it back down the aisle. "You're a real inspiration, Sister. Thank you for showing me how to always stand up for what's right," the girl said. The nun looked overcome. She burst into tears, not because she was touched, but because she knew it to be a lie.

In the row behind Sister Maria, Ms. Bromine stood among the other faculty, but was conspicuously *not* clapping. She couldn't. Her forearms and hands were wrapped in heavy-duty white bandages, making them as thick as snowman arms. The report at school about her being absent due to illness was true. The weeds she had scrambled through during her fight with Davidek had turned out to be poison sumac, and every exposed inch of her arms and legs was now covered in an explosive red rash. For Bromine, it was an agonizing reminder of a moment she'd rather believe never happened. For everyone else in the faculty, it was just one more reason to stay clear of her.

As the blue-robed graduates poured out of the church like a polyester flood, Hannah Kraut remained invisible among her classmates. She expected to be shunned—she knew it would happen after surrendering her fabled notebook at the picnic. But it didn't hurt anymore. A few of the more disgusting boys had muttered the old name "Fuckslut" at her in low tones as the graduates milled about the parking lot after tossing their caps into the sky.

Mostly, her old tormenters were too preoccupied with their own self-congratulation to notice her anymore. She overheard plans for a late-night bonfire along the river in Brackenridge, where one of the kid's parents had a cabin. The passing of plans and directions always hushed when Hannah drew near, not that she wanted to go to any of their parties anyway.

She was searching for someone, and her overlong graduation robes brushed the ground as she walked. In her hands, she held a narrow rectangular package wrapped in bright red paper and tied with a silver ribbon. Inside was the framed picture she had planned to give to Mr. Zimmer on prom night; the one with Hannah cheesing broadly as she squeezed in next to the only person at St. Mike's who could make her smile. Zimmer looked goofy, but was smiling, too, as she held the camera out with one arm and put the other over his shoulders, their faces pressed side to side. On the cardboard backing of the frame she had written:

Thank you for seeing something beautiful in me.

Hannah had meant to give it to him before the ceremony but hadn't seen him with the other teachers. Someone said he'd been out sick. Another heard he was visiting a relative. Ever since prom, she knew Mr. Zimmer wasn't the most reliable person, but she didn't believe he would miss graduation—their last night, the big good-bye. At the Hazing Picnic, he even said he wanted a photo with her in her graduation robes. He had promised.

Then she saw him, on the periphery of the crowd, moving toward the parking lot. Hannah hurried toward him, holding her gift in the air as she squeezed through the mob. She called out his name, but Zimmer seemed to move away faster. Then John Hannidy stopped him and said, "Hey, how ya feeling, Mr. Z! Have a nice summer, okay?" as he slapped Zimmer's shoulder and walked off.

That's when Hannah caught up.

She held out the package, but Zimmer was looking elsewhere, scanning the crowd, hoping to avoid Sister Maria, Father Mercedes . . . everybody. He'd already been seen by too many people.

"Hell-o? Earth to Mr. Zimmer," Hannah said, poking him in the arm with the wrapped frame. "I got you something. To say thank you—"

He raised a hand and said, "That won't be necessary, Hannah." His voice was strange, businesslike. He looked everywhere but at her.

Hannah pressed the package under his arm. "Come on, it's a gift," she said. "I know you'll like it."

Zimmer took the package and held it against his leg, like a secret agent accepting stolen microfilm. "Thank you," he said, not very convincingly.

"Aren't you going to open it?" she asked, but he was already disappearing into the crowd again.

Hannah started following him, but that's when she came face-to-face with Davidek, who was just standing around, looking as confused as always. She rose up on her tiptoes and saw Zimmer rounding the other side of the church. "Hey!" she said, and slipped a hug around Davidek. "Did I see you, like, skip out in the middle of church, altar boy? What was that about?"

Davidek mumbled some nonexplanation.

Hannah said, "Listen, you want to come with me over to Kings? Maybe get a hamburger or something? Celebrate graduation with one of those Kitchen Sink Sundaes they have? Those have, like, six different ice creams, and sauces and bananas and strawberries and fudge. . . . *Huge!* I've always wanted to get one, but, you know . . . don't think I could kill one by myself."

A voice in the crowd cried sharply: "Peter! . . . Peter!" like a knife slashing against tin. It was Davidek's mother.

People were jostling all around them, but she pushed through and grabbed her son's arm—but all he had to do was look at it to make her let him go again.

Hannah said, "Is this your mom? Hi, I was Peter's senior mentor this year."

Davidek's mother shook her hand tersely. "Pleasure," June Davidek said, her face suggesting an opposite emotion. "Come on, Peter. Time to go."

Hannah laced her fingers with Davidek's. "Aren't you going to come with me, Playgirl? We'll have some fun—"

"I'm sorry, but my little son is still grounded," June Davidek said. She checked her watch. If she left now, she could deposit Peter at home and still make it to Dingbats for mojitos with Celia and Kay before the movie.

The boy told his mother: "Listen, I'm going with my friend, Hannah, for ice cream. It's graduation night. So back off, all right?" It was strange to call Hannah his friend after all they'd been through—all she'd *put* him through—but some part of it felt true.

Davidek's mother clenched her teeth, and got close enough to her son to whisper in his ear. "You. Are. Grounded. . . . Remember all the shit you caused us?" she said. "And I can't make you move. But I can *slap* you. I can *scream* at you. I can pull at your shirt and cause such a scene that everyone in this parking lot will stop and stare. Is that what you want? Do you want to be the boy whose mommy spanked him outside graduation? Do you want your little girlfriend over there to see that? Because I'll do it, Peter. I'll make an ass out of you like you've never imagined."

She pulled his arm again. This time, her son began to walk.

Hannah's parents found their daughter in the crowd as she searched for Mr. Zimmer, and delayed her by insisting on some photos. "Could you get one of your friends to take one of all three of us?" her father asked.

Hannah said, "Let's just take one at home with the timer."

"Aren't you going out to celebrate with your chums?" her mother asked.

Hannah smiled. "Nobody says 'chums,' Mom." She told her parents that she actually wasn't feeling well, and suggested they take off and she'd be right behind them. Her father laughed and said, "Oh, our little girl is just trying to get rid of us!" as he linked arms with Hannah's mother, who kissed her daughter on the forehead and joked as they walked away: "Just try to be back by next Thursday." They would be saddened in an hour when they saw her arrive back at their house alone.

With almost no one left outside, Hannah was still searching. He couldn't have left without saying good-bye. But when she approached a handful of teachers still talking by the school entrance, no one from that group, which was heading to the Anchor Inn to drown the school year in Yuengling, knew Mr. Zimmer's whereabouts. "Was he even here?" Mrs. Arnarelli asked Mr. Mankowski and Mrs. Tunns.

Hannah was the last student to leave the school. She walked along the side of the gymnasium church, trying to see if Zimmer's car was parked on the street there, and she passed a trash can overflowing with plastic wrappings from carnations, candy wrappers, soda bottles, and mimeographed graduation programs. A flicker of silver ribbon fluttered over the lip, still lashed around some bright red wrapping paper, which was partially torn away.

The picture of a pigtailed schoolgirl and her favorite teacher smiled from the trash.

Hannah lifted it out. She even considered rescuing it. But the glass was cracked now. And someone's half-finished Mountain Dew had seeped pale green stickiness all over it. And what did she want with this fucking photo anymore anyway?

Hannah pressed her palm against the picture frame, wedging it deeper into the trash, where no one would ever see it again.

Davidek's mother was steering her minivan toward the Tarentum Bridge when Michael Crawford's black 4Runner streaked past along the shoulder of the road. On the back door was a short metal ladder, and clinging to the ladder was Bilbo Tomch, his graduation robe fluttering behind him like a superhero's cape, one arm clasped around the ladder for dear life as he whooped and shouted.

"God. He's going to kill himself," Davidek's mother said, but her son didn't reply. He was staring through his faint reflection in the window glass to the river below, with the long shadow of the bridge stretched out across it. The dark spot of their car traced along the glistening surface of the water.

"I don't know why you had to fight me back there," his mother said. "Can't you try having a civil conversation with me one goddamn time?"

Okay, how about this for "civil conversation"? he wanted to say. *The way you tried to bully and embarrass me back there? That's the last time. I'm done being pushed around by anyone—and that includes you and Dad. Do you understand? Or do I need to say: "Do I need to repeat it for you"—again . . . and again . . . and again . . . until it sinks in?*

But he was tired of fighting. And anyway, she'd find out soon enough. Stein's first rule of combat was secrecy. *Don't declare war, just wage it.*

Things had changed. A boy learns a lot in his first year of high school.

One was a simple lesson that a lot of people figure out around his age: Surprise, surprise—the good guys don't always win. Sometimes, they're lucky if they just get to keep on being good guys.

Davidek wasn't sure if he still counted as one or not. He hoped so.

But now he also knew that it's not enough to step in front of other people's bullets; you have to be bulletproof, too. You have to be harder than anything anyone else can throw at you, and sometimes you risk losing yourself just trying to save yourself.

Davidek could feel himself there now, on the edge of becoming someone he didn't recognize anymore, and he didn't like it very much. A year ago, he risked his life running out to save some kid he didn't even know; and now that he knew a *lot* of kids at St. Mike's, all he wanted to do was see them get what was coming to them—what they'd been dishing out to everyone else. He'd always assumed that as you got older, you became better, that you learned how to be brave, or wise, or do what was best for other people. Now he believed the opposite was true.

He guessed that's how someone turned into a Ms. Bromine, or maybe even his own mother and father—who wanted to start over so badly, but had no idea how. It was hard for him to remember a time when his mom and dad seemed happy, or even interested in anything about their two boys except unloading their own frustrations on them. Whether it was the clip-on tie, or begging for a late-night ride to find out what happened to Stein, they never listened when he asked for help, never trusted him. And so he had quit asking, and quit trusting them, too. That part was his fault, he supposed. All he needed was a friend, but you can't find that in people who hate where they've ended up but still expect you to follow in their footsteps. The upperclassmen of St. Mike's certainly proved that.

Davidek felt sorry looking over at his mother. All she wanted was to be loved—she just had so little to give in return. So now she was trying her best to make conversation, but a parent can't leave a child alone for so long and expect the occasional nicety to count for much. Those bonds break away much more quickly and permanently than most people would like to believe.

He wanted to tell her everything. He just couldn't.

But Stein had it much worse. His mother had caused more agony for her boy than anyone Davidek could imagine, and look at what Stein had sacrificed to try to save her—even after she was gone. Maybe you can't blame people for the pain that makes them who they are. Maybe that was just one more bullet you had to step in front of for someone you were supposed to love—even if you didn't want to. Even if it hurt. Maybe that *was* love.

"*Answer* me when I talk to you, Peter . . . ," June Davidek said, her fake friendliness edging away with every bump in the bridge span. "Can you at least tell me what the hell was going on back at that school that had you all worked up?"

The minivan reached a red light at the end of the bridge, and Davidek thought about unhooking his seat belt and turning to put his arms around his mom. Instead, he shook his head and looked out the window.

"It was nothing," he said. "Just kid stuff."

ACKNOWLEDGMENTS

This is a book about friendships, and it wouldn't have happened without some extraordinary ones in my own life: Anil Kurian passed an early draft to my editor, Brendan Deneen, who liked it well enough to spend a few years of his life fighting for its publication. Without him, no one else would have believed in it.

Helen Estabrook introduced me to Graham Moore, who recommended me to his formidable reps at ICM, Jennifer Joel and Clay Ezell, and with them came Roxane Edouard, the warrior agent fighting to get this book translated into other languages.

The people who made this stack of paper look so amazing include art director Rob Grom, who turned an innocent school uniform into a simmering metaphor of adolescent rage, and production editor Kenneth J. Silver, copy editor Eliani Torres, and proofreader Steve Roman—who saved me from many stupit mistakes. Thanks, guyz.

Thomas Dunne gave this project his blessing, and Nicole Sohl, the associate editor, expertly shepherded the book toward its final form. In publicity and marketing, John Karle, Marie Estrada, and Kerry McMahon have been tireless flag-wavers and drumbeaters.

A few colleagues at *Entertainment Weekly* gave me the platform of a lifetime to introduce *Brutal Youth* for the first time: Tina Jordan, Stephan Lee,

Steve Korn, and Jeff Giles. And an army of friends and relatives shared this book far and wide on Facebook and Twitter.

Nobody gets anywhere without a vouch, and I want to thank the story-tellers who read this novel and provided the blurbs you see on the jacket. They have spent their lives building reputations with readers, and gener-ously shared that with me. Jason Reitman was the first to pen a blurb, a true friend who also offered sanctuary when I needed to lay low and rewrite.

A note on music: Stein's father is a They Might Be Giants fan, which is where he heard that term Rabid Child. Credit where due. Another lyric that stuck in my head came from a 1994 Elvis Costello song called "Favor-ite Hour": "Now there's a tragic waste of brutal youth . . ." It summed up my early years rather perfectly, and has haunted me ever since. I owe Declan MacManus for the inspiration.

Many civilians read the book in draft form, and a handful spent hours helping me make it better: Susanna Eng-Ziskin, Erica Canales, Thea Okonak, Dan Snierson, and my brother, Greg Breznican (who came up with the shorthand description *Fight Club* meets *The Breakfast Club*.") Just before we started printing, my old schoolmate James Elkins noticed a scene where I had Stein's scars on the wrong side of his face. That kind of Indiana-Jones-grabs-the-hat rescue merits a shout-out.

Another early reader was John Carosella, my former teacher, my pres-ent teacher. When I was fourteen and wrote a freshman essay about want-ing to be a writer, he started encouraging me and has never stopped. He is not Mr. Zimmer, but is one of that rare breed of teacher who finds pieces of garbage among his students and says, "This is worth something; I can fix this." He fixed me. And I'm just one of many.

Finally, here's to the librarians of the world . . . you radical, militant bastards. My wife, Jill, is one of you, and when she started working on her masters in library science, I started working on this novel. You are the keepers, protectors, and sharers of stories, and stories are how we find each other in an existence that is tragically short of call numbers.

All I've ever wanted is to give Jill a book for her shelf that was written just for her.

Here it is, kiddo.